Swimming with Serpents

MERCER
UNIVERSITY PRESS

Endowed by
TOM WATSON BROWN
and
THE WATSON-BROWN FOUNDATION, INC.

Swimming with Serpents

A Novel

Sharman Burson Ramsey

MERCER UNIVERSITY PRESS
MACON, GEORGIA

MUP/ H854
H854e

© 2012 Mercer University Press
1400 Coleman Avenue
Macon, Georgia 31207

First Edition

Books published by Mercer University Press are printed on acid-free
paper that meets the requirements of the American National Standard
for Information Sciences—Permanence of Paper for Printed Library
Materials.

Mercer University Press is a member of Green Press Initiative
(greenpressinitiative.org), a nonprofit organization working to help
publishers and printers increase their use of recycled paper and
decrease their use of fiber derived from endangered forests. This book
is printed on recycled paper.
ISBN   Print   978-0-88146-391-0
          e-book   978-0-88146-379-8
Cataloging-in-Publication Data is available from the Library of
Congress

"Your coming is not for trade, but to invade my people and possess my country." —Wahunsonacock, Chief Powhatan (1545–1618)

"What's past is prologue." —*The Tempest, 2.1*, William Shakespeare

I dedicate this novel to my mother, Jean Bronson Gillis Burson, and honor our Native American heritage:

Jean Bronson Gillis (m. Dr. Elkanah George Burson)
Eunice Clair Jernigan (m. John Patrick Gillis)
Joseph Jernigan (m. Narcissus Charlotte Black)
John Joseph Jernigan (m. Josephine Cotton)
Joseph Jefferson Jernigan (m. Caroline Dixon)
Edith Jernigan (m. Lofton Cotton)
Vashti Vann Jernigan (m. Benjamin Jernigan)
Edward Ned Vann, Jr. (m. Mary King, daughter of the Squirrel King of the Chickasaw)
Mary Barnes (m. Edward Ned Vann, Sr.)
April Tikami Cornstalk Hop (m. Richard Barnes)
Big Turkey Cornstalk (m. Daughter of Great Hopper)
Hokolesqua Opechan "Stream " Cornstalk (m. Nonoma)
Opechan Stream Opechancanough (brother of Wahunsonacock, m. Cleopatra Powhatan the Shawano)
Ensenore Powhatan (m. Morning Flower, parents of Opechancanough)
Wahunsonacock Powhatan (Great Chief, brother of Opechan Stream, m. Amopotuskee Shawano Bear Clan) is the father of Cleopatra
Ensenore Powhatan (m. Scent Flower, parents of Wahunsonacock)

Prologue

1803

Snow Bird on Gentle Wind paused for a moment to watch the snowy white egret settle on the lowest limb of the spreading moss-laden oak. The bird was her totem, and it always appeared at momentous times of her life. She'd seen it when Jason appeared, and once more at the birth of the twins. And now.... Snow Bird swallowed her apprehension.

She lowered herself awkwardly onto the wooden bench in the cool shade. Gently, lovingly, she stroked her swollen belly and wondered as always at the miracle and gift of creating life. She tensed as her womb hardened with another of the slight contractions she had been feeling for weeks now. Damp tendrils of ink-black hair clung to her face. As the pain relaxed, she leaned back against the trunk of the oak tree. Her light-flecked amber eyes glittered with tears of discomfort—and fear. She must be strong, she told herself. But she could not help wishing Jason had not left her knowing the babe was due so soon!

Was that a movement in the forest behind her? Snow Bird shifted painfully to look around. Her husband's warning rang in her ears. But when a soft breeze caressed her cheek and rippled the oak leaves, dappling the shadows about her and giving respite to the unrelenting heat, she breathed in relief. Only the wind, she thought, and offered a silent thank you to the Great Spirit.

The boys' laughter was a blessed distraction from her discomfort. Her twin sons darted between the pines on the opposite side of the trading post clearing, pretending The Hunt. Their ten-year-old bodies, clothed only with deerskin flaps, glistened from the heat. They were lithe and agile as she had once been, and their chase gave her pleasure. Cade lifted his bow and took aim. Gabriel, covered with a deerskin and holding antlers to his forehead, scampered away, daring his brother to shoot, shouting insults as he ran. Cade stalked quietly on bare feet, remembering High Head Jim's lessons in the hunt. Gabriel lost sight of his brother and, in that moment of letting down his guard, caught the glancing blow of the dull arrow dead center on his chest. Though surprised, Gabriel played his part well. He collapsed and went dramatically through the death throes of the deer. Cade planted his foot on the dying deer and shouted out a well-practiced Indian victory cry.

"Admit it, Gabe. I'm the greatest hunter in the forest."

Gabe grabbed Cade's foot and flipped the proud hunter on his back. "The finest hunter can easily be defeated by the weakest animal when his arrogance leaves him unprepared," Gabe said, reciting High Head Jim's oft-repeated words.

Cade rolled on top of Gabriel, and the battle began anew. Afraid that the struggle was getting too rough, Snow Bird knew a distraction was called for.

"My warriors," she called, "come to your mother." The two dirty boys glanced up from their rolling clench and only then noticed her obvious discomfort. Immediately recalling their father's command to "grow up and take care of your mother," they scampered over to her.

"Are you all right, Mother?" asked Gabriel.

"Can we bring you water, Mother? You are sweating even here in the shade," Cade said, looking at the dampness that made her blue calico dress cling to the rounded bulge. That stomach was now so large that it obstructed her usually frequent hugs—the hugs she grabbed whenever she could catch them. She knew they tried to scamper far enough away to play hard-to-get but close enough to enjoy her loving embraces. She reached out and ran her fingers through their long hair.

"Such a cunning hunter you are, my son," she said, cupping Cade's face. He looked at her, so innocent and concerned, with his father's eyes, as blue as the cloudless summer sky, his skin pale with a Scot's ruddiness. Thoughts of their father quickened her heart with a love her people could not understand...or forgive.

"My son, the deer, you must always be alert. This is a good lesson for all in the forest, both animal and man. But never has a deer died so convincingly," she assured Gabe lovingly. Clear amber eyes like hers looked up at her, and his skin was dusky, like her own.

She pulled them down beside her there on her wooden bench in the shade and savored the feel of her sons as she cuddled them next to her. Their vitality gave her strength. She held them tightly as long as she could until she felt their impatience and released them. "Run," she said unnecessarily. "Each of you take a bucket to the stream and bring me water." She had learned long ago to have two of everything, for whatever one had the other wanted.

The water run became a challenge of speed and dexterity. Cade and Gabe must handle the buckets with care so that the one who returned quickest with the most water won. They sped across the clearing where packhorses had hardened the red clay in front of the trading house, grabbed their buckets from the front porch bench, and raced through the dogtrot to the rear of the cabin and down to the stream.

Snow Bird rested a hand on her protruding belly through her calico shift, a white woman's dress that her husband insisted she wear, made of cloth that they sold at the trading post. As she listened to her boys' voices at the stream, she thought of how active they had been even before they were born. Their birth had been difficult and she had recovered slowly. The wise woman of the village who had been with her through their birth had warned her of the danger of having more children.

But a man is a man and she was his woman. Jason too had been warned of the dangers of another pregnancy, but Snow Bird yearned for the closeness of their intimacy and passion and assured him that the herbs provided by the wise woman would prevent another child. They worked until the life force of the one now in her womb became stronger than the herbs. The concern in the older woman's eyes when she offered Snow Bird a potion that would end the life-threatening pregnancy haunted Snow Bird, who desperately wanted to see her sons become men. But Snow Bird decided the child within her had a life force strong enough to overcome the herbs and deserved a chance to live. She had loved the unborn babe from the moment she discovered she was pregnant.

Snow Bird watched Gabriel trip as he rounded the skin house and spill the water from the bucket. Cade laughed and taunted his brother until he saw the tears gather in Gabriel's eyes. To Snow Bird, Gabriel's awkwardness seemed strange in the son who looked most like her people.

"Here," Snow Bird heard Cade say as he poured water from his own bucket into his brother's. "We tried to carry too much. Mine is too heavy also." Cade usually assumed a warrior's bravado because it

3

brought rare approval from his father. But it did little to conceal the tender heart that Cade tried so hard to hide. Snow Bird's own heart swelled watching Cade try to ease his brother's embarrassment.

There had always been an unconscious competition between the two. Cade, eldest by mere minutes, took naturally to the hunt, reading the signs of the forest as readily as he was taught. Gabriel learned the lessons of the forest along with Cade, but she knew his heart ached to see the animal suffer. Gabriel was drawn to the stables to care for the horses, whispering to them as he brushed and nourished them. Even as a small child toddling along beside her, Gabriel had attracted animals that would have run from others, calling them to him and then babbling in a language that only Gabe and the animals understood.

Gabriel loved to sift the rich black soil of the bottomland near the Oconee River through his fingers and smell its pungent promise. Snow Bird and Gabriel planted seeds and nurtured young seedlings while Cade rebelliously wandered away into the woods, refusing any part of "woman's work" and constantly being rescued from brambles and streams by the young girls in the village assigned to watch the children. Gabriel's patience and empathy sharply contrasted his brother Cade's aggressive impulsiveness, natural grace, and athletic prowess. Although not identical twins, both would have their father's height and muscular build.

The sudden stabbing pain in Snow Bird's back caught her unaware, and she gasped with its intensity. The insignificant contractions she had been experiencing turned into one mighty thrust. She forced herself to breathe easily and calm down.

Not now, Yahola. Please. Let me see my husband once again.

Last night before Jason had left her to look for Bowles, she had clung to him and made love to him in the moonlight with a passion that was exceptional even for her. Unable to sleep, she then lay spooned with him on a pallet of furs on the hilltop above the river where she had first seen him paddling toward her village. She remembered how he had spotted her standing there on the hill. When his sky blue eyes had lifted and captured hers, she felt instantly the attraction that had bound her to the bold, determined, devastatingly handsome man she had defied her family to wed. But the night before, as she lay watching him sleep, she had shivered despite the warmth of the summer night as she felt the spirits gathering. Then she chastised herself for being a coward. She lay against his tall, muscular body, memorizing the taste, the smell, the look of him. Memories for eternity.

He must go. His work was that of a man. Bowles had challenged his trading territory, and the challenge must be met. Hers was a woman's battle. By morning she had done with tears and faced the rising sun and his departure with courage. Only she could fight the spirits that were weakening her and pulling her from this world.

"Stay close to the cabin and keep the gun handy," Jason had warned her before leaving. "Bowles and Savannah Jack want this trading territory, and they'll stop at nothing to get it. I'm just gonna get them first." Merely hearing those names brought a chill down Snow Bird's spine. Savannah Jack's vicious cruelty and horrifying mutilated face had made him famous, the villain of tales mothers told children. And *her husband* was out to catch him.

"Men from the village will come later in the morning to tend the post. It isn't the season, and I don't expect any activity. Just keep the gun near and stay close. They'll be here soon," Jason had commented off-handedly, already focused on capturing Bowles and Savannah Jack. He kissed her, insensitive to her apprehension, and set off with the men who usually tended the post.

The pain of the contraction subsided once more, and Snow Bird's mind wandered as she thought of the men her husband sought. The self-styled "Director General of the Creek Nation," William Augustus Bowles, a British sympathizer, had just returned to Perryman's village from his Spanish captivity at Manila. He and Perryman, his father-in-law, had captured the Spanish fort at St. Marks. Bowles now wanted control of Jason Kincaid's trading business as another step toward wresting power from the much-beloved Benjamin Hawkins, the American agent to the Creek Indians who had been appointed by the Great Father Washington as General Superintendent of Indian Affairs in 1796. Bowles's associates were bloodthirsty and ready to fight.

Savannah Jack, on the other hand, cared nothing for politics. The father of this renegade Shawnee half-breed was, strangely enough, the white trader John Hague, an adopted Creek through marriage to a Shawano-Chalaka woman. Savannah Jack simply hated white people who settled on and fenced in the traditional hunting lands. He had recently ambushed and brutally massacred a family traveling down the path to the Lower Creek villages from Charleston. His association with Bowles seemed to be a contradiction, but Bowles had promised to unify the Indians and fight the encroachment of the Americans, boasting that he would halt the adoption of the white culture promoted by Benjamin Hawkins and help revive the traditional Indian way of life.

Another contraction. Snow Bird closed her eyes and felt perspiration bead on her forehead.

Only the sound of the boys tussling penetrated the dark veil of her pain. Her expression brought the boys to her, their eyes round with fear. Snow Bird forced a smile and clenched the sides of the rough wooden bench tightly.

"Boys, I want you to run to the talwa and get my cousin Polly and her mother who is visiting. Tell them to come quickly." Sophia Durant, Polly's mother, was the sister of Alexander McGillivray, who had been known as the "Emperor" of the Creek nation. He had died ten years earlier, about the time Cade and Gabe were born, leaving the power vacuum Bowles intended to fill.

Sophia's courage and boldness were legend. Snow Bird needed her strength.

"Mother, is it the baby? Let Gabriel stay with you while I run into the village. I run faster."

"You do not! Let me go!" Gabriel demanded.

The two glared at one another.

"There is no need, my son," Snow Bird said in a soft, calm voice. "It takes a long time for a baby to make its way into the world. Just let me lean on my big strong warriors as I walk to the cabin. I will lie in the cool while I wait for you to bring Sophia."

Snow Bird's feet and ankles were so swollen that her moccasins no longer fit and her feet were tender. Gabriel was nearly as tall as she was, his body thin and gangly. Cade was slightly shorter, stockier, and more muscular.

The high ceilings in the cabin let the heat rise. A breeze blew through the dogtrot that separated the two sides of the cabin. Sitting on the rope bed with its down-filled mattress, Snow Bird ran her fingers along the smooth cheeks of the boys who stood before her, memorizing each curve.

"The little one longs to meet its brothers," she whispered to them. "Female child or male child, this one will need your guidance and protection." Her look was so intense that Cade put his arm around her to reassure her. Gabe sat close on the other side and clasped her hand.

"I love you both so very much," she said.

"I'm the oldest. I'll teach the baby," Cade promised, lifting his earnest gaze to meet her own.

"Me, too," said Gabriel.

Sensing the argument to come, she commanded, "Now go."

Not wanting to transmit her fears, and before another of the excruciating pains ripped through her body, she sent them away. Through the window of the cabin she watched them disappear into the brush of the pine thicket, still arguing about who was most fit to take care of the new baby and teach it everything it would need to know. Hunters bringing their deerskins and furs from the long months of the hunt here to her husband's trading post had worn a distinct path from the talwa, but the two boys had their own shortcut through the forest, and she was glad. She needed Sophia to arrive quickly.

"Yahola be with you, my sons." Alone to battle the spirits and the pain, Snow Bird allowed herself one cry to be heard by no one else and then clenched her teeth.

Sophia McGillivray Durant would be there soon. Snow Bird looked forward to her presence. Trained as a leader to her people by her uncle Red Shoes, who was Snow Bird's grandfather, Sophia was one of the few women who attended tribal councils at Hickory Ground, where she had often spoken for her brother Alexander. Her courage was well known. Once, when Alexander was in Washington with a delegation of Creeks, Sophia had learned that his plantation home at Little River was to be attacked by his enemies. Even in an advanced stage of pregnancy, Sophia had straddled a horse and rode from Hickory Ground to Little River in the Tensaw country, spending four days on the road and traveling a distance of almost 200 miles before she finally reached Apple Grove, McGillivray's plantation, and warned his family of the impending attack.

And then she had given birth to twins, Elizabeth and Rachel Durant. Their older sister Polly was Snow Bird's dearest friend and cousin. Later, when Snow Bird's mother died, Sophia came and got her and brought her home to raise with her own large brood of children. Now, alone and in pain, Snow Bird longed for the comfort Sophia would bring.

As if her thoughts had summoned help, Snow Bird felt a gentle touch on her hand. She looked up through a fog of pain and saw the still beautiful and much loved face of dear Sophia. Sophia's large, expressive olive green eyes caressed Snow Bird with love and concern.

"You've come," Snow Bird whispered with relief. She was no longer alone in her battle. "The boys brought you back."

"Be still," Sophia said. "Save your strength." Tender hands turned her onto her side with pillows supporting her stomach, and then Sophia massaged her lower back and helped ease the pain.

Snow Bird thought she heard Sophia speak to someone else in the room. "The boys. They never reached the village. Send someone to tell Polly's husband, High Head Jim, to look for the boys." Snow Bird sensed that this information should alarm her, but she was too consumed by her pain.

"Snow Bird, where is Jason, your husband?"

A contraction gripped Snow Bird, and she bit her lip to keep from crying out. "Bowles," she gasped. "Perryman's village." She could tell by Sophia's expression that she thought this was reckless of Jason, but at the moment she didn't care.

Snow Bird moaned as she rocked back and forth. Cousin Polly mopped her brow with cool cloths. The candles were lit and burned low as Snow Bird labored for hour upon hour, until at last she was too weak to push.

Her face drawn with worry, Sophia ran practiced fingers over Snow Bird's tightly stretched abdomen. The baby's head had not descended. She felt more gingerly. The infant lay horizontally in its mother's womb. If the position did not shift, neither mother nor child would survive. Through her haze of exhaustion, Snow Bird saw the wise woman of the village who had attended the twins' birth shake her head.

"We must turn the child, or neither mother nor child will survive," Sophia said as she assessed the situation.

The woman administered an herb to put Snow Bird to sleep. The maneuver had to be done quickly before the drug got to the infant. Snow Bird faded and was unaware of her surroundings.

Sophia stood back while the wise woman manipulated the child with slender agile hands from below, and when she nodded, Sophia pushed on Snow Bird's abdomen. With a burst of fluid and blood, the child emerged. Snow Bird moaned as the blood gushed from her body. The baby did not breathe or cry. "A girl," the woman noted. Sophia nodded and cried hopelessly as she watched the life blood flow from the body of her precious Snow Bird.

The medicine woman cleared the child's mouth and throat, then held the infant upside down to slap her bottom. Still no sound. Limp and lifeless, the child was a death-mask gray beneath the white vernix.

Sophia grabbed the child and prayed, "Yahola, please! Snow Bird sacrificed herself so she might live. Please!" She put her lips to those of the tiny baby and blew her own breath into the babe's mouth...then breathed and blew again. At last, a whimper. Once more she breathed into the little one, and with a jerk, the child cried out. Snow Bird's eyes flickered open when she heard the cry that grew stronger and stronger.

"Child of my heart. What a joy Yahola has blessed me with," she whispered as Sophia brought her little girl for her to see. Though swollen and bruised with the punishing birth, the child now looked pink and squirmed strongly. The medicine woman started a chant.

"Sing to me," whispered Snow Bird as she lifted her arm for the child. Sophia laid the baby girl in her mother's arms. With tears choking her throat, Sophia sang the song she'd sung as she rocked a lost, confused little girl crying over the loss of her own mother. Snow Bird smiled her love, and then her eyes fluttered closed. With a sigh, she was gone.

Her heart breaking, Sophia leaned down and pressed a kiss on Snow Bird's face. She gently closed the eyes of this child of her heart and pulled the baby and Snow Bird's lifeless body to her chest. Then she cried out in her anguish, giving over to great rolling sobs. Polly held her mother as they shared their grief. Snow Bird was the little girl who had danced into Sophia's heart, whose sweet singing had brightened every day she'd lived with them, and who had broken her heart when she married the man whom Sophia knew did not deserve her love.

The baby lay still, looking solemnly into her mother's face. Polly lifted Snow Bird's baby from the mother's lifeless arms. "It was as Snow

Bird wished it. She told me if there had to be a choice, her child must have the opportunity for life." She looked down at her cousin's peaceful face. "She must have thought she would not survive."

"Sarilee just lost her own child. She's still got her milk and needs a babe to hold. Call her here to nurse the babe," Sophia said sadly. "The babe's name must be as Snow Bird spoke. The baby's name is Joie."

Polly nodded. "Jim has already left to track the boys. I'll send a messenger to tell him to find Jason Kincaid and bring him home to bury his wife."

Then she went to fetch the slave girl while the medicine woman cleaned Snow Bird and prepared her for burial.

Sophia, holding Snow Bird's daughter close, stood at the window where Snow Bird had watched the boys disappear into the forest. An owl hooted, and a white bird visible in the moonlight fluttered from its perch on the highest limb of the ancient oak and flew into the night sky.

Hours earlier, the two boys had scampered through the pine woods toward the village. The shortcut led to a challenging jump over a deep gorge where a stream had cut its way down the hill. Cade sped up to leap the gorge. Gabriel was close on his heels, but he tripped on a tree root as he was about to jump. Cade heard his brother call out to him and looked around in time to see Gabriel's head disappear from sight. His heart lurched and he turned to run back. He lay down, stretched on his stomach to peer over the edge of the gorge. There he saw Gabriel clinging to a root protruding from the side of the bank.

"Hang on, Gabriel. I'll get you!"

Cade got up and looked around for a long branch or vine to throw down to Gabriel. Unfortunately, he had not thought to bring a knife. When at last he found a vine, it seemed like it took forever to bend and bite it to breaking. Anxious tears ran down his face. Gabriel was not strong. If he let go, he could be badly injured on the creek bed below.

Why had he led Gabe over that jump?

Cade swatted at the tears as the vine at last gave way. He hurried, dragging the vine along, listening intently for his brother's voice. Back at the ravine, Cade again lay flat and looked down before extending the vine. But Gabe was not there. Nor was he lying on the creek bed.

Cade's chest clenched when he heard the crunch of a footstep behind him. He jerked back to look up and see the most unusual man he had ever encountered. He was tall, with clear blue eyes, a chiseled nose, and a dimpled chin, and dressed in a combination of Indian garb and British officer clothing. Silver armbands encircled his upper arm above the ruffled white linen shirt he wore loose over breeches of deerskin and colorfully woven flaps.

The man reached out to help Cade to his feet.

"Where's Gabe?" Cade demanded.

"We have your brother. My name is Billy. We have come for the two of you."

Cade was familiar with these woods, and he knew the people who should be in them. His mother would never have sent this strange man for him and Gabe. If Gabe hadn't been missing, Cade would have run to the talwa to warn his kinsmen.

But he might *really* have Gabe.

The man said nothing, only turned and set off down a path that was seldom traveled by any in the village. It was obvious he expected Cade to follow, which he did without question. Gabe might need him. He soon heard the sound of flowing water and felt the cooling breeze as they walked toward a leafy bank in the shadows of moss-laden river oaks. There, sitting in a large canoe pulled up next to the shore, he spotted Gabriel. Cade could tell he was trying to communicate something to him with his eyes. Cade felt his fear.

And then a chill went down his spine as he recognized the large, muscular man steadying the canoe. Battle scars crisscrossed his body. He wore a red cotton handkerchief tied about his head, with feathers bobbing about that, oddly enough, only enhanced the effect of his menacing scowl. His cropped ears and the scar across his forehead intensified the startling effect and identified him.

Cade's blood ran cold.

Savannah Jack!

And then he realized that "Billy," the man he had followed, was none other than William Augustus Bowles—his father's archenemy and the man his father now sought.

"Get in the canoe," Billy ordered. "We've got a ways to go."

Cade's worst nightmare had just begun.

1

August 28, 1813

The day had finally arrived. Lyssa felt his approach though she knew he was still miles away. Her thick-lashed violet eyes sparkled with excitement in the morning sun. Her straight, glossy, blue-black hair lifted with the soft breeze drifting up the Hobuckintopa Bluff above the old Spanish fort at St. Stephens. Below, the Tombigbee River wound its serpentine way down to join the Alabama and then hurried past Mobile into the big waters beyond. From the shadows of the pine thicket there on the bluff, Lyssa would watch *her boy*, as she continued to call him, approach Oklahannali, the Six Towns District of the Choctaw, and the village of their chief, her grandfather Pushmataha, further up the Tombigbee River.

Beauty whinnied her objection to their stillness, indeed to Lyssa's whole plan. They'd been in position since before daylight, watching and waiting.

"Shh," Lyssa whispered, leaning over to stroke Beauty's graceful snow-white neck. "I know your feelings about this. But it is the right thing to do." Beauty shook her mane.

"Besides, it is too late to back out now," Lyssa said as much to herself as to Beauty. When she and her little brother Lance had planned this, it had made perfect sense. Now, with the knot in her stomach and the lump in her throat, she was not quite so certain.

"Lance *is* prone to being impetuous," she muttered to herself.

Beauty snorted. Beauty knew who the impetuous one was.

"Shh! He'll see us!" She certainly wasn't ready for that yet! Of course, he was nowhere in sight, but Lyssa had heard enough of Beauty's opinion of her endeavor.

Besides, sound carried over water. She did not want anyone to see her until her plan was accomplished. Anyone could ride past on the road behind her to downtown St. Stephens. A slight motion of her hand kept Samson and Delilah her ever-present bull mastiff companions, still and on guard. She sighed deeply, and her thoughts drifted to the events that had led to her first encounter with Cade Kincaid.

Beauty, Samson and Delilah, and the raccoon Ophelia, who had upset her father by stowing away in a basket on one of their packhorses, had come with Lyssa from the Savannah trading post that had been her family's home for the first eight years of her life. Then, ten years ago after her mother was nearly raped in their fields by men who took exception to the successful squaw man and his beautiful Indian wife, her father decided to accept the offer of his wife's father, Chief Pushmataha, to help the family settle in Choctaw country. Lyssa's father, Jacob Rendel, had parlayed trading with his love of horses and gotten involved with the Pebble Spring Jockey Club near the rocky shoals of the Tombigee River, where his friend George Gaines now had a Choctaw trading post.

Her father was the handsome, black-haired, green-eyed scion of a Virginia First Family. His own father's family in England had reluctantly accepted their younger sons's decision to settle on land they had acquired through investments in the London Company in Virginia, a move made more agreeable since he would live near other members of their family who'd come earlier to the colonies. Jake's father had come to America to seek his fortune, leaving his father and older brothers to their English titles and estates.

Jake had fought in the Revolution in the Savannah area and decided to stay there, much to his Virginia parents' dismay. Until he took his Indian wife, they'd had plans for him to come home and accept his rightful place in the upper echelons of Virginia society.

As a little girl, Lyssa had begged her father over and over to tell her the romantic story of the day he met her mother, Malee. He always began with, "I glanced up from counting the hides brought by what I thought was just another group of Indians." Then he continued, a smile playing around his eyes. "Stroking the colorful materials was a beautiful Choctaw princess who had come with members of her tribe to trade at my post on the Savannah River. Later, I learned it was her first trip away from her father's village. Her companions were so fascinated by the wares—silver mirrors, fabrics, pottery—that they didn't notice our instant attraction to each other."

13

Lyssa could just see it. Malee's playful, sweet spirit and grace had struck her father as he watched her interact with her friends. Then Lyssa's mother lifted her amber-colored, almond-shaped eyes and looked straight at Jacob. Her shy smile lit her face and warmed his heart so that suddenly, it seemed that only he and she existed.

"Mr. Rendel, Mr. Rendel!" The clerk finally got his attention. Only then did Jake realize he was gawking like a callow young man. He was thirty-five and a confirmed bachelor, a hardened veteran of the Revolution. Malee was only nineteen. Still, with one look he was smitten.

Jake was adept at the *ligua franca* needed for successful trading, and they communicated well enough with a lifetime to learn more. The two of them married at Christ Church in Savannah before his family or her father Pushmataha could object. They lived happily, content and complete in their own company and that of the daughter who for eight years was their only child. That fairy tale never grew old.

Then Lyssa remembered the fateful day when her mother was saved only because Lyssa spotted the smelly fur traders who had made her so uncomfortable the day before—with their rude comments and leering looks—lurking near the barn when she went to take Beauty an apple. Seven-year-old Lyssa had eluded the nasty men herself only because Samson lunged and growled at them, giving her the space to run away and find her father.

When she reached him, she breathlessly pulled him from the storeroom where he was taking inventory.

"Hurry. Come quickly!" she had cried.

Faintly, in the distance, they heard the frantic screams of her pregnant mother from the cornfield where she'd gone to pick ripe corn from the stalks. Jake ran faster than he had ever run before. Lyssa and the dogs followed close behind. Her mother's skirt was rucked, and though she fought and clawed, one of the men was positioning himself between her legs. Samson reached Malee first and went for the attacker's throat. Jake arrived in time to rip the man from Samson's powerful jaws and toss him to the other side of the cornfield with his pants still down around his knees.

"Maybe I ought to let Samson finish the job," Jake said, holding Malee in his arms.

"You came in time, my love," Malee said, tears dripping from her eyes. Sensing his thoughts, she entreated him, saying, "He is not worth the trouble it would cause. Your white man's law would side with him."

Jake felt that death was too easy for the son of a bitch. Unfortunately, the law probably *would* convict him instead of the perpetrator since he had attempted to rape an Indian woman. At least the man's friends had sense enough to scatter.

"Help me up and distract your daughter from that awful sight!" Malee commanded, catching sight of Lyssa's preoccupation.

Jake looked at his daughter. Lyssa was staring as the man ran and pulled at his pants, his white buttocks only inches from Samson's snapping teeth. She was mesmerized by his swolleness the fur trader was just now attempting to cover. His daughter could be scarred for life by the sight of the crudeness and brutality that man had almost perpetrated on her mother! Jake Rendel whistled for Samson and gathered his two girls close to lead them back to the post. They would not leave his sight again.

Had the man planned to stick that rod into her mother? Lyssa wondered and worried. The very thought caused her nightmares for weeks afterward.

His wife's near rape had a sobering effect on Jake Rendel. He realized that his wife and daughter, and the baby his wife carried, would know a respect in their Choctaw heritage that they would never know growing up in the white world. Lyssa was becoming more beautiful—and more vulnerable—by the day. Jake and Malee waited until after the birth of their son, Lancelot Arthur Rendel, and then they and their children moved to the safety of her father Pushmataha's Six Village territory west of the Tombigbee.

Sitting there on the bluff, Lyssa had nothing else to do but think. Her mind put away thoughts of her mother's assault and drifted to the moment later that year when she had first set eyes on Cade Kincaid.

For more security, her father had brought his family and their possessions on packhorses from Savannah to join a pack train led by Major General John Twiggs. From the meeting point at the Cedar Shoals trading post on the Oconee River, they would follow an old Cherokee trail that had become the postal riders' horse path, traveling from Cedar Shoals on the Oconee River, through Hawkins Creek Agency on the Flint

River, and finally through Creek territory to the Tensaw area where they would leave the pack train. Others would travel on to Mobile and New Orleans.

Lyssa had overheard her father tell her mother that with all the unrest in the Creek Country, he was sure grateful to be with John Twiggs, even if the man *was* fifty years old. His eyes twinkled, for Jake Rendel was nearly fifty himself at the time.

Malee had indicated the infant Lance in her arms and said, "The years have not slowed this woman's man." They both laughed and exchanged their special look.

Major General John Twiggs had been a Justice of the Peace in Burke County, Georgia, a state senator from Richmond County, and, as they discovered when they arrived at the Cedar Shoals trading post to join the train, had just been named a trustee for the University of Georgia that would be built on land nearby. The men laughed heartily about John Milledge, another trustee, grandly calling the 633 acres on the hill above the post—little more than a pine thicket—*Athens*, after the cultural center of ancient Greece.

A university! Just the word thrilled Lyssa. Looking longingly up the hill, she tried to imagine being able to attend a university like her father had done. But it was a dream she would never know. She was a girl and she was an Indian.

It wasn't long after they left Cedar Shoals that Lyssa met Cade.

Though Lyssa was only eight years old at the time and Cade was ten, it took just one look for her to *know* that boy was hers—whether he wanted to be or not. He was skinny and hungry because his father neglected him. His hair was tangled and filled with briars. But in those sad, sky-blue eyes, she recognized a kindred spirit—one half of her whole. Others might have thought her instant attraction to the boy was odd, but Lyssa had always been considered odd. Born with unusual intelligence and a canny sensitivity that put her in tune with other creatures, she was what some called "a whisperer." Perhaps it was that gift that drew her to him on the pack train. She was just a girl, younger than he, and actually had more more in common with his twin brother— and that was how Cade saw her.

Not that Lyssa hadn't struggled with being so different. Her Princeton-educated father (he made sure she knew it had been the

College of New Jersey when he attended) had taught her Latin at age four. The *Iliad* and the *Odyssey* were her bedtime stories, and she was reading Cicero's works by six. She read Shakespeare for pleasure, getting so distracted by his plays that Samson and Delilah had their work cut out for them herding her away from danger while she wandered with a book in her hand. Her vocabulary set her apart from the other children. She was so quick with mental calculations that she helped her father keep the books at the post by the time she was seven. The sight of her sitting on the high stool behind her father's counter, quill in hand, set queer on the minds of many. Most folks couldn't write their names, yet the little breed could not only read, write, and calculate, but she could literally talk the birds out of the trees.

As a toddler, Lyssa had watched eagerly, smiling and laughing when other little girls came into the Savannah post. But their parents guided them away from her, and as they grew older and entered the post, arm in arm with their friends, they rebuffed her friendly smiles and offers of sweets. Smiles turned to tears so often that, eventually, in spite of her sunny disposition and sociable personality, Lyssa had stopped trying. At an early age, she had experienced the pain of dismissal encouraged by the girls' parents, who didn't want their daughters "'sociating with breeds."

She didn't need them anyway when she had her animals. She was content. But her father and mother looked at one another over her head, and their hearts ached over her isolation and loneliness.

"She is special," her mother said.

"My little fairy," her father said, remembering his grandmother's pride in her Irish ancestry and tales of her family's fey gifts.

"A seer," both her grandfather and the village shaman said.

They made her "gift" sound positive and special. But then, they all loved her.

Her life changed when the son of the headman of a nearby talwa decided to make her his against her will and shifted the perception of her gifts from good to evil. Savannah did not have a monopoly on evil men, but Lyssa did not share that with her father. The young Choctaw pressed himself upon her and she nearly panicked, remembering her mother and the horrible man in the cornfield ten years earlier.

As small as she was, she *knew* she had little to fight with, and so—at a crucial point—she threatened to wither his man parts with her evil eye. Much to his (and her) surprise, Straight Arrow had suddenly become Bent Arrow, and Lyssa's virginity had remained intact. She later heard that, to the amusement of other women he had harassed, his arrow remained bent. That was fine with her. Why, she had performed a public service. But when old men started blaming her for their difficulties, life that had never been easy because of her differences became even more difficult. Straight Arrow went so far as to call her a witch!

Of course, Lyssa hadn't helped the situation by quoting Shakespeare's witches' speech while she stirred the sofkee, a cornmeal porridge, outside over an open fire. She'd spotted Straight Arrow soon after the incident, standing at the edge of the woods watching her. Unfortunately, some of his friends were watching as well.

Lyssa bent over the bubbling cauldron and allowed her hair to fall about her face. She hunched her back and stirred with vigor.

"Double, double toil and trouble;
Fire burn, and caldron bubble."

She ventured a glance at the gawkers. Their faces were priceless! She almost burst out laughing. But she controlled herself and continued on, quoting Shakespeare.

"Fillet of a fenny snake,
In the caldron boil and bake;
Eye of newt, and toe of frog,
Wool of bat, and tongue of dog,
Adder's fork, and blind-worm's sting,
Lizard's leg, and owlet's wing,—
For a charm of powerful trouble,
Like a hell-broth boil and bubble."
She closed her eyes and lifted her face to the sky.
"Scale of dragon; tooth of wolf;
Witches' mummy; maw and gulf…"

Taken in by her acting, the men had begun to move back step by step, inch by inch into the forest, putting distance between them and the Rendel cabin. But Lyssa was having so much fun that she took it to the end, dramatically lifting her arms above her and twirling around the cauldron as she recited the witches' words.

Of the ravin'd salt-sea shark;
Root of hemlock digg'd in the dark;
Liver of blaspheming Jew;
Gall of goat, and slips of yew
Sliver'd in the moon's eclipse;
Nose of Turk, and Tartar's lips;
Finger of birth-strangled babe
Ditch-deliver'd by a drab,—
Make the gruel thick and slab:
"Add thereto a tiger's chaudron,
For the ingredients of our caldron."

She tossed in a few more ingredients and gave the sofkee another stir. Then she lowered her voice for the grand finale.

"Double, double toil and trouble;
Fire burn, and caldron bubble.
Cool it with a baboon's blood,
Then the charm is firm and good."

In retrospect, perhaps she should have left off her final cackle that set them falling over their feet to get away. But their reaction and the look on their faces, horrible as the repercussions had been, still made her laugh!

Not long after, Lyssa could not raise her eyes when she walked in public or she might accidentally gaze upon some male—young, old, middle-aged, whatever. They shielded their man parts and quickly headed in the opposite direction. If she'd known how sensitive men were about those parts, she would have just kicked Straight Arrow's breech-clouted package and been done with it.

She could have done it, too. Her grandfather, Pushmataha, had secretly taught her everything he had taught her little brother, Lance. Use your wits first, he'd said, and then resort to force. She could handle a bow and arrow and shoot a gun as well as any warrior. But words could be more powerful, and in this instance they surely had more far-reaching consequences. Her and her grandfather's "secret" remained secret.

Her father knew something was wrong and thought her rejection of Straight Arrow, who had made known his intention to make Lyssa one of his wives, might have something to do with what she had seen in the cornfield. Did she think all men were like the rapist in Savannah? Lyssa would not talk about it. Of course, Straight Arrow's version led all to believe that Lyssa was a witch who had cast a spell on an honest admirer and that it would affect all men in the village.

Noticing her difficulties, her father had moved the family away from his father-in-law's village to a home near the Pebble Creek Jockey Club about a mile from St. Stephens, a town of 3,000 citizens that served as the seat of government for the Mississippi Territory. Life there was little better. Sally Carson, whom Lyssa had hoped would be her friend, had whispered "Choctaw breed" loudly when Lyssa sat next to her at school, and pullled her books far to the other side of the desk. Sally's contempt spread like wildfire. Soon Lyssa's time at school consisted of solitary lunches and bullying, and it did not help that she was smarter than any of them!

Lyssa now spent most of her time at the racetrack with her father, mainly in the barn tending his horses. She liked her work, for horses made better companions than people most of the time. Sometimes, however, she still longed for the friendships she saw other girls have. As she grew older, in spite of herself, she began to admire the stylish clothing of some of the young women her age, and a strange longing would take hold of her to feel the soft fabric and rustle of silk petticoats against her own skin, to smell a fragrant soap rather than pungent horse liniment. Had she told her father, he would have immediately dressed her in silks and satins and bought a mountain of perfumes and soap. But that would have kept her from her anonymity and her horses.

Then, one day before a race, keeping to the shadows of the horse barn and camouflaged in boy's clothing, she caught sight of the bright colors and intricate hairstyles of a group of stylishly dressed young women who were strolling through the track. Two girls entered the barn and snapped their umbrellas shut as they came into the shade. Hortense, the horse Lyssa was brushing, stepped back abruptly on her foot. Lyssa hopped soundlessly about in the deep shadows of the barn before she tumbled into the hay. She restrained herself from uttering the expletives on the tip of her tongue. She did not want to be discovered.

Other horses skittered at the girls' high-pitched voices. The girls took no notice. Their heads were together, and they were intent on sharing their gossip. Lyssa peeked through the rails and recognized her least favorite female in the world.

White world. Red world. The story was always the same. "You're different."

Lyssa held her breath. She did not want Sally Carson to see her, dressed like a boy, sweaty as she was, with hay sticking out of her hair. How did that girl always make her feel so awkward and ugly?

Sally minced around the muck of the stalls, her pale pink dress with a pink flowered overlay swishing as she walked. She inclined her bonneted head as she listened to her blonde-haired friend, who wore a turquoise and blue creation and adjusted the lace fichu lower in the already extremely low-cut bodice. From her spot on the floor, Lyssa peered between the wooden slats and took note of every detail of their beautiful dresses.

"Everybody talks about how handsome William Weatherford is," Sally said as she practiced a pose, poking the end of her fancy umbrella into the ground. As if on cue, a breeze lifted one of her natural curls, making it float casually about her face, and she smiled a smile no man could resist. Then she wrinkled her nose. "But he is so *old!*" The other girl giggled.

"And then there is Cade Kincaid." Lyssa's ears perked up. Hortense joined her, sticking her head though the railing. Lyssa tried to push Hortense back toward the middle of the stall. The horse was breathing so loudly that Lyssa was having trouble hearing!

"Even though Cade Kincaid got wounded at Burnt Corn Creek when the Red Sticks attacked, he still helped my father find those lost in the swamp before he would allow them to tend to his wound!" Sally continued, clasping her hands melodramatically to her heart. "He was a hero at Burnt Corn! My father said so."

Lyssa bumped her head as she fell back in surprise. The two girls glanced her way and saw only Hortense's head sticking through the railing.

Cade Kincaid? Wounded? Lyssa sat up again and listened more carefully.

Sally modestly dipped her head, then opened and twirled the parasol. "I think he might be the man I'm going to marry. I just haven't decided."

Lyssa's heart clenched, and she held her breath so as not to miss a word. Hortense nuzzled her, but Lyssa ignored the animal for once.

The other girl giggled again. "And how do you plan to accomplish that? You know he seldom attends any social event."

"Sometimes a girl must take matters into her own hands," Sally said provocatively as she led her friend from the cool of the barn and out into the sunshine once again.

Lyssa could not believe her ears. Cade Kincaid? *Her* Cade Kincaid?

"Hortense, Cade is wounded," she said to the horse nibbling on her ear. "My boy is wounded. And he is about to be ensnared by that—that—Jezebel! That—Sally Carson!"

Hortense whinnied in shared dismay.

"He is in *danger*, and here I am hiding away in a barn!" she said, looking around her in disgust. Hortense nodded her understanding.

Suddenly Lyssa's future hit her in the face. She realized that if she didn't do something, she would be kicked out of the competition by not even being in it! This would never do. Her dream was about to be shattered. The one thing that had kept her going through the years of isolation was the knowledge that one day her boy would come for her.

"Remember, Delilah, the first time we saw my boy?" Lyssa asked, sighing and forgetting her own admonition about being quiet. She patted the dog's head.

That first sight of her boy remained clear in her memory. She remembered it being as hot that August day as it was this day in August ten years later.

"Good Lord, Delilah, the devil must be close because it is as hot as hell here today," Lyssa said, using one of her father's favorite sayings.

Delilah licked her leg with her wet tongue in response. Delilah didn't waste words.

That evening ten years ago, daylight was fading as eight-year-old Lyssa headed toward the river with apples for her horses hobbled and belled to forage by the river with the other horses during the night.

Snow-white Beauty and ebony Beast, both thoroughbreds, were her father's most valuable investments. The pack train had ridden hard all day, and it was time to rest.

"Samson, come back here. Leave that squirrel alone," she called.

Samson, the more stubborn of the two mastiffs, slowed only to look over his shoulder at her, causing him to stumble in a gopher hole and tumble over his big feet. The squirrel chattered expletives and scampered up a tree. Samson recovered and barked his menacing version of "I meant to do that" before returning to Lyssa's side. It was then that she noticed the silence of the packmen. She turned to see what they were watching.

And then she saw *her boy*.

Her heart stopped.

She *knew* him.

Not that she'd ever laid eyes on him before in her life.

But she *knew* him. Not from dreams or visions or anything.

She simply knew him. That was it.

And suddenly she was hit with the most excruciating pain and knew it was *his* pain she felt. Her boy was being lashed with a whip by his own father. Cade Kincaid, staggering, his ice-blue eyes glazed with fever, had thrown himself between the man with the whip poised and the other boy, tall with gentle doe's eyes and scrawny to the point of emaciation, who lay on the ground with his arm upraised in anticipation of the coming strike.

Not a whimper escaped her boy as the lash ripped through the suppurating stripes already on his back, probably the cause of the glazed eyes and fever-flushed face. The onslaught of total awareness of another human being left Lyssa shocked into an unaccustomed inaction. She watched as the boy staggered and then regained his balance, bracing himself to receive another lashing.

Delilah, the female bull mastiff her doting father had trained to guard his careless and impulsive daughter, moved closer to Lyssa and began to growl, catching Samson's attention.

Suddenly a woman's voice shrilled through the night, "Teach those breeds a lesson about respect for their betters."

Lyssa's heart clenched and she felt the pain, greater than that of the lashes raining down on the boy wavering before her. The boy looked into his father's eyes, and Lyssa knew the shame he felt—not at the woman's words, for the woman meant nothing to him—but that his own father shared that horrible woman's judgment of him.

The packmen who ranged about there by the river, hobbling their horses for the night, were obviously disturbed. But they hung back, unwilling to involve themselves in what was perceived as a family affair, a man disciplining his sons. "Kincaid," she heard them whisper in explanation and exasperation.

The whip whistled through the air. Kincaid's methods might be offensive, and those nearby might have to turn their eyes, but his right was unquestioned.

The boldness with which Cade faced his drunken bully of a father was an image Lyssa would never forget. Nor would she forget the contempt in the voice of his father's woman when she urged him to beat some respect for his betters into that "half-breed" son of his.

"Move away, Gabriel," Cade ordered his bleeding brother.

Gabriel's eyes flickered with pain. He was on the verge of passing out, yet he was struggling weakly to rise, refusing to leave his brother to take the anger of their father alone.

"I can take it, Cade. You're sick with the fever. Go. Tend the horses. I can take it!" Then Gabriel's eyes rolled back in his head and he hit the ground unconscious. Their father barely took note of his son's condition. He only heard the words "half-breed" that the woman had uttered and let the black whip unfurl.

Lyssa literally felt her boy's despair at the contempt of his own father, knew his emptiness at the loss of his loving mother, and sensed his determination to protect his family, including the baby girl in that woman's arms. His eyes continually flicked between the baby and his father, whose arm drew back to unfurl the whip once again. Cade's unwillingness to cower before his father's anger seemed to stir Jason Kincaid's blood lust further. Samson and Delilah growled ominously at Lyssa's side. Lyssa was prepared to launch herself onto the drunken man when her father's hand grabbed her by the shoulder and his commanding voice stilled her.

"Strike that boy one more time, Kincaid, and you're a dead man," Jacob Rendel called in a voice of accustomed authority, chilling with its calm. "I'd sure hate to have to break in my new Baker rifle putting a hole in you."

Kincaid's arm stopped in midair.

"When did the hero of Cowpens become the bully of little boys?" Lyssa's father asked.

As the words sank into his alcohol-sodden brain, Jason Kincaid dropped to his knees and bowed his head. He looked up and glanced from his sons to the tall angular Scotswoman who held his baby against her bony chest. On any other man, the faraway, longing look in his eyes would have been heartbreaking. But the condition to which his madness had brought his sons wiped away any compassion Lyssa might have had for him.

Motherly Nicey Potts, who was from the Clan of the Wind like the twins, had rushed to them and had her big bear of a husband Herman carry Gabriel back to their wagon. Cade refused all help and staggered as he followed his brother.

Nicey's salves had healed the physical wounds, but Lyssa knew Cade's soul still bore the bruises.

Lyssa's did as well.

Could he have forgotten his childhood promise? Apparently she could no longer sit back and just *wait* for him.

She was still embarrassed by her behavior. Possessed by some horrible foreboding of what could happen to him without her there to protect him, she had actually clung to his leg with her father trying to pull her away until he promised to come for her when she had grown up. How could she have been so foolish? And yet—he *had* promised. Slowly a very smug, self-satisfied smile lit her face. She now had a plan.

That single moment had set Lyssa about her mission. She'd waited long enough for Cade Kincaid come to get her. If he would not come for her, she would find a way to get to *him*. She agreed with Sally about one thing. *Sometimes* a girl had to take matters into her own hands.

Unfortunately, that was easier said than done. Her father kept a close eye on her. But Lance.... Her brother was now nearly eleven years old and had the full freedom of the forest. He could go places she could not.

Lyssa felt like a different person when she stomped out of the barn. By the time she found Lance, she had already devised a plan. Always ready for an adventure, he was eager to help. Fortunately, Lance had a naturally devious bent of mind.

Little did Lyssa know that her plan dovetailed nicely with Nicey Potts's own covert planning with Cade's twin brother Gabriel. Nicey, a friend since their childhood journey from Georgia to the Tombigbee, was fired up about getting Cade and Lyssa together again. Cade carried scars from his time in captivity with Savannah Jack and Bowles that he would not share with anyone. They erupted in nightmares that, in the beginning, only his brother Gabe could calm. Because Gabriel came frequently to the racetrack, he had been able to keep in touch with Lyssa, informing her on Cade's whereabouts over the years and later confirming to Nicey that her affections remained true. Falling in with Lyssa's designs was simple, since the plot had already been set in motion.

Some of Lance and Lyssa's older cousins would pretend to be a raiding party, and Lance would be "captured." The cousins readily agreed to assist in the plan because they would be accomplishing two good deeds: getting Lyssa married off...and sending her away to a place where she would no longer be a threat to the village men. Her parents would not be told of the plot until it was complete.

Lance insisted to his cousins that their plan would prove that their superstitious concerns were wrong and stupid. Just because Lyssa could read and speak five different languages, run columns of numbers in her head, and talk to animals didn't mean she could level curses on people like one of those witches in Shakespeare's *Macbeth*, which none of *them* had read but Lance and Lyssa knew by heart.

With help from Gabriel, Lance and his cousins managed to get Lance safely "captured" in time to be there when Cade visited the Potts plantation. This way, Mrs. Potts could request Cade's assistance in getting the "poor little Choctaw boy," who had been captured in a raid, back to his people before he got killed.

Lyssa was now sitting on Beauty on the bluff, awaiting Lance's return. Her thoughts went back to Cade.

2

Time seemed to stand still as Lyssa waited and waited…and waited. The sun lifted from the east to its zenith on the other side of the river, the Creek side, and was now halfway to its descent in the west, the Choctaw side of the river. Beauty, Samson, and Delilah were growing more and more restless, shifting and whimpering their question.

"Soon," Lyssa promised, though her own anxiety had settled on her like a heavy mantle. Once again, Lyssa Rendel allowed her mind to drift back.

The next morning, after the battered twin boys had been taken into the Potts's custody, fat little hands had patted Lyssa's cheeks, and juicy kisses followed as Little Lance carried out his only duty: aggravating his big sister awake.

"Go back to sleep!" she grumbled as usual, all the while pulling him under the blanket in which she nestled in the welcome cool of the morning. "Here, let's cuddle a while."

Sometimes that would even work. At eighteen months, Lance was a good cuddler.

That day, however, Samson had decided to help Little Lance and licked her cheek with his rough tongue to Lance's vast amusement. Lance giggled. Samson sat back, giving them his pleased doggie smile. Lyssa swiped the slobber off her face with the back of her hand, her eyes still determinedly scrunched shut.

"It's too early! Go away," Lyssa complained, giving Lance a gentle push. Ophelia the raccoon scampered out of the way of Little Lance's rump as he tumbled back and giggled.

Then Lyssa's sleep encrusted eyes jerked open. Today was special. Her boy was nearby, and she would see him. She stumbled to the cask and splashed some water on her face and then, followed by her motley crew, made her way to the bushes while her mother kept Lance, who squalled in anger at not being allowed to follow. Lyssa blushed as she glanced over the bush to see Samson, Delilah, and Ophelia watching her intently and, of course, alerting anyone who glanced that way of the personal business she was attending to.

Please let the boy not be watching!

Her mother was heating the sofkee over an open fire and offered the spoon to Lyssa when she returned. Then she handed Little Lance over to Lyssa. Lance immediately ceased his earsplitting yells and planted another wet kiss on Lyssa's cheek, smearing sofkee all over her face just as he had already done to his own.

"Finish feeding Lancelot, too," her mother said as she set about gathering up their blankets and baskets into the bundles to load again on their horses. Her father was already gathering the packhorses. Impatiently, Lyssa obeyed her mother.

As soon as she had seen Lyssa's mother up and about, Mrs. Potts had ventured into their camp and asked Malee Rendel if she had seen a willow tree nearby so she could brew the tea that Cade needed. Apparently, his fever was due to more than the infected lashes down his back.

"Poor boy," she'd said. "The swamps those awful men took him to are breeding grounds for that kind of sweating sickness. I have found that the tea from the willow bark can help." Cade still had the glazed and burning look of fever, but he was already up and about. "Can't keep 'em down," Mrs. Potts said with pride as she headed in the direction Malee pointed. "Clan of the Wind, you know. It's in the blood."

Day had not yet crested the horizon, and already the air was filled with the curses the rough backwoodsmen directed toward the stubborn beasts of burden that had to be caught. The packhorses were small, raised in the Creek nation, but they were capable of bearing heavy loads and enduring great fatigue. At night, their packs were removed and covered with skins, the horses belled so they would be easy to locate and then turned out to feed on grass and young cane. Now it was time to gather them back together and reload them with packs of up to 180 pounds.

While she shoveled the sofkee into Lance's mouth, Lyssa watched the packmen settle the peculiarly shaped saddle that carried three bundles onto the horses. Two bundles were suspended across the saddle and came down by the sides of the pony, while the third was deposited on top of the saddle. Then they covered the whole pack with a skin to keep off the rain. It took quite a while to pack the horse correctly.

Lance decided to make bubbles with the sofkee, and Lyssa decided he'd had enough.

By then, the packmen were loading small kegs of tafia rum onto the horses along with poultry in reed cages. Other favorite wares included cloth, beads, mirrors, salt, binding, and petticoats that were secured in the horses' packs.

Lance was usually fascinated by the horses and men, and Lyssa entertained him by sitting with him and watching the packmen while her mother tended to the camp chores. As a result, when Lance spoke his first words Malee was shocked, but Jake just threw back his head and laughed. Lance was neither the first nor the last little child to learn rough language by listening to packmen.

Driving ten ponies in a lead, the packman used no lines but urged them on with hickory sticks and curses. Accustomed to their burdens, the ponies trotted docilely about their daily routine. Those who traveled with the traders knew that the Indians wanted the goods the traders brought to the different villages so badly that their safety was almost assured. But with renegades like Little Warrior, who had recently murdered a family he had trapped in a nearby canyon, and Savannah Jack on the loose, you could never be sure.

Lyssa held Lance's hand tightly so he did not escape and get trampled by the skittish horses. She had heard her parents talking and knew that they should be at the Indian agent Benjamin Hawkins's post by evening. Jake Rendel was looking forward to seeing his old friend Benjamin again. Lyssa knew her father was concerned about the epidemic of yellow water that had killed many of the Indians' horses last year. He was also worried about the growing dissension with the Creek nation over the increasing numbers of whites encroaching on Creek lands. He wanted to discuss the danger of taking his own thoroughbreds into the territory because of the risk of contagion as well as the danger of having them stolen by Indians desperate to replace the horses they had already lost.

Lyssa kept these issues at the back of her mind, but, the morning after watching Jason Kincaid take the whip to his sons, her concern was mostly for *her boy*. Lance grabbed her hand to drag her toward the horses. Lyssa glanced over at Mr. and Mrs. Potts's camp with studied nonchalance.

Mrs. Potts spotted her and answered her unspoken question. "They're tending the animals. Couldn't keep 'em down."

Lance laughed happily when Lyssa grabbed his hand and headed toward the horses, just where he had been trying to pull her. Considering his condition the night before, she was surprised to see Cade lingering at the edge of his father's camp, talking agitatedly to the black woman who tended the baby. Lyssa grabbed Lance just as he was about to latch hold of Ophelia's tail and settled him onto her hip, standing back to watch the interaction. Cade had obviously snared a rabbit and cooked it early that morning to bring to the slave girl tending the baby. What Lyssa observed was a heated debate as the slave girl attempted to refuse the food.

"Quit fussin', Sarilee," she heard Cade say. "If you keep making a racket out here, that Loughman woman will see me with this rabbit that I refuse to eat and she will take it for herself. Eat this to give you strength to feed the baby. I am the oldest. It is my responsibility to care for my brother and sister. I will provide the food for you and the baby that my father stays too drunk to think about."

Lyssa looked at his scarred, scrawny body and admired the spirit that remained untouched despite his father's lashings. Pride was evident in his fierce eyes and the nobility of his bearing. Sarilee took the rabbit and hid it within her cloak where she cradled the child. She then headed for the privacy of the trees. They needn't have worried. Leona Loughman remained curled in the blanket sound asleep in spite of the bustle around her. Lyssa watched her boy fade away into the woods, undoubtedly heading back to help Gabriel load the packhorses.

Like a wraith in the forest, Lyssa trailed Cade whenever she had a moment free from watching Lance. She was too shy and scared of rejection to make her presence known.

Although Lyssa thought she was undetected, Cade was aware of her every move. He hadn't been mentored by one of the best warriors and trackers in the Creek nation for nothing. Saying that High Head Jim was stealthy and undetectable was the truth, but the real surprise was that Jim accomplished this in spite of his size. He was six feet, eight inches, strong and well built, and extremely handsome if the soulful looks all the women sent his way meant anything. High Head Jim, in the prime of his life in his early thirties, had taken the time to teach Cade and Gabriel things their father could not...or would not. Cade had been an excellent student, much more so than Gabriel, who was constantly distracted by his empathy with the animals they tracked.

The skinny little girl reminded him of Gabriel. How she thought she could be undetected, followed as she was by two giant bull mastiffs and a chattering raccoon, amused and irritated him at the same time. He fought the protective feeling she engendered within him. Didn't she know it was dangerous to wander around alone? Many of those who had joined General Twiggs's train were renegades from the states, a rough-and-tumble lot.

He allowed her to follow him only so he could keep an eye on her. He'd spotted her father watching her from afar and gave him a nod to let him know he realized what she was doing and would also look out for her. Meanwhile, Lyssa naively believed she was expertly camouflaging herself and her little entourage. It was all Cade could do not to laugh out loud at the four sets of eyes—two mastiffs, Lyssa, and Ophelia—lined up, peering out of the shadows as he tended his father's horses.

"Your audience is in place, Cade," Gabriel teased under his breath.

"How do you know she's not watching *you*?" Cade countered.

"*You're* the ladies' man in the family," his brother said, grinning.

"Am not!" Cade said, for if he were, it would make him too much like his father.

"Are too," Gabriel said.

"Am not!" said Cade, lightly punching Gabriel's arm. Gabriel, of course, punched him back, and both boys winced. Though Nicey Potts's potions and stews had strengthened them, and her bear-grease salve protected their wounds, it would be days before they fully recovered. Leona Loughman had finally stirred and rode past the boys, clucking her disapproval of their fun. Rubbing his sore arm, Cade unconsciously looked back to where he'd last seen the girl, but she and her coterie had disappeared.

He shook his head. She wasn't any of his business. He had enough to take care of without adding a skinny little waif of a thing, more eyes than body. Still, he found himself scanning the bushes for a glimpse of her.

Lyssa had seen the Loughman woman ride past toward the twins. Mrs. Potts had told Lyssa that, regardless of her posturing, Leona

Loughman was merely a poor relation, attached to Forbes & Company only by a distant family relationship. Apparently, though, Cade's father was impressed and thought to elevate himself through some relationship, however tenuous, with the powerful company.

Turning her attention back to Cade, Lyssa noticed that Mrs. Potts's tea hadn't had time to make much difference. The boys' eyes still glittered with the fever. Herman had finally insisted that the two of them ride one of the horses. Cade must not have gotten much sleep at all last night, Lyssa thought, what with tending the horses, setting traps, and then cooking the rabbit he'd caught to provide for his little sister's nursemaid.

As the Loughman woman rode by, Lyssa hunkered back in the bushes. She felt guilty for her attitude toward her mother about helping care for Little Lance. Suddenly, she desperately wanted to give her mother a hug, something Cade and Gabriel would never be able to do again. She turned quickly, only to stumble over Delilah face first and hit her head on a rock.

Cade saw her at that moment. When she didn't get up, he wondered if she had broken her neck and went running to her side. By the time he got to her, Lyssa was sitting up holding her head in her hands, her elbows propped on her knees.

She looked up, clearly astonished to see him there.

"Little girl, are you all right?" he said as he gently felt her neck and head. Lyssa was so embarrassed that she started crying. "Aw, now, does it hurt that bad?" Cade asked. "Can you stay right here while I run and get your father?"

She tried to shake her head, but the shooting pain inside her skull made her groan. "I'm all right! Don't go—" She was going to say "...get my father," but right then he put his arm around her and she lost her breath. Not because he was holding her too tightly, but because his stormy blue eyes were less than a foot before her face and she simply couldn't breathe.

"Breathe, little girl. Did you fall that hard?"

She couldn't breathe and she couldn't quit staring into his eyes. What was happening to her? She'd never felt like this before.

"My name is Lyssa. Not 'Little Girl'!" she said indignantly with what little breath she had.

She knew she had dirt on her face, but she couldn't wipe it off and she couldn't spit out the dirt in her mouth. It was bad enough that she had fallen on her face, bad enough that she thought she was hidden and he knew she was there all along (otherwise he wouldn't have seen her fall), bad enough that she couldn't breathe and suddenly there were black spots in front of her eyes. But then everything started spinning and she threw up.

All over him.

Oh, God.

Maybe she would just pass out and die.

Covered in vomit, he picked her up, squashed her tiny body against him, and ran with her back to her mother with Delilah growling and nipping at his heels.

"Back, dog," Cade yelled. "Can't you see I'm trying to help her?"

By then her father had seen what was happening. He had jumped off his horse and was running toward Cade by the time her mother had slid off her horse with Little Lance. At last, Lyssa was breathing again, appalled by what she had done and by the fact that her face was smashed against Cade's bare, vomit-covered chest.

Puking in your hero's face was enough to shock you into breathing again. Her father's face spun around before her as he reached for her and laid her on the ground.

"She fell, sir. Tripped over that big dog there." The big dog pushed herself between Cade and Lyssa and began licking Lyssa's face where a big, blue knot was growing on her forehead.

"Move, Lilah. That hurts!" she said, slapping Delilah away. Lyssa rolled on her side, more mortified than in pain, although the pain was now to a level that mortification was about to take second place.

Mrs. Potts came running with one of her little cups of remedies. "Drink this, dearie. It'll help the pain." To Lyssa's mother she explained, "It's tea I made from the bark of the willow tree you directed me to. It helps with pain and swelling."

Lyssa's father held her up to take a swig, and she prayed she wouldn't throw up again. She couldn't even look at Cade now, she was so embarrassed. When she heard Mrs. Potts tell him to follow her so she could clean him up a bit, Lyssa didn't open her eyes or say thank you.

After a few minutes of watching her breathe, her father lifted her up in front of him on his horse. Beast's rhythmic gait and the warm day put her to sleep. The sun was setting when her father woke her up as he had done intermittently during their ride. He had ridden back down the line to point out the cluster of buildings ahead of them to her mother. Lyssa was mortified when she jerked awake to realize that she had been straddling her father, her mouth hanging open, and had actually drooled on his chest.

What if the boy had seen her! She felt the knot on her head and grimaced. Her head still hurt, but her father's excitement at being at Hawkins's agency made her forget about her embarrassment. To her mother's relief, she shifted in her father's arms so she could also see the fort ahead of them.

3

The sun had dropped close to the horizon by the time Twiggs led the pack train through the gate of Hawkins's agency. Looking westward through the gateposts down the central avenue to the Flint River beyond the settlement, Lyssa could see the striations of brilliant pinks and purples with its remaining rays outlining the clouds like gilt.

Throughout their journey, her father had dwelt endlessly upon the subject of his friend Ben Hawkins and what an admirable leader he was. The agency was intended to be a model of how successful animal husbandry and land cultivation could actually be. Lyssa knew all about this model of progressive agriculture through correspondence between Hawkins and her father. Jake Rendel discussed these things with his daughter, who had always been interested in the world and asked many questions in order to understand.

A different child would have been bored to tears, but Lyssa could hardly wait to meet this friend and classmate of her father's.

Benjamin Hawkins had been a prosperous landowner and state senator from North Carolina before accepting the job as agent to the Creeks. When he agreed to be the principal agent for all four southern nations of Indians in 1796, he had brought his slaves with him from North Carolina to the agency. They had cleared and fenced the rich fields and planted orchards as examples to show the Indians. Hawkins even had a cotton gin, a wonderful new invention that automated separating the cottonseed from the cotton fiber. One of Hawkins's favorite projects was teaching Indian women to spin their own cloth out of the cotton they grew, thereby decreasing their dependence on credit at the factory, the government-operated trading post. This gave women something they could trade so they wouldn't have to be completely reliant on the skins their men provided.

Unfortunately, that self-reliance didn't sit well with the men. In fact, it stirred quite a few of them to violent actions.

Shrinking lands had cut back on the amount of hides the men could bring home from the hunt, and the demand for deerskin had decreased, meaning they needed more credit to buy their goods at a time when the cost of goods was going up. This concept of the changing value of a good relative to the demand of the good was difficult for Indians to understand. The traditional sex roles were rigid. Unfortunately, Lyssa's father told her, the men considered working in the fields women's work. The white man's ideas of civilization and domestication provoked traditionalists, and Ben Hawkins was having a hard time convincing the Indians that this new way might be better for them.

Twiggs guided the pack train to the field beyond the village, stopping just outside the enclosure to camp for the evening. Otis, Jake Rendel's ostler, organized the nine other packmen who tended their many packhorses, while Lyssa's father led her and her mother and brother into the agency. Lyssa noted that Cade and Gabe were helping the Potts family with their horses, but she knew they'd be seeing to their father's horses immediately after. Jason Kincaid would probably have found a tree to sprawl out under and a jug of tafia with which to drink himself into oblivion.

Lyssa thought she was prepared for the Creek Agency, but the sight was more than she could have imagined. After entering the gate to the fort, they crossed the causeway bridge with low wetlands to the left and garden, tents, and smokehouse to the right. This led to a street lined with a hatters shop, a blacksmith shop, houses for the slaves Hawkins had brought with him from North Carolina, an Indian tavern, a joiners shop, and a weavers shop. Beyond that were the office, the kitchen, and Hawkins's two-story white-washed frame home, complete with a wide front veranda. His assistant Christian Limbaugh's home was directly across the street to the south. The broad street ended at the ferry across the Flint where they would pick up the path to Pensacola and New Orleans should they continue to its end. While the organization and beauty of the fields and orchards was impressive, it was the throng of visitors that crowded the streets, stores, office, and the porches of Ben's home that truly amazed Lyssa. Reds, blacks, whites, and mestizos milled about everywhere.

Her father lifted her down from Beast and then went to help her mother and brother down from Beauty. They all mounted the stairs to Hawkins's white house. Long, lace-curtained windows that could swing open like doors lined the veranda. When her father knocked at the front door, a child crawled between the curtains and the window and peered out at Lyssa. A tall, graceful woman with a dusky complexion and dark hair plaited and pulled into a coronet around her head greeted them, clutching a baby on her hip.

"Is Benjamin Hawkins here?" Lyssa's father asked, hat in hand.

"Follow me," the woman said with a smile and led them down a hall with whitewashed plaster walls and an ebony-stained heart pine floor. She opened a door to reveal a private study where the craggy-faced Hawkins sat, quill in hand writing a letter, oblivious to the noise and activity that poured in through the open window. Right outside on the veranda a group of old men sat cross-legged, passing a pipe and watching the women's activity at the kitchen and washhouse.

"Is it always such a madhouse, Ben?" her father asked.

Hawkins stood immediately, pleasure wreathing his face, and embraced his old friend. Lyssa was prepared to be impressed with the man who had assumed such a thankless job, leaving home and family to serve his nation by attempting to bring peaceful change in such a cauldron of culture clash. But now that she was actually in his presence, she found that Benjamin Hawkins evoked an even stronger emotion with his bearing. He was a handsome man, well built and clean shaven, with blue eyes bright with warmth and intelligence. Deep dimples accentuated his broad, ready smile. His voice was deep and cultured. He clasped her father's hand in both of his own.

"Unfortunately, yes," he said. "You see, I travel frequently throughout the Nation and receive quite generous hospitality. It is only expected that I should return that hospitality. My home always has visitors. And yes, it is quite wearing at times."

Jake Rendel noted the lines of worry and fatigue in his friend's face. He knew Hawkins suffered frequently from gout. The rigors of sleeping in the elements on the trail exacerbated his ailment. From their correspondence, Jake knew the responsibility of the job was dampening Hawkins's usually optimistic outlook. Hawkins caught a glimpse of Lyssa as she pressed close to her father, her thumb in her mouth and the knot growing bluer on her head. She knew she was much too old for the thumb in her mouth, but when she was tired (and she was very, very tired), it somehow took on a life of its own.

Hawkins smiled at her.

"My, my, what a beautiful little girl. Looks like you've had an accident," he said. Lyssa nodded and shyly hid her face against her father's leg.

"She had a little fall and gave us a scare, but everything seems to be all right." Jake looked around for Malee.

"Ben, I would like to introduce to you my wife and my children." Malee hung back, her shawl shielding her and Little Lance. "Here is my wife, Malee Rendel, and our son, Lancelot Rendel," he said, pulling Malee into the shelter of his arm. "And this is Lysistrata Rendel, our daughter."

Hawkins smiled at them and lifted his eyebrows at their names.

"Lance and Lyssa," her father said. Hawkins nodded.

Lyssa felt her father tense, knowing Hawkins assessed Rendel's situation—happily married to an Indian woman—and was probably relating it to his own.

With warmth and grace, Hawkins said, "So this is your lovely wife and your son. And what a fine family you have!" Then he leaned down and chucked her under the chin. Lyssa grimaced. Hawkins chuckled. "Jake, you lucky man. What a beautiful family!"

Malee smiled shyly at the man about whom she had heard so many good things. Among the Creek Nation, he was a great man with a powerful voice that had been heard by the Great Father Washington, by whom he had been appointed to this position. She knew from her husband that the new president, Thomas Jefferson, listened to Hawkins regarding Indian affairs. While she had not been tutored in academics as Lyssa had, one could not be married to Jake Rendel without absorbing history, politics, and current events. After dinner, as she sewed or nursed Little Lance, her husband read aloud from the newspapers he acquired in Savannah and Charleston. Often he had Lyssa read to them while he carved or wove hemp into rope for use on the post.

"So why have you left your post near Savannah, Jake?" Hawkins asked.

Lyssa's father related the incident that had led to their removal to the west. Hawkins nodded as if he sympathized.

"Malee is the daughter of Pushmataha," Jake Rendel said. "They will be safer closer to his protection and influence." He looked at his wife and children with love evident in his green eyes. Malee smiled back with just as much love and affection but shifted Lance on her hip, reminding Ben Hawkins that he had left them standing without offering refreshment.

"Forgive me. Where are my manners?" Ben turned to the woman who had greeted them at the door. "Jake, may I present to you my housekeeper, Lavinia Downs." He pointed toward the baby and at the child they had seen at the window, who had snuck in during the conversation. "These two scamps are Georgiana and Muscogee. Lavinia will make sure you are comfortable."

Lyssa, wise beyond her years, had noticed the woman watching Hawkins as he and Jake had talked. Ben might call her his housekeeper, but the tender way she looked at him betrayed her true feelings for the man, and the way the child whose face she had seen at the window pulled at Hawkins's trousers and held her arms up to be held betrayed his relationship to the children. She liked Hawkins, but she wondered why he was reluctant to acknowledge his children and their mother with the same respect her father showed her mother and his children.

Lyssa watched her mother follow Lavinia, aware of a bond they had in common—their love for men forbidden by their own cultures to love them in return. Lyssa's father had found no barrier there, but Hawkins was apparently still battling convention.

Lyssa lingered in the library, awed by the number of books on shelves and stacked by chairs and on the desk. There must be over a hundred, some with which she was familiar but many she'd only heard of...and one by Jonathan Swift that she had longed to read. She looked at it reverently but dared not touch it.

Hawkins noted her interest. "She looks hungry for that book, Jake," he commented.

"She has been reading since she was four and can read and write five languages," her father said with pride.

"I'm impressed but hardly surprised, with a scholar like you for a father," Hawkins responded.

"Well, it hasn't made her life any easier. It's only been another barrier to friendships, as if she didn't have enough to contend with," he said, noticing the three pairs of eyes staring in at them from outside the library window.

Hawkins followed his gaze. "What do we have here?"

Lyssa's father explained, "Lyssa has this 'gift' with animals. Those are three of her most faithful followers. Samson and Delilah are bull mastiffs, gifts from my sister, the only family member I have that did not treat my family with disrespect and contempt when I took them to Virginia to introduce them to my parents."

Hawkins nodded with both understanding and resignation.

"I'll never take them back," Jake said with asperity. Hawkins's look turned to sympathy. He could imagine.

"The other is Ophelia," he continued, "the raccoon I thought we had left in Savannah with the rest of the menagerie only to find she had stowed away and didn't reveal herself until it was too late to send her back."

After receiving a nod of permission from Ben Hawkins and her father, Lyssa sat cross-legged on the floor, leaning against the bookshelves with the book open. The book had banished her fatigue, and she barely heard the men talking about her. Not even the arrival of the silver tea tray laden with sweet cakes and sandwiches could distract her.

Hawkins offered Jake a brandy, and her father readily accepted. The men sat in the two federal rocking chairs with the tea tray between them.

Knowing Lyssa was oblivious while she was reading, Jake leaned toward Hawkins and said softly, "Lyssa is lonely and has no friends." He took a puff on the pipe Hawkins had provided. The smoke drifted slowly and companionably toward the ceiling. Then he sipped the brandy Hawkins had handed him.

Hawkins sat in his well-worn rocker, listening intently.

"The whites call her half-breed," Jake said. "She is growing, and soon those boy's clothes she insists on wearing will not hide the fact that she is too pretty for her own good."

Hawkins observed the ebony brows and thick lashes that framed Lyssa's violet eyes, her creamy skin, her rosebud lips pursed with concentration, and the lustrous thick black hair that rippled over her shoulders. He also saw the potential for great beauty in the little girl with her unusual coloring and perfect features.

"She doesn't understand that she might be in danger from anyone or anything because it is in her nature to see only good in people. I had to get them away from there!" Jake's face clouded as he remembered how they had been treated.

"I am so sorry. They deserve much better," Hawkins said. Lyssa's father realized he was talking of more than just the Rendel family.

Indeed, Ben Hawkins understood their dilemma. His own family wanted him to return to North Carolina where his prominent family lived and become involved once again in national politics.

"Do you ever think that if John Witherspoon hadn't left Scotland to become president of the College of New Jersey and insisted that modern language be taught as well as classical, you wouldn't be here?"

"That did get me onto George Washington's staff, and the rest is history, as they say!"

Hawkins laughed. The two of them swapped tales of their former friends at Princeton. Aaron Burr had served with Hawkins in the United States Senate as senator from North Carolina.

"Burr introduced James Madison to his wife, Dolly," Ben told Jake, the two chuckled. "The Constitution James wrote got passed has given our new country the foundation it needed," Jake said. "That was a lifetime ago," Ben said.

A return to his former life would not be a life for Ben's Indian family, which was probably one reason he was reluctant to leave his job as Superintendent of Indian Affairs. The problems Jake Rendel encountered involving his own family confirmed Hawkins's concerns.

"It is much more of the tradition for the Indian to assimilate others into the tribe," Hawkins commented. They sipped their drinks in the comfortable silence only longtime friends can enjoy, smiling at each other as they watched Lyssa's animated face shift with emotion as she read *Gulliver's Travels*.

"That is one book that transcends time, Jake," Ben Hawkins said. "Swift wrote it in 1726, and it is still one of the best stories ever told."

Jake nodded and sat back, relaxation evident on his face. "You've built an impressive site here, Ben," he finally said, awed by the vigor and activity of the agency, its organization and productivity.

Hawkins shrugged. "Sometimes I feel like Don Quixote, tilting at windmills. The Indians are like little children who will not look to tomorrow. They do not understand so many of the concepts that govern the white world, like land ownership. They laugh at the white man's belief that land can be owned. It is like air, a gift from Yahola, they tell me." He chuckled sadly at their innocence and lack of understanding.

"They reason that there is so much land, so why stay in one spot? Unfortunately, they are now beginning to feel the pinch as settlers encroach from the north and east in increasing numbers, traveling down the Three Notch Road through the Creek country to settle in the Tombigbee area. With Jefferson's purchase of Louisiana, the security of a mail route connecting Washington to New Orleans makes the expansion of the road even more critical. Of course, the promise of more land will bring more settlers. Seeing this, the War Party is gaining strength." Hawkins's ominous words settled about them as he once again filled their glasses.

Jake told Ben about the boys in their party who had been kidnapped by Savannah Jack and William Augustus Bowles and then tracked by Little Warrior, the son of Mad Dog who was raised by Big Warrior, chief of Tukebatchee.

"I didn't realize they were with this train," Ben said, surprised. "We sent out trackers to find them before Little Warrior did. He is so filled with hate; their lives would have been worthless had he found them. You heard what he did to that family at Little Canyon."

Rendel nodded. "I must admit to having quite a bit of trepidation about bringing my family into the Territory at this time. Traveling with General Twiggs gave us a fair sense of security. Do you think you can enforce peace, Ben?"

Ben shook his head. "The young resist the encroachment of civilization. They long for the past of their grandfathers. The old have seen much and accept more readily what they have been unable to resist. The young think they can do without the things with which they have become so accustomed. Even the bullets with which they shoot the deer are a part of what they despise. Yet they are not ready to return to the bow and arrow in their hunting. They cannot understand how the shift in demand in Europe and the states affects the value of the hides they bring in to the trading posts."

"Yes," Jake said. "I have had the same trouble myself on my post. They are accustomed to being able to buy a certain number of goods as we tally one chalk mark per deerskin. Unfortunately, the European market for fine gloves and book bindings made of deerskin is down, and a pound of deerskin can no longer be considered the equivalent of twenty-five cents. Yet my Indian suppliers still make the same number of moccasins from that skin and therefore cannot understand my saying it no longer has the same value."

That got them to talking about how vocabulary represented ideas and how important it was to understand the precise meanings of words. Both men were linguists. Hawkins showed Jake the Comparative Grammar and Dictionary of the Muscogee or Creek Language he was writing at President Thomas Jefferson's request.

Lavinia brought them more food in the study, and Lyssa joined them in eating, careful to clean her hands well before going back to her book. Lavinia realized how tired their guests must be and had already guided Malee and Lance to one of the guest rooms.

Jake and Ben stayed up late into the night talking of the friends and interests they had in common. They finally noticed Lyssa yawning, and her father took her to the room where Lavinia had already settled Malee and Lance. After carefully closing the book and placing it reverently on the mahogany dressing table, Lyssa tumbled onto the trundle bed. Hawkins had assured her she could borrow the book and he would retrieve it at his next visit to St. Stephens. After making sure Malee and the children were comfortably settled, Hawkins and Rendel returned to the library, where they visited into the early morning, when Rendel realized he had to get some sleep.

Unfortunately, the family could not linger at the agency. All rose early the next morning to the delicious smells of fried potatoes cooked with onions, ham, eggs, and fresh-baked bread. Lavinia and Malee had found that they had much in common and parted with fond goodbyes and promises to meet again soon. They met up with the pack train already engaged in crossing the Flint River.

Lyssa eyed the fast-running river anxiously. Already she could see several of the packhorses struggling for footing. She felt their agitation. Her strange "gift" alerted her to their fear at stepping into the current. But now there was more.

With the sensitivity she had known from the moment she met him, Lyssa sensed that Cade Kincaid was in danger. Frantically, she scanned the shoreline and the horses bunched along the trail awaiting their turn to cross. She spotted Gabriel, his attention focused on soothing his father's horses, but Cade was nowhere to be seen.

Then a shrill whinny captured her attention, and to her horror she saw the frightened horse stumble and fall on a figure that had tumbled onto the sand, still holding the reins. Without a second thought, before others could think to react, Lyssa slid off the back of the horse on which she rode with her mother and dove in, swimming through the muddy water to the shoals where boy and horse now struggled. Malee's scream attracted her husband's attention. She could only point to her daughter, who had now grabbed the reins from Cade's hand and spoke as only she could to calm the frantic horse whose eyes rolled in fear. Quickly, Lyssa had him calmed and standing while Cade lay still in the sand. She dropped the reins as her father approached and knelt beside Cade, lifting his head from the water and pulling his body across her lap to pommel his back.

"Wake up, boy. Don't you die on me," she pleaded. When at last the water gushed from his mouth and he began to cough, Lyssa began to cry and hit him harder.

As soon as his eyes opened, he gasped and said, "Little girl, you'll finish what the river couldn't do if you don't quit hitting me."

"If the sand hadn't been soft here, you fool, that horse would have killed you, don't you know?" she cried. "And I'm Lyssa! Not *little girl!*"

"Mary Beth saw a snake," he said. Lyssa pushed him out of her lap and started jumping around in the water, her eyes darting back and forth.

When her father reached her she climbed into his arms. "A snake scared the horse, Daddy. Do you see it?" Her father chuckled and cradled her high above the water. While Lyssa frantically searched the water at his feet, Cade sat mesmerized by Lyssa's panic.

"Lyssa's afraid of snakes," Jake Rendel explained. "That's the only critter that I know won't wind up as one of her pets, much to her mother's relief. Nothing else I know of can scare this girl."

"I'm right here," Lyssa said regally, still eying the water. "You're talking about me as if I were not here, you know. And you can put me down now."

"Yes, Princess," her father said, the edges of his mouth threatening a smile. He stretched out his hand to Cade and pulled him up. "You all right, son?"

"Yes, sir," Cade responded. "I got some bruises for sure, but I don't know whether they're from Mary Beth falling on me or your daughter pounding on me."

Lyssa sniffed, and with all the dignity she could muster, she swam cautiously from the sandbar to the shore and her waiting mother.

Watching her go, Jake said to Cade, "I reckon you've noticed my daughter has decided to add you to her orphan menagerie."

The boy looked at him questioningly.

"All those animals that follow her around—they're just a few of those we had back at the post in Savannah. She adopts strays and orphans. Once she becomes attached she never lets go," Jake explained.

Cade's eyes widened with the implications.

"Just a warning: she'll be watching out for you. Which means she never sees the danger to herself when she's protecting her little family. And that means she needs you to watch out for her because she's careless with her own safety and more than a little clumsy."

"But I don't *want* her following me and watching out for me," Cade said plaintively. "I do just fine taking care of myself."

He stood there with feet wide apart and his hands spread wide, a skinny boy with startling blue eyes too big for his emaciated body, his hair long and dripping with water. He sure didn't look like much. But Jake knew his daughter saw something there.

"Sorry, boy. That doesn't seem to matter to Lyssa. Once you find a place in her attentions, you can't seem to ever get loose." Lyssa's father looked almost sorry for him.

Cade took Mary Beth's lead and continued across the river, looking back over his shoulder only once. Sure enough, Lyssa was watching his every step from her perch on the back of her mother's horse. Just for a moment he allowed himself to be touched that someone cared about him, but tears started to spring in his eyes and he stifled the feeling. Then the barriers went up again.

As if he didn't have enough to do, taking care of his father's packhorses *and* those of the Pottses, watching out for Gabriel *and* the baby, making sure Sarilee had enough to eat...and now he had to watch out for that little girl who was bound to get hurt watching out for him!

He kicked the dirt. He didn't want anyone watching out for him. He didn't want anyone caring about him. He didn't want to care about anyone else.

As Lyssa watched, he seemed to grow taller and stronger as he purposefully led the reluctant horse to the other bank and up the sharp incline. Lyssa caught her breath with the rush of emotion she felt for this boy, this stranger, who suddenly had become so important to her. She hugged her mother tighter, confused by the strange emotion.

Day after day, she watched how Cade kept Gabriel and the baby Joie within his sight. She saw him make sure his father's horses were hobbled safely near the best grass and freshest water, just as he did the Potts's livestock, though he steered clear of his father. She knew the play of the deep dimples in his cheek as he fought the smile she could see in his eyes, never permitting it to reach his lips. She observed other children watching Cade to imitate his walk and the proud way he stood. She noted the patient way he taught the small boys who crowded about him to lure the fish from their shadows so they would bite the hook tied to a length of vine and baited with whatever was handy. Leadership was a mantle he wore as naturally and unconsciously as breathing.

There were times, though, when Cade would sit still and listen when Lyssa read to Gabe. He watched when she taught his brother to read and eventually learned himself. Lyssa and Gabe grew close during that time. They both loved Cade and had much in common with each other. Gabe's flutes fascinated her; he made such beautiful instruments and played such haunting music. Even Samson sat at his feet and listened for as long as Gabe would play.

Too soon, it seemed, it was time to cross the Tombigbee River to go to St. Stephens and into the Choctaw country. That was where their paths diverged. Her father would take his family into Choctaw country, and Lyssa's boy would remain with the Pottses in Creek country.

Lyssa remembered every word she had said to Cade that day when she was finally convinced to release her grip on him.

"I will wait for you, Cade Kincaid. You will come for me when I am all grown up! Promise me!" Strong, proud, and stubborn, she had stood there waiting until he finally agreed.

"Okay, I will come for you," he said, rolling his eyes—which fortunately Lyssa did not see.

Satisfied, she had pressed her precious dictionary into his hands. "Come for me," she demanded again.

That was ten years ago. She was now almost nineteen years old. Gabriel had confirmed to her when she had seen him at St. Stephens recently that Cade was about to make a big mistake. He was indeed looking with interest at Sally Carson.

"Sally Carson has gone for an extended visit with Harriet Mims, according to Mrs. Potts," Gabe said. "The Mims home has become a fort. Sally figures with Cade being in the militia there, she's bound to be able to maneuver the relationship to a satisfying conclusion...for her, anyway." Gabe's expression had turned sour.

Though he didn't know it yet, Cade was about to marry Sally Carson, the most beautiful girl in the Tombigbee area, with a face as beautiful as Helen of Troy and a heart as black as the river Acheron. Lyssa had to save him for his own good. She knew it was time to take fortune into her own hands and bring her boy home...to *her*!

She had taken no notice of the satisfied look on Gabe's face when he turned away. He had seen the resolve in her expression and was glad she would do something about this. His tormented brother deserved a chance for happiness. He wasn't sure exactly what had happened to Cade when they were held captive by Savannah Jack and Bowles. All he knew was that Cade had been besieged by nightmares ever since. Sometimes, Gabe had discovered, the music he played on his homemade flute could speak through the horrors of the dreams and soothe Cade. But seldom were Gabe and Cade together. Nicey Potts told Gabe that between Cade's recurring malaria fevers and the nightmares, she was truly worried. When Lance told Gabe what Lyssa had overheard in the barn, Gabe had told Nicey. Between them they came up with the plan, and then Lance had led Lyssa into thinking it was her idea.

And so Lyssa watched. And waited.

There, at the turn in the river. It was a canoe. Her brother looked up at the cliff, knowing she would be there, and grinned.

Her mouth fell open. Her eyes widened in awe. The man sitting in front of Lance in the canoe looked nothing like her boy. This was no skinny, half-starved youth. Nor was it the teenager she had observed riding up to the Mims home several years before. It was a fully grown man with a chest so broad and arms so powerful that her mouth went dry as he pulled the oar through the water. He was the most beautiful man she had ever seen.

And there in the canoe was the red material that would bind the two forever.

4

It was hot as hell, and the August dog flies were biting the shit out of him. Cade Kincaid was aggravated. The air was muggy and hard to breathe, and the current in the damned 'Bigbee was running fast after the recent downpour. That meant that as he paddled the canoe upriver against the current, the damned canoe was going backward almost as fast as he could pull it forward. There were probably 10,000 Red Stick Creek warriors aiming their guns at him from the east shore of the Tombigbee and 10,000 Choctaw aiming at him from the west shore, and he and the young Choctaw boy were sitting ducks.

If it hadn't been for Nicey Potts acting like it was the most important thing in the world for this little Choctaw and that damned bolt of red cloth to be returned to his people right now, if not yesterday, then he'd be training with Dixon Bailey and the militia at Fort Mims. One of the scouts from the Tensaw militia unit who'd already been in the fort told him Sally Carson had asked him when he was going to join them. She was staying with her friend, Harriet Mims, in the beautiful Mims home in the center of the one-acre enclosure that was now Fort Mims.

Sally Carson at Fort Mims, and here Cade was in the middle of the damned Tombigbee River heading in the opposite direction!

But he'd gone and gotten wounded at Burnt Corn Creek. It was supposed to have been an easy task when 180 men had answered Colonel James Caller's request to intercept the party of Indians that had gone to Pensacola to procure arms and ammunition from the Spanish to fight the Americans. You'd have thought they were headed out for a picnic. Caller had led the militia dressed in his finery—a calico hunting shirt, top boots, and a high, bell-crowned hat. He rode his best horse, a fine bay. Cade, Sam Dale, and Jeremiah Austill had felt vastly underdressed in their frontier garb of coonskin cap, bearskin vest, short hunting shirt, trousers of homespun, and buckskin leggings. As always, the three of them came equipped with a wallet to hold parched corn and coal flour. He and Austill carried their long rifle and hunting knife. Dale brought his double-barreled shotgun.

The militia had initially routed the Red Sticks. Then, led by Peter McQueen and High Head Jim, Cade's mentor who had become a prophet of the Red Stick movement, the Red Sticks had regrouped and attacked the undisciplined men of Caller's militia, who had resorted to looting the Indian camp. They ran for their lives. Cade, though wounded, had to search the woods to rescue Caller, who had gotten lost.

After that debacle, when Gabe told him Nicey wanted him home, it had seemed like the right thing to do. She needed to see he was okay, Gabe had said. So Cade had succumbed to Gabe's persuasion and gone to the only real home he had known since the death of his mother.

Just so he could mend a little bit. (He'd never admit to wanting the attention Nicey Potts would give him.)

Then, once he'd been home and received her pampering, Nicey had started in on him about returning that damned kid and the red cloth to the Choctaw. Just as he was about to say hell no to delivering that damn cloth (which probably would have made her grab him by the ear and wash his mouth out with soap), her chubby chin had quivered and her brown eyes, now clouded with age—those eyes that always glowed with love when she looked at him or Gabriel—had filled with tears. Though Cade was a man fully grown, a warrior among his people, and immune (or so he perceived) to the wiles of women, Nicey's tears had melted his resolve. There was no way he could deny her anything.

So here he was rowing and cussing.

Herman and Nicey Potts, much to his relief, had finally agreed to seek refuge at Sam Mims's place near the Cut-off between the Alabama and Tombigbee rivers. They would be safe with Dixon Bailey, the man Cade had voted for as leader of the Tensaw militia. Cade knew him to be a man of integrity and courage, the kind of man you wanted at your side in a battle. Coincidentally, Dixon Bailey was married to Cade's cousin Sarah Louisa Durant, the sister of Polly Durant, who had been Cade's mother's best friend. Polly's husband was High Head Jim, the man who had been closer to Cade than his own father.

High Head Jim was also the Red Stick who had shot him during the battle.

How had things gotten so out of control?

Nicey Potts didn't have an answer to that, but she did fill him in on the details of the family relationships of those who had become the major players in the conflict. She loved doing this because, as she explained, "It's family."

Both Nicey and Cade were of the Clan of the Wind. "If you can't talk about your relatives, who can you talk about?" Nicey said, though if truth be told she didn't limit her talking to family.

It was hard to follow her recitation of family connections, but he tried because Nicey thought it was so important.

"Let's begin with Sehoy," Nicey said, pouring Cade a cup of tea as they sat at her kitchen table together. "She was a Tallassee village Indian maiden who bore a daughter, also named Sehoy, by Jean Baptiste Marchand, the commander of the French fort Toulouse. She also had a boy, Red Shoes, by a Choctaw Indian chief. " Nicey paused, frowning.

"There are so many Sehoys I'm going to number them," she said.

"Sehoy II married Lachlan McGillivray and bore Alexander, Sophia, Jeanette, Elizabeth, and Mary. Malcolm and Elizabeth are hers by Malcolm McPherson. Their sister, Sehoy III, was fathered by Chief Eagle Wings of Tukabatchee.

"All of Sehoy Marchand's children—that's Sehoy II—were close to their uncle Red Shoes, your great-grandfather. By the way, Red Shoes Marchand also raised David Francis after the death of David's mother, who was the sister of the famous Shawnee chief Cornstalk."

"That's how they're so closely related to Tecumseh and probably the reason McQueen and Josiah Francis have become prophets of this Red Stick movement," Herman threw in from the adjacent room. Cade hadn't realized Herman was listening.

"That's right," Nicey continued. "Red Shoes was married to Susannah, an older daughter of James McQueen, the father of Red Stick leader Peter McQueen. That makes James McQueen Josiah Francis's grandfather, just as he is the grandfather of Tecumseh, who you went with William Weatherford to hear speak last year."

Cade nodded.

"Your friend Will Milfort's mother Jeanette McGillivray, sister to Sehoy, Mary, and Sophia, found her love in LeClerc Milfort," Nicey told him.

Will Milfort was just three years older than Cade and Gabe, and William Weatherford often took the three of them with him when he went hunting, knowing the fatherless boys needed his guidance.

Herman walked into the kitchen and reached for a teacup. "Will's father was a soldier of fortune," he said, "and a French adventurer who had dueled with and killed a servant in the household of the newly crowned Louis XVI, king of France. He served as a war chief for Alexander McGillivray before going back to France in 1796."

"Will was about six at the time," Nicey added.

Herman continued, "LeClerc Milfort had lived here for twenty years before returning to France. He sent back word that Napoleon needed his advice on how to deal with the natives in the French Territory." And so he stayed."

Continuing her recitation on Alexander McGillivray's sisters, Nicey had told Cade, "Sehoy III took to husband the Hollander, William Dixon Moniac, and bore Hannah, who married Josiah Francis; Jessie, who married William Colbert, a Chickasaw chief; and Elise, who married her uncle Alexander McGillivray. By John Tate Sehoy III had David, and by Charles Weatherford she bore William, who you tell me has joined the Red Sticks; Elizabeth, who married Sam Moniac, her sister Hannah Moniac's half-brother; and also Rosanna, Jake, Major, and Washington.

"Mary McGillivray got her a solid, steady English trader, Richard Dixon Bailey," Nicey said with a nod and a lift of her eyebrows as if to say, make up your own mind who got the short end of the stick. "Her son Dixon, along with his wife Sarah Durant, Ben Durant's daughter by Sophia McGillivray, and her other sons Daniel and James are already at Fort Mims with the militia, as is her daughter Elizabeth, who is married to Lachlan Durant, Ben and Sophia's son. Ben Durant is at Fort Mims with his and Sophia's children.

Nicey ran a hand over her eyes. Cade felt as exhausted as she looked, just listening to the tangle of connections that made up his family. "Sophia has joined the Red Sticks," Nicey said, her lips pursed in disapproval. "She's now with her daughter—another Elizabeth—and that Elizabeth's husband, Peter McQueen. Also Polly, High Head Jim's wife…and Sophia's sons Sandy and John Durant.

About then, Mary Bailey herself appeared. Nicey settled her with a cup of tea.

"My Dixon commands the militia, you know," Mary told them all proudly, stirring her tea.

Cade knew. He was glad for that. He'd feared that the honor of being commander might be laid on him and he sure didn't want that level of responsibility. What if all hell broke loose and he made a mistake and he was responsible for people's lives? He'd had enough of that kind of "honor."

Cade excused himself and followed Nicey's instructions to lie down so his wound could heal, but he lay in such a way in the nearby darkened room that he could see them, though they could not see him.

Nicey told Mary that she Herman were considering Cade's suggestion that they seek safety at Fort Mims.

"I've gone and checked it out," Mary said, "but there are just too many people there, and the smell and mosquitoes and those punky no see-ums are awful!"

"Cade's headed to Fort Mims soon as he heals up a bit, and he thinks he can look after us better if we're there with him," Nicey said, puffing up with pride in the young man she considered her son.

Her words that day had touched Cade's heart. He could tell how much it meant to her that he was concerned about her and Herman. It humbled him. She and Herman had given him so much. A home. A family.

But now it was a family divided. He frowned.

Cade shook his head in wonder at how crazy things had gotten!

Pulling the oar through the muddy river and ignoring Lance's chatter, Cade pictured the Mims plantation. Situated on the bank of what was referred to as Boatyard Lake, the 524-acre plantation was located in the Mobile-Tensaw delta where the Alabama and Tombigbee rivers came together and flowed around Nannahubba Island, an area referred to as the Cut-off. Samuel Mims operated a ferry across the Alabama River to the island there on the south end of the Cut-off. Travelers would then take the path across the island to the Tombigbee side, where Adam Hollinger's ferry would transport them across to the western shore of the delta. The home itself was a spacious, whitewashed, two-story building with a wraparound veranda and second-story dormers.

Only now, Cade had heard, the home, the outbuildings, and the recently constructed dwellings for neighbors who had sought shelter were surrounded by logs upended in a trench encompassing about an acre. The beautiful place where Cade had attended many a lively dance had been turned into a fort. The whole Tensaw area was now a hornet's nest of enraged Red Sticks!

And Nicey and Herman were headed there because, at last, *they had listened to him*!

So why didn't he feel better about their well-being? The fort was a safe place for them to be, he told himself. Why was he so apprehensive? Maybe he just needed to know they'd arrived at Fort Mims safely. He needed to be there! Not rowing up the damned Tombigbee!

He thought about how the militia had been preparing for the worst. Since the skirmish at Burnt Corn Creek, the Red Sticks had already attacked several settlers' homes. Set fire to them. Destroyed the crops. Stole their horses and killed the cows, sheep, goats, and chickens. Including Sam Moniac's herd of cows, and that was a lot of cows!

Before he'd arrived at Nicey and Herman's place after getting shot at Burnt Corn, Cade had run into Sam Moniac on the Wolf Trail to Pensacola. Forty-three-year-old Moniac, also known as Totkeshajou, was Weatherford's deceased wife Elizabeth's brother. He had just been to his still burning plantation home and saw what had happened to his cows. Sam had told Cade that the rumors he had heard about Weatherford committing to the Red Sticks were true. Cade supposed he should have told Nicey, but he was afraid she would be worried about Gabe, and he hadn't heard from his brother recently himself.

Sam had also told Cade that Captain Isaacs, the husband of Alexander McGillivray's daughter Lizzy, had taken much of the ammunition Peter McQueen had gotten from the Spanish at Pensacola before the battle at Burnt Corn Creek and high-tailed it to the safety of Tukabatchee and Big Warrior. To top it off, Peter McQueen had burned Sam's house and destroyed the cattle because Sam had refused to join the Red Sticks.

Word was out that the Red Sticks were ready to attack one of the forts in the 'Bigbee area or the Upper Creek capital at Tukabatchee under Big Warrior, who wouldn't "take the talk" of the prophets. That they were out to retrieve the ammunition that they felt Captain Isaacs had stolen from them and planned to wreak a little vengeance at the same time.

Cade shook his head. It was hard to know from one day to the next who was on which side of this conflict.

Cade swore. Once again, he felt totally out of place rowing up this damned river when he needed to be with Nicey and Herman. He wondered where in the hell Gabriel was now that Weatherford had gone over to the Red Sticks.

The deal was that Cade would deliver the boy and the red bolt of cloth if Nicey and Herman would agree to seek safety there at Fort Mims, where Cade knew his militia had been assigned. As soon as he completed this task, Cade would be there to protect them.

Ten years ago, when Cade had first come into the Tombigbee area with Nicey and Herman, he had been confused by the tangled web of interconnectedness of the people he met. He was of the Wind clan because his mother was. But now not even clan loyalty bound them. Brothers and sisters, mothers and fathers, and children had turned against each other as this war fever had possessed the entire Tombigbee area.

With a loud sigh, Cade glanced back at the Choctaw boy. Why was he wearing such a smug expression? The boy didn't look the least bit concerned, sitting against the rear of the canoe. *Damn!* Cade swore to himself. At least rowing and cussing gave him time to think...and wonder at what the hell had happened between all these people who once cared for each other.

One thing he knew—Dixon Bailey and William Weatherford hated each other. Though their mothers were sisters, the women had never been close, William's mother Sehoy being eight years younger than Mary McGillivray Bailey. Nicey had told Cade that Alexander McGillivray had sent his nephew Dixon Bailey to Philadelphia to be educated along with some of McGillivray's other nephews. Unlike the others who were taught by the Society of Friends, Dixon was schooled under the direction of Secretary of War Henry Knox and came home with contempt for the Indian way of life. That attitude may have been why the Baileys were forced out of their mother village of Autossee twice, though when the village realized they were deprived of the goods Richard Bailey provided, they invited them to return.

As jovial a person as Mary, Dixon's mother, usually was, she could be too opinionated for her own good. Mary considered herself a role model and advocate for Hawkins's programs, and she started preaching his domestic agenda with a vigor that could only be matched by Lorenzo

Dow in the pulpit during a revival meeting or maybe Josiah Francis in the middle of an ecstatic vision. Her own family continued the Creek tradition of bathing daily in the sometimes frigid water, but Mary took it a step further, expanding her cleanliness standards to include a woman's responsibility to ensure her family's clothes, which she had weaved and sewn, were *clean* as well! For some women, all that progress was going a bit too far, and so they felt justified in booting the busybodies out.

Cade had heard Nicey and Mary talking about it one afternoon when he went to the water pail for a drink before heading back out to the field to work with Herman.

"Most folks now wear clothing made of the materials sold at the trading posts or woven at home," Mary pointed out. "You hardly see people wearing skins anymore. Why is it so difficult to understand that woven cloth—rather than clothing fashioned from skins like we used to wear—needs washing and mending?"

Nicey shrugged and crossed her arms to hide her own frayed and stained cuffs.

Mary took another sip of Nicey's apple cider and pretended not to notice.

Cade knew that not many folks could live up to Mary Bailey's standards. At that moment, he would probably have banished her himself for making Nicey feel bad. That was probably why the Baileys had moved to the Tensaw area where they could live among other Métis people in the Tensaw area. The Pottses had experienced the Baileys' same dilemma of finding a middle ground between their two cultures. Nicey could relate to that, which was probably why she and Mary remained friends in spite of Mary's critical spirit.

As he checked his position on the river, Cade recalled that Benjamin Hawkins spent a lot of time with women, trying to push his pet projects. Both Mary and Nicey were receptive and enjoyed his visits. Cade had always been amused at the sight of the lanky agent to the Creeks sitting on Nicey's settle with one of her prized collection of teacups balanced on his bony knee. Hawkins seemed just as at home there as he did sitting on the ground by a fire, taking a slug of corn mash with the men he also visited. Hawkins had the gift of making everyone with feel at ease, but he was particularly fond of Mary and Nicey, particularly because they had proven how applying the domestic skills he endorsed could benefit the family for comfort and profit.

Hawkins had bragged on Mary to Nicey, telling her, "Mary is one of my success stories...perhaps my best weaver. She is a role model for the young women of the tribe with her industry." Then he added, "Mr. Bailey was a good farmer, had many conveniences about, with his lands fenced, stable, garden, lots for his stock, some thriving trees, and a small nursery. When he got thrown from that horse in 1798, he left Mary in pretty good shape, and she's managed it all quite well by herself. And, I'm glad to see that Mary's daughters follow her example. Mary Bailey is as neat and economical a woman as I have met. I have only heard her to be agreeable and happy in conversation. She's kind to everybody, yet firm."

Nicey had rolled her eyes his way as Hawkins bent to take a sip of tea. When he looked back up, she gave him a prim but tight-lipped smile. Far be it for her to ruin her own reputation by being contrary.

But just as Cade had feared, Nicey had misconstrued Hawkins's simple comments on Mary Bailey's accomplishments as criticism for her and Herman's efforts. Nicey took it to heart, and she worked Cade hard the summer after that. Herman had to remind her that the Baileys had lots of sons! She only had two adopted sons, and since Gabe was living with William Weatherford and working his stables, that left Nicey with Cade and Herman, and she was about to work them to death. Besides, inheriting from Mary's wealthy brother Alexander was bound to have contributed to the Baileys' prosperity.

It was little wonder Dixon Bailey and William Weatherford had wound up on opposite sides in the conflict. If Nicey kept rattling off the two men's accomplishments to *Cade*, he might want to go to war with Dixon Bailey *and* William Weatherford.

Cade shook his head. How had his friend, relative, and mentor, William Weatherford, become his enemy almost overnight? He did not doubt what that meant. He'd learned the hard way. He was still stunned that it was High Head Jim who had turned, aimed directly at him, and shot him at Burnt Corn Creek. That he was not dead was probably proof of High Head Jim's affection.

The night before when they had camped before taking to the river, the boy he was returning to the Choctaw had asked a question that brought back memories Cade had thought were long buried. In proficient Creek, he had asked, "Why must Creek fight Creek?"

Cade wondered that himself. But this rebellion had long been brewing. Some might say he and Gabe had been two of the first victims of the movement to bring the Creek Nation back under the control of its old leaders and ways. The conflict had led to his and Gabriel's capture. William Augustus Bowles and his ally Savannah Jack had wanted to wrest control of the Creek Nation away from the Americans. Bowles and Jack included Cade and Gabriel's father Jason and the Creek agent Benjamin Hawkins among those Americans.

Cade and Gabe had heard Bowles's story firsthand during their capture. The man liked to talk about himself.

Bowles had jumped off a British ship in Mobile and followed a small band of Indians back to Perryman's village at Miccosukee during the Revolution. The former Boston actor had assumed his greatest role when Chief Kinache, Thomas Perryman, became his father-in-law. He then styled himself Eastajoca, "Director General of the Creeks," and sought not only Jason Kincaid's trading alliances but also the power Alexander McGillivray had wielded among the Creeks before his death, power that Benjamin Hawkins had assumed.

As his delusions of grandeur grew, Bowles had aligned himself with the bloodthirsty Savannah Jack, another man Cade knew all too well. Savannah Jack Hague's mother was from Sauwonoga, a Shawnee settlement within the Creek Nation. So Jack of Sauwonoga became Suvanner or Savannah Jack in most folks' parlance. His father was John Hague, and many people claimed Hague's father was Simon Girty. Jack was just as mean as Girty.

Cade had once heard Benjamin Hawkins say, "No other country or age ever produced so brutal, depraved, or wicked a wretch as Savannah Jack's grandfather."

Cade disagreed with Hawkins and would have told him so. That distinction could only belong to Savannah Jack himself. But he could not bring himself to speak of that time because to do so meant to relive it outside his nightmares.

While looking straight at Cade with his cold, steely eyes, Savannah Jack had boasted that he had killed so many women and children on the Cumberland and Georgia frontiers that he could swim in their blood if it was collected in a pool. He said this as he sliced the skin of Cade's arm with a razor-sharp knife, giving the boy his signature.

Cade shivered involuntarily and ran his fingers over the scar he'd made cutting it away.

Then his thoughts jumped forward to the fall of 1811 when the Shawnee Tecumseh came to the Creek Nation and Cade and Gabe saw Savannah Jack for the first time since their captivity. The boys had accompanied William Weatherford to Tukabatchee for the Grand Council where Tecumseh would speak.

Weatherford, as the leader of their Clan of the Wind, had become his and Gabe's mentor when they came into the Tensaw country. When Weatherford discovered Gabe's gift as a horse whisperer, he offered Gabe the opportunity to live with him and work with the stable of horses at his racetrack at Hickory Ground near the junction of the Coosa and Tallapoosa rivers. He'd invited Cade also, but Herman Potts had broken his leg about then, and Cade knew he could not leave Nicey and Herman to their own devices.

Nicey and Herman encouraged Cade to go with Gabe and Weatherford to hear Tecumseh. Weatherford was a highly respected war chief and a great role model for a young man. He straddled two worlds well, a skill Nicey thought her adopted sons needed. The Grand Council was an event Cade would never forget. Thousands had made their way to Tukabatchee for the much-anticipated talk. Tecumseh, their hero, a Shawnee with a great reputation as a warrior, hunter, and speaker, had earned his legend among his people. His father Puckenshinwa was the grandson of both Shawnee Chief Rising Sun and James McQueen of Tallassee, who was also Peter McQueen's father. Tecumseh's mother Methoataske—Turtle Laying Its Eggs—was a Souvanogee Creek.

Tecumseh had come south hoping to build a coalition against the white man with the help of his cousins. All the young warriors knew that Tecumseh's father had fought valiantly with Chief Cornstalk in 1774 at the Battle of Point Pleasant and had died there. Chief Cornstalk himself had gone to Point Pleasant, hoping to assure the Americans, or the "Long Knives" as the Indians called them, that he intended to honor their treaty, but he was murdered along with his son at the hands of the Americans. Tecumseh's lesson was that the white man's word was worthless.

The murder of Cornstalk, along with the death of his beloved older brother Cheesekau, gave Tecumseh all the motivation he needed to try to achieve a union among all Indians to push the "Long Knives" back to the shores upon which they had first set foot. Sikaboo, Tecumseh's prophet, was also a descendant of James McQueen. Sikaboo attended the Grand Council at Tukabatchee to recruit prophets. The prophets claimed that the Master of Breath had called them to turn away from evil and renounce the ways of the white man and their civilization. Those who stood against their cause stood against the Master of Breath.

Before Cade left with his brother and Weatherford for Tukabatchee, Nicey drilled him with the family connections so he would not embarrass himself—or her—by saying anything in the presence of the wrong people. Aggravating though that woman talk was, Cade absorbed it all in spite of himself. Much of it he had heard before, but he didn't want Nicey thinking he'd paid attention to women's chattering.

As if telling him for the first time, Nicey had emphasized the strong ties between the Shawnee of Ohio and Pennsylvania and the Creek, reminding him that disease and war often brought the Shawnee south to take refuge among their relatives, sometimes for years.

Cade had heard tales of the great valor and heroic deeds of great Shawnee warriors. The elders intended to inspire young warriors to emulate these heroes' courage against the oncoming, seemingly never-ending encroachment and onslaught of the white man. Cade always found this a bit odd since, as Nicey pointed out, so many of them were descended from James McQueen, the white man born in 1683 who came into the Territory in 1711 as a British soldier under Oglethorpe, married a Creek woman named Katherine Fraser, and stayed. He had many wives and begat many children. He was still alive at 128, and Nicey noted that he could possibly be at the meeting at Tukabatchee, watching the interplay of many of his descendants.

"That's interesting, Nicey," Cade has said impatiently, "but I've got to get on the road." But then big tears formed in Nicey's eyes, and his resolve crumbled. "Okay, I missed what you said about Josiah Francis's and Tecumseh's relationship to Chief Cornstalk."

"Josiah's mother and Tecumseh's father, Puckenshinwa, were brother and sister," Nicey said, wiping her eyes. "James McQueen is their great-grandfather."

The clouds passed and the sun shone again on her face. It was at least another half hour before he was able leave.

Finally, the twins had set off with Weatherford, Moniac, and their entourage that September. The horses on which they rode were the finest in Creek lands. Cade and Gabe's dappled Appaloosas were known for their strength, speed, courage, and intelligence. An occasional horse of Arabian descent appeared in Weatherford's stable, like the one Weatherford rode that was trotting along in the center of the group. It was his favorite horse, a lofty, elegantly formed, durable, and distinctive gray called Arrow. Their horses pranced through the crowds that lined the path to the center square, aware that they were the center of attention as they entered the village.

Gay and festive, filled with anticipation, the population of Tukabatchee had swollen to five thousand, consisting of a large number of mixed-blood Métis like Weatherford, Moniac, Gabriel, and himself, along with a scattering of blacks and whites.

Weatherford honored the occasion and attended as Red Eagle, wearing the Scottish Tam of Clan McGillivray with a sweeping red egret plume. His hair had caught the midday sun, and flashes of red reminded Cade of how Weatherford had acquired his sobriquet, Red Eagle, Lamochattee Hopnicafutsahia. Weatherford stood six feet two inches tall and was intensely muscular, as were the others of their group who also ranged close to Weatherford's height. They were warriors, all naked to the waist, their chests glistening with the heat of the day, wearing only buckskin pants and moccasins. Weatherford's white buckskins shone as a startling contrast to the silver gray of the magnificent horse he rode. Red Eagle, a war chief of the Creek Nation, nearly glowed as he rode amid the impressive group of warriors.

Sam Moniac rode beside Weatherford, the medal George Washington had placed around his neck in 1790 glinting in the sun's rays. At the time of the Grand Council, twenty years had passed since Moniac had accompanied Alexander McGillivray to meet with the Great Father, and he had never removed that medal.

Out of respect, Cade and Gabe had hung back behind the illustrious pair. Cade sat proudly erect, aware that the crowds parted and the women stopped what they were doing to follow the party with their eyes. Cade found it disconcerting that the young women's eyes slid past

Weatherford and landed directly on him. It was a new and unsettling experience.

"I am an old man, Sam," Weatherford said in a voice only they could hear. "Thirty-three summers have I seen. And now the women have eyes only for our young kinsmen."

Moniac nodded nearly imperceptibly, and said, "Ten years ago, you were their age. That was when we attended the council at Hickory Ground with your father and captured Bowles."

"At the command of Hawkins," Weatherford added at the sight of Ben Hawkins standing with Big Warrior before the Council House. Cade remembered catching an odd tone of resentment in Weatherford's voice. A slight lift of Moniac's brow was the only indication that he might question Weatherford's inclination.

Benjamin Hawkins, white-haired and craggy faced with gentle blue eyes, stood before the Council House with long-armed, square-shouldered Sam Dale and also Big Warrior, the largest man Cade had ever seen. Big Warrior, chief of Tukabatchee, stood six feet, eight inches tall and was as spotted as a leopard.

Nearly sixty at the time of Tecumseh's visit, Benjamin Hawkins did not stand so tall as when Cade had first seen him eight years prior at his agency on the Flint. In retrospect, rowing the canoe down the Tombigbee River, Cade realized it was more than the man's slight stoop and the cane he used because of his gout; it was that Cade had grown. Hawkins had also acquired snow-white hair and many wrinkles over the years. When Cade had last seen him, Hawkins had charged William Weatherford's father, Charles, with the task of capturing William Augustus Bowles. It was suspected that Bowles would attend the Grand Council that year, and he did, boldly declaring himself king of all the Indians assembled for his "State of Muskogee," of which they were now subjects. He also informed them that he had declared war on Spain with Britain as their ally, which of course made the Americans their enemy. Hawkins had told Weatherford that the Spaniards offered a prize of $6,000 and 1,500 kegs of rum for the capture of the nuisance pirate Bowles. In debt as usual, Charles Weatherford had decided that capturing Bowles could be satisfying and profitable.

The younger Weatherford had brought Gabe and Cade along, thinking to help heal the wounds of their captivity by letting them assist in Bowles's capture and deliver him to the Spanish. Bowles had managed to escape when they were on the way to Pensacola. But only briefly. Cade was instrumental in recapturing him by tracking him into the marsh where he hid. The man finally died at Moro Castle in Havana, Cuba, in 1805. Perhaps Weatherford's goal was achieved. Cade's nightmares were no longer centered on William Augustus Bowles *and* Savannah Jack. Bowles was finally out of the picture.

But Savannah Jack remained free, and, what was worse, he might possibly be at the 1811 Grand Council. Cade hoped that he would have the opportunity to deal with Savannah Jack now that the playing field was more level.

Weatherford had halted and slid to the ground near Big Warrior. Cade and Gabe joined him. Alexander Cornell, Hawkins's interpreter and Big Warrior's cousin, stood near Benjamin Hawkins. He nodded to Cade. Cornell traveled frequently with Hawkins as he made his rounds through the Territory. Together they had often experienced Nicey's hospitality and were familiar with the Kincaid boys. Once, while Hawkins was helping Nicey plant the peach saplings he'd brought her, Cornell had amazed him and Gabe with his famous buck's horn that resembled a man's hand.

Attending the Grand Council was apparently an occasion that called for Alexander Cornell's finest attire. He wore his thigh-length, buckskin Iroquois jacket that sported fancy fringed body strips and a very colorful yoke and cuffs beaded in turquoise and red. Cade had heard others joke that Cornell's wife, Big Lizzie, Mad Dog's daughter and Far-Off Warrior's sister, liked to wear that jacket also when company came. Now that was a sight Cade would like to see.

Mad Dog had until 1799 held the position now held by Big Warrior as speaker of the Upper Creeks in the National Council at Tukabatchee. He cited his advanced age as the reason for his resignation. Cade had heard Hawkins tell Cornell that he thought his father-in-law was "one of the best informed men of the land, and faithful to his National engagements."

With a bit of corn mash to loosen his tongue, Cade remembered hearing a disgruntled Hawkins sitting on the bench on Nicey and Herman's front porch complaining to Herman, "Mad Dog has five Black slaves and a stock of cattle and horses that are of little use to him. French and British agents encouraged the red chiefs to live on presents from their white friends. Mad Dog now claims those presents as a tribute due to him, and one that never must be dispensed with. How can I get the Creeks on the road to independence when the old ways bind their leaders to dependency?"

Herman just shrugged, passed the corn mash and puffed harder on his pipe.

Cade figured many presents had already been handed out before the National Council began. The Americans had a lot at stake with the decisions that would be made at this Council and the opinions that would be formed when Tecumseh spoke. The great men of influence among the Creek would surely be there

And while that would surely include 81 year-old Mad Dog Nicey was sure that if he was still breathing James McQueen who was 128 years old would attend. So would Sam Moniac's father, 63 year-old William Dixon "Jacob" Moniac.

Moniac had come to Creek country from the Netherlands around 1756 by way of Sainto Domingo. He accompanied a ragged band of Nachez Indians who had been captured by the French to be slaves back to their village. Most who had been taken to the island had sickened and died there. Upon their return they found that the French had pretty much destroyed or confiscated all they had left. So, those who remained followed Moniac into the safety of Creek Country, a confederacy of displaced tribes, where they settled near the Tallassee Old Fields at James McQueen's invitation

McQueen and Moniac feared what had happened to the Nachez in their old land would happen once again. The threat to peace in the Creek Territory was greater than ever. They had managed to guide and restrain the Tallassee up until that point ... at least that was Herman's opinion when he had finally gotten a word in while Nicey took a breath.

"Moniac and McQueen will be there! I'd bet my tea cup collection on that! So Mad Dog will be there even if Mad Dog's son Far-Off Warrior and his daughter Tuskenua, Big Warrior's wife, have to prop him up!" Nicey said, laughing. Herman laughed as well envisioning the two siblings kowtowing to their elderly father's demands.

"Big Warrior could lift the shriveled old man with one arm," Herman stated with dry humor between pulls on his pipe. "I'd hate to be sitting next to those two who now can barely hear demand 'Now, what did he say?'" Herman and Nicey got a big laugh out of that.

Cade schooled his features, stifling a smile, remembering.

Big Warrior's brother, Davy Cornell, also known as Dog Warrior, had been killed by the Americans in 1793 while carrying a flag of peace at a treaty meeting at Coleraine. The killing had horrified Benjamin Hawkins though he was not at that time Agent to the Creeks. Nicey had told Cade that Joseph Cornell, Dog Warrior's father, had been glad to get the 600 piaster indemnity and had sent his son Big Warrior to collect. Their sister Vicey Cornell had been Alexander McGillivray's wife at that time of Dog Warrior's death. McGillivray himself died not long after that, Nicey had recalled.

"That was a sad day for our people," Nicey said.

As he entered Tukabatchee, Cade had seen Dog Warrior's son, David Yargee Cornell, also known as Dog Warrior in the crowd in the midst of a group of fine looking young women. Davy Cornell scowled as the women turned to watch Cade and Gabe ride in with Weatherford's entourage. He was of the same age as Cade and Gabe and Cade knew him well. He would be attending the National Council. Cade scowled back.

Then Cade spotted Will Milfort who grinned happily at Gabe and Cade as they passed by. He sported a black eye, lots of cuts and bruises but had a smile so wide that Cade knew that Will's team in ball play on the plaza that morning *must* have won. There must have been pretty good competition, Cade thought from Will's appearance. Little wonder they called it "the little brother of war." Maybe Davy Cornell had been on the opposing team he thought, pleased that Will had beaten him if his assessment was true.

As usual, Will had a woman tucked under each arm. Will had benefited from his father's reputation. When LeClerc Milfort had first come into the Creek territory he had to prove that a French warrior was equal to a Creek warrior. Though he had felt it prudent to refrain from such activities initially, he was accosted by one amorous maiden who apparently made a good report and, when he moved into her accommodations, four other young women appeared chiding him for his modesty saying they had never seen a "capon-warrior," a castrated rooster. Whether that meant size or prowess, Milfort was unsure.

"What man, particularly what *French man*, could refuse such a challenge?" Milfort had said to Weatherford when he noticed the attention Weatherford was getting from the young ladies. When Weatherford laughingly asked him how that evening turned out, Milfort delighted in telling him that he came out of that incident "with honor." He married Weatherford's aunt Jeanette McGillivray soon afterward ... perhaps an act of self-defense, Cade thought, chuckling to himself. Jeanette McGillivray had remarried after LeClerc Milfort returned to France and was now Jeanette McGillivray Milfort Crook. She was a formidable woman.

Of course, Will felt "honor" bound to live up to his father's reputation.

Cade turned his thoughts from Will Milfort and onto the Council meeting. Nicey and Herman had speculated on how Big Warrior would take Tecumseh's talk. Well, mainly Nicey speculated and Herman nodded every now and then giving her all the encouragement she needed to express her own feelings on that subject. Of course, she would always conclude with a nod toward Cade and the words, "Well, that's what Herman and I think about it," making Herman's eyes twinkle and his eyebrows lift.

Weatherford had introduced Cade and Gabe to Big Warrior and then addressed Benjamin Hawkins.

"Do you remember Cade and Gabe Kincaid?" he asked.

"I know these young men well," Hawkins said, smiling and extending his hand.

Weatherford then greeted Sam Dale, embracing him as an old and beloved friend. Dale had earned respect one warrior to another when he had served with the militia, seeking out Indians who conducted raids into Georgia. He also had a wagon business that he operated out of Savannah, and he transported goods into the Territory when he wasn't helping his seven orphaned brothers and sisters on their farm in Georgia.

Cade, hesitating briefly as he paddled, now realized that it was Sam Dale who had led the initial attack at Burnt Corn Creek at Caller's command and was grievously wounded.

The Choctaw boy eyed him strangely, seeming to wonder at this sudden stillness, and then glanced toward the shore and looked for the danger he thought Cade had seen. Cade quickly dipped the paddle once again in the rushing river, pulling them further toward the boy's home.

But his thoughts remained on the Grand Council of 1811.

5

Grand Council 1811

Located in the center of Tukabatchee at one end of the plaza, the Council House was obscured by all the other dwellings as they approached, especially with the throngs of people who had gathered to hear Tecumseh. When they were at last upon it, the house looked almost as big as a hill itself, with a thatched roof nearly touching the ground and then rising from walls four to six feet deep and approximately four feet high to terminate at least twelve feet high inside in a point in the center. It was a massive building.

A wall rounded the Council House in front of the door, the only opening in the house, for the purpose of blocking winds that might blow out the ceremonial fire. Big Warrior led them into the Council House to smoke the pipe while slaves took their horses to the paddock to care for them. Tall as they all were, especially Big Warrior who nearly filled the aperture, they had to crouch to enter what felt like a tunnel, making the vast, spacious room seem even larger when they came into the light that streamed from the opening at the center of the room through which smoke from the ceremonial fire would escape. Seating for two to three thousand warriors on the tiered bamboo benches was determined by clan, rank, and other considerations, which was probably one reason Nicey had been so careful to make sure Cade knew some of the people she anticipated being at the meeting. Weatherford took a prominent seat among the Clan of the Wind. Cade and Gabe were included less prominently. Big Warrior allowed Benjamin Hawkins a seat of distinction beside him.

Cade and Gabe warmly greeted their mentor High Head Jim, Polly Durant's husband. Though nearly fifty years old, High Head Jim, also known as Mustaushobie Coochman and Jim Boy, remained a formidable warrior. He arrived dressed in his full ceremonial attire.

Big Warrior's son, Checartha Yargee, twenty-eight-year-old husband to Peter McQueen's daughters, Millie, Tallassee, and Nancy, handed Big Warrior his impressive pipe. The pipe had a four-foot stem, was sheathed in a speckled snakeskin, and was hung with wampum, strings of white shell beads fashioned from whelk shell and white and purple beads made from quahog. Big Warrior passed the pipe to all the chiefs solemnly and with great ceremony. Cade proudly watched Weatherford partake of the pipe as war chief of the Taskigi, Cade and Gabriel's own mother's home talwa.

The Beloved Man of the Creeks, as Hawkins was called by many, was also resented by many. His purpose for attending the Grand Council of the Creek Nation in the midst of the growing discontent only added fuel to the situation. Hawkins presented a request that the postal riders' trail down which Twiggs's pack train had traveled be widened further to become a *wagon* trail they now called the Federal Road. The assembly realized what that meant—more intrusion into their traditional land and hunting grounds. When they objected, Hawkins, who had grown cantankerous with his poor health and discomfort, told them it would be done regardless of their decision.

The council remained polite. Though Tecumseh arrived at Tukabatchee on September 20 just in time for the Grand Council, he and his warriors waited Hawkins out. Each morning they would announce that Tecumseh would speak that day. Each afternoon a message would be sent that "the sun had traveled too far" and that he would appear to speak the next day. Eventually Hawkins had waited all he could. He was ill. He was irritable. He wanted to go home.

As soon as Hawkins left, Sam Dale going with him, a muttering arose about the changes Hawkins wanted to make in their lives.

Cade heard one man grumble, "He's got my woman spinning cloth to make her own clothes. What does she need a man for to hunt the deer for their skin if she is spinning her own cloth for her clothing?"

Another said, "I bring the same number of skins to the post and receive fewer goods in return. Yet the same number of moccasins can be made from that skin. How can it trade for fewer goods?"

Cade understood both sides of the argument. He remembered his own father had complained about how the international economic situation dictated the value of deerskin. Deerskins were not bringing the same price, and the trader was unable to buy supplies to trade with the hunter at the same price. That had caused hard feelings between Cade and Gabe's father and the men of the village.

At noon on the last day of September 1811, Tecumseh at last chose to appear. The crowds parted as the Shawnee warriors and their prophets came out into the square. Silence fell as they strode forth, armed with rifles, tomahawks, and scalping knives at their belts, their faces and bodies painted black like demons, eagle plumes dancing above their heads, and white buffalo tails suspended from bands around their waists. Silver bands encircled their wrists, above and below their elbows, and elaborately wrought silver gorgets were banded about their necks. Above the red flannel that encircled their foreheads, they wore another silver band. Their hair was close shaven with three plaits adorned with hawk and eagle feathers hanging between their shoulders. Only a flap covered their loins. In addition to the streaks of red paint from their eyes across their cheekbones was a small red dot on their temples and a large red spot like a target on their chests.

The warriors circled three times about the square, led by a limping Tecumseh who wore both a white crane feather symbolizing peace among the Indian tribes and a red one as the emblem of war against their enemies. He had been injured in battle, leaving his leg damaged, and a childhood mishap had given one tooth a bluish cast. Those flaws only enhanced the legend of the warrior. The Shawnee emptied pouches of sumac and tobacco at each corner and finally into the ceremonial fire, sparking flames that licked high up the ceremonial pole in the center of the square.

Upon entering the Council House, Tecumseh let out a war whoop that was echoed by his followers. They approached the assembled Creek chiefs. Those who had been reclining now sat erect, cross-legged upon the tiered cane benches in the Council House to exchange tobacco in a display of friendship. Only Captain Isaacs, also known as Tourcada, a Coosada chief, his head adorned with buffalo horns, refused the offered pipe of friendship. Knowing that he later took the talk and claimed prophetic powers made his single act of resistance curious as Cade thought back on it.

Captain Isaacs shook his head and said, "Tecumseh is a bad man and no better than me."

Although Weatherford remained aloof and noncommittal, he did smoke the pipe. With dramatic flair, the six-foot Tecumseh stood before the Creek assembly and waited until not a sound could be heard. Even those outside the Council House, including Sam Dale who had left Hawkins to return surreptitiously to hear Tecumseh, quieted, straining to hear what might be going on inside.

Commanding the room with his imperial mien, Tecumseh spoke. His delivery was such that Cade would have understood the meaning even though Tecumseh's northern dialect had to be translated by his cousin, the prophet Sikaboo. Cade was mesmerized by his speech.

"Let the white race perish. They seize your land; they corrupt your women; they trample on the ashes of your dead! Back, back, ay, into the great water whose accursed waves brought them to our shores! Burn their dwellings! Destroy their stock! Slay their wives and children!"

Weatherford's jaw tightened at those words, and Cade watched him visibly stiffen. A warrior knew it was one thing to fight another warrior, but to kill the women and children who could not fight back? Yet Cade knew that Weatherford was as aware as he of the fever that was building to cleanse the Nation. Much could be justified in the name of a sacred cause.

Tecumseh's naked painted body trembled with emotion. The expressions on his face shifted from sneers in contempt of the white people to captivating smiles that drew his audience along on the ride down the rapids of his challenge.

"The red man owns the country, and the palefaces must never enjoy it. War now! War forever! War upon the living! War upon the dead!"

Tecumseh's eyes burned with the fervor of his words. Passion played in every cadence. Cade watched and saw that same passion reflected in the eyes of Josiah Francis, forty-nine; Little Warrior, forty-three; Peter McQueen, fifty-four; and the many *young* braves who had become his followers. Tecumseh's words ignited an almost fanatical gleam in their eyes and, as if mesmerized, they sat straighter, their gaze focused on the speaker who had come not just to set a fire in their hearts but to ignite a conflagration. Even Captain Isaacs, who had refused Tecumseh's pipe earlier, seemed to be responding to his words.

"Kill the old chiefs, friends to peace; kill the cattle, the hogs and fowls; do not work, destroy the wheels and looms, throw away your ploughs and everything used by the Americans," Tecumseh challenged.

The men behind Cade who had been complaining about Hawkins's effect on their women stomped and shouted as Tecumseh spoke those words. He'd read their discontent, known their disgust with the new corruption of their traditional ways, and played to their prejudice and feelings of powerlessness.

When Tecumseh spoke, even Cade's heart beat faster with pride in his heritage as this man of noble bearing—this warrior who wore well and honestly the mantle of courage, honor, and dignity—spoke from his heart. The words fell like music on the ears of his listeners. Even Weatherford sat straighter before him as he listened to this man so honored among the people.

"No tribe has the right to sell, even to each other, much less to strangers.... Sell a country! Why not sell the air, the great sea, as well as the earth? Didn't the Great Spirit make them all for the use of his children?

"The way, the only way to stop this evil is for the red man to unite in claiming a common and equal right in the land, as it was first, and should be now, for it was never divided.

"We gave them forest-clad mountains and valleys full of game, and in return what did they give our warriors and our women? Rum, trinkets, and a grave.

"Brothers, my people wish for peace; the red men all wish for peace; but where the white people are, there is no peace for them, except it be on the bosom of our mother. Where today are the Pequot?

"Where today are the Narrangansett, the Mohican, the Pakanoket, and many other once powerful tribes of our people?

"They have vanished before the avarice and the oppression of the white man, as snow before a summer sun."

Tecumseh concluded, "The British, our former friends, have sent me from the Big Lakes to procure our help in expelling the Americans from all Indian soil. The King of England is ready handsomely to reward all who would fight for his cause."

Cade had heard of the offer of five dollars a scalp by British agents if the scalps were brought to Pensacola. Both the Spanish in the south and the British in the north wanted war between the Indians and the Americans. The Americans fought the British in Canada at the moment, and Cade already knew from listening to Hawkins that the British had promised Tecumseh support in his effort to unify all tribes against the Americans.

Big Warrior remained still and silent, seemingly unmoved even after Tecumseh's stirring talk. Tecumseh addressed him directly.

"Tustannuggee Thlucco, your blood is white. You have taken my red sticks and my talk, but you do not mean to fight. I know the reason. You do not believe the Great Spirit has sent me. You shall believe it. I will leave directly and go straight to Detroit. When I get there I will stamp my foot upon the ground and shake down every house in Tukabatchee."

Big Warrior said nothing, but puffed his pipe and enveloped himself in clouds of smoke.

Sikaboo spoke next.

"I communed with the Great Spirit, who sent Tecumseh upon this mission. Those who join the war party will be shielded from all harm—not one warrior will be killed in battle. The Great Spirit will surround our enemy with quagmires, which will swallow up the Americans as they approach. We will finally expel every Georgian from the soil as far as the Savannah. You will see the arms of Tecumseh stretched out in the heavens at a certain time, and then you will know when to begin the war."

Cade perceived Big Warrior's reaction not by any nuance of facial expression but by the way he clenched his knife handle. But was it acceptance of Tecumseh's words—or concern with Tecumseh's call to kill the old chiefs who urged restraint? All had listened closely to Tecumseh's words. Their impact was visible on the faces all around him.

Tecumseh sat down. He passed the pipe once more. And then, suddenly, the Shawnees leapt to their feet and, sounding their war cry, began the Dance of War.

Scout. Ambush. Combat. They enacted all the elements of war in their dance.

The crowd responded with loud whoops.

While the assembly still shouted, Tecumseh strode from the Council House leading his warriors, his limp barely noticeable. When finally the tumult that followed Tecumseh's words died down, Weatherford stood. The red egret feathers contrasted with his white buckskin pants and reminded Cade of blood and innocence, an image that made his heart beat faster. But he was no seer, and he thrust the thought from his mind.

The Creek had gotten what they had expected. Tecumseh was everything a great speaker should be. He fulfilled their expectations and more. The Creek leaders had gathered at Tukabatchee to discuss the issues that now separated brother from brother. What effect would Tecumseh's words and performance have on their decisions? Cade wondered would they fight together to rid the Nation of the growing dependence on the white man's ways. Although the question was not a new one, the wave of discontent had grown more powerful.

Gabe and Cade, novices to the council, sat quietly and just listened. Many agreed with Tecumseh that it was now or never. They must fight now or lose their identity forever by the constant encroachment of wagon after wagon of whites settling on their land and claiming it as their own.

The assembly stilled as Weatherford stood to speak. His words were few but eloquent, seldom but meaningful. He looked into the eyes of those who regarded him—some of those eyes glowed with a dangerous fervor of zealots now fueled by Tecumseh's powerful oratory.

"When the Americans were weak and few, they defeated the British," he said. "Now they are stronger and greater in number. They will surely conquer again. The English bear no more love for us than do the Americans. Both are white. All whites are enemies of the red man."

The Autauga village silversmith, Tecumseh and Sikaboo's cousin, Josiah Francis, nodded and looked about him to see how others were responding to his kinsman's words.

But Weatherford's next words took them by surprise. "We should remain neutral. But if we are forced to go to war, let it be with the Americans."

Then Weatherford sat, leaving the Council House bewildered. His words lingered in the air, punctuating the emotionalism of Tecumseh with the reason of a man who weighed the inevitability of the power and numbers of those his people wanted to fight—and realized the futility of the battle.

Inspired by his cousin Sikaboo's talk, Josiah Francis stood and began to shake. Sikaboo hurried to Francis and guided him from the Council House.

"He is now blind, but he will again see, and then he will know all things that are to happen in future," Sikaboo promised.

Sikaboo placed Francis in a cabin by himself, around which Sikaboo danced and howled. Francis was from this point forward a major prophet for the Red Stick cause.

Cade bumped into Will Milfort as he left the Council House and discussed briefly Tecumseh's talk with him and Sam Dale. Weatherford, Dale, and Milfort had shared many fires. Weatherford and Moniac joined them. Cade had been disturbed by the emotionalism of the movement that appeared to be taking shape right before his eyes. He could tell Weatherford and Sam Moniac were disturbed also. Weatherford stood aloof from Sam Dale, though he had embraced him when they had first arrived. Cade caught a speculative look in Dale's eyes. They did not waste words, and all were soon once again on the path toward home. Cade glanced back at Tukabatchee with a feeling of foreboding.

Gabe was just ready to get back to the stables and his horses.

As they left Tukabatchee, Cade glimpsed Savannah Jack. Jack lifted his knife and pretended to aim it at Cade's heart. Weatherford accidentally moved between them. Cade knew it was a warning. He had thought himself immune to Savannah Jack after all these years. But the reptilian glare reminded him of how bloodthirsty and unrestrained by any morality he was. Cade glanced at his brother Gabriel. Mercifully, Gabe had not seen Savannah Jack. But Cade knew that Savannah Jack would take whatever opportunity he had to kill them both, reminders of his failure and the power he could have had if William Augustus Bowles had prevailed.

That night as they lay on their blankets around the fire, Cade overheard Weatherford and Moniac talking when they thought their companions were asleep. Moniac asked Weatherford which side he would take if it came down to a fight. Weatherford replied, "Are my loyalties with the Americans? I asked myself today. And I thought of Ben Hawkins. Or are my loyalties with my people, and I looked at Far Off Warrior, High Head Jim, and Peter McQueen. My mother is Sehoy, Clan of the Wind. My grandfather was Eagle Wings a Tukabatchee chief. I am a war chief of the Taskigi. As a man, a warrior, and a chief it is my duty to bring victory to my people when they decide upon war." He spoke with an air of frustration.

"If I cannot talk my people out of this hopeless cause, perhaps I can at least keep them from doing what Tecumseh said and killing the women and children."

Moniac nodded, understanding. Weatherford was above all else a Creek warrior. Moniac stroked the medal he had gotten from Washington. That vow of friendship was a vow he never forgot.

When Cade returned home, Nicey and Herman wanted to hear about everything that happened, who said what, how they were dressed, and Cade's reactions to it all. Then Nicey filled him in on the details he had only half-listened to before Tukabatchee that now seemed much more important. People, their relationships, events, and perhaps fate had led to the situation in which Cade now found himself as he paddled up the river to deliver the Choctaw boy back to his people.

"Josiah Francis is now one of Tecumseh's prophets," Cade had told Nicey. "His brother Joseph Francis has also gotten caught up."

Josiah followed in his father's footsteps and had become a silversmith. As a symbol of his prophetic powers, he now wore an intricately designed serpentine-shaped armband of silver with eyes of a bezoar stone in the center on his upper arm, calling it his talisman. The bezoar stone, a precious stone formed in the intestine of a deer similar to the way a pearl is produced, was a valuable commodity in the European market because it had long been thought to be an antidote to poison and a source of magic powers.

"'Tecumseh is a bad man and no better than me' were Captain Isaacs exact words, Nicey," Cade reported.

"He's jealous of all the attention Tecumseh is getting," Nicey said. "Captain Isaacs is a sly, deceitful man. You know that Captain Isaacs's wife, Lizzie McGillivray is Mary McGillivray Bailey's niece. Years ago Captain Isaacs accused Dixon, Mary's son, of not being a 'true' Creek. Personally, I think Sam Isaacs was jealous of Dixon. Dixon had the advantage of being educated."

Surprisingly, after his words and rejection of Tecumseh at the Grand Council, Captain Sam Isaacs had joined Francis in the prophet movement. He had gone north on a trading trip and came home a changed man. He'd explained his sudden change of heart regarding Tecumseh by saying, "We'd pulled the canoes ashore and made camp. I was awakened by a horrible noise, the river roared and rocked as if a violent storm had struck. The noise was nearly deafening. Trees fell and the birds screamed in the trees. And then...*the Mississippi River ran backwards*!

Captain Isaacs told Weatherford in Gabe's hearing that he had fallen to his knees at that point into a trance during which he "dived down to the bottom of a river and lay there and traveled for many days and nights receiving instruction and information from an enormous and friendly serpent that dwelt there and was acquainted with future events and all other things for a man to now in his life."

The violent upheaval had been felt in the Tensaw area as well. They all knew when Tecumseh had arrived home. Josiah Francis and Sikaboo gathered many converts as a result of Tecumseh's prediction coming true. The Master of Breath had given a sign.

It was Tecumseh's brother Tenskatawa who had originally predicted the comet that had appeared in March 1811 and the earthquake. The town he established called Prophet Town overflowed with new disciples who came to hear his message. In the Tensaw area, Lorenzo Dow's camp meetings attracted hundreds if not thousands. Both Dow and Tenskatawa preached repentance and urged their followers to turn from their wicked ways. The comet in the sky and the shaking of the earth had convinced many folks that *someone* was trying to get their attention and the end of the world was at hand if they did not repent of their evil actions.

Feeling the earth shake and seeing the Mississippi River run backwards as Tecumseh had predicted led to Isaacs following Little Warrior north to the Great Lakes to learn from Tecumseh's brother, the prophet Tenskatawa, and to fight with Tecumseh. He was *with* Little Warrior when he led the attack on settlers at Duck River thinking that the Creek had declared war on the Americans. Later, when at Benjamin Hawkins's insistence, Little Warrior's execution was ordered by the National Council for the killings, Isaacs defected and testified against Little Warrior to save his own neck.

As a prophet, Captain Isaacs gained too many followers for his own good. Cade had heard that after the skirmish at Burnt Corn, Josiah Francis, taking his lead from the prophet Tenskatawa, Tecumseh's brother, had started calling Captain Isaacs a *witch*. It had worked for

Tenskatawa, who had successfully eliminated opposition and competition for power by putting many "witches" to death in the north.

With the passing of James McQueen in 1811, the movement against the Americans gained strength, and Peter McQueen had joined the Red Sticks. The families of those who had been executed for the attack on Duck River demanded justice on those who had killed them. Led by Peter McQueen, Captain Isaacs's house was burned to the ground. On the run from Francis's accusations and those who would burn him as a witch and to wreak vengeance upon him for his part in the order to execute those who had participated in the Duck River killings, Captain Isaacs took supplies he had gotten when he had gone with Peter McQueen to Pensacola and took refuge with Big Warrior at Tukabatchee, providing those Indians friendly to the Americans with much of the Red Sticks' direly needed ammunition.

Friend today, enemy tomorrow, Cade thought. He knew about that firsthand.

He paddled faster and harder as he thought of Nicey and Herman heading toward Fort Mims. He needed to finish his errand with the Choctaw boy and get on to his duty. Thoughts of Tecumseh's words stirred his anxiety. Who would protect Nicey and Herman, watch out for Gabriel, and find out if their little sister Joie, who would be almost twelve years old now, was alive and safe?

He knew that the Creek who had ventured from their village to settle in the Tensaw area were considered daughters of their mother village who had to be disciplined for allowing themselves to be influenced by the white man. They spun cloth. They raised cows, pigs, and chickens. They were quickly becoming nearly indistinguishable from the Americans with whom they lived. Thus, the Red Sticks reasoned that they must be punished.

Cade's mother's spirit haunted him. He must find Joie. To honor the promise he had made his mother, he would find her now that he was a man and assure himself of her safety.

The only good thing about this fool's errand was that, in spite of his youth, they'd probably have elected him captain of the damned militia if he'd been at the fort—just because he'd been shot at Burnt Corn. Cade never wanted to be a leader. That meant you were responsible for others. They didn't know just how little leadership he had in him. His mind nearly went back to Miccosukee until he heard the boy behind him clear his throat.

Cade turned and held up a hand to quiet him. He cocked his head to the east shore. The boy nodded. Sound carried on water.

The boy was good with an oar. Cade had to give him that. They dipped and pulled harmoniously as they paddled upstream.

But that glance at the boy set him to thinking about a certain daft, violet-eyed bit of trouble he'd long tried to forget. And the thought of her made him want to smile. The long dimples in his chiseled face deepened as he forced his mouth into a frown and sent the memory of her to the back of his mind. She was gone, probably married by now. Heaven help the poor cuss that took her as his wife.

Hell if that kid didn't remind him of Pipsqueak. But she had those crazy-colored eyes, and the boy's were brown. What could be making him think of that accident-prone little girl that was such a pest?

Back when he'd come to Creek country with the pack train, she had followed him everywhere. Trouble—that's all either one of them was. It must be why the kid made him think of her. The girl had literally stalked him after she had spotted him when his father was beating him there by the river. After that, he couldn't shake her. Cade had even complained to Nicey Potts.

Nicey had just clucked, understanding in her eyes, and said, "Girl's afraid your father's gonna take the whip to you again."

He could not disguise his dismay, and Nicey saw it. Warriors did not have little girls protecting them. Their father's whip was the least of the hell he and his brother had known.

"As long as she's watching out for you, you can keep an eye on her. You've seen how absent-minded that girl is, just as likely to walk off into a river with her nose in one of those books she's always reading," she had added, stroking his ego a bit.

That did make sense to him at the time, since he had just fished her out of a river, two creeks, and a small ravine because she'd been doing exactly what Nicey said. So Cade had nodded and accepted the inevitable. If he had his way, he'd never be responsible for or care about anyone else. Until they parted at St. Stephens, the little girl with the sparkling indigo eyes who used big words, read books thick as his arm, and was followed by critters most folks would not get near was added to his list of those he had to watch out for.

Shit.

His muscles bulged as he pulled even harder against the current, sweat dripping and stinging his eyes and the still raw flesh where the bullet had grazed him at the battle at Burnt Corn. He didn't have time to swat the damned flies biting and bringing big welts to his skin. But he'd learned early to ignore pain.

So he wasn't brave and he could barely read. What reading he could do was what that little girl had taught him when he finally gave up resisting her.

The militia was mighty lucky they had Dixon Bailey as captain and not him. Why would anyone want to promote someone whose own father didn't think he was worth having around?

Now where did that thought come from? He hadn't thought of his father in two forevers—or at least today.

Cade sat straighter and fought the lump in his throat. The wound from Burnt Corn had weakened him more than he wanted to admit. Too much pain. Too many memories. In his dreams, the time he and Gabe spent with Savannah Jack and Bowles tormented him relentlessly.

A time when he was helpless.

But he was helpless no longer. Cade was now taller than William Weatherford. He was broad shouldered, muscular, and powerfully built, quick and fast, incisive in his thinking, and competitive to a fault. He would never again be at another man's mercy. While he did not pick a fight, neither did he turn from one.

That was it. He nodded with a quick jerk of his head that probably made the boy behind him wonder what he was thinking. Cade turned and took the boy aback by practicing his fiercest look.

He never spoke of the time he spent with Savannah Jack and Bowles—tried never to remember it.

Gabe had helped settle his torment by making flutes that could bring the birds from the trees to light on his shoulders. Amazingly, the music he brought forth from those pieces of reed calmed even the most ornery horse. Gabe played a mesmerizing, almost haunting tune that actually soothed Cade when his memories troubled him and the fevers returned, though he'd never admit it to Gabe. Cade had seen things, experienced things, that Gabe did not know of due to his delirium at the time.

Gabriel could talk to the horses and said they talked back, something he and Pipsqueak had shared. Something that had made Cade think those two belonged together. Who was Cade to say whether man, or girl, could communicate with the animals? He just knew he'd seen enough to believe it.

Cade wondered if Pipsqueak had ever heard Gabe play the flute.

Whatever made him think of that?

For some reason, that little bit of bother kept popping up in his memories. Must be because he was so close to St. Stephens, where he had last seen her. She wouldn't go until he promised to come back for her when she had grown up.

Surely such a promise didn't count.

Cade knew there was a special bond between Gabriel and Pipsqueak. He'd sensed it, and he was not usually a sensitive sort. Why the idea should make him jealous was beyond him. He and Gabe had met Pipsqueak on the heels of their captivity. The two of them had acted like he was fragile and might shatter. It disturbed him that they had whispered—about him, he knew—and hovered about him as if they thought *he* needed protecting! Gabe and Pipsqueak belonged together.

Damn it all to hell and back! He hated for folks to act like they knew so much more than he did.

It was unsettling that they had thought he needed anyone. It was he who had protected them! They were both odd with that strange sixth sense of theirs that made others wary of them. He'd kind of expected Gabriel to go seeking the girl one day; they had so much in common. Whenever he'd mentioned her to Gabriel, Gabriel would give him a strange, oddly compassionate look.

He really should encourage Gabe to look her up now and see if she had married.

He shrugged off a sudden piercing sadness and focused on paddling.

After a few minutes, he glanced back at the boy behind him who didn't have the sense to look scared or intimidated by him. It only took one look at the kid's coloring to tell he was in the same fix Cade had been when he was his age. Half in and half out of two worlds. And that meant he didn't really fit in either one.

Shit.

Why the hell did he care, anyway?

He didn't care.

About anyone or anything.

He rowed and scowled.

Unwillingly, Cade remembered how scared he and Gabriel had been when William Augustus Bowles and Savannah Jack had kidnapped them.

Their fleeting joy after returning to their father was quickly shattered by the overwhelming pain of their mother's death and their father's rejection. And then there was the contempt his father shared with the woman he took up with—that Loughman woman. It hadn't been so bad for Cade, but after what they'd been through, how could his father not know how *Gabriel* needed him? He needed his father's reassurance that he had not been the reason for his mother's death. Yet his father blamed them!

Snow Bird had been all that was loving and gentle in Cade's life. He missed her soft voice, her sweet hugs, and the security of her presence. That day on the river when the damned horse had balked at the sight of the snake and the little girl had saved him was the first time the tears he had mastered for so long threatened to appear. Gabe saw it and knew the little girl had touched Cade's fiercely guarded heart. But Cade had pulled himself together and thrown back his shoulders, all tears and emotion suppressed, unconsciously mimicking High Head Jim's confident grace. He would not weaken. He would be as stoic as High Head Jim, his mentor.

"Get the bear grease out and smear it on, boy," he said softly to the Choctaw boy, remembering Pipsqueak's soft touch when she'd rub Nicey's salve over his back while he pretended to be asleep. So many times he wanted to sink into the oblivion of forgetfulness, but her touch brought him back. "It stinks to high heaven with all the shit Miz Potts puts in there, but if you don't, those flies will bite the hell out of you."

He'd said "shit" to the boy. Nicey would tan his hide for that, big man though he was. She didn't bide with him talking like the trappers he'd heard on the pack train. When Lorenzo Dow, with his scraggly hair and beard, had come into the territory, Nicey had gone and gotten herself some religion. Dow's harsh voice and wild gesticulations excited the wonder and curiosity of the crowds he attracted. While Nicey wouldn't take a strap to him like his father had, she could make some hellfire of a bar of soap to wash his mouth out with. He didn't dare stop to rub any of the bear grease on himself. If he did, the damned current would take them back to where they started, or they would drift over to the rushes where those bull alligators liked to hide, and there was no damned telling whether or not the crazy "prophets" had set the their sights on him.

So he steered his course down the middle of the river and suffered the bites of torment.

He thought about how the earth had literally shaken in December 1811 after Tecumseh's visit, how the great water of the Mississippi River had flowed backwards and changed its course. With events like that, it was inevitable that the prophets of Tecumseh would find followers. Suddenly, the Creek Nation had become a place where you couldn't tell who was your friend and who was your enemy. A place where brothers swore blood oaths against their brothers.

Maybe he could have told the woman who'd become like the mother he'd lost "no."

No, he wasn't a babysitter.

No, he didn't have time to run her errands for her. There was a war going on.

No, that little boy would just have to stay in a place that was about as safe as a nest of moccasins.

He'd already fought and been wounded in this goddamned brothers' war—and by High Head Jim, a man he trusted, a man he thought cared about him. It was a hell of a world where you couldn't trust a soul.

Any man who was with the Americans was against the Red Sticks, and friend or foe they would be dealt with the same. The friend of the enemy was the enemy, friend or brother be damned.

Where in the hell *was* his brother, Gabriel?

While thoughts and memories kept Cade absorbed and maneuvering the river kept him silent, Lancelot Rendel felt his own excitement grow. Once he got Cade into Pushmataha's domain, whatever happened next was up to Lyssa.

And they were nearly there.

Light glinted off something white, and Lance knew Lyssa and Beauty were on the bluff watching and waiting. She would follow the trail along the river until they came to the first of the Six Towns villages where her grandmother Chamay, also part of the plan, awaited.

The game was on. Lance's amber eyes sparkled at the thought.

6

August 28, 1813

Lyssa stood inside the hut, dressed in the white deerskin she had lovingly fashioned for her wedding night, wringing her hands, biting her lips, and waiting for her bridegroom.

She heard the shouts and cheers that came like a wave from the village and knew that he was coming—and she grew more and more apprehensive. Her mother had told her grandmother, Chamay, of the nightmares Lyssa had after seeing her mother's assault in the cornfield. When the young men started paying notice to Lyssa, her grandmother had taken her aside and talked to her about the ways of men and women.

"There was a raid on my village when I was young. I was raped by a white man," Chamay had said. "Your grandfather arrived in time to save my life, but the white man's seed lived within me. It was the will of Yahola that your mother be born. It was the love of your grandfather Pushmataha that made me whole, Little One. Love can be a beautiful thing. Do not let what you saw in the field rob you of that."

Though Lyssa knew with her mind about the ways of men and women, she could not comprehend the why. She knew her boy, now fully grown and the most beautiful man she had ever seen, would expect her to submit. Would she have the courage?

What would she say to him?

And then he was there, pulling the skin door aside to enter the hut. Tentatively, she smiled at the stranger...who now only vaguely resembled her boy.

What had she done? What would *he* do? She bit her lip and forced herself not to run.

The man took one step forward and the skin door fell closed. With the second step, he stumbled. And then he fell, hard, like a tree hewn in the forest, and passed out facedown on the pile of deerskins she had arranged for their wedding night.

Unconscious.

What now?

Tentatively, Lyssa stepped forward to study him. This was the gangly boy she had fallen in love with at eight years old? She could not help noticing that this nearly naked man stretched out on the floor of her hut had shoulders that would be the envy of any warrior in the talwa. With his hands palms down beside his face where he'd caught himself as he fell, she noted that his body tapered enticingly to the breechclout, his only clothing.

Lyssa waited for him to move or speak...or something. Could he have drunk so much that he'd keeled over dead?

A very undignified snort answered that.

Well, if he wasn't dead, he *was* dead out. Lyssa tapped her finger on her lips, pensively eying her prostrate hero. Regardless of the drool slipping from the side of his mouth, he was one *handsome* man. His long sable hair had come loose from the leather tie and now covered the stubborn angular chin she'd noticed as he'd tumbled to her feet. She watched him warily, yet he did not move.

Hmm. Perhaps this was an unforeseen opportunity.

Lyssa approached him cautiously. She knelt and sat back on her heels. Still no movement. The scars she had once tended crisscrossed his back. The boy whose fevered body she had rubbed with Nicey's salves had now become a man.

Her hand was drawn irresistibly to pull his long hair back from across his face. Now she could look at the chiseled jaw with those deep dimples she remembered so well. What a gorgeous man her boy had become!

Her one shy touch was not enough.

Growing bolder, she ran her fingers through his thick dark hair. He still didn't move a muscle.

This was not how she had envisioned their reunion. She wasn't exactly sure what to expect, but an unconscious bridegroom had not been it.

But then, truly, in her planning, getting him into the hut was about all she had dared let herself think of.

All in all, having him passed out was probably for the best. She was almost certain he didn't realize he was a bridegroom.

For hours she had peeked through the crack between the deerskin and the door frame trying to gauge how much time she had before she had to explain herself to the man she had tricked into marriage. She had tried explanation after explanation as she paced, twisting her hands and biting her nails.

The entire village had lined the path from the river to her grandfather's dwelling where her grandmother, Chamay, the matriarch of her clan, accepted the red cloth, knowing full well the meaning of her acceptance. Chamay had been Lyssa's closest confidant and friend from the moment she had come into Pushmataha's village.

Chamay had met and liked Gabriel Kincaid, Cade's twin, who because of business association with Weatherford had learned the *lingua franca* and could now communicate with just about anyone. When Gabe ventured into Choctaw country searching for horses suitable to racing at Weatherford's horse track on the Alabama River, Chamay had spent hours with him unknown to Lyssa, learning of the young man for whom Lyssa still carried such devotion.

Chamay knew her daughter, Malee, would not approve of Lyssa's plan because her husband Jake would be so violently opposed. She reasoned that Lyssa's father remained too much the Virginia aristocrat, whether he believed it or not, to approve of the methods of the Indian women in helping men along in their decisions. Jake Rendel would be happy to keep Lyssa with him as his little girl forever.

But Lyssa was a woman. A very lonely, fearful, and unhappy woman forced to straddle two worlds.

Perhaps the Great Spirit had intended this union and needed a helping hand from a loving grandmother. Chamay convinced the great chief Pushmataha that his "little heart," his name for his beloved granddaughter, needed their help. He agreed. The idea that he was bypassing Malee's Englishman, the man who had stolen away his own Malee, the daughter of his heart though not the daughter of his flesh, was appealing to him as well. Though Pushmataha had taken Chamay as his own wife immediately after the battle during which a white man had raped her, it was obvious that the child born nine months later carried the blood of another race. It never mattered to Pushmataha.

The long, silent line of men and women gathered by the riverside wanted to see the one brave enough to marry the girl responsible for withering the man parts of the most ardent Choctaw brave of the village. Cade casually carried the bolt of red cloth that everyone (but him) knew was meant to be a bridal gift. To Cade's wonder, Lyssa's grandfather had greeted him warmly and offered tafia rum all around. Lyssa had watched through the hut door as Chamay moved from Pushmataha's side to accept the red cloth and then held it high with great ceremony. Cheers came up from the crowd, and the bewildered Cade accepted the offered tafia, proud to still be in possession of his hair. He figured the little Choctaw boy he had delivered was much loved. He looked around for the boy. Lance, whom he knew only as "Little Arrow," had disappeared.

The evening had progressed well with ever-increasing high spirits. Lyssa had watched from the hut in which she awaited her bridegroom in the ceremonial white deerskin of a virgin. The jug of tafia went around and around, and Cade was wary enough of his circumstances to be sure not to offend the hospitality of this jovial group that seemed so thrilled to have the young captive returned. Of course, all the toasts and hilarity that the other braves enjoyed had been carried on in the Choctaw language—a language of which Cade was totally ignorant, to their even greater amusement.

Cade laughed when the others laughed. Unnerved as he was being alone in a Choctaw village, he also drank freely of the tafia that was passed around. He figured most of what they laughed about had some sexual connotation because of their focus on his breechclout and the finger motions: straight...bent...straight...bent...ha ha ha.

They were Choctaw after all and not exactly known for their wit or intellect by the Creek. At last they'd all led him, stumbling, up the hill to a hut set apart from the village. He pulled aside the skin curtain. There before him, lit only by the moonlight, stood the most beautiful woman he had ever seen wearing white doeskin so finely cured and fashioned that it sheathed her body like a glove. While he felt there was something familiar about the woman with the ebony hair and violet eyes, he decided he could only have known her in a dream.

Before he had seen her, his brain had already been foggy and his feet unsteady. But now his breath caught in his chest. Then she smiled a smile that completely took his breath away. He'd stumbled inside and then, as the skin fell to close the view from the outside, he pitched forward and passed out.

Lyssa knew this was definitely not part of the plan. Though originally, the plan had only extended to getting him here. At least that part had been accomplished.

Lyssa felt only the slightest guilt knowing that Cade Kincaid thought the festivities were because he had brought home the young Choctaw boy. She had thought long and hard on what she would say to explain their situation. Now she had a reprieve. She chewed on her lip and looked at him lying there unconscious. Yes, this was best.

But what to do next? She chewed on her fingernail.

He was here, her boy, and suddenly all she wanted was to be as close to him as she possibly could. For ten years, she had felt that a part of her was missing. Now he was here, and she wanted to hold him to her heart and never let go.

Her grandmother had told her about the ways of men and women, and Lyssa knew it didn't involve clothing. Emboldened by the darkness and the fact that her intended was totally unconscious, Lyssa untied the soft doeskin shift and let it drop.

If he were awake, would he find her pleasing?

With only the light of the full moon shining from around the coverings of the windows and door, Lyssa looked at the man lying on her deerskin. He was hers. Wasn't he?

Her eyes shifted from his glorious eyes, thickly lashed and firmly closed, down his body to the fresh scars from the gun wounds he had gotten at the Battle of Burnt Corn Creek. Gently she traced the wounds, one on his forehead and one lower down his side. Then her eyes ventured further to the belt of his breechclout. Good Lord, he even had dimples there! Her fingers slowly made their way to the enticing dimples.

She caught her breath and trembled with her own boldness. From that point, somehow her hands ventured under the clout. Lyssa held her breath at her audacity. Cade snorted and she jerked her hand away.

Only vaguely was she aware that on the other side of the skin door, braves were taking bets on whether the crazy Creek would be able to do the deed. The bets were on.

Twenty to one she'd wither his man parts. Then once more the jug of tafia was passed around.

Morning would come and Lyssa would have to venture from the hut. Everyone would know at that point whether there was truth to the fact that she was the cause of the curse for the villages' bent arrows. But at the moment, that thought did not distract her. She took a deep breath and untied the belt, loosing the breechclout. Slowly, she slid it away from his body, revealing an impressively taut set of buttocks beneath those enticing dimples.

It was as if some brazen stranger had somehow come to inhabit her body. A strange compulsion guided her hands to touch him while he slept. His legs were spread, and, unable to help herself, she touched him, causing an odd reaction. Suddenly she Lyssa jerked back, remembering the man in the cornfield who had almost raped her mother. She glanced up to make sure Cade's eyes were still closed. His breathing retained the steady rate of a sleeping man. She was safe with him. She knew it.

An aching fullness in her own body increased her fascination. She gently turned Cade onto his back. Driven by the wonder of what his smooth chest would feel like against her, Lyssa straddled him. Her waist-length hair became a curtain around them, teasing his chest. She gently brushed his chest with her own. He groaned and she sighed.

She laid her head on his chest and absorbed the beating of his heart—her own adopting his rhythm. This was the boy who'd filled her heart when she was only a girl, and it seemed right that now he was the man for whom her body yearned. She was so focused on her intense feelings that she missed the shift in his breathing.

Suddenly, he had her by the hips, and the man she'd thought was still sleeping was one with her. She cried out with surprise and a sudden pain, though it was fleeting.

Her heart filled with knowing this was her destiny. This total oneness. This boy become man. And immediately she was overwhelmed with such fierce love that it seemed her heart would burst. She was totally consumed with the man who now shifted their positions and covered her. And then she felt his touch and his kisses covered her body. He took her with him to a crescendo of passion that crested in waves until at last he stiffened and cried out.

And then he did it again. And then once again.

Finally, exhausted, he rolled onto his back, still nuzzling her hair, planting kisses behind her ear and down her neck, holding on to her tightly, as though he would never let her go. And then with a deep snore he was once again asleep. Lyssa smiled as she tenderly stroked the face so changed from the boy he had been, but yet still so beloved. She reached for the white deerskin she had worn to welcome him, and with it she covered the two of them.

She now knew the "why" of the ways of men and women.

She drifted into a sleep of complete assurance that the world was right and all would be well.

And then came the morning.

"Lyssa! Lyssa!"

Slowly she came awake, aware of her father's voice calling, coming closer. Her head was not on her pillow. Whatever she slept on was much too hard. As if in a fog, she pulled back the hair that covered her eyes and discovered that it was also trapped beneath the shoulder on which she lay. She looked straight into cerulean blue eyes that knew immediately who she was. At that moment, the flap to the hut was flung open, and there stood her father. There was little doubt what had taken place between the two young people in the hut.

Too late, Lyssa grabbed the white deerskin to cover the two of them once more. A shout of exultation came from the gathering outside the hut, where all was revealed to the crowd gathered. Women laughed and hugged their men. Men jumped and thumped other men on the back before grabbing their women by the hand and dragging them back to their dwellings. Bent Arrow, now most assuredly Straight Arrow once more, herded his first wife into the nearest hut. The curse was lifted!

At the door and beside her in the hut, in unison, the two men said, "Lyssa?"

Then Cade uttered incredulously the name he had always called her. "Pipsqueak?"

Cade could not believe that the beautiful woman who now reclined on his outstretched arm was the little girl he had left at St. Stephens years earlier. Nor could he believe it was she lying naked under the white deerskin after having engaged in activities of which the evidence was obvious for anyone to see! And probably *had* seen! He felt her silky hair on his arm, the womanly feel of her ample breast against his side, her smooth cheek against his chest, and now her arm around him. Her ~~sweet~~ lips touched his chest as she gazed up at him with sleepy, adoring violet eyes.

Her father growled.

That got Cade's attention.

"What is going on here?" Jake Rendel shouted.

They both just looked at him. Cade was confused. He vaguely remembered the beautiful woman standing at the door of the hut, but nothing after that. How could she possibly be Lyssa...Pipsqueak?

He looked at her again, incredulous.

Lyssa felt the situation was obvious and needed no comment.

Rendel found *himself* blushing. "Let me try this again. Lyssa, your grandmother tells me you are married."

"Married?" Cade exclaimed. "You're married?" Would her husband burst through the flap next?

"Yes, Father," Lyssa said. "You know Cade promised he would come for me ten years ago. I know you thought he only said that so that I would leave him alone. But he finally came. And he brought the red cloth, the bridal gift, and he gave it to my grandmother."

"I did?" Cade said.

"And last night he made a woman of me."

"I did?" No use denying it. The evidence was on the deerskin.

"I did," he said again, struggling to get up. He was in a difficult position, naked on a pile of deerskin and holding the man's naked daughter in his arms.

Lyssa leaned back on her elbows, suddenly angry and rebellious.

"Get up from there, girl," her father ordered. "We're going to Fort Stoddard. Judge Harry Toulmin will marry the two of you and make it legal."

"But," Cade attempted before fiery purple eyes flashed his way. "Sir, I'd like to talk to Lyssa. Alone if I may."

Rendel hesitated, and then he said, "Just get dressed and get out here fast."

Cade managed to find his belt and breechclout from which he had been divested during the night. He then crossed his arms and stood silently, just waiting, a stance he had seen Weatherford take with effect many times. He appeared to be in control.

But inside, his mind was racing.

Married? He couldn't get married. He was never going to have a wife. He had to get to Fort Mims. He ventured a look at the girl—no, woman—pulling over her head the long shirt she'd taken off the night before to put on the now-stained doeskin shift. This was not the skinny little girl he'd left at St. Stephens ten years ago. She leaned over to pull a moccasin from beneath a table, and he couldn't take his eyes away from her. Cade groaned. He was a very sick man.

"Did you say something?" Lyssa asked.

He raised an eyebrow, hoping she would not notice his physical reaction to her.

"All right, all right. I guess you deserve an explanation," she said, looking at him and hoping he would tell her it only mattered that they were finally together. But he didn't say that. All he did was stand there. Arms crossed. Saying nothing. And making her more and more uncomfortable in the silence. What if he actually loved Sally Carson?

Tears gathered in her eyes.

"I waited and waited for you! You did say you would come for me, you know."

His eyebrow lifted again.

"I know. You were only ten," she conceded. "And I *did* refuse to budge until you promised. *And* you're going to tell me that no ten-year-old boy can be held to a promise made to an eight-year-old girl." She looked at him, saw that his eyebrows was still raised, and decided to continue.

"But I was standing in my father's barn one day, worried to death about how the men in the village thought I had cursed them so their man parts withered. I heard Sally Carson say she planned to trap you into marrying her, and I simply could not let someone do such a lowdown, dirty thing to someone I loved," she said, glancing over her shoulder as she leaned down to retrieve the other moccasin she had kicked under the pile of deerskins.

His eyebrow went higher. She thought the reaction was because of her proclamation of love—her undying, never faltering, unfailing, totally selfless love. Had the man lost the power of speech?

In truth, Cade hadn't a clue of a word she had said. All the blood had left his brain when she leaned over to find her first beaded moccasin.

Now she was standing so close that he grew lightheaded. He had no choice.

He managed to move them to the only piece of furniture in the hut, a table that held a candle that was thank-you-god unlit—causing the candle to topple to the floor. She gasped with the unexpected pleasure. And suddenly it was only the two of them again, and the sensation was so fierce and the waves of pleasure so strong that she nearly passed out.

Her father chose that moment to throw back the damned skin and reveal all once more to the throngs who had gathered outside the hut. With all the noise coming from inside the hut, he thought Cade had taken exception to being tricked into marriage and had become violent. What he saw was the last thing he had expected to see. He'd better get those two legally bound before the blood left Cade's head again.

Another cheer came from the crowd. More dancing and hugging and kissing. More running off into nearby dwelling places. And Lyssa's grandfather's deep voice resonated through her foggy brain, saying, "Now you know how I felt when Malee married you."

Then came her grandmother's voice. "You should thank me for getting them married before they saw each other again."

Was her entire family standing there?

Her father groaned. She knew that sound.

"Just think," her grandmother said with relief in her voice, "there are bound to be grandchildren soon."

The shaman had apparently followed and stood with them at the door. "In fact, I predict a surge in the population of the entire Choctaw nation in about nine months," he commented.

Of course, all of this was said in the Choctaw language, so Cade didn't know what they were talking about. The groan he understood, but the rest seemed like a threat. He stood there, with fists clenched and knees bent in front of Lyssa in a stance so purely protective that Jake Rendel could not help smiling. Cade Kincaid reminded him of Lyssa's dog Samson—all heart and devotion. He figured the boy didn't have a clue. Of course, at this moment he was acting more like Samson did when Delilah was in heat.

Jake's scowl returned.

"He's quite impressive, really," Chamay commented.

Good Lord. "Put the Kraken back under cover, Kincaid," Jake Rendel commanded in English.

Cade looked at him, bewildered.

"Cover yourself, man," Rendel said. "The women out here are all but swooning as it is."

Kraken? That was what they called it? Another crazy Choctaw word. Cade immediately straightened his breechclout.

Cade stood there bewildered. What had happened to him? He was a man of discipline, always in control. He was immune to the wiles of women.

And this was Pipsqueak! He shook his head in confusion. He was indeed a sick man.

Lyssa blew a strand of blue-black hair from her eyes, focusing in the opposite direction from the door and the obvious audience. Finally she turned her head. The entire Choctaw nation could be at the door. But all she saw was the gorgeous rear view of the man who took her breath away with a single glance. Why had she never noticed how enticing such a view could be?

But she knew. No other man was Cade Kincaid.

"Lyssa." Her father's voice. Reluctantly, she shifted her gaze. He pointed two fingers toward her, capturing her attention, and brought them back to his own sparkling green eyes. "Focus," he said to her.

To the others around him, he said, "I'll take the boy with me. If we leave the two of them alone in there, we'll be here waiting the rest of the day."

Chamay nodded and went into the hut. Rendel pointed at Cade and gestured at him to follow.

"Did you get all the 'talking' done you needed to do?" he asked Cade.

"Talk?" Cade responded.

"That's what I thought," Rendel muttered, taking the young man by the arm.

Chief Pushmataha, a strikingly muscular man who wore an air of authority and commanded respect, pushed away the smile that would mar his usually impassive countenance. But he could not control the twinkle in his warm brown eyes. He could imagine what was going on in the hut now with Chamay and her beloved granddaughter. No man would be good enough for their Lyssa, but her heart had been set on this one. From what he knew of Cade Kincaid, the young man had possibilities. Especially now that he'd had the opportunity to see with his own eyes Jake Rendel's reaction. The Great Spirit had a wonderful sense of humor, he thought, chuckling to himself, though not one glimmer of his thoughts ever showed on his expression.

Pushmataha glanced down toward the river and noticed another canoe being pulled ashore. He recognized Gabriel Kincaid as he jumped from the canoe and ran up the hill. "Your brother is here, Kincaid," he said to the man who had Lyssa's heart.

Cade immediately whipped away from Pushmataha and Jake Rendel and ran toward Gabriel.

"You were in on this," he said, jumping on Gabriel and pummeling him.

"From what I saw when you walked from that hut, I gather you are a married man, now, Brother," Gabe said, laughing as he gained the upper hand and rolled him over.

"What am I going to do with a wife?" Cade said with an air of desperation, and then, when Gabe reacted with uncontrolled laughter, he blushed and tumbled, rolling over and over with Gabe down the embankment.

Gabe pulled away long enough to catch a breath and to look his twin in the eye. He smiled at what he saw there. "I think you know," he chortled.

They tussled with each other into the shallows of the water.

"Calm yourself, brother. You do not want these people to think you aren't happy with your new bride. Do you?"

"I just don't need any more responsibility right now, Gabe."

"There's never a good time for you, Cade. Since losing Mother, you don't let anyone to get close to you," Gabriel said as they continued to struggle. "But your marital status is not why I am here," he continued, his face red and his muscles straining as he pulled Cade's hands from around his neck.

Cade sat back, straddling his brother, whose head was nearly submerged in the water. "The Red Sticks are about to attack Fort Mims," Gabe said.

"Then why in the hell are you here and not warning Nicey and Herman?" Cade said, suddenly growing still with shock.

"I can't. Weatherford has joined the Red Sticks but is trying to prevent a massacre. He sent word by several of the slaves that the Red Sticks are approaching, but Major Beasley has put the slaves to the lash for lying. Captain Middleton did not see the warriors himself. You know Dixon Bailey hates Weatherford, and he knows about my close relationship with him. He thinks I am with the Red Sticks because of my connection with Weatherford and won't let me near the fort."

Gabe grabbed Cade's hand as it descended for a punch. He said seriously, "Cade, Joie is there. I watched our father take them all into the fort. And then Nicey and Herman refused to listen and went into the fort themselves."

Cade was suddenly mobilized with the thought of what could be happening even now. He jumped off Gabriel and splashed through the water to the canoe. "Come on. We've got to save them."

Gabe jumped in after him. They left Jake Rendel and Pushmataha standing on the bank. The two men had heard Gabriel's words.

"God help us all," Rendel said.

Pushmataha nodded. Six days ago, he had told a mail carrier headed for Toulmin that he had heard warriors were gathered on the Black Warrior River and were dancing the war dance. He had not known then what their target would be, but knew an attack would probably occur within eight days. A conflagration was about to begin, and he knew the conflict would not be confined just to the Creek. He must ready his own people. He had rejected Tecumseh's talk, but others within the Nation had agreed with Tecumseh. They must be controlled.

"I must go to Malee and make sure she is safe," Jake said.

The chief nodded again and then went on to see about his duties as a chief. His role as a grandfather had receded.

Jake turned back to see Lyssa come toward him, flushed with happiness and anticipation. Chamay followed Pushmataha into their dwelling.

"Where is Cade?" Lyssa asked. She'd only taken time to pull up her usual boy breeches before running after him. How could he have gotten away in such a short time?

"Lyssa," her father said, "Gabriel brought news that there is an imminent attack on Fort Mims where Cade and Gabriel's sister is, and Nicey and Herman Potts have headed there as well."

He took her by the arms and looked directly into her eyes when he said, "Cade and Gabe have gone to try and save them."

Lyssa's face drained of all color. She suddenly felt so weak; she didn't think her legs would hold her up. She dropped to her knees in the path.

"I must go to St. Stephens to your mother and make sure she is safe. We may have to go on down to Mobile. Prepare yourself. I will find Lance."

Lyssa sat back cross-legged on the path, her elbows on her knees and her hands over her face.

He was hers! Her boy. He was on the way into danger, and he had left her here. She felt like half of herself was on the way into a death trap. Her heart clenched and her ears pounded. How could a person be so gloriously happy one moment and so much in despair the next?

She could not go with her father to St. Stephens. She had to go to Cade at Fort Mims. She could not let him face that danger alone!

She stood slowly, thinking all the while.

"I cannot go with you now, Father," she said. "Lance and I are safe here. We will stay with Grandfather."

Anxious now to make sure his beloved Malee was safe, Jake Rendel nodded. Lyssa breathed a sigh of relief as her father headed for the horses. She heard Beauty nicker an objection as her father leapt up on Beast. Samson and Delilah barked a reminder that the two of them were still tied, a precaution Lyssa had taken to make sure her bridegroom was not attacked by her protectors on their wedding night.

Once her father was out of sight, Lyssa strode determinedly toward Beauty. She had just found Cade. Now he was merely a shadow on the water receding beyond the curve in the river. She was not about to lose him. Her father thought she was staying with her grandfather. Her grandfather thought she had gone with her father.

She, Samson, and Delilah were about to follow her husband into Creek Country.

7

Gathering at Fort Mims

"Carrie Joy, get your lazy ass here right this minute," came the shrill voice of Joie's stepmother Leona Loughman Kincaid.

Joie hated being called Carrie. Sarilee said that her mother had named her Joie. She told her that her mother had said she was her joy and a blessing...and then she had died. Leona said the French spelling of that name was too fancy for the half-breed she was forced to keep in her household. And that she certainly was no joy. Carrie was a name plain enough for her lot in life.

That was a mean, hateful thing to say, but her stepmother said it frequently. Her language was as colorful as that of the packmen who brought trade goods to her father's post. Joie couldn't understand why Leona hated her so much. She had tried to win her love. When she was younger, she thought it was her fault. But when Joie's half-brother J.J. was born, Leona seemed to hate him as well. With her head, Joie realized that the woman's insults came because it was simply Leona's way, part of her spiteful character. Her heart was not reasonable. But the damage to Joie's self-esteem was done.

Sarilee said Joie reminded Leona too much of Snow Bird, Joie's mother, the woman Jason Kincaid had never stopped loving. When Sarilee brushed and arranged Joie's black hair into a single long braid in the morning, she always whispered to her that she looked more like her mother every day. She told Joie over and over that she had her mother's kind and gentle ways—and that she, Sarilee, loved her like her own child, the child she would never have.

Since Joie refused to answer to Carrie, her stepmother had finally learned to shriek the double name to get her attention. But spelling it "Joie" was her act of rebellion. A French priest who had stopped at her father's trading post showed her how to spell it correctly. When he traveled their way, he often stopped for a while. He even taught Joie to read, which infuriated Leona.

All pretense of refinement had gone by the wayside as the woman grew more and more bitter about her life with the hard-drinking man who yearned for a long-dead wife. It was a moment of colossal weakness when she had allowed him into her bed only to hear him cry out Snow Bird's name. Soon after, she had discovered she was pregnant with the crying, puking, pissing, pooping infant that now wailed for the slave girl Jason had managed to buy to nurse him when Leona refused.

Joie hated Leona Loughman Kincaid. But she loved her brother more than life. As her father had told her in one of his drunken stupors, James Jason Kincaid, "J.J.," was named for a grandfather Joie would never meet.

Joie stood still for a moment to catch a breeze, a rare occurrence in the miserable fort. The heat was a torment. Flies, mosquitoes, and punky no-see-ums swarmed in the cattails in the swampland near Boatyard Lake, competing with each other to be the most irritating varmints attracted by the refuse of nearly four hundred adults and one hundred children—the settlers, slaves, Mississippi Territorial soldiers, and Tensaw militia who all gathered in that one-acre enclosure. Add in the romping dogs and the nauseating fumes of the outhouse with several months' use, and it was sometimes hard to breathe.

Joie shook her head. Thinking about it didn't make it better. She poured another pot of boiling water into the pan where she washed dishes.

She didn't mind washing dishes. She could do that and pretend she was a part of one of the other families in the crowded fort. Vicariously, she could join the happy lives of those people.

The Randons were a large family living in a cabin near the place where Joie's father had pitched their tent. Viney Randon was a pretty girl of seventeen, about five years older than Joie. Joie dipped a dish in the hot water and watched Viney run through the west gate, where she was headed to Boatyard Lake to meet Peter Durant. Joie had overheard them making plans to go muscadine picking over on Nannahubba Island, a small area of land that formed where the curve of the Tombigbee River was made complete by the Cut-off.

Joie envied Viney. She had managed to get out of the sweltering fort, and she knew other girls were jealous that she had caught Peter Durant's eye. Peter Durant was the dream of every girl in the Tensaw area, though Joie had also heard girls whispering about Cade Kincaid. Cade just happened to be Joie's brother, though she could not remember meeting him. Leona would have a fit whenever anyone mentioned Cade or his twin brother, Gabe.

One day, though. One day Joie knew her brothers would find her and J.J., and…well, now she just had to get through today.

Earlier, Elizabeth Randon, Viney's young cousin, had begged to go muscadine picking with Viney. Joie laughed to herself, thinking of what Viney had told Elizabeth and the resulting look on Elizabeth's face!

"Well, I would take you, 'Lizabeth, you know I would," Viney had said, "but those bushes have the biggest rattlesnakes hiding in them I have ever seen. Now, you know I'm tall enough to see them, but little short folks like you—why, you're right on their eye level."

Joie chuckled, knowing exactly what Viney was up to.

Elizabeth had run away from Viney and jumped into her mother's lap, where she stayed put until coaxed out by the arrival of Mary Louisa Randon Tait, Tura Hollinger Randon's stepdaughter. Joie thought it was amusing that Tura and Mary Louisa were nearly the same age. Mary Louisa was married to David Tait, William Weatherford's brother.

"We're bound to be safe here," Mary Louisa assured Tura. "Surely the Red Sticks won't attack. Billy Weatherford dotes on these girls, his little nieces!"

Joie thought it sounded like she was trying to convince herself.

She listened to the women talk and Leona snore. Apparently David Tait had not wanted Mary Louisa to come to the fort and had even gone to the trouble to prepare a cave nearby in case of emergency. According to Mary Louisa, her husband had gone to check on the cattle he'd hidden from the scavenging Red Sticks. But when Mary Louisa's father, Viney's uncle John, saw smoke rising from plantations all around them, he sent word that he wanted her to be with them within the security of the fort at the Mims plantation.

Joie had heard Mary Louisa say, almost hysterically, "I wish I knew what was best. Why would Davy insist we stay on the plantation? This fort is so well defended; surely we are safer *here* than on the plantation where smoke is rising all around us. The Red Sticks have set fire to other plantations!"

That made sense to Joie as well.

Wringing her hands, Mary Louisa said, "Billy warned Davy that the mixed bloods who hadn't taken the talk would be targeted for punishment. They are blamed for taking up the white man's ways and not keeping the lands and the traditions of their people. Those who have prospered most are the ones most likely to be attacked."

"Where is Davy?" Tura asked.

"He's gone to Pierce's Mill to check on cattle he hid there."

"Oh, Mary Louisa," Tura said. "That's where the Red Sticks are supposed to be heading!"

Mary Louisa, who had tried to be brave, now broke down sobbing. "Oh, God. I want Davy and my girls safe! I just don't know where *safe* is!"

"Look at all the militia here!" Tura said. "Even the Mississippi Territorial militia are here with our Tensaw militia. We have experienced fighting men—the best of all! Why, they've already fought those Red Sticks at Burnt Corn. They know the enemy!"

Mary Louisa was crying in earnest now.

"We are in good hands," Tura assured her as she gave her a hug.

"Are we? Major Beasley is not paying attention to the warnings, Tura," Mary Louisa said. "When I came in the gate a while ago, I noticed how hard it would be to get it closed in a hurry. Isn't that why you said Pa went down there? To try to talk Beasley into paying attention to his slaves who have reported seeing suspicious things? Maybe all of you should pack and come home with me."

Tura could only shrug helplessly. They sat pensively for a minute, watching their little girls play with their dolls. Mary Louisa burst out, "Oh, God. Now I wish I'd stayed at the plantation."

Tura picked up a shirt that needed mending and said, "Your Pa calls them a bunch of religious fanatics."

Mary Louisa ventured to the door and looked toward Joie, who pretended to focus on drying the dishes. "That's what makes them dangerous," she told Tura. "They can justify whatever they do on the grounds that the 'Great Spirit' commanded them!"

"He also says their real motivation is jealousy," Tura said. "The families who realize they must learn to work with the world as it is and adapt have prospered, while those determined to hold to the old ways are still poor. The Red Sticks want what we have, and they are just striking out in anger."

Mary Louisa turned back toward Tura and nodded. "And so they burn our buildings and steal our cattle. They could have it all; just leave us alone!" she wailed, her brown eyes filled with tears.

Tura snipped the thread and tied it off. She picked up a thimble and started stitching. "It's all so complicated. Davy's brother, Billy Weatherford, for example. He's rich. He doesn't need anything anyone else has. Besides that, he lives in the white world as readily as the red man's. Something else has driven him to pick up a gun and aim it against his brothers," she said pensively.

"Sapothlane," Joie heard Mary Louisa say.

"I heard Sam Moniac tell Davy she had him by his"—a quick smile touched her lips—"you know."

Tura grinned and nodded.

Then Mary Louisa sniffled again. She looked around at the distressed expressions on the women's faces. Her luminous brown eyes filled with tears. "I'm sorry," she said. "I'm just trying to understand. I just want my family to be safe."

Tura stuck her needle in the cloth and put it down. She lifted her arm and swiped her forehead with the sleeve of her shirt. And then she gave Mary Louisa a pat. "We can't think of anything else, anyway," she told her stepdaughter. "These are the sorriest stitches I've ever made! Uncle William is visiting with his wife and daughters who are with Mother over at their cabin." She leaned forward. "He's been a guide, spy, and interpreter for General Claiborne. Maybe he has news."

William Randon Hollinger had grown up in David Tait's home, having been taken in to live with the Taits when he was six years old after death of his mother, Elizabeth Moniac, Davy Tait's half-sister. Adam Hollinger, William's father and Tura's grandfather, was an Irish trader. He operated a large cattle ranch and a ferry from Nannahubba Island to the west bank of the Tombigbee while Sam Mims operated the ferry on the east side of the island.

Joie knew just about everyone in the fort—at least by appearance and by listening to her father and stepmother talk. She'd only met a few of them, since she was isolated by her chores and the alienating personalities of her stepmother and father. Leona spoke of them as if they were her friends, though none of them bothered to speak to her. Leona was impressed if they had money or position, and Adam Hollinger was said to be a wealthy man.

"Thank goodness William is here," Mary Louisa said. Since she had helped raise William, she still felt motherly instincts toward him. "That is another member of our family who should be safe, at least. Let's go to your father's cabin."

The Dyer cabin was about 200 yards east of the Mims house in the center of the fort, just opposite the Mims's kitchen. Rosa Zuba Tait skipped along beside Mary Louisa and Tura as they made their way. She'd heard that Tish McGirth would probably get to the fort today, so she carried a rope for her and Tish to skip when she arrived.

Susan Hatterway ran toward the Randon tent, calling for Tura. Hurrying after her, her husband Henry shouted, "Tura and Mary Louisa are at the Dyers'. I'm headed for the east gate to see what's keeping John!" When he caught up to Susan, he gave her an absentminded kiss and then left her to find her friends while he headed off to join the men.

Joie watched while the women made their way through children rolling hoops, slaves doing their chores, men gathered in groups speculating on the possibility of the Red Sticks daring to attack their well-manned fort, and women just standing and fretting. Beside her, Sarilee cut up vegetables to add to the stew pot.

In a cabin nearby, Joie glimpsed sweet Sarah Summerlin lying just inside the door. She was probably the biggest and most miserable pregnant woman Joie had ever seen. Suddenly, Sarah looked straight at her and smiled, startling Joie. Could Sarah read her mind?

Shyly, Joie smiled back. Not many folks noticed her.

More than anything at this moment, Sarah Summerlin wanted to go down to the river and float—just float—in the shallows where her monstrous pregnant body would not weigh her down so heavily...and she could cool off. She would have gone with Peggy Bailey down to the river, but was having slight contractions and decided to stay put. She thought enviously of the women who had gone to wash pots and clothes who were now probably splashing along with their children in the cool water. She pulled the sticky shift away from her sweaty body.

Joie was glad that Sarah would soon have the baby she and her husband John had longed for. She knew John had gone with Sam Mims's sons, Mims's wife Hannah, their daughter Harriet Mims, and their guest Sally Carson down to Mobile for some supplies they needed. With the contractions and all, Sarah had decided she would be safer within the fort. The baby wasn't due for several weeks, but Sarah was so big and miserable.

"They've hung Jo to the whipping post," Joie heard Elizabeth Bailey Fletcher say. Elizabeth stood in the door of Dixon Bailey's makeshift cabin closest to the west gate where Sarah Summerlin lay. She tossed up her apron to wipe the sweat away, seething with anger and frustration as she watched from the door. She had just returned to the cabin after following her husband Josiah to the east gate, where Major Daniel Beasley of the Mississippi Territorial Guard, now the commander of the fort at Claiborne's orders, had accused their slave of lying about seeing Red Sticks around and insisted he be flogged!

"Josiah's done all the arguing he can do with that cocky Beasley. Beasley threatened to kick us out of the fort!" Elizabeth exclaimed. "Josiah told me Beasley is famous for seeing flogging as a way to deal with rebellious blacks. Mainly he was a lawyer, but he was sheriff in Jefferson County in the Mississippi Territory before being appointed to his position by General Claiborne, a friend of his. He ordered flogging with thirty-nine lashes for many a slave."

Sarah looked up and said, "There's lots of folks who are worried that the Red Stick war will bring about a slave rebellion. They don't trust even their oldest and most faithful slaves not to reveal strategic information about troops and the condition of the forts and such."

Elizabeth wiped her hands on a cloth hanging from the waist of her skirt and blew back a damp hank of dark hair. She couldn't get over Major Beasley's arrogant disregard of a valid warning. "Red cattle, my hind foot!" she said. "We trust our Jo! Does Beasley think our Jo would take a chance on being punished like that black was yesterday when Beasley decided he was lying? Jo has to be telling the truth!"

Elizabeth's brother Dixon Bailey was captain of the Tensaw militia stationed there at Fort Mims and was the reason they had such a stout cabin at their disposal. Dixon and Elizabeth's brothers, James Bailey, twenty-seven, and Daniel Bailey, fifteen, were housed there with them in the cabin near the east gate opposite the river gate. Joie had seen their sister Peggy go with other women out the east gate down to the river to wash clothes and pots and cool off. Everyone's nerves were on edge.

The children who had gone with Peggy Bailey had returned, and now they played near the cabin door. The oldest boy swatted his ball with a stick, a serious expression on his face. He was practicing for the day when he would be allowed to play with the men. The younger children were being entertained by a slave girl who was hiding a pea under one of several moccasins and having them guess which moccasin covered the pea.

They were lucky. Joie had seen Bailey's man Mango bring supplies to them from their plantation earlier in the week.

"Josiah's Ned took some of Dixon's blacks down to the river this morning to a fishing hole he found, and they've brought back a pretty good mess of fish," Nancy Summerlin Bailey said to Elizabeth, trying to change the subject and lighten the mood.

"We can make gumbo with some of those tomatoes Mango brought back and put it over some grits tonight," Elizabeth said.

Joie's mouth watered. She wished her father would quit drinking and go hunting or fishing.

While the women did their work in the huts, tents, and cabins inside the fort, the men either stood and watched or were busy playing poker near the east gate. "Keeping an eye on things," Josiah Fletcher told his wife Elizabeth when he'd kissed her that morning and then went to join the men. She hadn't seen an eye flicker from their cards in the past thirty minutes.

Two of John Randon's slaves had returned from his plantation yesterday and reported that Red Sticks were wreaking all sorts of havoc. They said they saw Red Sticks on the way to Pierce's Mill to destroy whatever they could find there. But when Major Beasley dispatched Captain Middleton and his soldiers to investigate, they found nothing. So now John Randon's men had been strung up and flogged too.

Dixon Bailey had drilled his men earlier before the heat of the day, but with it being nearly time for the noon meal, they now milled around at the east gate near the outhouse and the flagpole where the unfortunate slave now hung. A game of cards was underway while they waited for the call to eat.

"Indians don't attack in the middle of the day," Joie had heard Dixon assure them all earlier.

"Wish I could have gone with Viney," Joie heard Ralph Bailey say from where he leaned back against the cabin door, watching the children play. The fourteen-year-old shivered with the ague that had weakened him for a week now. He had a fever and chills that would not go away. Dr. Spruce Osborne, West Point graduate and garrison surgeon, had taught Ralph's mother, Sarah Durant Bailey, to make a quince tea and had the boy chewing quince bark. That seemed to help some, but he was weak as a baby, and Joie knew that worried Sarah and her husband, Dixon.

Joie glanced over to the east gate where Benjamin Durant, Dixon Bailey's father-in-law, leaned against the pickets beside Dixon and watched the card game.

Edward Steadham, arms folded across his chest, stood with Godfrey Lewis Winkel, that son-of-a-bitch fifteen-year-old New Yorker who thought he was better than all of God's creation. They were listening to the men arguing over where Major Beasley oversaw a slave's flogging. Joie did wonder why she should hate him so when he was only telling the truth. She really was just an ignorant breed just as she had overheard him say, and why should it hurt more when Godfrey Lewis Winkel said it than when Leona Loughman Kincaid said it? Joie couldn't understand it.

It looked like all the men were nearly salivating as they watched the beautiful Betsy Hoven.

Betsy held her baby brother with his downy head tucked beneath her chin, swaying while she hummed some soft tune and watched her siblings, Jason, Cornelius, and Lena, shooting marbles. Her silver-white hair was captured in a knot, and the tendrils that escaped hung damply, framing her pale skin that was now flushed with heat. She bit her lush bottom lips. Her sisters Katia, Laura, and Corinne were pouting because their mother would not let *them* go muscadine picking like Viney Randon.

Joie thought it was a toss-up as to who was the prettiest—Betsy Hoven, Harriet Mims, or Sally Carson. They were all best friends.

In truth, the men were watching Betsy, but at the same time Edward was telling Godfrey that his brother William had sent a warning to the

Steadhams that they should leave their plantation because of the danger. They had not heard from William Steadham since. "Matthew thought William meant for us to leave the Creek country," Edward said, "but our father and Uncle Moses refuse to abandon all they have built. Coming to Fort Mims for the safety of our family enables them to continue to go out and bring in some of the crops and care for their cattle."

Joie watched as Edward pointed out the members of his family participating in the revelry around the east gate.

"Elijah, Jesse, Moses Jr., the twins, Matthew and Thomas, and Uncle Moses' six daughters are all here with us."

While Joie watched Edward and Godfrey at the east gate, a tall, strikingly handsome, oddly familiar man entered the gate and hurried toward Herman and Nicey Potts, who were camped close to the gate. They greet each other affectionately. As they talked, the man got visibly upset. Nicey and Herman turned and pointed to her camp! The man rushed up and hugged the frail, toothless Sarilee, swinging her around. Sarilee laughed and hugged him back. As they spun, the man whispered to her. When he put her on her feet, Sarilee turned and pointed right at Joie!

The man looked at her with eyes the same sky-blue color as her own, and Joie knew. "Cade?" she asked. He opened his arms and she rushed in.

"I've come for you, Joie," he said.

"Sarilee said you would," she said. "And I waited and waited."

"Ah, the prodigal son!" roared a voice.

Cade's voice had brought their drunken father out of his stupor. Jason Kincaid staggered to his feet. Angrily, he yanked Joie away from Cade, tossing her like a ragdoll to the ground. She hit her head on the water bucket and sat stunned.

"You good for nothing breed!" Leona shouted from where she sat. "You ain't been around to help your father a bit in your sorry life. What do you want from him now?"

"I don't want a damned thing from him," Cade said, rushing to help Joie to her feet. "I've come to get my sister away from you." He felt the lump rising on Joie's head. "I hear you've treated her worse than you treat your slaves, and from the looks of Sarilee, that's pretty bad."

Leona swelled with anger.

"You go with him, brat," the woman said smugly, too lazy to move from the shade. But her shrill, grating voice carried over the noise of the fort as she shouted at the girl. Joie's big eyes held Cade's momentarily. He saw the glimmer of hope dim, knowing what was coming.

"But you'll never see your baby brother again," Leona finished.

Hope faded, though Joie's eyes held a pleading look for understanding...and unearned, undeserved love. Then she pulled away from Cade and looked down at a frail young black woman with a bundle in her arms. Barely more than a child herself, the slave held a white baby to her breast. Cade had not realized it was a child until that moment. He had a half-brother! Suddenly, Joie's reluctance to leave the hell she was in became clear. He'd felt the same way when he was forced to leave Joie.

The noise attracted the stocky, florid-faced, dapperly dressed Major Beasley, who took time from swigging on his jug of tafia and watching the card game by the gate to assert his authority over the domestic argument.

"Here, Kincaid," he commanded, nodding toward Joie's brother. "*You* take this letter to General Claiborne. Maybe it'll give you time to calm down. Got too many people in this fort to have fighting going on."

"I ain't in *your* command," Cade said angrily.

Looking up, he saw Dixon Bailey approach. Bailey was a tall, well-built man, with long sandy hair tied in a leather thong. His size and height lent him a commanding demeanor. Bailey's light-colored eyes were piercing and intelligent. Along with Colonel Caller, he had been in charge of the militia at Burnt Corn Creek, when they had run off the Red Sticks led by Peter McQueen, High Head Jim, and Josiah Francis.

"Looks like you're recovered from the wound, Kincaid. I guess you're reporting again for duty. I say *you* take the letter."

Cade threw his hat in the dust. Dixon Bailey picked it up and handed it back to him, along with the reins to a fresh horse he'd taken from Matthew Steadham, whom Beasley had originally told to deliver the report.

"Even a blind pig finds an acorn every now and then," Bailey said. "Beasley's right about this."

Cade looked at Joie helplessly. She glanced toward the baby with such love that he knew the only way to get her out of this was to take the baby as well. He would do it! But first he had to deliver the letter Major Beasley thrust into his hand. Cade jumped on the horse.

At the gate, he turned and shouted to Beasley, who was making his way back to his original spot near the east gate. "I'll be back, old man. And when I do, I'm takin' Joie with me. I promised my mother I'd take care of her, and she won't be abused by that woman anymore."

Then Cade wheeled his horse around and looked once more at the couple he'd greeted when he entered the fort. They clung to one another as they watched him kick the horse into full gallop out the open gate.

Her brother had come for her!

Leona indicated a basket filled with soiled clothes. "Go wash the damned clothes, and don't get any foolish ideas about leaving. Your *little brother* needs you," she sneered.

Jason Kincaid returned to his bottle. Joie wondered how he managed to provide for them at all, as drunk as he stayed. Leona returned to her usual spot, reclining in the shade of a lean-to they'd contrived near the pickets, while the nurse fed the new baby, sitting in the sun and trying to shield the child with her own body. Leona made a show of whining about ungrateful sons and how childbirth had left her an invalid.

Soldiers lay about, waiting for meal call as the sun rose toward noonday. John Rigdon, one of the musicians for the militia, played his fiddle, and the girls and a group of hardy and profusely sweating young men danced. Happy children played, rolling hoops and shooting marbles.

But Joie wanted to get out of the fort before she broke into tears. Her brother had come for her and she could not leave. Would she ever escape that horrible woman?

"I was the scribe for Beasley's dictation this morning, so I know what the note said," Godfrey Lewis Winkel was saying. The boy had the gift of total recall and recited verbatim what Major Beasley had dictated that he write: "*Mims Block House, August 30th, 1813. Sir: I send enclosed, the morning reports of my command. I have improved the Fort at this place, and made it much stronger than when you were here.*"

"Bullshit," Edward said. Godfrey looked around them and nodded. He continued, "*Pierce's stockade is not very strong, but he has erected three substantial blockhouses. On the 27th, Ensign Davis, who commands at*

Hanson's Mill, wrote me: 'We shall by to-morrow, be in such a stait of defense that we shall not be afraid of any number of Indians.'

There was a false alarm here yesterday. Two Negro boys belonging to Mr. Randon, were out some distance from the fort minding some beef cattle, and reported that they saw a great number of Indians painted, running and whooping towards Pierce's Mill. The conclusion was that they Knew the Mill-fort to be more vunerable than this, and had determined to make their attack their first. I dispatched Captain Middleton with 10 mounted men, to ascertain the strength of the enemy, intending, if they were not too numerous, to turn out the most of our force here and march to the relief of Pierce's Mill. But the alarm has proved to be false. What gave some plausibilty to the report at first, was that several of Randon's negroes had been previously sent up to his plantation for corn, and had reported it to be full of Indians committing every kind of havoc. But now I doubt the truth of that report.

I was much pleased with the appearance of my men at the time of the alarm yesterday, when it was expected every moment that the Indians would appear. They very generally seemed anxious to see them."

"That is it," he told them."Just about word for word."

Edward couldn't seem to help saying, "Look at this fort. Does it look prepared to you?"

Godfrey shrugged again and looked out the east gate.

The dense cornfield beyond the clearing glistened with a brilliant haze in the near-noon sun. Godfrey shielded his eyes. Not a Red Stick in sight.

Matthew Rigdon chortled over the hand he had been dealt, and Edward was drawn to the card game to see if their "drummer," Matthew Rigdon, was going to lose his pants again. Rigdon's best friend and buddy, Nehemiah Page, the hostler for the Mississippi Volunteers and a regular at the card games, was missing this morning.

"Where's Nehemiah?" Godfrey had asked Rigdon earlier.

"He's sleeping it off out in the barn with the horses. Be quiet or you'll bring his absence to Major Beasley's attention. Beasley's in a foul mood this morning what with those slaves lying and Fletcher arguing with him."

"Beasley's been drinking ever since dictating his report to you this morning," Edward said.

Godfrey felt a chill. He left Edward and followed Joie.

Sam Mims and his seventy-six-year-old brother, David, sat on the veranda of the house smoking their pipes. Joie ducked her head as she hurried past, embarrassed by her father and stepmother and the drama that had just unfolded. She glanced up briefly and thought once more of the amazing family resemblance between the two brothers. In spite of the ten-year difference in their ages, both had a thick mane of white hair. She knew they were aware of her discomfort. They made a point of looking past her out the gate toward Boatyard Lake, where the charming scene of Peggy Bailey and several other women with their children frolicked near the water's edge.

Joie wanted to get to the river and just be alone.

She was about to leave the west gate when Vicey and Zachariah McGirth and their children pulled their keelboat ashore. Vicey climbed from the canoe and stretched. Her children jumped from the keelboat and dashed through the shallows to run up the hill. Hot as it was, whatever had gotten wet would dry quickly, Joie thought, looking forward to getting wet herself as she washed the clothes.

Vicey Cornell McGillivray McGirth looked past Joie, watching her six daughters and only son, James, head up the hill from the lake for the gates at Fort Mims. This was a lark to them. Excited about seeing their friends, they scampered quickly up to the fort. Joie could not help being a little jealous.

James, a handsome, redheaded eighteen-year-old, was probably looking forward to seeing his friends Peter Durant and Viney Randon. Joie had heard Viney tell Sally Carson that they'd all attended Lorenzo Dow's last camp meeting meeting together, and Viney thought James was sweet on her.

She'd also heard Dixon Bailey tell his brother James that Zachariah had barely avoided being captured by the Red Sticks in Mobile through the intervention of Sanota.

"I had forgotten that Zachariah and Vicey raised him," James had responded.

"After High Head Jim, Peter McQueen and their men fought us at Burnt Corn Creek and saw the battle as a victory," Dixon said. Sanota joined the Red Sticks because he admires High Head Jim so much."

"He even looks like Jim," James had agreed, nodding.

Joie saw now that James McGirth had brought a new deer rifle.

"Don't worry," he yelled to his sister Sarah. "I'll take care of you!"

Sarah yelled back, "The Red Sticks are safe if your skill at hunting deer is any measure!" James chased her up the hill and into the fort. Zachariah, carrying the baby, Lolly, who had just turned one, turned to share a smile with Vicey.

Lolly clung to a quilt her mother had probably pieced for her.

"Vicey," someone called. Joie looked up to see Vicey's brother, James Cornell, ride from the stable at the south of the fort. Vicey walked toward him.

Joie wondered how Vicey could even smile at her brother, who had actually *sold* her to Zachariah. She guessed Vicey had gotten over her anger at James for trading her to Zachariah for Zachariah's ferry after the death of her husband, Alexander McGillivray.

Perhaps Vicey's brother James was bitter over the terrible disease that had disfigured his face. Maybe he had seen how Zachariah adored her.

From the way Vicey looked at her tall, green-eyed, dark-haired, gloriously handsome husband holding their baby, she owed her brother for seeing something she'd been too grief stricken to realize. Her brother James had made her happy *and* made a profit from it. That was the Cornell way, Leona had said. That was what had made the Cornells one of the wealthiest families in Creek country.

Recently, Joie had heard Dixon Bailey say, James Cornell had traded his sister Lucy's daughter, Polly Kean, with Sam Jones to acquire his own woman, Betsy Coulter. And then the Red Sticks had torched James's trading post, his plantation, and his cowpens at Burnt Corn Springs, where the Wolf Trail intersected with the trail to Tukabatchee. The Red Sticks had been on their way to Pensacola to acquire the guns and ammunition the Spanish had promised. Madame Baronne, who owned a brothel, had bought James's wife from Peter McQueen and High Head Jim. Fortunately, a citizen of the city saw what happened and rescued Betsy from the brothel.

There was no doubt the Red Sticks were angry with the mixed bloods who had not chosen to rise up against the white men in their midst. They were particularly angry with those who had prospered in their association with the whites. The descendants of the French Huguenot Joseph Cornell had surely done so.

Joie watched Vicey, who was still standing there enjoying the breeze outside the river gate before entering the sweltering fort. Suddenly, her husband slipped up behind her, swept her off of her feet, and planted a big kiss on her mouth. Vicey clung to him when he finally set her on her feet.

"Sarah has Lolly," he said to her. "I'll be back soon with more provisions for the militia. There's a lot of hungry people in there. Ned's coming with me. All the children are playing inside the fort."

"Be careful," she said. "Hurry back."

She watched as Zachariah maneuvered the keelboat out onto Boatyard Lake. Ned followed in the canoe he'd brought along to get provisions for the family.

Joie wondered if her family would have been like that if her mother had not died. Her heart ached for what might have been.

Vicey hesitated before the west gate. Joie watched as she changed her mind and rounded the corner toward the east gate.

It was still. Too still. There were no bird songs or rustlings in the cornfield to the north of the fort.

Joie was at last down on the bank of Boatyard Lake. The sun shone brightly, making a light show on the water. The sky was a clear blue. Fish jumped and skipped.

Joie dropped the clothes basket and dipped her feet in the cool water near where the canoes were banked. She looked north and watched Viney round the bend. Peter looked up from where he stood, his arms folded with one foot on a canoe to steady it. He grinned at her and stepped back to offer his hand and help her into the boat. She took it with a smile, and they pushed off to go berry picking on Nannahubba Island on the other side of the lake.

Joie looked back toward the fort. Godfrey Lewis Winkel stood at the gate, watching her with a look that might have been contemptuous or pitying.

Though the sun shone and a breeze actually rippled the water, she could hear no birds.

Martin Rigdon beat the call to the noon meal.

8

Gathering Red Sticks

William Weatherford, "Red Eagle" to the one thousand warriors he, Paddy Walsh, and Far Off Warrior led that day, had stripped to his breechclout and painted his face black and red for war. He and his warriors had drunk the Black Drink and danced with the prophets during the night. He was now prepared to go into battle.

He crept through the cornfield and paused to await the signal to attack, crouching in a thickly vegetated shallow ravine of tupelo gum and cypress on the southeast side of Fort Mims. He was part of one wing of the two columns of warriors positioned for the attack on the fort. He lay between Paddy Walsh, the prophet who was to lead them, and Far Off Warrior, the venerable principal chief, now sixty-two years old. Though an old man, Far Off Warrior had a warrior's heart and a love of the Creek Nation that would not allow him to stay out of the battle.

Far Off Warrior was the son of the famous Tukabatchee chief Mad Dog, who had died the year before in 1812. Mad Dog was one of the great medal chiefs who had gone to Washington with Alexander McGillivray, serving for many years as the speaker of the Nation at the National Council. Years earlier, Far Off Warrior had married Hannah Hale, a white woman rescued as a child by his father during a raid. His half-brother Little Warrior, Mikko Thulukka, also known as Fustache Mikko or Birdtail King, had been adopted by Big Warrior when his mother left Mad Dog and married Big Warrior. Little Warrior had been sentenced for execution at the National Council in 1811 for following Tecumseh and murdering white settlers in Ohio. At the time, Far Off Warrior was one of the old chiefs who supported that vote. Now that Far Off Warrior had joined Peter McQueen and Hopithle Mico of Tallassee in taking the prophet's talk, he regretted voting for his half-brother's death sentence.

Weatherford also knew that Far Off Warrior's brother, Tustenuggee Hopola, was serving as a guide to the Americans. Far Off Warrior's half-sister Big Lizzie was married to Alexander Cornell, Benjamin Hawkins's right-hand man and Big Warrior's first cousin.

Several days earlier, before planning their attack, Red Eagle had reconnoitered Fort Mims. He and Paddy Walsh had snuck up to peek through some of the five hundred portholes cut into the pickets three and a half feet from the ground all around the fort. They could actually *hear* the conversations from the complacent inhabitants inside. Their defenselessness actually made Weatherford's blood run cold. Portholes three and a half feet from the ground? The gate blocked by sand? What was Beasley thinking? Was he mad? How could Claiborne have allowed such a fool to command a fort?

As much as he hated Dixon Bailey, Weatherford would have given him credit for having better sense than to allow such recklessness at something called a fort! Bailey had been taught by the Americans' Secretary of War Henry Knox, whom Bailey quoted over and over. Surely the man had said something wise in all the time Bailey had been with him. LeClerc Milfort only had contempt for the Americans and told Weatherford that Knox was little more than a bookstore owner with a fascination for military history. Knox had joined the Continental Army and rose quickly when he befriended George Washington. Bailey had told Milfort that Knox said the Americans could and would take by force the lands the Indians were unwilling to sell. Dixon Bailey warned of this repeatedly until they were all sick of hearing it. No true Creek warrior believed an American could best him.

But Weatherford resented Bailey for a much more personal reason. Dixon Bailey and his mother, Mary, showed only contempt for Mary's sister, Sehoy, who was Weatherford's mother. Sehoy had eleven children by three different men; her father was an Indian, not a white man; and she lived a comfortable life with the slaves she had inherited from her brother, Alexander McGillivray. Weatherford realized that his mother and his father, Charles Weatherford, lived far beyond their means and owed vast amounts of money to Forbes and Company.

Still, he also knew that his mother longed for the closeness that others enjoyed with their sisters. This yearning and her family's harsh, critical words had often brought tears to her eyes, and that was reason enough to hate Dixon Bailey and his gossip of a mother.

Weatherford had concluded that Mary Bailey was a petty, jealous, vindictive woman. Her sister Sehoy was beautiful and attracted men with little effort. She lived graciously in traditional Creek style. Weatherford thought the embers of Mary's bitterness and contempt had spilled over to Dixon Bailey early on and had only been fanned by Henry Knox, who cultivated an ally in an exceptionally intelligent young man when Bailey's uncle, Alexander McGillivray, sent him to Philadelphia to study with the Quakers.

Still, what had Bailey learned living there with Henry Knox, the Secretary of War, about building a fort? After many Indian victories, Washington had replaced Knox in Little Turtle's War in the northwest with General Anthony Wayne. The arrogant Dixon Bailey would learn a lesson from his Creek brothers today.

There were over 500 people in there! Women and children too!

Milfort had taught Weatherford to use the enemy's weakness to formulate a strategy, so he used the deficiency in the location of the portholes to plan the attack. Weatherford had ordered the first wave of warriors to take command of the portholes. They could shoot in, and then the inhabitants could not shoot out. He had learned much about the everyday activities inside the fort from one of Zachariah McGirth's slaves. The slave had come into the fort before Vicey and Zachariah to make preparations and had seen another slave getting flogged. When he got sent out to bring back provisions and saw Red Sticks himself, he decided not to chance a flogging and simply surrendered to the Red Sticks. He then described in detail all the activities in the fort.

Peter McQueen helped Weatherford plan the attack. Earlier, a messenger had arrived in camp with news from Chattachufaula, Peter McQueen's town. William McIntosh and a party of Creeks friendly to the Americans had burnt the town of 375 people, destroyed the corn, took fourteen head of cattle, and looted what did not burn. McQueen's warriors were enraged and eager for battle. Josiah Francis, another Red Stick prophet, lay in wait with Peter McQueen.

Soon after they arrived and settled in the ravine under cover of the night's darkness, Weatherford repeated his approach to the walls of the fort and looked in once more, unobserved by the relaxed guard. The men inside were totally unprepared and unsuspecting, despite the reports he knew would have come from the blacks he had allowed to escape. He knew the slaves had spotted the war party and warned those inside the fort!

To his dismay, he realized some of the children looked familiar.

Upon returning to the camp, Weatherford addressed the warriors. "There are women and children known to us all in that fort. Let us wage war upon the warriors and show mercy to the women and their children."

"Red Eagle becomes a woman," Savannah Jack said, his lips curled in contempt. Blood dripped from the cut he had inflicted on his forearm with the blade of the knife with his hand-carved handle. His action signaled his oblivion to pain and just how greedy he was for the sight of blood. Jack maneuvered the knife aggressively toward Weatherford as if prepared for an upper thrust that would gut an opponent. Weatherford did not flinch.

"Does our 'leader' betray us with his white heart?" sneered Savannah Jack. His naked body, scarred from many battles but honed to pure muscle, was even more ferocious looking than usual now that it was painted for war. Weatherford stared into Jack's soulless black eyes that glittered with venomous hatred for those of their fire who sided with the enemy—and for whites in general.

Weatherford knew Savannah Jack had never been sure of his loyalty. To Jack, Red Eagle walked too easily in both camps. Jack remembered well that Weatherford and his father, Charles, at the command of Benjamin Hawkins, had captured Augustus Bowles and delivered him into Spanish hands for the bounty money.

"Weatherford has family in that camp," said the chief of Wewocau, who was to lead one prong of the attack into the fort. "So do many of the rest of us."

Some nodded and looked into the distance.

Others cried out, "Remember Burnt Corn Creek! The blood of our brothers cries out for revenge!"

Weatherford raised his hands and waited until silence fell. Only then did he address the one thousand Alabama, Tallapoosa, and Abeka warriors assembled there on Flat Creek. Weatherford felt their tension. Of course they wondered how committed he was. Much of his family lived there in the Tensaw, though Weatherford's residence was 150 miles away on the Alabama River at Taskigi, the mother village of these recalcitrant children now about to be disciplined by the village's representatives.

"I am a man. I *fight* with my brothers," he said, reaching down to Far Off Warrior to help him to his feet. Far Off Warrior stood and surveyed the warriors before him. All were armed with gun, war club, or bows and arrows pointed with iron spikes. They were naked but for the girdles about their waist. Buffalo tails hung suspended from the girdles of the Shawnee who fought among them, and cow tails hung from the others. All of their faces were painted red and black for war.

"Our prophets have spoken," Far Off Warrior said. "They have seen the visions and done their magic. We will fight and bullets will not pierce us."

Paddy Walsh, a small, slight man whose claims of mystical powers and visions had served well to enhance his stature, wore an elaborate costume consisting of a headdress with split buffalo horns, ermine, natural dyed feathers, a deer skullcap with rabbit skin, and feather drops with a hand-beaded brow band that bobbed and swayed about his head. The rabbit fur encircled his ankles. His scarred, tattooed, and ornamented face was also painted black and red.

Walsh stepped forward with the four warriors he had made invulnerable to bullets. "These men will enter the fort and fight for as long as they see fit," he said, "and then the rest will enter and take the fort. I will run around the fort three times, and my magic will paralyze the men within the fort."

He shook his staff, and his eyes rolled back in his head, revealing only the whites and conjuring visions of spirits inhabiting his body. His body trembled. His actions mesmerized the now-eager warriors.

When at last he recovered, Walsh said, "It will easily be taken, and the women and children will not be injured."

"It will be as Paddy Walsh says," Josiah Francis assured them. He wore the headdress of a buffalo with raw horns, a beaded band, and feathers, along with the mantle of a prophet.

High Head Jim unfolded from where he had sat cross-legged, standing to his full height of six feet, eight inches. He was a powerful warrior, well respected for his strength and courage. The warriors stilled to hear his words. "We avenge our brothers murdered at Burnt Corn," he said. A war cry went up. The memory of their humiliation still burned. Their subsequent victory at Burnt Corn seemed to assure them of their ultimate victory over those who had contributed to their shame.

David Yargee Cornell, the son of Dog Warrior, who had been murdered under a white flag by the Americans in 1793 at Coleraine, looked jubilant. He would at last get retribution for his father's murder. "Five dollars a scalp," he whispered to Sanota. "Tomorrow I will be rich!"

"Tomorrow we will be pulling shot from your butt!" Sanota teased.

Captain Isaacs, who would have stood with Walsh and Josiah Francis as a major prophet, was notably absent. As the husband of Alexander McGillivray's daughter, Lizzie, Isaacs had standing and had gained many converts early on. Under the influence of Shawnee prophet Sikaboo, Isaacs had followed Tecumseh north when he had come in 1811 to speak at the National Council. He had seen the Mississippi River flow backwards when Tecumseh stomped his feet and made the earth shake. Back home, they felt the tremors in their villages and heard from others of the deaths and the change in the channel of the Great River. The sign appeared in the sky just as Tecumseh foretold.

Captain Isaacs returned from the Great Lakes claiming to have gone swimming with serpents and had visions through which he acquired supernatural powers. Recently, however, Walsh and Francis had grown jealous of Isaac's large number of followers and plotted against him. Francis accused him of being a witch and then sent men to capture him. They burned Isaacs's houses and destroyed his stock. Captain Isaacs was now at Tukabatchee with Big Warrior, along with much of the ammunition that had come from the Spanish in Pensacola.

Walsh and Francis had intended to take the ammunition they had gathered from Pensacola, capture Tukabatchee, and then punish Captain Isaacs and Big Warrior for their disloyalty. But the families of the five Red Sticks killed by Caller's men at Burnt Corn demanded retribution and urged the attack on Fort Mims. So here they were at Fort Mims instead of Tukabatchee as so many had expected.

Red Eagle knew Dixon Bailey was inside the fort. He had been a leader of the militia that attacked and nearly retrieved the guns and ammunition Peter McQueen and High Head Jim had gotten in Pensacola. Weatherford's blood also burned for vengeance.

But not on women and children.

The last of the ceremony of war had been observed. Through the night, they had all partaken of the Black Drink ceremony, the emetic of willow bark and button snake root, ingested to purify the warriors and prepare them for war. They had moved to their positions outside Fort Mims under cover of darkness.

All the while, Weatherford worried over the glimpse he had gotten of two little girls that looked remarkably like his nieces. But he'd told his brother Davy to keep his family away from the fort! He had let slaves escape that he should have killed just so they could report seeing the Red Sticks. How could his nieces possibly be in the fort? Surely those little girls who loved him and ran to him to throw them into the air when he visited their father could not be there!

Weatherford knew his brother didn't think the Red Sticks would attack a fort filled so many of their kinsmen, but his brother did not know the fervor of the prophets. He had gotten caught up in it himself, convinced that it was better for everyone if the white man took his civilization back where it came from and let the red man regain control of his traditional lands, ways, and beliefs. But had Weatherford, as Sam Moniac had said to his face, allowed himself to be influenced by a beautiful woman?

All things considered, Weatherford would rather be at his Hickory Ground racetrack than lying here nearly naked, waiting to destroy those he knew to be friends and family. Some in there were actually his family. He knew that. But now he was committed to participate in a war he had stood against until the choice came down to his clan and his village—or what he thought was an occupation force supported by faithless clansmen who must be disciplined.

Early in the summer, he and Sam Moniac, whom he had heard was on his way to Mobile, had gone to Chickasawhay, the southernmost Choctaw town, to enlist the help of Mushulutubbee for the Red Stick cause. Their trip, except for the livestock they brought back, was fruitless. The Choctaw under Pushmataha's leadership would not fight the Americans. Upon their arrival home, they had encountered Far Off Warrior, or Hopoie Tastanagi of Taskigi; Peter McQueen of Tallassee; High Head Jim, or Tustenuggee Emathla of Autossee; Josiah Francis, or Hillis Hadjo of Autauga; and Sikaboo on the Tellewassee Creek taking the Black Drink.

"Take the Black Drink with us," Francis demanded. Knowing the meaning of the drink, Moniac had refused. Francis lifted his war club to strike Moniac but was momentarily blinded by the light reflecting from the medal George Washington had personally given Moniac years earlier. Moniac jerked on the reins and his horse pawed the air while Francis grabbed for the bridle. Moniac grabbed Francis's war club and knocked him out. Then he rode away with bullets flying about him.

While others went to Francis's aid, Weatherford looked straight into Far Off Warrior's eyes and downed the noxious liquid. "You raised me," he said, "and I will fight with you or be put to death."

Far Off Warrior was the son of Mad Dog, who had been chief of the Upper Creeks after Alexander McGillivray's death at which time the title went to Big Warrior of Tukabatchee. He was known by many names, two of which were Micco Thlucco, meaning Little Prince, and Tustunnuggee Hopoie, meaning Far Off Warrior. Born in 1751, he had lived long and had known Puckenshinwa, Tecumseh's father. Puckenshinwa had been a head chief in Ohio when the first trickle of Americans came into the land, and he foresaw the eventual removal of his people if they did not stand and fight. Now Tecumseh had told his father's venerable friend that more than 500,000 Americans lived on Shawnee lands in Ohio. To Far Off Warrior, that number sounded as large as the grains of sand on the shore. And they had arrived just since Puckenshinwa's death in 1773!

Those lands had been ceded illegally by treaties like that at Fort Wayne in 1803, Tecumseh said, which were headed by the general against whom Tecumseh fought in Ohio, William Henry Harrison, then governor of Indiana, a land where some Shawnee had moved when their Ohio lands had been confiscated.

"Whisky chiefs signed away what belonged to all for trinkets, promises, and whisky," Far Off Warrior remembered Tecumseh saying with disgust. Fort Wayne was the last straw for Tecumseh and the first step on his road for a unified Indian front that he would lead against the land-hungry Long Knives, as he called the Americans. That was what brought him south.

Tecumseh had said these words to Far Off Warrior before a fire, right after Benjamin Hawkins demanded a wagon trail through the Creek lands at the Grand Council in 1811. Two years later, as they sat before another fire, Far Off Warrior had told William Weatherford that he could envision the endless stream of wagons described by Tecumseh that would come to fill *their* land down the four-to-six-foot Federal Road that had been slashed through Creek territory from Cedar Shoals, now known as Athens, Georgia, to Fort Stoddard just north of Mobile. It had begun as a postal rider trail years ago built for the Americans as a small concession just after Hawkins became the agent.

They must make a stand now or forfeit for their children the heritage the Great Spirit had intended for them.

"My brother, Little Warrior, returned home with Tecumseh after he spoke at Tukabatchee," Far Off Warrior had said, scowling at the memory. "Prophet Town, established by his brother, the prophet Tenskatawa, had been destroyed by General William Henry Harrison. Harrison had come to Prophet Town to discuss the cession of *more* land.

"Infuriated by Harrison's demands, Tenskatawa foolishly promised his followers that they would not be killed by white man's bullets and allowed his warriors to attack Harrison. The wily Harrison knew Tenskatawa's arrogance and impulsiveness. He was prepared for the attack. Tecumseh also knew Tenskatawa's quick temper, and he had told him to be patient and wait until he had the support and strength of all tribes united. Ignoring Tecumseh's words and in Tecumseh's absence, Tenskatawa ordered his warriors to attack Harrison's encampment, and they *were* killed by white man's bullets."

Far Off Warrior stared into the fire. "Many who had taken Tenskatawa's talk were disillusioned and immediately returned to their own villages."

Weatherford nodded. "That pretty much destroyed Tecumseh's dream, I guess," he said. "But what choice have we but to fight when, as you say, wagon after wagon filled with land-hungry Americans invade our territory?"

Far Off Warrior puffed on his pipe and exhaled slowly, watching the smoke lift into the sky. "Tecumseh has not given up. Since Tecumseh went north and the order for his execution was issued, Little Warrior has fought along side Tecumseh at Brownstown, Monguagon, 1st Amherstburg, Frenchtown, Ft. Meigs, the 2nd Amherstburg battles. As for the accusation that he murdered settlers, he tells me that at that time,

123

he truly believed that open warfare had erupted between the Americans and the Creeks."

"Captain Isaacs was with him and gave evidence," Weatherford said, shaking his head slightly in disgust. They were both angry with Isaacs, the cunning deceiver who had claimed to be a prophet and wound up running back to Big Warrior, who remained a friend of the Americans, meeting up with him at Tukabatchee with badly needed ammunition.

"To mollify Benjamin Hawkins and remain true to the treaty the old chiefs of the National Council held with the Americans, I was among those who ordered Little Warrior's death," he said.

"Captain Isaacs led the war party to capture and execute him," Far Off Warrior said. "He failed, of course. But Hawkins and Big Warrior have now sent McIntosh to hunt him down."

"I now wish Little Warrior were here with us to fight this battle. He was right. It is a fight I now believe we must fight. It is a fight he fights by Tecumseh's side," said Far Off Warrior.

Then he looked directly into Weatherford's eyes and said, "Tecumseh is of our blood. He is a man."

Weatherford acknowledged him with a slight nod. He knew all of this, of course. Far Off Warrior merely chronicled what had led up to this day. Which had ignited the war? The order to execute Little Warrior, the demand to widen the Federal Road for wagons, or the attack on Peter McQueen's band at Burnt Corn Creek?

No one could answer the question for certain.

The two men had sat together lost in thought, watching the smoke from Far Off Warrior's pipe lift in white clouds into the night sky. Weatherford remembered that night well.

But today, in the throes of the ecstasy of Walsh's eloquence and the promise of his magical powers, Weatherford and the others chose to believe the unbelievable. It seemed that Josiah Francis and Paddy Walsh might actually be able to conjure their invisibility. Earlier, while the war party rested near a cool stream, a militia patrol had ridden past on their horses only about 300 yards from where the large body of men was gathered. The men of the patrol were in such deep conversation that they were oblivious to the war party on the other side of the bushes. Surely the Red Sticks would have been discovered had it not been for the power of the prophet's magic. His warriors grew more confident.

Rather than risk being seen, Far Off Warrior signaled the warriors to move out. They followed the patrol down the Federal Road, where they camped only three quarters of a mile from the fort for the night.

Now, lying in the noonday sun with a thousand warriors, waiting to attack the fort, Red Eagle thought he was prepared. Tonight he might be with his ancestors. When he saw James Cornell gallop from the fort, look their way, and wheel around to reenter the fort, he tensed and prepared to call the attack. But the Red Sticks could hear Cornell yelling inside the fort—heard both his words *and* Beasley's response—and then saw him wheel again to gallop past. Red Eagle looked down the ravine toward David Cornell, also called Dog Warrior, as was his father who was murdered at Coleraine. David was James, Vicey, and Big Warrior's nephew, and all were descendants of the Englishman James Cornell and a Tukabatchee woman. Red Eagle saw the blood drain from the face of the young man who had been so bold just moments before. If James Cornell had been in the fort, could more of his relatives be there? Weatherford watched as Cornell spotted his father's sister, Vicey Cornell McGirth, round the corner of the fort.

Sanota, now lying flat beside David Yargee Cornell in the cornfield had followed his eyes and also watched as Vicey stood at the gate with her hand shielding her eyes. He thought she sensed his presence. She was the mother who had taken him in after his own mother had died of a snake bite. Sanota had been wandering, and the Great Spirit led him to her. She and Zachariah McGirth had just married at the time and were headed to McGirth's home, as Vicey's brother had sold her to McGirth. She was still mourning the passing of her first husband, Alexander McGillivray, and the death of her hope of having a child. She had decided she was barren and should never marry again. Her heart had turned to stone, and she hated her brother James for selling her to McGirth.

Was she chattel to be sold?

Vicey had told Sanota that she was ranting to Zachariah, who merely continued on his placid way. She who had been the wife of one of the wealthiest and most powerful men in Creek country...sold? But she was not of McGillivray's clan and, because of the matriarchal lineage and

125

traditions, that meant his sisters inherited from him, not his wife or his children. Vicey returned to her own clan and once again became the property of her brothers.

She told Sanota that she was so depressed at the point of her marriage to Zachariah that she believed she mattered little. And then Sanota had stumbled from the bushes into their path. He had melted her heart, she told him. He had lifted his mournful brown eyes to hers, and when she slid from the horse on which she rode beside the stranger she must now call husband, he reached out for her—that little boy, thin, bramble scratched, broken after sitting with the corpse of his mother for days before venturing forth without her—and her heart had shattered. Zachariah gave the little boy his hand and lifted him onto his horse before him. When Vicey mounted her own horse, she saw the big man beside her gentled by the expression on his face when he held the child. The hardened heart she thought would never love again grew to envelop them both. Where there was not room for one, there was now space for two—and more.

There had never been a question, when they discovered what had happened to the boy's mother, wehther he belonged with them. They took him home, where Vicey found that Zachariah had a son, Jamie, that she had not known about. The hard shell of a heart with which she began that journey opened and expanded as she watched Zachariah with the children. Vicey had told Sanota that he was the beginning of their family.

Sanota loved Vicey and Zachariah with a love beyond gratitude.

But this was war. Sanota was bound to his talwa and his people. Still, as Weatherford said, he had come to fight warriors, not women and children.

Sanota watched Savannah Jack nearly vibrating with the blood lust he longed to inflict on those who had assumed the white man's ways and rejected the old ways. Sanota thought Savannah Jack just liked to kill. Most among the one thousand warriors now shared Jack's emotion, whipped up as they were by the prophets' promises and the effects of the Black Drink.

Sanota breathed deeply. "I am a man," he said.

Further down the line, Weatherford exchanged glances with Will Milfort. Weatherford's heart clenched. Would Milfort, his young kinsman, survive the day? And all those other eager young warriors?

Weatherford had become a mentor to fifteen-year-old Will Milfort just as Will's father had been for him. LeClerc Milfort had taught Weatherford theories of war that he had learned from his tutors in Rheims, France. While sitting in camp by the fire after a long day on the hunt, LeClerc Milfort would tell Weatherford tales of great warriors with strange names like Julius Caesar and Hannibal. Milfort inspired Weatherford with their courage and the wisdom of their strategy.

He also taught him Spanish and French. Both Milfort and Weatherford's uncle, Alexander McGillivray, had impressed on him the power of the spoken language. He welcomed these teachings because he knew they would improve his understanding of those who spoke that language as well as improve his ability to communicate.

So how had he failed and wound up lying here in a cornfield preparing to kill family and friends for a cause he knew was unwinnable? According to Sikaboo, Paddy Walsh, and Josiah Francis, bullets would not kill him and his warriors because of the power of their magic. Red Eagle schooled his features not to display his doubts. Bullets *would* kill, reason told him, and on this day, many he loved would awaken to another existence beyond this current knowing.

From the fort they heard the drum beat the noonday call. Weatherford brought his mind back to the battle at hand.

Paddy Walsh nodded, his eyes gleaming. Far Off Warrior tensed for the onslaught. Weatherford swallowed and reminded himself, "I am a man."

He lifted his war club, and suddenly one thousand Red Sticks shook the earth with their silent run to the fort. Then, with a yell, Paddy Walsh and the four men he had made invulnerable to bullets started circling the fort.

The attack had begun.

9

Earlier that day, while the Red Sticks bided their time, the sun had reached halfway to the zenith in the sky when Gabe and Cade beached the canoe in a tangle of cypress roots on the banks of the Cut-off below Fort Mims. They had landed there many times before when visiting Sam Mims's boys or trading horses with William Weatherford. Fish still skittered over the surface of the calm water, but everything else seemed strangely silent—something High Head Jim and Weatherford had taught them to note. This time, they had a serious mission—to rescue their sister Joie along with Herman and Nicey Potts before the Red Sticks attacked Fort Mims.

Cade put on the clothing that Gabe had the foresight to bring. He pulled down his hat. With just a look, Cade and Gabe acknowledged the ominous silence and the danger it signaled. Cade indicated his intent to leap ashore and motioned for Gabe to hide the canoe.

Pumped with determination to find Joie, Nicey, and Herman and take them to safety, Cade jumped from the canoe and disappeared up the slippery hill. Gabe was glad his brother had changed clothes. He himself wore only a breechclout, but Cade didn't need to look like an Indian going into the fort! Watching as Cade headed east, Gabe was blinded by the sun's rays.

And then a shadow blocked the sun. Gabe looked up and saw Old Interpreter, painted in the red and black war colors and brandishing his tomahawk. Old Interpreter was also known as James Walsh, the South Carolina native and Swamp Tory who had adopted the prophet Paddy Walsh after the death of Paddy's father. Gabriel fell back in the canoe, trying to avoid the blow he knew would come. But when Old Interpreter recognized Gabriel, he lowered the tomahawk and stared menacingly down at him.

"Weatherford's Gabriel," he said.

"Yes. I've come to join the Red Sticks," Gabe said, searching quickly for a reason for being there. He pretended he had just arrived in the canoe at the bayou. He guessed it was possible that Old Interpreter had not seen Cade disappear up the hill and into the copse of trees. "I've come to find Weatherford and follow him."

Old Interpreter looked at him speculatively, and then he accepted Gabe's explanation. It was logical, after all, since Gabe had been so closely associated with Weatherford.

Gabe secured the canoe, hiding it under some brush. Then he followed the Red Stick up the creek, through the woods, and back down toward the bayou and a creek that flowed into it behind the cornfield.

"You must prepare for battle," said Old Interpreter. "You have not purified yourself for war. You must take the Black Drink and paint for war, or the prophet's magic will not work."

Gabe followed him to Flat Creek and struggled to show no signs of hesitation. No warriors remained in the camp, but evidence of their numbers was easy to see.

Old Interpreter read his expression. "The war party is in the field awaiting the command to attack," the older man said. Cocking his head, still doubting Gabe's allegiance, he said, "Weatherford has planned the attack and leads the army."

So Fort Mims *was* to be the target. And Cade was walking straight into a trap! Knowing he would have gone in the river gate, Gabe could only hope his brother had not been seen by the warriors in the field.

All along, Gabe had hoped his information had been wrong or the target had shifted to Fort Sinquefield or Tukabatchee, as he had first heard—not that he wished the attack on anyone. But Joie and Nicey and Herman were at Fort Mims.

Gabe fought against running after Cade to the fort to warn the settlers. Old Interpreter would kill him before he left the camp. The Red Stick had not taken his eyes off Gabe since he first spotted him in the canoe. Clearly he did not trust Gabe.

Gabe drank the Black Drink and immediately began the cleansing, allowing the emetic to force its extreme reaction, impressing even Old Interpreter with the distance he could vomit. Perhaps even now Cade had Joie and had gotten her out of the fort. The Pottses would be more difficult, he knew. They were old and slow. Gabe was so nervous for his brother that he was sweating, but Old Interpreter took that as proof that the Black Drink was taking effect and purifying him for the job ahead.

Gabe continued the process of purification and preparation, watching the sun rise in the sky and hoping Cade had been successful at least in rescuing Joie. In the distance, he heard the drum in the fort beat for the noon meal. Old Interpreter tensed and looked toward the fort. Gabe took another swig of Black Drink and projectile-vomited once more for the benefit of his "friend." Then, through the sweltering haze of the oppressive heat came the sound of a drum, followed by blood-curdling yells that told them the attack had commenced. Gabe felt weak and feared his legs would not support him.

Gunshots and shouts of confusion drifted above the noise of pounding feet and fleeing wildlife. But what was that shrill, raucous sound that pierced the air above the sounds of battle?

"Bagpipes?" Gabe asked incredulously.

"Peter McQueen continues the tradition of his father," Old Interpreter said, nodding toward the fort. James McQueen had died just after Tecumseh's visit in 1811, so his son Peter had become heir to the bit of Scotland that McQueen had retained during his long tenure in the Creek nation. Old Interpreter's eyes darted between Gabe and the fort. Gabe knew Old Interpreter wanted to be in the battle, but he'd been assigned to lookout and rear guard, and until Gabe proved himself to be a true friend, Old Interpreter would be on his guard. The sound of the bagpipe was irritating enough to drive an army to violence, Gabe thought.

He felt helpless and forlorn. Had he led his brother to his death? If he had not gone to get him, Cade could be safe in Pushmataha's care, enjoying newly wedded bliss. Now he had probably lost Cade *and* Joie. Yet still he must pretend to be a part of this murderous act!

By the time Gabe had performed the full required ceremony and applied the war paint, it was mid-afternoon. Some of the warriors were coming back to camp, waving scalps and carrying their wounded, their booty, and the captives and slaves they had taken hostage. Gabe's heart beat faster as he searched among them for his small sister. He realized there was little hope for Nicey and Herman. They were too old to be any good as slaves.

Otee Emathla ran and jumped into the stream to join the others in washing off the blood that covered his body and cleansing his wounds. "Count your scalps," he challenged to those who returned behind him.

"I was one of the first into the fort! I am undoubtedly the most successful warrior of the day! And I have the scalp of Sam Mims!" Indeed, there was a hoary-haired scalp hanging from his belt, still dripping with blood. "He fought hard. But he will not see another sunrise."

Soon the stream ran red with blood. Gabriel fought to keep his expression stoic, yet his heart raced within him with the fear that the blood of his brother and sister mingled with the blood of others from the fort, now staining the stream before him.

Old Interpreter stood silent and watched the young bucks prance about, waving their war clubs and proudly displaying the number of scalps they had taken. The Brits had promised five dollars a scalp, so they had taken as much of each scalp as possible. That way, they could divide them and make it appear that they had taken more than they actually had. Old Interpreter was not happy. He had no scalps. He glared at Gabriel as if blaming him.

"We surprised them," said the chief of Wewauca. "Walsh promised us an easy victory." That made him happy. But then his countenance changed."Yet our warriors lie dead in the fort," he continued, incredulous that all of the incantations and promises of the prophets had come to such a result. His disillusionment was clear.

"Paddy Walsh, your son, ran around the fort twice before being shot on his third time around," Davy Cornell told Old Interpreter. "Still he lives. But when he called for his followers to throw aside their firearms and fight with clubs and knives, I recognized Dixon Bailey's voice call through a porthole, 'I wish you'd try it!'"

Gabe cringed inside, thinking what a stupid thing that was for Bailey to do. It was obvious those words had become the Red Sticks' rally cry, exhorting them to return to the fort and finish the job. Outwardly, Gabe still presented a fierce countenance, successful thus far in convincing them he was on their side.

"Far Off Warrior fought bravely," said Dog Warrior sadly.

"He was old. He died a man," said the Old Interpreter.

"Your brother was with the Americans at Burnt Corn," Peter McQueen said, challenging Gabe.

"And I was making sure Weatherford's horses were in the right hands," Gabe said boldly, though his heart fluttered in his chest. This was the truth. He had taken those that had been sold to Jake Rendel to the Pebble Creek Jockey Club.

He looked past McQueen and saw that many injured warriors now lay along the bank of the creek. Gabe's ministering heart longed to go to them, but such was not a warrior's inclination. He must remain firm in his deceit.

"Tell me more," said Old Interpreter. "I was told to stand guard and have no scalps." Gabe's skin crawled as he imagined Old Interpreter considering how many scalps he could make from Gabe's. But Old Interpreter indicated him and continued, "That was how I discovered this latecomer."

"Weatherford will be glad to know of your loyalty," said the chief of Wewauca. Gabe inclined his head, acknowledging the words. He stood with arms crossed, feet spread, balanced and ready, his own tomahawk in his hand.

"Three of the four Walsh had said his magic would make invulnerable to the bullets now lie dead inside the fort," said Davy Cornell.

Gabe looked about him and watched the anger grow as more Red Sticks gathered. The discussion grew heated as they argued whether to take the losses they had incurred and leave or return to the battle. Those who had been attacked at Burnt Corn Creek were determined to succeed. They were here now instead of at Tukabatchee or Fort Easlie because of the Red Stick families who wanted vengeance on those who killed their loved ones in Caller's surprise attack at Burnt Corn Creek. Dixon Bailey himself had led the American attack at Burnt Corn.

The Red Sticks knew that the militia that had attacked them was in the fort. Now Dixon Bailey's mockery became their rally cry. Their resolve to go back was made firm when some of the slaves they had captured told them about the valuables buried inside the fort. They were determined now to go back in and destroy those damned traitors.

"Far Off Warrior was killed as he entered the fort," Davy said, watching Weatherford walk into the camp with the old warrior lying lifeless in his arms. "He was one of the first through the gate. It was he who killed Daniel Beasley as the fool tried to close the gate. Too late."

The battered Red Sticks parted as Weatherford walked among them, bearing the body of his mentor.

"Far Off Warrior lives, though barely," Weatherford said, surprising them all. "I am taking him to the women." They watched solemnly as he strode to the horses and gently deposited the old warrior across the back of his horse.

Gabe followed Weatherford to the river. Weatherford felt his presence behind him and stepped back, bumping into Gabe and taking the opportunity to whisper quickly to him. "I leave to tell my brother Davy Tait of his wife and children." He turned mournful eyes on Gabe. "My warriors were like famished wolves, and the first taste of blood made their appetites insatiable."

He had time to whisper only a few more words—enough to make Gabe sick to his stomach—before others closed in around them.

Weatherford turned to address the men. "I fight warriors. We have won the day. I will not butcher women and children." He looked at the long blond hair dangling from the collection of scalps that hung from Socca's breechclout. Then he whistled for Arrow, who came running. Weatherford grabbed Arrow's mane and pulled himself up onto his back. Grabbing the reins of Far Off Warrior's battle horse, he rode proudly away from the gathering.

Gabe hoped the others would follow him. Let the battle be over.

But friends of those who had fallen in the attack stood to speak. The sun was halfway to its descent.

Paddy Walsh, supported by kinsmen, made his way to the bank of the stream.

Davy Cornell spoke first. "The magic Walsh claimed would protect us has not done so," he said. "My brothers lie dead inside the fort." Gabe felt the emotions of the crowd shift. "He is a false prophet."

Walsh himself had been shot three times and looked near dead. He did not have the strength to defend himself. Sensing the shift in the gathering of warriors, some of his fellow Alibamos picked him up and quickly left to take him back to their village. Old Interpreter, his father, remained.

Savannah Jack then rose before the assembled Red Sticks who squatted by the creek's edge, arguing, cleaning their wounds, and slaking their thirst. All quieted to hear the words this fierce and dangerous opponent would speak. Gabe had not noticed him before that moment, standing as he did behind most of the Creeks who had returned. Savannah Jack was spattered with blood. His tomahawk protruded from his breechclout, red and shiny with the blood of his victims. He did not wash away the stains but lifted his hands, palms out, and quieted the crowd.

"Hear me," Savannah Jack cried, his coterie of blood-hungry warriors urging him on. "Our enemies think they have won. They mock us. They call us women. Let us purify our land with fire."

He pulled back the bow in his hand and sent a flaming arrow into the air. Then Savannah Jack looked straight at Gabriel. "We must not let our enemy live beyond this day," he continued. "Take their gold and hoarded treasures. Remember Burnt Corn."

The warriors echoed his cry. "Remember Burnt Corn!"

"Follow me!" shouted Otee Emathla. "I will show you the way of many scalps. The cowardly Spanish deserters who thought Fort Mims was safe from the brave Red Sticks have much hair, much scalp. They just knelt, making the sign of the cross, and made it very easy to take a knife to their throats. I'll bet these crosses that they wore are pure gold!"

Sikaboo, the prophet who had come south with his cousin Tecumseh and stayed to train other prophets, encouraged by his grandfather's brother Peter McQueen, stepped up to make the incantations and dance the dance.

Even though the numbers of the Red Sticks had dwindled, at least 700 warriors returned to the fort, this time shooting fire-tipped arrows into the wooden buildings. Gabe could hear the women and children scream.

"I am going with Weatherford," he told Old Interpreter, trying to control his countenance.

Old Interpreter said quietly but ominously, "No." The threat was obvious. "We will search the shore line to find those who might have escaped."

Gabe swallowed hard and mastered his fear. Unnatural sounds drifted on the wind from the fort, and the smell of blood surrounded him. It had driven all the animals of the surrounding area into hiding. The natural sounds of the forest were silent, but the horror of what was going on inside the fort—combined with the sweltering heat, the swarms of mosquitoes, and the effects of the emetic—made him weak. Flames now licked the sky as the fire arrows found tinder, and the acrid smoke justified the tears in his eyes. In truth, he wept over the depredations those he knew would suffer by the ravening beasts of Savannah Jack's band of followers. Some he loved might be their victims, and he was helpless to save them.

And so he followed the steps of Old Interpreter while his heart broke.

They were heading toward the fort when Gabe saw motion and knew someone had escaped and made it into the brush near the woods.

He must attempt to distract the Red Stick. Old Interpreter squatted near some brush and lit his pipe. Sitting back on his heels, he drew deeply on the pipe, looking calmly at the flames that licked the sky where the fort now burned. He exhaled the smoke and lifted his hands to the Great Spirit.

"This day marks the strength of the Red Sticks, Weatherford's Gabe," he said before emptying his pipe onto the brush.

Gabe saw a slight movement from the hidden escapee as the fire kicked up. "I see the warriors return," he said, quickly leading Old Interpreter from the place where someone hid. The main body of warriors with their captives and slaves were headed toward the path to Hickory Ground.

There was no way to know if his family were among the captives— or lying dead or dying within the fort from which flames now leapt and cries and shrieks of agony still came.

Old Interpreter chose to join in the raiding and burning of the nearby plantations and the killing of the signs of civilization—all the domesticated animals—and he took Gabe with him. They headed north toward Davy Tait's place. It was desolate. Everyone had gone. Not even a single slave remained. Old Interpreter ordered them to shoot the livestock. It seemed a waste to Gabe, shooting all that cattle. They could have fed an army with the meat. But he guessed that was the point. No need to feed Americans, the Red Sticks rationalized. Even if Creeks went hungry, too.

Night was falling, but Old Interpreter decided to retrieve Gabe's canoe and head down the bayou to Lake Tensaw. He wanted to see if any survivors lurked about from whom they might take valuable scalps before they made camp for the night. Gabe had led the search for the domesticated animals, so Old Interpreter became less suspicious of his loyalties. But Gabe's mind was consumed with thoughts of Cade and Joie, and he watched for an opportunity to search alone for his brother and sister. He had little doubt of their fate should Old Interpreter find them.

"I heard a nanny goat," Old Interpreter said as he balanced the canoe for Gabe to get in. "There are probably lots more where that one is." Several other warriors jumped in to aid them in their search.

As they navigated down the stream and out into Boatyard Lake with the reflection of the brilliant sunset on the waters and the acrid smoke of the fort burning his eyes and nose, Gabe spotted smoke rising down the river and cringed inside. He hoped no one still lingered near the areas where the Red Sticks continued to roam, pillaging, killing, and burning. So far, all Gabe had killed or seen killed was animals. That was bad enough.

10

Cade galloped from Fort Mims thirty miles northwest to Fort Easley, where Claiborne had come with thirty territorial militia men as reinforcements. He arrived in record time late that evening of August 30, 1813.

Cade had looked for Gabriel at the bayou where they had landed and where the two of them had planned to reconvene to take Joie out of danger. He'd come back to tell his brother that plans had changed—that Beasley wanted him to deliver a message north to Claiborne—but Gabriel was nowhere to be found.

Cade sure as hell didn't have time to linger looking for him.

Where the hell was he? Goddammit, would he have to save Gabe too? Cade couldn't help but remember losing Gabe before and finding him with Savannah Jack, a man who had haunted him ever since. Jack was close by with the Red Sticks; Cade had no doubt. Cade knew Savannah Jack hated any Kincaid and hated the twin brothers most because he thought Cade had bested him.

Bested? Hell, he had escaped! Just the memory still gave him nightmares.

Gabriel had chosen to stay behind with the canoe and let Cade attempt the mission because he knew Beasley wouldn't let him leave the fort with his well-known connections to William Weatherford. Dixon Bailey, captain of the Tensaw militia there at Fort Mims, hated Weatherford and anyone associated with him. Cade, though, had earned Bailey's respect because of his loyalty to Bailey's mother's friend, Nicey Potts. But since Gabe figured prominently in training Weatherford's horses and had not joined the local militia as Cade had, it was clear that he shouldn't be the one to enter the fort. It was well known that Weatherford had sided with the Red Sticks, and while many of Weatherford's relatives were in the fort, unlike him, they had rejected the wild notions of the prophets. So the plan was that Gabriel would withdraw to a nearby bayou to wait for Cade and Joie and possibly the Pottses. Only now Cade was headed north and Gabriel did not know it. Had Gabe done something rash?

Cade jumped from the sweating horse soon as he got to Fort Easley and stormed straight into Claiborne's office. He threw Beasley's letter onto the desk, shouting, "The damn east gate at Fort Mims won't even close, General. And the blame fool ain't got sense enough to dig it out and prepare for an attack. He's got Josiah Fletcher's black who reported seeing Red Sticks in the fields tied up...and had him flogged! Said what he saw was 'red cattle.' Arrogant son of a bitch!" he shouted, flinging himself against the desk and glaring at the half-dressed general.

"Hold on, Kincaid," Claiborne sputtered. "I left orders—"

"I don't give a shit what you ordered," Cade exclaimed. "You appointed Beasley! The man ain't got the sense God give a gnat! He's too busy drinking and playing cards to pay attention to what's going on around him. And he's so damned cocky he can't accept the fact that the Red Sticks ain't one bit impressed with whatever high and mighty connections he might have in the west to get him that appointment."

"Hold on, boy, I'll send reinforcements back with you."

"I ain't got time to wait. I've got to get back and see to my sister. My Pa moved his family into that goddamned fort, and I aim to get my sister out of there! Nicey and Herman is just sittin' ducks there in that hellhole. You appointed an incompetent commander for that fort, and the blood of those defenseless people will be on your head." Cade pointed his finger at the chastened officer. "Just what goddamned credentials qualified that worm of a thieving lawyer with no military experience for you to think he could command a fort?"

Claiborne was still tying his robe around him, having been roused from a deep sleep by his adjunct. "Hold on, Kincaid," he sputtered again. "Some of our friendlies told us the Red Sticks were massing to attack Fort Easley. We're thirty miles northeast of Fort Mims. But just in case, I left orders to secure the defense at Fort Mims. Lieutenant Spruce Osborne is a West Point graduate."

"I told you I don't give a shit what you ordered. Beasley ain't going to listen to Osborne, and Osborne ain't got no experience fightin' Indians! And besides, that fort is about as secure as a boy's tree house! Even that's high enough that Red Sticks wouldn't be able to shoot straight in. The portholes in that fort are three feet off the ground. What protection is that?" Cade exclaimed. "The enemy can just as easy shoot in as the defenders can shoot out. What damn fool designed that defense?"

By now Claiborne was beginning to sweat.

Cade picked up a chair and threw it against the wall. Then he flung himself out of Claiborne's office before Claiborne could have him locked up.

As soon as Cade could saddle a new horse, he headed back to the fort. He stopped only to water the horse and throw water on his own face to stay awake. Smoke drifted on the wind. At last, with day nearing its end, he drew close to the fort and spotted buzzards circling around in the wisps of smoke and the stench of burning flesh. Except for the crackle of the burning embers, there was silence. His stomach curdled and his chest clenched.

"Oh, God," he whispered to himself. "Oh, dear God in heaven, am I too late?" His horse whinnied and pulled at the lead. Horse has better sense than me, thought Cade. He wants to high tail it out of here.

Fighting his own fear, Cade slid off the horse and tied him to a tree. Then he approached the fort warily, remembering all the lessons his kinsman High Head Jim had taught him. The irony did not escape him that High Head Jim had probably been a leader of this battle. Red Stick war clubs littered the grounds, each one representing a dead warrior. As he neared the west gate, he spotted a man through the fog of smoke. The tinges of pink and purple of the setting sun backlit the veil of fog, hinting of the glory to come for those who had met their Maker that day. It was the beginning of one of the most glorious sunsets Cade had ever seen.

But nature didn't take notice of the tragedy beneath it.

The man stood just outside the gate, watching a black man pat down the dirt on a grave on the bank above the river. The limbs of a river oak spread like protective arms, with moss dripping like tears over yellow swamp daisies too cheerful for the sad burden laid in their midst.

Cade thought the man was Zachariah McGirth, but he wasn't sure. "Zach?" he questioned.

Startled, the man crouched and reached for his gun, tears still streaming down his face. Then, recognizing Cade, he said, "Damned Red Sticks. Damned stupid Beasley."

Zachariah McGirth either didn't think the Red Sticks would return or didn't give a shit. And looking around, there didn't seem to be much reason to care. Any noise of approach would be obscured by the sounds emanating from the crackling wood of the devastated fortification. The place was destroyed. Why would the Red Sticks need to come back?

From Cade's angle, the gate to the fort, with its charred and broken posts, looked like the gaping yawn of an old man with black and broken teeth.

Once McGirth got started, he kept talking.

"I was in a keel boat on the Boatyard Lake going back for more provisions. They came in the east gate, just like Fletcher's black, Jo, said. I heard the drummer beat the call to the noon meal, and it warn't long after that that I heard shooting." He flapped his hand toward the east gate. "Beasley's lying scalped there beside the gate. The damned fool *finally* tried to close it. Too late."

McGirth shook his head mournfully and looked over at Cade. "Vicey sent me back to the plantation for provisions. Family had to eat. Hell, I had just brought them into the fort to add to the numbers. We saw what a poorly provisioned place this was. Five hundred people all living together in a one-acre compound. The smell! What we had brought warn't near enough. Vicey sent me back to bring more to share.

"Last I saw my children, they were running into the fort greeting their friends, the girls making eyes at those young militia men. Vicey and I talked here by the gate. I looked up and she waved, then she turned to talk to someone and walked around to the west gate. I just saw her turn the corner...don't know why she was going toward the east gate." Tears streamed down his cheeks. He shook his head again, still not believing. "Then me and Ned put the canoe in the water and paddled off.

"I heard gunshots, and soon I saw the smoke rising and the flames licking at the sky just as we reached the Cut-off. We turned around and headed back. The sounds. Oh, God, the sounds. Screams and yells, babies crying and then whimpering. The horrifying war cries made by those men whipped up by the crazy incantations of the prophets. And then the strangest sound. Made my skin crawl, and I know it must have scared the hell out of those inside the fort...like the wailing of banshees."

"Peter McQueen," Cade said.

"What the hell was a damned bagpipe doing in the middle of a Red Stick attack?" McGirth asked. "He whipped 'em up just fine from the looks of things."

"Much as McQueen and Weatherford hated Dixon Bailey, I figure it was as much a message to Bailey to reveal who was coming at them as it was a way to stir up the warriors," Cade said.

"We were miles away when we first heard that godawful sound," McGirth said, wiping his eyes. "We pulled the boat up into a bayou and continued back through the swamp. Middle of the afternoon, the sounds settled for just a while. I guess they carried off some of their dead. But the whooping and hollering started up again. Then came the flames that shot up mid-afternoon and on through the night. We heard shooting and shouting all night long. We couldn't sneak in till just about an hour ago. Made it into the fort through a hole somebody'd cut in the north wall behind the block house."

The days of summer were long, and daylight was just giving way to dark. He looked behind him into the fort, his shoulders slumping.

"I know Bailey never thought they would attack in the middle of the day. He'd a been more vigilant, despite that pissant Beasley. This ain't their way."

"You remember we attacked High Head Jim and Peter McQueen at Burnt Corn Creek at noon," Cade said quietly.

Cade and McGirth had both been there. They remembered Caller's confident order to attack when he spotted the Red Stick group stopped for a meal. Everything went fine in the initial attack, and they routed the Red Sticks. But they did not follow up, just commenced to plundering. The Red Sticks regrouped and ran the militia so far into the swamps that some got lost. Cade even had to lead a search party out to find Caller. When they did, he was half dead, wearing only his shirt and drawers. That was not a day any man among the militia wanted to remember.

McGirth looked up quickly. "That's it," he said. "This is payback. You know some of the militia bragged about making tobacco bags out of the dead Indians' ball sacks."

McGirth's eyes stared into the distance, seeing again a horror that couldn't be spoken. In words simply too inadequate, Cade said, "I saw the smoke long before I got here and knew they had attacked."

"They came in the east gate, just like Fletcher's Jo said. Poor bastard, he's still tied to the damned post. His body riddled with shot and torn limb to limb. They deballed the man! Probably while he was still alive. Then they scalped him like every other poor soul. Some Red

Stick will make a tobacco pouch out of his ball sack, too, I'll bet." He looked pale, and when he staggered Cade reached out to steady him. His hand was clammy and cold even in the steamy heat of the long August day.

McGirth shook his head and began to repeat himself. "Vicey, once again thinking she had to take care of everybody like that first husband of hers trained her to do, sent me back for more corn and the meat that we had hid in the woods before the Red Sticks came to the plantation the first time. We hid in the woods then, but Vicey thought they'd found our hidey hole and we'd better come to the fort now. If I'd a been inside the fort, maybe I coulda...."

Cade felt helpless. He wished he'd been there too. He also felt guilty to be alive.

"We searched and searched," McGirth continued, "but I cannot find my family. Only my boy. Cut to pieces. Or what I think is my boy. And then burned. Sixteen years old, but I could tell he fought like a man. He held the gun I'd give him and that was how I knew it was him. Protected his sisters and his mama best he could."

McGirth sighed and gulped. He covered his eyes and his voice quivered. "We buried him—what we found of him—over yonder." He indicated a fresh grave beneath a river oak, then leaned over and took a deep breath. Cade worried that the big man would pass out, and he drew closer, reaching out again. Over his shoulder, Cade caught a glimpse of the hell inside the fort.

Joie! Nicey! Herman!

Images of their faces came flooding back into his mind, and he rushed past McGirth, gagging as he entered the fort. He'd walked right through the jaws of hell. He'd only thought he'd been there before. Women butchered, raped, tortured, scalped, and burned. Babies with their downy heads bashed in and tossed carelessly aside like rag dolls. Blood everywhere. The stench of death was overwhelming, and the sight of their black and bloated bodies and empty, staring eyes was surreal.

How could such horror have occurred in this place where lanterns had once lit the gracious home, beckoning travelers with a warm welcome? Cade passed the still glowing embers of the home with its wide verandas and saw the bodies of sixty-six-year-old Sam Mims and his seventy-two-year-old brother David Mims—at least he thought it was probably them, big as they were—lying where the front porch would have been. In Sam's death grimace, he saw a gold tooth. It was a wonder the Red Sticks hadn't taken that! But his distinctive white mane of hair was now in the possession of some Creek warrior.

His eyes burned with the smoke and his eyes watered, though whether truly from the dense smoke of the fire or the overwhelming sorrow that filled his heart, he could not be sure.

Cade remembered the bright lanterns that once were strung around the grounds and the gaily dressed ladies who had flirted and danced in their furbelowed gowns, their hair twisted into dangling curls and woven with ribbons and flowers. He recalled Sam Mims regaling them with recollections of his time with the Swamp Fox, fighting the British in the Revolution. Hannah Mims, Sam's wife, had played the "Soldier Rest" on the harpsichord Mims had shipped up the Alabama from Mobile, while their daughter Harriet sang a nostalgic song that appealed to her father as he remembered his friends who had fallen in battle. The lyrics she had sung in her sweet, soft voice played again in Cade's memory, a sharp contrast to groans of the charred timbers and dogs' howls as they prowled through the burnt and mutilated bodies before him.

> Soldier rest thy warfare o'er.
> Sleep the sleep that knows no breaking
> Dream of battles fields no more
> Days of danger, nights of waking
> In our life's enchanted hall
> Hands unseen thy couch dethrowing
> Fairy strains of music fall
> Ev'ry sense in slumber dewing
> Soldier rest thy warfare o'er
> Dream of fighting fields no more.

Turning in a circle, he looked around him and could not believe the nightmare before his eyes! His friends in the militia with whom he had fought at Burnt Corn Creek. The beautiful girls with whom he'd danced. Sam Mims's daughters Harriet, Prudence, and Sarah. The Mims boys Joseph, David, and Alexander. Sally Carson, whom he had heard was visiting with them. He stumbled away from the sweet memory that was now obliterated by the carnage.

Midway through the fort, Cade recognized the old men Moses Steadham and William Tarvin, both bullet-ridden, scalped, and mutilated. They must have really put up a fight, he thought. He recalled seeing Steadham's son Edward just inside the gate when he'd come riding in the day before. Brave men. People he knew.

Steadham had six daughters whom he'd apparently fought like the devil to protect. Unsuccessfully.

Blood poured like tiny rivelets from their bodies, turning the hard, baked dirt into black mud. These were his friends, his playmates, his relatives. Now they lay like broken dolls, their eyes open and unseeing, while vultures settled and picked away at them, gorging on their flesh.

A woman wearing a necklace he knew belonged to Mary Louisa Randon Tait slumped near the charred bodies of two little girls. Cade leaned over once again, gagging, and vomited.

Good God almighty. Weatherford allowed this to happen? Had he watched while the Red Stick force killed and mutilated his own brother's wife and children?

McGirth had followed Cade. "I've buried my boy, but...."

He indicated the massive job ahead of them. No decent man would leave their friends to the animals, the ravening dogs already gathering. But there were hundreds of people massacred here.

It was more than Cade could comprehend. How could this happen? Where was Joie? Was she lying dead or nearly dead nearby? He had failed his mother's last request. Cade made himself scour the fort. What he saw would haunt him forever. But if he could find his sister, he could at least bury her.

There was no sign of Joie or the baby, but then there were so many people burned beyond recognition that he could not be sure who was who. Indians, white and black men, women, and children lay in one promiscuous ruin. All were scalped, and the females of every age were butchered.

He ran out through the gates and searched around the fort but found only more bodies, more horror.

The sound of horses' hooves sent him running toward the river gate where he had left Zachariah McGirth. The man was so distraught that he was likely to throw himself into the middle of whatever Red Stick band might show up. But the flag flying above the mounted men identified them as militia. But they were too late. Too late.

"General Claiborne will send a detachment to deal with the dead," the commander of the militia said. All around him, brave, experienced men averted their eyes from the sight in the fort, tried to stop their tears, or vomited from the stench. The horses all shifted uneasily and were difficult to control. Death filled the air.

"We've got to go reinforce Fort Madison," the commander continued. "We heard a party of Indians hit there. It's nearly dark and we've got to get to the fort. There's nothing we can do here now." He looked at the two men sympathetically. "They could return anytime. You men should join us."

Tired, bitter, and determined, McGirth said, "If any of my family got away, they've gone to Fort Stoddard. I'll go there first. Then I'll find you and join the fight. I've got some Red Sticks to kill."

"Take my horse," Cade offered. "I got something I got to take care of first." He inclined his head toward the fort. "I'll take the canoe your man came in back across the river, get a horse, and meet you at Fort Stoddard. Ain't nobody left out of the militia that was assigned here to serve that I can see."

"Better hurry, boy," the commander said. "Them injuns is riled up now. Another scalp is just another scalp."

The militia pounded past the entrance to the fort. Zachariah retrieved the horse from where Cade had tied it. "I'm leaving Ned with you, Cade," he said, indicating the black man beside them. "He can't swim, and I'm taking this horse across the river. If you can find your sister, he'll help you bury her. But you'd better leave soon as you can. Ain't no telling who might come back to see if there's anything left to take."

Cade nodded and made himself search for Joie. He approached the place where he last remembered seeing her and his father. There lay his father, sprawled on his back, his body riddled with wounds made from both tomahawk and gun—and scalped. He was ripped open and castrated, lying there in his own blood. A chill ran through Cade's body. Savannah Jack's distinctively carved knife jutted from his father's chest.

Cade could imagine his father's fear. He relived it himself nearly every night in his dreams.

Jack had gotten partial revenge. He'd left the knife for Cade to see—a reminder that he'd come for him next.

"Well, Pa, no man deserves to die this way," he said with a lump in his throat. At least it appeared that he'd fought hard trying to save his family.

As Cade stood over his father's remains, he remembered when he and Gabriel had stood with their father, who held the newborn Joie at their mother's grave. That day, they had been a family. Their beautiful, loving mother had been the bond between them all. Her loss had devastated them.

Sarilee lay mutilated beside the overturned water cask. Leona Loughman Kincaid was buzzard meat. Literally. The grim sight of the big black bird balancing gracefully and delicately picking at the woman's eyes gave Cade no pleasure, even though she had cost him whatever hope he'd had of reconciling with his father.

Ned wouldn't come back into the fort. He was hiding behind a tree. Cade went out and said, "Dig a couple of holes, Ned. Dig them big enough for a man and a woman." He would bury his father because he knew his mother would want him to.

The big black man nodded, swiped his face with a rag, and commenced to digging.

Cade went back into the fort and dragged his father to the tree. Then he returned once more and, after pulling the lance from her body, lifted Sarilee tenderly in his arms.

"Oh, Sarilee," Cade whispered. "If there's a heaven, you're already there. You were the only mother Joie ever knew. If you could make her safe, I know you did it." It was only then that he recalled the infant he'd glimpsed.

Ned had already put his father into the hole he'd dug and was waiting to throw the dirt on him. He gestured at Sarilee's limp body. "She was a good woman."

Cade nodded. "The best. But we ain't got time for no formalities, Ned." He gently laid Sarilee into the ground.

"Don't know the words, anyway," Ned said gruffly. "Lorenzo Dow said there was a God. If there is, then where was he today?"

146

Cade shrugged. Then he felt his anger returning. "Where could Joie be?" he raged.

"Sometimes they take prisoners," Ned said.

In spite of all the evidence around them, it looked like Ned at least was holding on to hope. He was still hoping Vicey Cornell and her six daughters might be alive, in spite of the carnage they had all seen. For Zach McGirth's sake, Cade hoped so too.

He guessed there was a chance Joie was alive, but at that moment he was so stricken at what he had seen that he could hardly dare to imagine it. He wondered if that beautiful new mother cut wide with a babe on each arm had ever seen her babies. He kind of hoped not. That would have been too cruel.

Nicey and Herman?

He turned around, looking about him. Several generations of families were wiped out in just a couple of hours.

He needed to find Gabe. What if they had Gabe? He hadn't been where he was supposed to be. Cade fought the feeling of desperation that threatened to unman him.

Only then did he remember he had a wife. Son of a bitch, he said to himself. Her Pa had warned him...long ago when she was just a little thing. He'd do best to just get shut of her soon as he could. But that was one stubborn female, he'd say that.

Well, I'll just go back and tell her I'm gonna get shut of her, and then I'll go looking for Joie.

He nursed his anger. It was better to be angry than hopeless. He would return to St. Stephens and give Lyssa Rendel a piece of his mind. He would not admit to himself that he needed to make sure she was all right in this crazy world where everything and everyone he'd ever cared for was lost.

The wind had taken the smoke east. But in the west out toward Nannahubba Island across the Boatyard Lake was the glorious sunset, now a riot of color with mere tinges of light making the clouds look silver tipped. The last rays cast their final beam before waning day would pull its blanket of darkness over the devastation around him. Before he could leave, he had to search once more. The sun's last light bouncing off something shiny captured his attention.

Cade's heart clenched when the glimmer of gold caught his eye, and somehow he knew that he had found Herman. Unrecognizable except for his gold tooth, Herman lay on his back near to where Cade had last seen him when Herman had told him where to find Joie. Held in his embrace was the woman who had loved Cade like a mother...now silenced forever. Could that be a smile on Herman's face that he had maintained until the end, as he looked into Nicey's eyes for the last time? From their position, Cade could tell Herman had been hit and had fallen with a mortal wound. He could almost see Nicey run to him to shield him with her own body, pleading with him to live and trying to protect him from further injury at the same time. A spear protruded from her body, pinning the two together as their life's blood flowed as one. And so the two who were never far from each other in life met death together as well.

And it was he who had insisted that they would be safe at Fort Mims!

Cade's heart was breaking. How he loved these two people! Giving, loving, generous people who had offered him all they had and told him it was their gift to themselves. He lifted his head and finally howled his grief. If *this* was the will of Yahola, a judgment upon evil, why must the innocents perish?

He knelt beside their burnt, still bodies and whispered, "I love you. I will miss you every day. Thank you." He could not help adding, "I am so sorry!"

He would never forgive himself.

He was to blame for their death.

"Oh, God! If there *is* a God, if ever any two people deserved heaven, it is Nicey and Herman," he sobbed.

But there was nothing he could do for them. To separate them now, even to bury them, seemed cruel.

He made himself continue looking for Joie. As he stepped through shadows, he wondered if the spirits of those so horribly killed lingered.

He came again to the small area where he had found his father's body. He looked once more at the body of the woman who had so despised him. In death she was of course no threat, but he remembered her venom and the pain she had caused.

"This was hell, I know, woman, but if there is a hell after death, I reckon you found it."

Darkness fell swiftly then. Cade looked back to the tree beneath which he had buried his father. There, in stark contrast to the deep purple sunset and the darkening sky, a snowy egret stood on one leg and perched on the looping, moss-laden limb above his father's new grave. The bird cocked its head and looked straight at him. A strange peace settled on Cade. He was glad he had taken the time to bury his father.

"Goodbye, Nicey. Goodbye, Herman," he whispered, taking one last look toward where he knew they lay. He did not know grief could be such a horrible, physically painful thing. He had been so sick when he found out his mother had died that it took every bit of strength he had to hold Gabe aright and tend to Joie.

And that little girl needed him still. If he could find her. "Please, God, Yahola, Master of Breath, please let me find her!"

Cade and Ned headed toward the bayou to retrieve the canoe. Canoes with broken hulls littered the bank, but Ned had hidden theirs well. Cade stripped out of Gabe's trousers and tossed them into the canoe. Down to his breechclout and moccasins once again, he stepped in just as he heard a nanny goat bleat. Sound traveled well across the water, he knew. At least something survived, he thought, and pushed the canoe away from the bank to go to the place where he had expected to meet up with Gabriel. Maybe he was there by now.

What if he wasn't there?

Perhaps to keep his sanity, he thought of the wife he'd acquired the day before. It was all Gabe's fault. He'd helped plan the whole thing! If he could find that brother of his....

But what if he didn't?

What if Joie was one of those mangled and charred bodies he'd left behind?

Think of Lyssa.

And then the Kraken stirred. Lie down, you dang fool. It's indecent coming from where you just been. Ain't no justice in this world, he thought. He didn't want a wife. God knew he didn't need a wife. He'd failed his mother once again and lost the sister he'd promised to watch after. And now there was no Nicey to tell him everything would be all right. No Herman to wink at him to encourage him to indulge the woman who was his life. Their love was rare. Something to long for but too rare for Cade to ever dream of possessing himself.

The Creek had rose up, and he was in the militia, and now he had to go fight the damned Red Sticks—and that included his own kin that had raised him better than his own father. He had just left death and destruction behind him, and yet just the thought of Lyssa's soft skin and silky hair had him imagining her naked beside him again.

He was a sick man. He just wanted to forget where he'd been and what he'd seen, if only for a while!

He rowed faster.

11

Samson and Delilah hugged Beauty's flanks as they trotted silently beside Lyssa. They had crossed from the west bank of the Tombigbee, swimming across the current to Hollinger's ferry on Nannahubba Island, and found it abandoned. They took the trail across the island to Mims ferry and found it also abandoned except for a basket filled with berries that lay beside the drag marks where a canoe had once been pulled ashore. Lyssa glanced south down the river toward Mobile.

"Someone left fast," she whispered to Beauty, leaning down and weaving her fingers through the horse's snow-white mane, soothing her by stroking her neck. Flames had now become dark smoke still rising across Boatyard Lake to where Lyssa knew Fort Mims had once stood. Her eyes burned as the dense cloud of smoke drifted closer. She swallowed the lump in her throat.

The attack had already occurred! Did Cade rescue Joie? Were they alive?

Lyssa hesitated, wondering what to do now.

"If we were smart, we'd head south too," she said to the animals. "Report what we saw and then come back with reinforcements."

Three pairs of eyes looked at her. The hair on the back of Samson's neck stood on end as he reacted to the danger he sensed. Beauty actually took two steps backward.

Then Lyssa thought of Cade. What if he was injured and only she could save him? Sighing, she looked across the narrow slip of water where shattered canoes now lined the bank. There was no movement. She saw not a single living creature, but then she could not see much from the veil of smoke that seemed to get thicker and thicker.

She didn't even hear anything. The silence itself was frightening.

Lyssa tried taking a deep breath and nearly choked. She pulled up her shirt and covered her mouth and nose. One good thing, she thought, was that the smoke kept her hidden as well. What had started out as a beautiful, cloudless day was now so clouded with smoke it looked like a heavy fog had settled. She took another deep breath and then prodded Beauty toward the water and toward her goal—Fort Mims and her boy.

Beauty sighed also, and Samson sniffled. Beauty looked around at Lyssa, hesitated, and shook her mane. Lyssa prodded her with her heels. Beauty reluctantly proceeded forward into the water.

"You're right. I guess I'm not very smart. But if my boy"—she remembered the night before—"my *man*, is in that fort, I will find him," she said with determination.

Sound carries well over water. Though she could not see the fort through the dark smoke, she listened for activity. She heard only silence and the crackling of burning timbers. Lyssa lay low on Beauty's neck as they crossed the narrow slip of water that separated the island from the east bank. Then they swam silently across Boatyard Lake to come ashore in a cane thicket.

The fog-like atmosphere of the smoke that lay heavily about the fort only added to the ominous lack of songbirds or the presence of any wood creatures. Lyssa was driven on by a chill in her heart. Surely if her boy had been killed, she would have felt it. Instead, she only felt driven to press forward.

Buzzards navigated through the smoky umbrella toward the fort. Lyssa knew with agonizing sureness that Cade must have arrived at the fort just about the time of the attack. The presence of those scavenger birds and their great number foretold what they would find.

The very silence was threatening. All creatures great and small sensed the danger. Lyssa and her companions progressed as quietly as possible up the bank.

The sight of vultures picking at something that once was alive but was now unidentifiable brought her to a halt. Lyssa feared it was a dog, and then she prayed it was a dog and not a small child and looked away.

She slipped from Beauty's back, dropping the lead, and indicated a silent "stay" to her three companions. Something slithered in the shallows beside her. Lyssa shivered and sucked up her courage. Her man might need her. In her imagination, she could see him lying there, barely alive, thinking of her as he drew his last breath.

Her feet moved forward while her brain told her this was the craziest thing she had ever done. The Red Stick warriors could still be here! All she had to do was look around her to know that a bloodlust had possessed those who attacked the fort, and that lust wouldn't stop to ask questions about what her business was—a Choctaw in the middle of a Creek massacre.

Cautiously, she moved forward, slowly approaching the smoldering remains of the gate that had given entrance to the fortification around what was once a beautiful and gracious home. Here she had watched men and women in their finery dancing and romancing. Here she had witnessed Sally Carson steal a kiss from her boy years ago when they were children, and she had come with her mother and father to a christening and party at the great house.

Thinking of that time, almost hearing the music and remembering the graceful movements and the beautiful women, she stumbled flat onto an overturned canoe partially crushed by a rock that left a hole in the hull.

Lyssa caught herself in time to stifle a squeal.

Flat on the canoe, she peered down through the hole made by departing Red Sticks to make it unusable and was startled by a pair of terror-filled sky-blue eyes peering up at her. That familiar blue. It had to be....

"Joie?" Lyssa whispered.

Astonishment filled the girl's eyes, which were a startling blue in contrast to her dusky skin and inky black hair. The child nodded, put a finger to her lips, and indicated that Lyssa should join her under the canoe immediately. Joie lifted the craft and Lyssa crawled under and lay beside her.

"I came looking for your brother, Cade," she said.

"Are you crazy? There are some damned mean Red Sticks that will be back to do some more killin'," Joie whispered. "They took some hostages and slaves with them. But when the flames die down, they'll be back. I heard 'em. They took canoes all around me, threw rocks in the rest. The hole in this hull saved me."

Lyssa crawled to the hole in the hull and peeked out. The smoke lifted slightly, revealing the hell into which she had stumbled. Charred, scalped, and mangled bodies lay all about them. Lyssa imagined how those desperate souls must have run hopelessly into the flames to avoid a worse death.

What Joie must have seen! Joie, surviving in the midst of this, was a miracle.

The younger girl took a deep breath. "I have to go look for my little brother," she said, her voice quivering. "I seen folks run out a hole cut in the back of the fort. I'm going to crawl in through that hole and see if anyone is alive."

"It's still burning hot at some places, Joie!"

"Can't wait. They might come back any minute," Joie said.

"Wait a minute—your brother—Cade…"

"I seen him today for the very first time," Joie whispered. "He said he came for me. He didn't know about the baby. I would never have left the baby. Leona sent me to wash his clouts. I won't leave him now."

"Is Cade…?" Lyssa asked.

"Beasley sent him off just before noon with a report to General Claiborne. He ain't come back that I seen. It was right at the drumbeat for the noon meal that the Red Sticks attacked the fort. They was all around these canoes or I'd a gone in where I seed 'em comin' out." Tears leaked from her beautiful eyes. "That's a lie. I could'a goed sooner but I was so afraid. I seen what they did to—"

"Hush!" Lyssa said. "You're a little girl. They'd have done to you what they did to those others. Staying alive is the best thing you could have done to help your brother. And now I'm here. and we'll, well, we'll go together."

That sounded brave. Lyssa sure didn't feel brave.

But Cade was alive. Lyssa breathed a sigh of relief and "girded her loins." She didn't know exactly what that meant, but it probably meant she was trying not to shit in her pants with fear. At least, that was exactly how she felt right now.

"We'd better go if we're going, and then we'll get out of here."

"Why would you go in there?"

"I can't let you go in there by yourself. I married your brother, and that makes you my sister, something I never had before," Lyssa said matter-of-factly.

Tears gathered again in the girl's beautiful blue eyes and streaked her sooted face. Joie had been alone for so long, even though there was a house full of people. Her stepmother was always quick to let her know she didn't "belong."

Words didn't come easy for what she was feeling, and so she just grabbed Lyssa's hand and pulled her along behind as she dug down in the sand and crawled out from underneath the shattered canoe. They skirted the tree line before trying to make it across the clearing to the hole in the back wall. They hesitated, and then, hearing nothing but the crackling of timbers, they crawled quickly toward the hole in the back of the fort where in places the wood still burned and corpses were piled atop one another. There the roof had collapsed on the inhabitants of a cabin where they had retreated for refuge together against the back wall. The smell of burning flesh would have driven the girls back if they did not have the pressing need to act quickly to find out what had happened to the baby.

Lyssa knew Joie recognized many of the dead that they passed, charred, scalped, and bleeding, but it was the sight of a beautiful woman with large, thickly lashed, hazel eyes staring unseeingly, lying gutted and bleeding with an infant on each arm as the vultures circled, that finally broke them. Those two babies who probably had just breathed life had lost it in the next moment. Their heads had been bashed, and now they lay on each of their mother's outstretched arms without ever having had a chance to live.

Joie fell to her knees. She tried to stifle her sobs and cry silently. She swallowed hard to avoid throwing up. Lyssa was having a hard time keeping it together herself, and she hadn't known anyone here personally.

Lyssa knelt beside the child. "Honey, the Red Sticks will be coming back. You can't do anything for these people now."

"I know," Joie said. "But this woman smiled at me when I went past this morning. She was so happy, so excited that she was going to have a baby after waiting so long. I seen her watching her sister's children playing and seen the hunger raw and achin' in her eyes. She wanted these babies so bad."

"Joie…"

Joie took a deep breath and inclined her head to the left. "There's our camp."

Dear God, Lyssa thought as she looked to where Joie indicated.

"Sarilee," Joie said, and all the love and sadness a word could hold came out in the way she said that name. The black woman that had raised her lay beside an overturned water cask, the water spilled about mixing with her blood. An Indian lay nearby, dead with a knife in his back. Sarilee's dress was pulled up, and a staff protruded from her private parts. Lyssa gasped and stood to block Joie's view of the desecration.

Then they noticed a white woman, eviscerated, the coils of her entrails spread about her, a look of unspeakable agony on her face. All were scalped. Lyssa's skin crawled, and she knew a fear like she had never experienced.

They both tensed when they heard the sound, a slight mewling from inside the water cask. Lyssa knelt quickly and reached inside.

"It's him," Joie cried. "He's alive!"

Lyssa pulled the baby out of the cask, taking note of the cut on his head. It looked as if Sarilee had stopped the Red Stick in the act of attempting to scalp the baby by sticking a knife in his back. Stopping him cost her own life. Sometime before she gave over to death herself, she apparently had strength enough to hide the babe in the wet cask that would be the last to burn.

Lyssa handed the baby to Joie and pushed them both toward the hole in the wall just as they heard horses' hooves pounding toward the front gate. The bloodlust of the Red Sticks had not been sated, Lyssa thought. They had to get out of there. But what if Cade had returned and she hadn't found him? What if he was one of those who still clung to life and lay groaning just beyond them?

Before she could turn back, a white-haired girl child of about eighteen months crawled out from underneath a black man's body and tottered to her feet, stumbling toward them. Lyssa grabbed the child by the hand and pushed her through the hole, following quickly behind Joie with the baby. She would save those she could save. She thanked God for the obscuring smoke, as she could already hear the madness toward the east gate. Joie had been Cade's purpose for coming to the fort. Lyssa would serve him best by seeing to her.

Lyssa quickly scurried through the hole in the spiked stockade logs, and then they crawled from bush to bush in the fading light. Another child, black as night and about the same age as the one Lyssa had by her right hand, sat stunned, leaning against his dead mother. Lyssa grabbed him with her left hand and whispered, "Do not make a sound!"

The child lifted sad, brown eyes spilling over with tears and said nothing, but he ran as quickly as his stubby legs would go. Lyssa clasped the white-haired girl to her chest and pulled the boy, half lifting him along. They ran through the woods to where Lyssa had left Beauty, Samson, and Delilah. She put the toddlers on on Beauty's back. The little boy clenched Beauty's mane while the small girl clung to the boy.

"Hold on, tight now," Lyssa said, leadng Beauty away. "We've got to take a ride."

"Mama," the girl whimpered.

"Hold on, little one. Your mama would want you to go with us," Lyssa said gently.

"He ain't said nothing. He ain't cried or nothing," Joie whispered frantically as she hurried beside Lyssa, looking down at the flushed and naked baby clasped tightly in her arms.

Lyssa reached out to touch him. "He feels hot, Joie. But he's breathing. Let's get to a safe place where I can check him out better. We've got to keep going."

The sounds from the fort chilled her soul. The Red Sticks had come back for the rest of their dead and got caught up in the frenzy once more. Whatever barely living souls had remained in the fort were dead now, she was sure.

Samson and Delilah followed close behind, herding them forward. They sensed the danger behind them and wanted their people to move quickly. Every now and then Samson would look back and let out a soft growl. Lyssa knew they couldn't survive the currents of the river with all those children, so they skirted the banks. They had traveled for about twenty minutes as dusk became dark when Samson suddenly stood stock still and lifted his ears. The hair prickled on the back of his neck once more as a sound rustled through the underbrush. Lyssa pulled Beauty into a clump of trees and shushed the others. Joie huddled close with the baby held protectively to her chest.

Ragged and confused, with holes burned into his clothing, using a stick for support and walking with a limp on a leg turned wrong and obviously badly broken, a boy who looked about fifteen stoically hobbled from the underbrush. "Well, hell and damnation," Joie whispered, "if it ain't just my luck that that damned stuck-up Godfrey Lewis Winkel ain't gone and survived. If there was ever anybody that deserved to be scalped by a heathen Indian it's him."

And then the tall, lanky, redheaded, freckle-faced boy passed out right in front of them.

"Shit," Joie exclaimed. "I'll bet you're gonna make me help you put him over that horse, ain't you. I'll bet there ain't no way you're gonna let them heathen Injuns find the son of a bitch and give him just desserts, is you?"

And then, before Lyssa could respond, Joie thrust her infant brother into Lyssa's arms and rushed out into the path to pull Godfrey into the thicket.

"He's breathin'. Just passed out walking on that dadburn broke leg, like the damned fool that he is." Only then did she look at Lyssa. "Well, all right, let's rearrange the younguns and pull Godfrey onto the horse."

Beauty nickered and looked at Lyssa. If horses could raise an eyebrow, Beauty did. Then they both looked at the little girl they had thought was shocked and suffering through her experience. She had suddenly come to life again. Joie put both hands on her hips and just looked at them.

There was no time to argue and truly no choice in their dilemma. Lyssa just hoped that they didn't stumble across any others anytime soon. Anxious to get them all into a more secure spot, she laid the baby in the straw of the pine thicket, lifted the two little ones off the horse, and helped Joie pull the unconscious boy onto Beauty's back. Then she put the two small children behind the unconscious boy.

Lyssa opened her mouth to ask Joie who this fellow might be, and then shut it quickly. There was a story there, but this was no time to tell it. Joie picked up her brother and turned to Samson and Delilah for permission to head down the path again. Apparently Joie had a bit of Gabriel's special gift of communication, and she picked up on the permission Delilah gave with sniff and a step forward, figuring they were safe if the dogs didn't sense any danger.

Hell was behind them in the smoky death of the fort.

They walked until they could walk no longer, just following Beauty's lead through the darkness. The bleat of a nanny goat caught Lyssa's attention.

"Goat's milk. We're going to need that," Lyssa whispered. Samson, go find that goat." Samson headed off at a trot through the pine thicket. The others followed until they came to a clearing and discovered an abandoned dogtrot cabin leaning and rickety, planks aged silver, with the roof nearly collapsed. And nearby was a nanny goat in dire need of milking that had apparently gone running through the woods to get away from the melee and wound up here, just like they did.

"Thank you, Jesus," Joie exclaimed.

Lyssa was exhausted and sighed with relief. It looked like there had not been anyone around this particular cabin in quite some time. The fences were down and the thatch roof was in bad shape. The chinks had come out from between the logs and weeds grew everywhere.

"Well, if the snakes haven't taken over the inside, this will have to do," Lyssa said.

Joie looked up at her, wide eyed.

Lyssa swallowed hard. "Guess I'd better check it out."

She set the two little ones on their feet. They immediately plopped down next to each other onto their backsides. The flaxen-haired girl stuck a thumb in her mouth and put her hand onto the kinky hair of the black child, who stuck all four fingers into his mouth and quietly accepted the little girl's tight grasp of his hair.

Lyssa grabbed a stick and headed for the dark interior of the cabin. She paused at the door and listened hard. She'd almost rather face a marauding band of Indians than a rattlesnake. Then she thought of what they had just seen at the fort and decided maybe rattlesnakes were less dangerous.

She needed some light, so she backed out of the gaping maw of the unknown. Thankful for the reprieve, she set herself to making a torch. She took dry moss that had dropped from the canopy of oaks lining the river and wrapped it on the end of a thick stick. Whittling away on dry tinder brought a spark and then a flame to the moss. With the meager light of her small torch, her courage weakening, she stepped up to the door. Then she stepped back and looked around for a rock. Finding one the size she needed, she threw it into the cabin and listened hard for a rattle. Hearing nothing, she climbed the rickety step and stuck the torch inside. Then she brushed the floor with the stick. Finally, she stepped in and swept further into the shadows of the cabin beyond the area lit by the torch. She checked all the corners and the ceiling as well as she could and decided it was as safe as it could be before she went back for the children.

Lyssa and Joie pulled Godfrey off the horse and dragged him, groaning, into the cabin. The babies toddled after them. Joie retrieved her brother, who was burning up with fever.

Lyssa took the baby from Joie. "See if there's a well around, Joie. We've got to cool this baby down. What's his name?"

"Jason Junior," Joie answered. "Leona said my father's other children didn't count and this one should be named for him. I just call him J.J."

Cade's dad was a bastard, Lyssa thought.

"I'll call him J.J. also," she said. "Do you mind if I call you Joie? That's what your mother named you. It was that Loughman woman who insisted on calling you Carrie Joie. I guess the one time your father stood up to that woman was when he added Joie to the name she insisted on."

"I'd like that," Joie said. "I want to get shut as much as I can of that woman. I wished her dead lots of times. But I never meant...."

"Don't think about that. Nothing you thought hurt her. Nobody in there deserved what they got."

Joie nodded, and Lyssa looked around for something to carry water in.

"Rinse this and hurry back with the water," Lyssa said, handing the girl a gourd she'd seen hanging on the front porch. "And bring some moss off those oaks out there. We need something for diapering these babies."

This was a new experience for Lyssa, being the one that others looked to for answers and protection. Not exactly what she had started out to find yesterday. But she'd set one foot after another forward on her own choosing, and this was what the Great Spirit had put in her path.

"What fate imposes, man must needs abide; it boots not to resist both wind and tide," she whispered to Delilah, quoting Shakespeare. The dog looked up from hovering protectively over the two sleeping children.

Samson chased his tail.

Beauty hadn't approved of leaving the safety of the west bank of the river, Lyssa knew. But the dogs didn't seem to mind.

Joie hurried out the door. There was little Lyssa could do to make any of them more comfortable. The toddlers had spooned in a corner, taking comfort from each other. Godfrey, still unconscious, groaned in his sleep. Lyssa knew she would have to set his leg soon, and while he was unconscious was a good time to do that. But first she needed to cool the baby. She'd spotted a wooden bowl in which, from the looks of it, many a biscuit had been kneaded. When Joie returned with water, Lyssa set the bowl between them on the floor and poured some of the water on the baby. Immediately the baby squirmed. She poured more of the water down his body as she supported his head and then sopped up the water with moss.

Joie went to the well several times to get more water until the baby's skin had lost its intense flush and his breathing seemed more regular. Seeing no other options, Lyssa pulled off her shirt and swaddled the baby.

Then she passed the child to Joie and turned her attention to Godfrey. "I think that stick I brought in here poking around for snakes will do as a support," she said to herself as she considered what to do. She'd have to rip Godfrey's shirt apart to tie the splint.

"Lay the baby down, Joie, and come hold your friend while I straighten his leg."

"Ain't no friend of mine, goddamn son of a bitch."

"Joie, he is obviously your friend or you wouldn't have pulled him out of the middle of the road. And while we're at it, where did you learn that drover's language?"

Joie arranged herself across Godfrey Lewis Winkel's chest, holding down his arms with her body. Lyssa kept the girl talking while she went about cleaning Godfrey's broken, protruding fracture and setting the bone. Then she poulticed the open wound. It wasn't a pretty sight.

"Leona cursed Sarilee and me like dogs when my Pa weren't around," Joie said. "Sarilee said she warn't no lady...warn't no real Loughman neither. Just a whore who took a notion to latch ahold to somebody what'd take care of her. She knew just like every other whore how to keep from making babies, Sarilee said. Till something happened and her trappings didn't work. She made my Pa's life hell for putting her in the family way and took on like you ain't never seed about how miserable she was. When J.J. was born you'd a thought she'd been killed.

"Wouldn't put J.J. to her tit either. That nanny goat out yonder that Samson's been out rounding up is probably the one Pa brought with us to the fort. Dinah's baby died of the fever in the fort, and Pa paid her master to let her take little J.J. to tit, poor little thing."

Lyssa realized Joie had adroitly avoided answering her question about Godfrey, but she'd have to save the questioning, she thought, as she carefully pulled off the boy's shirt and used it to tie his leg splint. Then she turned back toward the baby, examining him more closely now that he was a bit cooler.

"We've got Godfrey as stable as possible for the moment, Joie," she said, "but we have got to get some fluid into J.J.! His lips are looking parched and his little fingers are shriveling. We've got a goat, but we've got to figure out how the little fellow can suck and get some milk." Lyssa looked at their sparse possessions. After having torn her shirt for covering the feverish infant and binding the boy's leg to the splint, there wasn't much left aside from the gourd and a few strips of her shirt.

"Joie, you think you can milk that nanny into this gourd?"

"I'll give it a shot," the girl answered as she bravely grabbed the gourd. After checking outside and listening carefully, she headed out after the goat.

Soon she came back in, sloshing milk from the gourd as she stepped.

Lyssa wrapped the gourd and tied it tightly to a nipple she formed out of cloth. As she inclined the gourd, the milk filled the makeshift nipple. She nudged the baby's cheek with it, and he opened his mouth in an instinctive root.

"Looks like a baby bird openin' its mouth for a worm," Joie said, smiling. "He's more a Little Blue Jay than a J.J. " She put the nipple to the baby's mouth and instinct led him to suck. Lyssa looked at Joie in relief.

"He's a strong one. She didn't want him, but he wanted to come. Here, let me hold him and feed him."

Fortunately, the other two had fallen asleep as soon as they hit the floor. But they would soon stir, and Lyssa had to find something to feed them all. Godfrey was breathing okay and didn't feel too feverish.

Now the rickety cabin that she had been so reluctant to enter seemed familiar and safe. Outside the door could be bloodthirsty Red Sticks...or snakes. And now it was full dark. They had used the moss Joie gathered to light a fire in the fireplace, and they had run out. They needed more, but Lyssa was exhausted and decided to rest a moment herself before heading outside. She crawled behind the spooned babies and cuddled them, patting them gently as they adjusted to her contours.

Was it only last night or a lifetime ago that she had found her boy...made him her man...and then lost him again. Lord willing and the Creek don't get her, she'd find him, and she vowed that when she did, he wasn't getting away again. And then she fell sound asleep.

After an hour's rest, Lyssa forced herself to get up and hunt for herbs and roots she would need for the wounds and fevers. The basics grew near the little cabin. She concocted the remedies just as she had watched the shaman in her village do. She had also read her father's copy of Nicholas Culpepper's *The English Physician Enlarged* out of curiosity. From it she had learned ways to make plasters, ointments, oils, poultices, syrups, decoctions, juleps, and waters and mix them according to the cause or afflicted body part. She never dreamed she would need the information, but now it served her well. For wounds, she knew she needed to stop the flow of blood with *hilis hatki*, "white medicine," which was ginseng root boiled in water and made into a potion. For nausea, fever, malaria, and swellings, she would need the root of the *miko hoyanidja*.

It was as if every other human being on the east side of the Tombigbee River had vanished except for these children that had somehow survived. Oh yes, and the Red Sticks whose fires lit up the night skies. They were brazen with confidence that their roving bands had killed all of their opponents.

Here at the cabin were Joie and her brother J.J., the older boy Godfrey, and the toddler girl and boy whom they called Meme and Mo. And now there was another. The little girl they now called Sister had been dragged into the cabin by Delilah. Lyssa could only guess she'd been hiding in some berry bushes because of the scratches all over her body and the tangles in her hair. Lyssa had looked up from sitting cross-legged on the floor feeding J.J., and there stood the little girl in remnants of a blue calico dress, one hand clutching a rag doll and the other on Delilah's neck, her face scratched and bleeding, and her hair matted with thorns. Lyssa had handed the baby to Joie and opened her arms.

"What is your name?" Lyssa had asked.

"Sister," the little girl whispered as she reached out and touched Lyssa's face. Then she fell unconscious into Lyssa's arms. The child was feverish, near starved, and dehydrated, and Lyssa was not sure she would make it through the night. When at last she became conscious, her eyes were vacant and she would not speak. But it had taken only one look into that child's beautiful face and sea green eyes and Lyssa had fallen in love.

She had come to find Cade and help him rescue his sister. Instead, Providence or the Great Spirit or God Almighty—her mixed culture seemed to have given Him lots of names—whatever His name was, He had sent her a flock. That was a problem. She loved them all. Now they were hers, and she was determined to protect them.

She kept them hunkered down, using what she could find in their immediate vicinity as they waited for the roving, ravaging Red Stick beasts to retire to their lair. Surely their women and children wanted them home, and surely they would want to store some of the booty and remaining livestock they had stolen.

Lyssa could not sleep. It simply would not come. If she fell asleep she might miss hearing one of the little ones when they needed her. She kept listening for sounds outside the cabin. Were Red Sticks creeping up on them even as she sat there caring for the children? Would there be enough to feed them tomorrow? Was the well water the cause of the toddlers' illness?

She was so tired.

It wasn't as if she did everything. On the contrary, Joie took the major responsibility for J.J. She kept him cool and continued forcing the goat's milk into his mouth. After several days, J.J. began to thrive. But Lyssa had her hands full with the constant care of the red-headed, freckled-faced teenager, Godfrey Lewis Winkel (as Joie referred to him whenever she spoke of him), who remained unconscious with a high fever and his leg in danger of putrefying. And on top of that, the two toddlers had taken sick.

"They've got what took many in the fort down even before the Red Sticks attacked," Joie said.

Lyssa turned, both babies in her arms. "And?" she asked.

"It killed 'em," Joie said. Lyssa's heart clenched at her matter-of-fact tone.

"Well, it will not kill these babies. They made it out of that fort alive, and I mean for them to stay that way."

Lyssa swayed with the hot toddlers in her arms. Then Mo, the boy, was jolted by a spasm and tensed with the pain. Another cry of pain and another bout with diarrhea left what remained of Lyssa's clothes stained and smelling.

It was so stupid of her to come across the river after Cade with nothing. Nothing! She would never travel without her medicine kit again. All she had brought was a book. A book! And it had gotten wet in the crossing. They needed clothes and medicine! No wonder her father always thought she required a keeper.

She could kick herself. Not even a change of clothes.

She would have to go back to the fort.

Mo moaned, and Lyssa knew she had to go. There was no one else. While her grandfather Pushmataha had prepared her as he did Lance for every emergency, she had never thought she would need to use those lessons. She had grown up sheltered and protected by adults who loved her and tried to shield her from the world's cruelties. And all the while, Pushmataha had trained her, along with Lance, as a warrior, as if it were their special game. Her grandmother Chamay taught her the skills of a woman, remembering that should she need to follow her man on the hunt, their supplies would be basic, and she must fashion what she might need from what she would find around her.

There was no way Joie could return to that fort. Just days earlier, Lyssa had discovered what brought on the nightmares that jerked Joie awake. Lyssa, wide awake with her ever-present insomnia, had seen the child sit straight up, staring into moonlight with her mouth wide open in a silent scream. Lyssa had gone to Joie and pulled her into her arms. Joie wore herself out with tears that night before falling into a deep sleep. Lyssa did not know if Joie had actually been conscious when she held her tightly in her arms and rocked her back and forth, big girl though she was. Joie awoke the next morning as if nothing had happened the night before, and nothing was said.

Later, while they gathered moss and rushes for the cabin while the children slept, Joie said, "Her ghost haunts that fort. She ain't gone to heaven like the others. She told me when I didn't want to wash the clothes that day that if I didn't get those clothes washed, when she died she'd come back and haunt me."

Joie looked up at Lyssa with her big blue eyes clear and serious. "I didn't get the clothes washed. I hid under the canoe."

The child wasn't as unmarred by the events as Lyssa had first thought. Lyssa knew how the mind wraps around something and turns it upside down, inside out, up and over till it seems reasonable enough to the one thinking it. And Joie expected the spirit of that evil stepmother to be waiting for her just so she could spring from the rubble. Lyssa guessed she was lucky Joie was as strong and helpful as she was. If Joie had been down and out, Lyssa didn't think she could possibly cope.

She pulled Joie into her arms. "I know right now you think that, Joie, but it just doesn't happen that way. You don't have to go back to that fort. Not ever if I have anything to say about it. That woman is burning in a hell worse than what happened in the fort that day for threatening you and meaning to scare you the way she did!"

She pushed Joie away just enough to look into her beautiful eyes and say, "I won't let anything bad happen to you. Just look around at our protectors." Samson was sniffing Delilah's butt at that moment. The two girls looked at one another and broke into laughter. The tension faded.

Later, Lyssa wrapped moss around the toddlers' freshly washed bottoms and laid them on the floor beside Joie, who sat cross-legged and rocked J.J., crooning softly something she must have learned from Sarilee. They all watched Lyssa clean up from their evening meal, fully expecting her to take care of them. Even Sister looked her way with growing awareness in her light green eyes.

Godfrey groaned and tossed with his fever. Lyssa had found a willow tree and would pound the bark to make tea. She loved them all so much. She could not let them down.

Surely some basic implements and bits of clothing had survived the burning and pillaging at the fort.

"I've got to go and gather some herbs," she said to Joie. "And I will have to go back to the fort because we've got to have clothes and some pots to cook in."

Joie nodded and commented grimly, "You'll find pots under the bodies. The women were washing them."

Lyssa shuddered. Her eyes grew enormous with anxiety, and Joie took her hand. "You don't have to go," the younger girl said. "We can make do here."

"They're dead," Lyssa said with false courage. "If I move them or take something they can't use anymore, it's not going to make them more dead." She looked around her at their stark surroundings and meager supplies. She wished for her mother, her grandmother, anyone but her to be in charge. "If I don't go, these babies will die. Plus, I need some clothes," she said, still convincing herself to go beyond the security of the little perimeter they had established with Samson and Delilah always alert.

"Well, Godfrey could wake up any time, and he don't need to see yore titties." Joie looked down at her own buds just beginning to strain at the coarse dress that was way too little, a reminder of the meanness of the stepmother who had raised her. Then she looked at Lyssa's breasts as if noticing them for the first time. "It wouldn't be prudent," she said, shaking her head. "Might set him afire and condemn him to the pits of hell for his devil's urges."

"Where'd you hear that?" Lyssa asked, as if she didn't know.

Joie shrugged.

Lyssa pressed her lips together. It wasn't a conversation for today. But she knew the little girl needed a friend to counteract the bitter, mean-spirited woman with whom she had lived for the past ten years.

Lyssa prepared the cabin as best she could to be gone a while.

"Stay, Delilah." Delilah sat in the door, her head cocked, alert and protective. Samson woofed his question. Lyssa hesitated. Then she lifted her head and took a step toward the door.

"It all begins with a first step," she said.

It didn't look like Joie was going to argue with her.

"Come with me," she said to Samson.

She swallowed her fear, climbed on Beauty's back, and maneuvered her way along the creek bank, trying to hide Beauty's footprints as much as possible. Beauty and Samson sensed the danger, and the training her father had given them kicked in. They would do their best to protect her.

It was probably her imagination, and she had a vivid one, she knew, but she thought she heard voices and horses' hooves beating their way in the distance.

She stilled, tightening her legs to signal Beauty, and sliced the air with her hand toward Samson, who lowered to his stomach. The dog tensed and listened. Then he wagged his tail. Lyssa sighed with relief. It must have been the natural sounds of the woods. Life had finally returned to the woods around the fort where the carnage was still scattered like broken dolls all around the landscape.

Lyssa had come prepared this time, having ripped the scarce remnant of her shirt to cover her nose and mask at least some of the smell of rotting flesh. Finally, within sight of the charred fort, she slid from Beauty's back at the tree line. With her feet once more on the pine needle carpet, she surveyed the open ground around the fort and down to curve of the river.

The squirrels chattered back and forth as they leapt from limb to limb. A heron flapped its wings and flew down to the rippling water to fetch a fish. Bullfrogs croaked from their lily pads. Mosquitoes swarmed through the cattails. Deer sharpened their antlers on the pine trees, and every now and then she heard the disconcerting roar of a bull alligator and the nerve-grating slither of a water moccasin.

Standng there at the edge of the woods, Lyssa gazed into the clearing at blackened remnants of a once-beautiful home. She was mesmerized by the devastation. Her skin prickled with a strange disquiet. She intended to go into the fort, but she got the willies watching the vultures circling around. Something evil seemed to float in the air. The hair on the back of Samson's neck stood on end, and he placed himself between her and the fort. He sensed it too.

As far as she could tell, she was alone in the human category. That was why she had brought Samson. As long as Samson was calm, she would be also. Or so she told herself.

"They're dead," she whispered to herself. "Can't hurt you now, I told Joie." That was easy to say back at the cabin. But here...looking at all those bodies. Thinking about how horrible their deaths had been!

Rationally, Lyssa knew they were dead, but what if—and she knew it couldn't be true—but what if spirits continued to linger around those dead bodies? Even if they couldn't hurt her, if she glimpsed something move she knew she would begin screaming. Every nerve in her body was tense. Every hair on her arms was standing on end. That was one damned spooky space...dead folks lying there and Red Sticks out where nobody knew. They could be hiding behind a tree and jump out and cut her throat. One could throw a tomahawk and cleave her skull just like she'd seen so many done inside that godforsaken fort!

All that was beautiful was gone. The bodies still rotted in the hot September sun. And as far as she knew, the Red Sticks could return before the militia did. So if she was going to find what she needed, she'd better do it fast, although it kind of felt like robbing the dead on the hallowed ground that had become the gravesite of so many.

Maybe she wouldn't have to go into the fort if the women who had come down to wash had left enough that the Red Sticks hadn't taken. The scavenging was necessary if she was to provide for her band of infants.

Too smart for her own good. Her daddy had always told her that curiosity and her impetuous nature would one day take her to no good end. Well, he was right. She looked yearningly across the Boatyard Lake to Nannahubba Island. Beyond that was the Tombigbee and then Choctaw country. She could swim to the security of a family that adored her. And who hadn't a clue where she was.

But if she had not come, who would have cared for those children? Joie couldn't do it by herself. If not for Lyssa, she might still be under that canoe.

Lyssa had asked if Joie knew of any who survived. She told Lyssa she couldn't swim and that was why she had not tried to reach Peggy Bailey when she saw her swim across the river, guiding a canoe filled with women and children who had been with her washing clothes. Peggy had seen what was happening at the fort and silently propelled the loaded canoe to safety through Boatyard Lake and into the big river.

A brave woman.

All her senses were on high alert. Lyssa kept expecting to find a military patrol come to bury the dead. The Red Sticks must be attacking the other forts and keeping them occupied. Maybe the Red Sticks were winning.

She took a deep breath. She would not turn back. Too much depended on her finding the supplies she needed.

She took the path down to the water and breathed a sigh of relief. The implements she needed littered the bank of Boatyard Lake, where the women had been washing clothes and pots when the attack occurred.

She scanned the lake but only saw an overturned canoe on the verge of sinking in the middle. The godawful smell was enough to make her gag in spite of her efforts to cover her nose with the fabric. She gathered the clothing, averting her eyes from the sight of the bodies (she would not think of them as women—as long as she did not recognize anyone it was possible), putting on a discarded blouse to replace the shirt she had torn for bandages, thankful for something to shield her from the horde of buzzing, biting mosquitoes that hovered in the swampy areas of the river side and the flies that swarmed about the bodies. She hurriedly tied pots and pans together with the arms of another shirt and slung it over her shoulder, bundling the remaining clothing for herself and the children in her arms. Then she hurried back toward Beauty.

But before she climbed the bank, she gave herself a moment to look up and down the river. Where was he? Her boy? Joie's version of the morning the horror struck had Cade leaving the fort long before the attack. Surely he was safe and she would find him—when she could move with her little flock.

A sight she could not avoid was the small animals that nibbled on the bloated bodies littering the bank. She forced herself to lean down and gather some of the herbs she needed, tucking them into the bundle. Her thoughts drifted. Some of the bodies had bloated and burst in the heat— a sight she hoped never to see again. She lowered her eyes, giving those people at least the dignity of privacy with this horrible indignity and tragedy of their death. She could do nothing for them. They were dead. But the ones she was determined to save could be the children of those women who lay dead on the bank. They would tell her, if they could, to save their children.

All of those people with hopes and dreams, just living their lives. Cut down in minutes. And now, no one was recognizable as the husband, wife, mother, daughter, son they had once been. Lyssa sat back on her heels. If she closed her eyes, she could imagine the music drifting from the old Mims house, laughter, the clink of glasses, voices. In her mind's eye she glimpsed the beautiful silk dresses that swirled and dipped as the girls danced inside the house.

Lyssa had watched such a party from the vantage point of a tree limb outside a window. Her parents had come to the christening as friends of the Mims and camped nearby. Tears spilled from her eyes now as she thought of her parents and wished they were there.

She looked across Lake Tensaw to Nannahubba Island, wishing she could backtrack to where she had begun several days before. And while she yearned to cross that river, her heart led her back to the children.

12

Sitting in a canoe full of Red Sticks, covered in war paint, Gabe looked toward Nannahubba Island where another canoe had suddenly appeared, skimming gracefully across the still water of Boatyard Lake, cutting through the blanket of fog and smoke, mere shadows against the sunset. But the sight chilled his heart. Enemy or friend, he wondered.

About the same time, Cade also spotted a canoe appearing silently from the entrance of the bayou where he'd left Gabe. The previously motionless waters now rippled, disturbed as when a gator quietly moves toward its prey. Instinct kicked in. Danger.

The fog cleared enough to identify the source. Personal reflection evaporated as a canoe full of Red Sticks painted for war cut its way through the amber waters of Boatyard Lake at the entrance to the next bayou. Before Cade could react, the lead oarsman in the other canoe spotted him and Ned, and suddenly the war canoe shot forward, heading straight for them.

"Goddamn it all to hell and back. Ned, you'd better row like you never rowed before," Cade yelled.

Ned's muscled arms corded as he pulled the oars as fast and deep as a man could pull, but they were no match for the six Indians in the other canoe. Both canoes raced through the water, slipping in and out of the smoky haze as Cade and Ned attempted to get through the Cut-off and into the Alabama River. If they could get there before the war canoe, there was a chance they could make it across to the other side. But there in the inlet known as Boatyard Lake, they were dead meat.

Cade could not row and shoot at the same time, and the Red Sticks drew closer. Finally, Cade pulled his gun from the bottom of the canoe, but as he sighted the gun toward the approaching canoe and got ready to pull the trigger, he recognized his brother Gabriel. Good God almighty. Gabriel painted for war? Sure as hell, it was him, and his face was painted half red and half black. Cade lifted his gun high over his head as if in greeting. He couldn't shoot. Gabriel might get hit.

Gabriel recognized him at about the same time. He said nothing, but suddenly the war canoe rocked and tipped, and out spilled the six

Red Sticks who sputtered and shouted and looked around for the fool that had upset the canoe. Cade looked behind him.

"Ned, pull your paddle out of the water!" Ned obeyed immediately. It seemed minutes, but could only have been seconds before a hand appeared at the side of their canoe. Cade reached down and grabbed his brother's arm, pulling him into the canoe and handing him an oar.

"Row! Dammit. Row!" Cade commanded. "I'll shoot."

He aimed for the canoe and shot a hole in it before reloading to shoot the threatening Indians. "What the hell were you doing in a Red Stick War canoe?"

"Shut up and shoot!" Gabriel shouted.

Thank God for the fog.

But there was such confusion among the Indians in the water having lost their oars and their guns that Cade, Gabriel, and Ned made the narrow aperture and shot out into the Alabama River. "Go north up the Bigbee, Ned," Cade directed.

That made sense. If the Red Sticks recovered their canoe, they wouldn't think the enemy would head up current. The three men rowed through the dark of night, hearing the bellowing roars of bull alligators and the occasional splash as one lowered itself into the water. From time to time, they saw a moccasin's ripple outlined by the moonlight. But they didn't hear or see any Red Sticks. Yet. They steered clear of the bank with the overhanging branches from which a serpent might flip into their canoe.

After rowing for several hours, they spotted a sandy beach in the light cast by the sliver of moon in the sky and steered toward land. They jumped from the canoe, pulling it up behind them and hiding it in a cane stand. They made their way inland through the woods, away from paths, to make camp for the rest of the night. At last they found a spot by a creek to stop and rest.

"Now, Gabriel, tell me what happened." Gabe had slurped some of the clear water from the running stream and now lay sprawled on the leaf-covered bank, looking up through the pines and moss-laden river oaks to the stars that twinkled in the dark night sky. Gabe explained that as soon as Cade had left the canoe, Old Interpreter had appeared, and from then on Gabe had been compelled to pretend support for the Red Stick cause.

"Anyhow, that is how I came to be in that canoe." Gabriel said. "I'm guessing you didn't find Joie."

Cade shook his head sadly. "Beasley saved my life by sending me to deliver his report just about as soon as I got into the fort. By the time I got back to the fort—well, you don't want to hear it all. But I found our father and buried him and Sarilee. The birds are feasting on that woman. I found nothing of Joie."

"Well, maybe she escaped if you didn't find her," Gabe said.

Cade shrugged and nodded. He didn't seem hopeful. "Did the Red Sticks say anything that might help us locate Joie?" Cade asked.

"I did hear them say they would eventually gather at Hickory Ground. But they want to destroy as much as they can in the Tensaw area to wipe away any sign of the white man's ways. Bands of Red Sticks still roam up and down the river. They will find any excuse they can to burn the plantations and kill the livestock of those they consider turncoats." Gabe hesitated. "They've taken lots of captives. I didn't get too close a look, but it's possible…. Let me tell you, Brother. Savannah Jack ain't forgot us. I could tell by the look in his eyes. If he'd caught me alone, he'd have used that hand-carved knife on my throat."

Gabe shivered, remembering Jack sitting in front of the fire and carving the handle of his knife, sharpening the blade, and trying its sharpness on his own skin, adding to the many scars on his body. "I tried to steer clear of him. He's still the scariest son of a bitch I ever saw what with only part of an ear and his nose nicked and all those scars! I'll never forget the first time I saw him. He's probably with the scavengers now. But he got close once and he said, 'If your brother hadn't left the fort, I'd have his scalp and his balls along with yore Pa's.'"

"I knew he was there, Gabe. He left his identifier. His knife was in Pa's chest," Cade said.

"At least his words let me know you weren't in that fort," Gabe said, looking at Cade with relief. Cade watched his brother's eyes grow moist and turned away before he embarrassed himself with some show of emotion.

"Then he pulled his balls out of the clout and commenced to shaking them at me as a threat. 'Took care of his woman too!' he gloated. 'Gonna make me a pouch out yore Pa's balls. Needs addin' to. Now's not the time, but I'm coming for the whelps of my enemy.'"

"If he'd seen Joie, he'd have said something, don't you think?" Cade asked.

Gabe nodded.

Cade closed his eyes then, trying to push away the mental image of the man who still gave him chills.

"When I saw you," Gabe said, "I decided to try to make a getaway. I got a glimpse of what happened inside that fort, and I don't want to be any part of that. I understand now why Weatherford looked as sick as he did and why he wanted to go to see Davy Tait."

"He told you he was going to see his brother?" Cade asked.

"Yep. Said he saw a tomahawk cleave into his little niece's head."

Ned's eyes bugged. Gabe's teared up again. He had known that little girl.

"Weatherford tried to get word to the fort," Gabe continued, trying to justify the actions of the man he respected so much.

"Word did get to the fort. They had Fletcher's black, Jo, tied to the post and were beating him when I left. He told them he'd seen Red Sticks. Beasley called them red cattle." Cade shook his head. "I saw Joie, Gabe. She's a pretty little thing—black hair and Pa's blue eyes. She didn't want to leave the baby, though."

"Baby?" Gabe asked.

"Yep," Cade said. "Pa's wife just had her a baby. They got a girl to feed the baby, but Sarilee was there too, taking care of it just like she did Joie."

"I guess Joie worried about that baby like you and me did her."

Cade nodded.

"I reckon she was taking care of that baby when the Red Sticks attacked."

Cade covered his eyes and rubbed his forehead. "That's how I see it. I buried Pa, what was left of him, and Sarilee," he told Gabe. "Saw the woman. Don't ever want to see anything like that again. Wouldn't wish it on my worst enemy."

Gabe looked away and wished his mind could block out what it imagined. But, even more, he hated seeing the return of the haunted look in Cade's eyes. He could never get Cade to tell him what happened during their captivity. Gabe had been delirious, but Cade had to deal with Savannah Jack and William Augustus Bowles. Gabe had not awakened until they were back at their village. He only knew his brother had rescued him—and nearly lost his own life doing it.

Cade stood, pushing the disturbing thoughts away. It was time for action. "I've got to look for Joie. If she got out of that fort, she'd have rode the current down to Fort Stoddard. And then I gotta see about a woman that thinks she took a husband. Hell if I'll let that little bit make a fool out of me. That wasn't a marriage?"

"Looked like to me it was you who might have took a wife there...."

"She took advantage of me!"

Gabe laughed, and the usually reticent Ned snorted.

"I mean, I was drunk...."

"You don't remember a thing?"

The betraying Kraken woke up then, just from the memory of Lyssa Rendel.

Gabe laughed and pointed. "Truth Teller don't lie."

Time to change the subject.

"Gabe, you said they took prisoners. Did you see who they were?"

"No, Old Interpreter kept me close. They didn't trust me. There were a lot of women and children and some slaves, it seemed, from the glimpse I got."

"Well, we need to get on to St. Stephens to report what happened to Judge Toulmin. And Lyssa Rendel—*Pipsqueak*—is gonna be sorry she ever tricked this man."

Gabe and Ned looked at each other knowingly.

The Kraken didn't hear a word Cade said. Just the thought of her made his man part try to get out of the breechclout. This could be embarrassing. Cade tried to think of anything but Lyssa, which of course had him thinking *only* of her, remembering the night they'd spent together, how beautiful she was, how she felt, and before long he could hardly breathe and he was in such pain...and then, thank God, they were climbing the Mobile and Vicksburg road to High Street on the Hobuckintopa bluff above the rocky shoals of the Tombigbee. Below, they could see St. Stephens.

"Let's go," he said, and he strode ahead of them down the wide dirt road up the limestone bluff into town. They passed tree-shaded lawns with elegant houses that Cade knew were furnished with imports from England and Spain. The town had a history with both countries and had flown the Spanish flag until 1796. It had always been a dichotomy of ramshackle and classic structures. Sexton's Tavern was a basic wood structure with a big gathering room and a kitchen with rooms upstairs for overnight guests. At the corner of High Street and River Road was Israel Picken's impressive Tombecbe Bank. Cade had attended a theatrical performance done by a traveling troupe with Nicey Potts at the new school, Washington Academy, which perched on a hill toward the end of the street.

But today Cade was fuming and took no notice of the town. He'd been tricked! Duped! His condition was perfectly natural. He was a red-blooded male. He really had no feelings—beyond the obvious—for that girl, Lyssa...Pipsqueak! He was going to tell her the trick hadn't worked. He wasn't married. He had to go fight the Red Sticks and see if his sister had been one of the captives Gabe had seen.

He recalled Lyssa's passion-filled eyes and loving smile, and suddenly he was lightheaded and wishing....

And then a shot rang out, and the three jumped behind the trees that lined the road and took cover. They'd forgotten that Gabe still wore the breechclout and the remnants of the red and black paint of a Red Stick warrior.

"Don't shoot!" Cade shouted. "It's Cade Kincaid, here to see Judge Toulmin. That ain't no damned Red Stick. It's just my brother Gabe."

"Hell, boy!" shouted George Gaines, the agent to the Choctaw stationed there at St. Stephens. "Ain't you got sense enough to dress American when you come into town? Got folks here that just escaped a massacre, and they're ready to get some blood of their own! Heard tell the Red Sticks might attack St. Stephens!"

They were finally led through town under guard. Gaines took them to the agency, where he cleaned Gabe up and gave him some breeches and a homespun shirt. The brothers told him what they knew and had seen. Gaines agreed to help them interview survivors to see if they could get news about Joie.

13

Lyssa felt desperate as she foraged at Fort Mims for necessities they needed to survive. Eyes and ears alert to every sight and sound, she skirted the fort and made her way to the river bank. She tried to remember the glory days and close her mind to the horrors. The oak tree rising, charred and bare, high above the remains of the fort next to where the Mims house once stood was now a morbid marker as she approached. In spite of the recent horrors that had occurred beneath its spreading branches, she was reminded of the night she had climbed this tree when it was green and full of leaves, shielding her from view of others.

Lyssa had not expected to see Cade that night four years ago. But she was drawn from their camp while her parents attended the party. She had climbed the tree to watch. Somebody inside played the Virginia reel on a fiddle, and figures glided past the floor-to-ceiling windows, casting shadows into the night. Lyssa watched all the dancing through the window, tapping her foot and wishing she had a dress that pretty, even if she didn't have any bosoms to hold it up.

Her parents had wanted to buy her a dress so she could attend the party, but Lyssa had refused, saying she didn't want to go to any old party. She would stay at the camp with her animals and Lance, who sure didn't want to get dressed up. He wondered why he had to leave his friends who were going hunting to go with his parents to some stupid "white man's" party. So after the christening earlier in the afternoon, the children had returned to their camp, leaving their parents to enjoy the party. It was her mother's first such party as well.

But Lyssa had slipped back after Lance had gone to sleep.

Curious, she had watched Sally Carson peek from a window, watching for someone. A young man galloped up and passed the reins of his horse to one of Sam Mims's waiting slaves. Lyssa watched Sally Carson time her own exit from the house in order to encounter the new arrival.

The door opened, and Sally rushed out and right into the man who reached out to hold her and steady them both. Sally looked up into his eyes and said, "Oh, my, I am so sorry. How embarrassing. I just needed some air and...." She trailed off, batting her eyelashes and trying to look surprised. "Why, it's Cade Kincaid!"

It was only then that Lyssa realized the man who'd galloped up was the one she knew as her boy.

She fumed from her perch in the tree, aware that Sally Carson knew exactly what she was doing despite her feigned surprise.

Even then, still not fully grown, Cade was so handsome that Lyssa's heart had nearly stopped when she saw him silhouetted in the doorway, about to step into the home from the broad veranda. Cade had changed, but she would have known him anywhere. He was taller, broader, and more muscular. His dark brown hair was longer and he was dressed in a shirt and trousers, probably made by Nicey Potts, who had apparently taken the twins as her own sons. For a moment, the moon had reflected on those startling Kincaid blue eyes, and Lyssa's heart flipped over in her chest. If she had not been holding on tightly to the limb, she'd have fallen out of the tree.

That was why Sally had spent so much time peeking out the window!

The beautiful young lady fanned herself and said, "It is just too hot to go back in there right now. Let's find a cool place for a moment." She took Cade by the arm and guided him to a "cool place," all right! They headed toward the shadows of the veranda, where Sally pressed her (even then) ample bosom against his chest and lifted puckered lips.

Cade responded as any young man would have done, crushing the girl to his chest and kissing her in such a way that Lyssa, just watching, went limp and once again might have fallen out of the tree if Sally's father hadn't come to the door and called for his daughter to come in. Sally hurried from the darkness breathlessly, claiming it was too hot in the house and she'd come out for fresh air. After she went in, Cade hesitated a moment and then followed. Later he had come out with Gabriel, Will Milfort, and William Weatherford, and they had all headed toward the horses.

That night seemed so long ago that it felt unreal, especially considering what lay before her now. Lyssa had been fifteen, and Cade and Sally just a little older.

As much as she hated Sally Carson, Lyssa hoped she had not been at Fort Mims. She looked beyond the charred tree and up at the sky, where a flurry of vultures circled. Following the water's edge, she watched as one settled and preened just beyond her on the bank. Then he turned and pranced back and forth, surveying the vast number of opportunities, selectively choosing his prey. Lyssa averted her eyes and swallowed her bile.

An alligator roared and splashed, pulling with it the body of one who had fallen nearby. But it was the howling of dogs that surprised her as she approached what had before been total silence but for the occasional crackle of the embers or the fluttering wings of a buzzard. The dogs, used to being fed by their masters, had now returned in packs to feed on the carrion of what had once been human beings. Their vicious growling as they fought over the flesh was as horrible as the sight of mangled and mutilated bodies. Her imagination of the continuous depredation upon those pitiful people would fuel her nightmares forever. She could not make herself take another step forward. She fell to her knees, weak with the horror of the place.

Don't look! Turn back! Or so her instincts told her.

But she had a mission to keep those who trusted her alive.

She tried not to breathe. The air was heavy with death.

Surely one day a force of militia would come and bury what was left of the dead, she thought as she glanced back at the ruin and decay up on the hill, feeling guilty that she had not tried to bury anyone herself. But there were so many! She could not endanger the children. It could just as well be Red Sticks who returned to the site of their "victory."

The Red Sticks *had* returned shortly after the battle and retrieved their dead. Lyssa was only grateful they had not noticed her and Joie leaving the fort. She stood up and straightened her shoulders. It was the living she must deal with. She was still worried about J.J. If he didn't make it, it would kill Joie. And Godfrey's leg bone had punctured the skin, with red streaks radiating from the wound. She had set the bone and secured it. But she would have to resort to poulticing it with wet red clay, then letting it air dry, doing another poultice with honey and pollen, letting it air dry again, then applying yet another poultice with wet red clay, alternating the process every fifteen minutes to battle the infection. She also needed to make a tea for the little ones for their diarrhea.

Fortunately, she found what she needed down by the bank where the women had been washing. She put red clay in one of the small pots and gathered what herbs she could find.

An alligator eyed her from the water, drifting closer and closer. Lyssa faced him boldly, never taking her eyes from his. And then he got distracted by something close by. An easier prey, she guessed.

Suddenly, noting the position of the sun in the sky, she realized that she had spent a long time gathering the things they would need. Fear had caused sweat to drench the clothing she had found on the bank. Lyssa whistled for Beauty. She had stood all she could stand of the smells that seeped through the handkerchief with which she had covered her face. Her stomach heaved. And nothing could block those sounds!

Had she had gathered more than she could carry? She did not want to have to return anytime soon. The death all around her without the respect of a decent burial made her skin crawl and her heart pound.

"Beauty," she called softly. Beauty would not come to her whispered call. Instead, Samson came and pushed against Lyssa's leg, nudging her to the rushes where Beauty stood snuffling something at her feet.

"All right, Samson. We're leaving," she said, following him to where Beauty stood transfixed. Samson watched the gator approach. Lyssa tossed her bundle to balance the weight across Beauty's back. The horse whinnied, and Lyssa shushed her tensely, looking all around. Samson took a defensive stance in front of Beauty, and at last Lyssa looked down.

There was another body. And until she saw the chest heave, she thought it was another *dead* body.

But Beauty had found a boy who still lived. From the looks of him, he was *barely* living. Just as she realized what lay at her feet, Samson bristled, watching the gator that had been eyeing Lyssa now approaching more aggressively. They were competition for his prey. Lyssa quickly laid the boy over Beauty's back and leapt up behind him. Samson barked loudly, but his bark was just one other among the frenzy from the fort. They escaped the gator, who had already opened its powerful jaws to secure its prey, by mere seconds. Dear God!

How the boy had survived that long without becoming a gator's meal was a miracle!

Red Sticks were as vicious as that gator, though, and Lyssa felt that every motion, every noise, was alerting someone of their presence, and she feared that someone would shoot her before she could get back to her children. Beauty sensed the danger herself and navigated the rushes quietly. Samson watched for more rogue gators. Lyssa finally guided them into the safety of the woods and toward the cabin.

There was no sight more beautiful than the sight of that peaceful cabin as Lyssa rode up with the fevered child in her arms. He looked to be about eight years old, smaller than Joie, with thick dark brown hair. A gorgeous child. Someone's pride and joy, she knew.

She carried the boy in, and Joie said, "Another one? How many more could be wandering around lost and alone?"

Lyssa's heart melted as she thought how cruel she had been to wonder how she could care for yet another child. Then she wondered aloud, "*Are* there others?"

But now she had these to care for. So she laid the boy down and went back for what she had recovered from the bank of Boatyard Lake.

The boy's wound was infected, and he was burning up with fever after days in the mucky rushes of the lake where he had hidden. Later in the day, when she had managed to get his fever down, he opened his thickly lashed hazel eyes and grabbed her hand as she wiped his brow with a cool rag. He whispered to her what had happened to him.

He had been laughing and splashing in the shallows with other children while their mothers did the laundry when the attack occurred. He looked up, and a Red Stick warrior, tomahawk held high, had come racing down the embankment. Others followed, and the war clubs came down upon one after another of his mother's friends and his playmates. There were few shots fired down at the water's edge. No need to waste bullets or arrows on unarmed women and children.

Heads rolled and blood spurted everywhere. The child told what he had seen in graphic detail. Lyssa would have shushed him, but she realized that telling his story seemed important to him. He had been near the bull rushes and fell back into them, desperately wiggling his way into the deepest parts, scared that any minute a tomahawk would get *him* in the back. He lay down and breathed through a bit of cane. As he wiggled, he'd seen some of the women and children escaping in a canoe that Peggy Bailey had guided down the river, swimming and pushing it in the right direction. He'd watched, but he was too frightened to show himself.

His mother and sister had both been looking around frantically for him and calling his name. He said nothing. They were both grabbed by the Red Stick he had seen first. He watched as the man slapped his sister until she quit crying. The Red Sticks carried his mother kicking and screaming back to the fort. Others threw rocks in the canoes and shot randomly into the rushes. He stayed hidden.

One of the shots got him. The water became bloody around him, mingling with the blood of others. Yet still he lay on his back in the rushes, breathing through that piece of cane. When dark finally fell, he managed to pull himself further into shallow water and passed out. And that is where he stayed, too frightened to move, until Beauty literally stumbled upon him while she fed on the cane by the river.

"I hear my mother and sister calling to me every time I close my eyes," the boy said. "Maybe if I had run to them, they would have run fast enough to get away! They stayed because they would not leave without me!" His little body shook with his tears and the pain of his guilt. Lyssa held him tightly and rocked him back and forth. "I was too scared to move!"

"They would have caught you all," she whispered to him. "Your mother and sister would have wanted you to live and grow to be a man. A fine man. You must live for them."

With the story out, the boy finally slept, though he screamed out again and again during the night. Night after night. Until he simply quit sleeping at night, afraid the Red Sticks would hear him scream and come for them. His name was Ben. Joie had recognized him because she knew his sister Virginia, who was probably dead now.

It was impossible to keep the children quiet. In addition to Ben's nightmares, Joie had her own, and the blond toddler constantly babbled "Mememememe" with her arms uplifted. The tiny girl seldom ventured far from the small black boy, sleeping with her hand in his hair and murmuring "Momomomo." Beyond these noises and the moans of the sick, J.J. made enough sound for all the rest. He was a determined and demanding child. He would survive.

Once fitted with utensils for housekeeping and having established a store of preparations for healing, Lyssa made it through each day with a routine that somehow kept everyone alive and fed. She fashioned a bow and made arrows sufficient for hunting the plentiful quail. Bone made an adequate hook for fishing, something Joie was reluctant to do because she could not swim. Lyssa wove a basket to trap fish instead. They made do with the vegetables that appeared in the abandoned garden and an occasional chicken that made the mistake of strutting back through the yard. Joie was proficient at setting traps for rabbits and squirrels.

The days turned into weeks. Each day dawned with the necessity of hunting for herbs to make the potions and poultices the children needed. Lyssa left the cabin on daily foraging trips, even venturing into the cornfields around the eerie abandoned Fort Mims that provided their major food source.

The first time she had done that, she had stumbled upon the bodies of some of the Creek warriors who had been killed in the battle. Apparently, the Red Sticks had returned and attempted to bury their fallen between the rows of corn. Then the sheer numbers of dead had discouraged them, and they'd simply left them there. Lyssa had fallen, and, where she lay, she looked directly into the unseeing eyes of a fallen Red Stick. The scream that had escaped her would have alerted anyone within a mile's distance of her presence. She'd shrieked and shrieked while she ran until she could run no more, and then she knelt in the rows of corn and cried.

Now, every time she ventured forth to forage, she gave a wide berth to the fort that she now considered a graveyard. She came at the cornfields from the rear and picked from the edges, never venturing close to the interior again. She did not know if those in the fort had been buried. But about six weeks after the massacre, the vultures disappeared.

Lyssa was able to grind corn and make the nutritious sofkee mixture that every Creek mother kept cooking and adding to every day. Lyssa now understood the wisdom of that. It was nutritious and available whenever anyone became hungry.

Every day she thought she would awaken to see her father or her grandfather there to rescue her, though rationally she knew that she had outsmarted herself by leaving and not letting anyone know where she was going. Each man thought she was safe with the other. They would not come to look for her until they spoke with one another again. That could take months.

But wouldn't they sense that she needed them?

She wanted to think Cade would return for her and realize she was with neither her father nor grandfather, and then someone would know to search for her. But she couldn't be sure he had even survived. Maybe he decided he didn't want her. Maybe he really loved Sally Carson and Lyssa had destroyed his hope of real happiness.

She was standing alone at the edge of the cornfield, frightened, exhausted, depressed, and desperate to feed the seven children who depended on her, now healthier and always hungry, when she broke down. Every doubt she had ever had in herself came crashing in on her. She knelt in the rich black dirt in a row of ripened corn on the edge of the field and shook with sobs until at last she lay back and looked up through the golden tassels of the corn at the blue October sky.

"God? If you're up there, could you possibly help me out here?" she whispered. Her father Jake Rendel had read the Bible with her and taught her to pray just as Malee had taught her of the Master of Breath. The differences seemed too trivial for the two entities not to be one and the same, and Lyssa had always thought those differences were probably manmade. It seemed to her that mankind was such a contentious lot. The present situation is a pretty good example, Lyssa thought, and she felt that God probably agreed with her.

"I came to find Cade, and instead you gave me a bunch of children to feed. I'm all alone here."

No voice from heaven. But perhaps it was God that planted the thought in her mind that it was just like her, impulsive and constantly stumbling into trouble, to have gotten into this fix in the first place. And while she was bound and determined to survive, he might as well take advantage of the situation to make a little good out of a bad situation.

She'd been so proud of herself for making such an adult decision to follow her man when he left, a decision she knew neither her parents nor grandparents would approve. But God's pointing out the fact that she'd gotten herself into this mess wasn't the kind of help she'd desired. She wanted something like a chariot to come down from heaven and take her and the children back to St. Stephens, but apparently God hadn't gotten the message.

Delilah nudged her. Lyssa pushed her away. She'd left Samson to guard the children, but there was Delilah, always sensitive to her feelings. She could almost see tears gathering in Delilah's eyes. Lyssa reached up and hugged her. "Well, maybe I am not *all* alone." She sighed. "I just found him, Lilah. How can I lose him now?"

She rolled over. "What if he is dead?" But she *felt* that Cade was alive. Surely she would feel it if he were not. What if he needed her?

But there was no way she could go to look for him, even taking the children with her. How could they travel? What would she feed them along the way? No one had ever depended on her before. It was a new and awesome feeling. She could not go. She could not search. She just had to survive and keep her little brood hidden as well as she could until at last someone came to find her.

She stood up and gathered the corn she had spilled from her skirt when she lay down in the cornrow.

Unconsciously, she glanced toward the charred remains of the fort. Friends and relatives had done this! It was more than she could comprehend. Tears trickled down her cheeks. She was tired. *So* tired. And she had been throwing up first thing every morning for weeks now, hiding it from Joie. She needed to sleep—to rest.

This was not like her! She didn't wallow around caterwauling about things! She had gotten Godfrey, Ben, Sister, Meme, Mo, and Jay well. Joie was alive. *She* was alive. Cade was *probably* alive. And she was lying here feeling sorry for herself!

So she was tired! *What the hell was the matter with her?*

Lyssa looked around her. The sun was shining. She dusted herself off, heaved her load of corn, and whistled for Delilah to follow her back to the cabin.

14

Joie pulled Lyssa's hair back from her face and tied it with a leather thong. Lyssa was on her knees, once again throwing up where she'd gone to the bushes to do her morning business.

No use denying it. Cade's child grew in her belly.

Joie had brought a dampened cloth when she followed her out. She'd gotten used to the routine.

"I'm pregnant," Lyssa said.

"Yep," Joie responded matter-of-factly.

"Well, hell," Lyssa said.

Joie quirked her eyebrow at Lyssa's uncharacteristic curse. "Yep," the child said again, dimples popping in her cheeks as she fought a smile. Lyssa smiled back in spite of her discomfort. Seeing a smile on Joie's face was worth it. Her dimples were little periods on each side that changed the usually serious Joie into a fairy-tale princess with her sky blue eyes and thick, wavy black hair. But Lyssa certainly would not mention that to the contrary Joie, or she might quit smiling altogether.

She took the cloth from Joie's hand and leaned against the tree. A breeze ruffled the oak leaves and set them to falling and littering the clearing that Lyssa swept daily to discourage snakes close to the cabin. Joie kicked dirt over Lyssa's mess. Lyssa sat still, fighting the nausea that threatened to make her vomit again.

"It *would* take the first time," she said. "Other folks have to try for years, but with me and Cade, it only takes once. Well, maybe twice. But if you count…then three times…." She realized what she was doing and said, "Cover your ears, Joie Kincaid. I'm babbling out of hysteria right now."

Joie shrugged.

"This is all we need now, another baby," Lyssa said, again to herself.

"I figure that's what Cade's gonna say also," Joie said.

Lyssa hadn't thought about how Cade would feel about a baby. She didn't really think he wanted *her*! Her heart ached thinking about Cade. Please, God, let him be all right.

Lyssa spotted Mo and Meme come crawling down the stairs of the cabin. Ben sat near the door, always ready to run and hide. Lyssa watched him and wondered what awful sights he relived when he reluctantly closed his eyes. She knew he wanted to venture out. It was written on his face—the longing to belong, to be with the others. But he held back. He had seen too much, and until he could trust again, he'd hang back and watch cautiously. He was around eight years old, Lyssa was sure, but his thumb was in his mouth—a comfort, she supposed. His dreams must be especially vivid. And so he fought sleep. Ben's eyes seldom closed at night. He sat wide-eyed, watching, waiting until the sun rose. Now, sitting there in the sun, his eyelids drooped and his head dropped back against the wall, his mouth falling open. Lyssa's heart ached for the silent boy with the awful fear. And his guilt over simply surviving.

Sweet Sister followed the toddlers, still clinging to the doll and sucking on three fingers. Sister seldom let Lyssa out of her sight. Lately, Lyssa awoke, extricated herself from the children who cuddled to her like a litter of puppies, and then ran to the bushes. Sister was slower, but she always came soon afterwards.

As for Godfrey Lewis Winkel, Lyssa had long wondered why Joie reacted to him the way she did. She figured now was as good a time as any to ask since Godfrey was inside. With the children dawdling toward them but not yet beside them, she and Joie had about as much privacy as they would ever have. Lyssa said, "Okay, Joie. *Now* is the time for the Godfrey Lewis Winkel story."

Joie pursed her face up like a prune. "Well, it ain't gonna be a happy story, that's for damned sure. The goddamned"—Lyssa looked at her disapprovingly—"the...Godfrey Lewis Winkel came to Fort Mims with the aunt and uncle he'd come to visit. His parents live in New York City. Godfrey, you see, has decided he wants to be a writer. One of those writers that writes for a new paper."

"Newspaper?"

"How would I know? I ain't never seed one!" Joie said. "He was standin' there talking with that fancy voice using those fancy words to Sophie Rigdon, and I ast 'what's a new paper?' and he laughed at me! Called me 'ignerent.' Well, hell...I mean my goodness! I ain't never had nobody show me no words. I coulda larnt 'em!"

Tears brimmed over in Joie's eyes. Lyssa patted her hand, still afraid to move. Now would not be an appropriate time to vomit.

"Godfrey Lewis Winkel said he'd come for an adventure that he was gonna write about and become a famous reporter for the new…newspaper. He'd pull out the nub of a quill, dip it in a little jar of stuff he carried in his leather pouch, and then, serious as you please, commence to making little squigglies on the page. 'Whatcha doin'?' I'd ask and he'd say, 'Takin' notes on the activities of the primitive settlers on the frontier of America.' Good God Almighty. He didn't lift a finger to help nobody nowhere. He was an observer, he said. His aunt, perty little lady, would smile and take care of all that needed doin' along with their slaves while him and his uncle sat back and discussed the goin's on around them. Would the Red Sticks attack? Was there really ever hope of civilizin' such a primitive 'ciety. All that mess.

"Hell, yeah, the Red Sticks were gonna attack! And no wonder when they got goddamn strangers invadin' and settlin' on their land. Get some weak man drunk on tafia from their village to sign somethin' he cain't read sposedly sellin' somethin' he don't own and never did and accordin' to the Red Sticks belongs to everbody not just one somebody. They make 'em build roads for folks to bring families down to settle on lands that once belonged to them and, yeah, I think, they're gonna fight for it."

That girl has been learning and listening beyond Leona and Jason Kincaid's cabin and conversation, Lyssa observed.

"And there sit those two calling on their slaves to bring 'em this or bring 'em that, holdin' their nose at the stench but not lifting a shovel to even dig a privy." Her eyes sparked with anger and she flushed with her memories.

"Then I heard him trying to impress Sophie Rigdon. He commenced to tellin' Sophie bout how 'primitive' that 'ciety here in the 'Bigbee is. And that's when he told Sophie how "ignerent" we all were.

"And you know the worst part? He was right. And I was 'shamed I can't read or write. And Sophie Rigdon was so perty and wore such perty clothes. And there I was lookin' worsern any slave there in the fort with baby throw up smellin' me up to boot, and he fixed those wire glasses perched high on his nose and looked down his hoity-toity nose at me like I warn't no bettern' one of them punky no-see-ums he was swattin' at!"

Joie had worked up a mighty fine mad. Her blue eyes snapped as she remembered how hurt she had been. "And now I know he ain't no bettern' me and he wouldn't even be here if I hadn't insisted we bring him with us. And now he's dependin' on me for his very pot to pee in! Mister High and Mighty.

"Well, I done learnt me a lesson. You know, ain't none of that matters. Pore old Sophie, she ain't got that perty hair no more or those perty clothes. In a twinkle she got shot down there on the bank right in front of me. And I saw some brave cut her perty yellow hair right offn' her head…and worse." Joie shivered and shook her head in wonderment. "Here today. Gone tomorrow. And when we go, it's the same for all of us, high and low.

"Aint much difference in any of us, really, 'sides the fancies we put on the outside. That fart'd be dead ifn' you and me didn't have a heart biggern' good sense. We've all still got to pee when we wake up in the morning. And he needs a ignerent half-breed like me to bring him the damned pot!"

She didn't say it poetically, but the essence of what she said had been the stuff of plays and poetry. It made more sense the way she said it.

Mo and Meme had successfully toddled over to them, and both plopped down in Lyssa's lap. Sister stood close and patted Lyssa's head. They were all offering their silent comfort while Joie paced angrily back and forth, gesturing wildly with her expressive hands. The tone of her voice had the babies sure Joie was yelling at Lyssa. Samson and Delilah assumed their protective stances around her, and Beauty whinnied a reminder that the baby had awakened and was crying.

And Godfrey Lewis Winkel was calling for a pot to pee in.

"I'll teach you, Joie," Lyssa assured her. "You'll out-read and out-write Godfrey Lewis Winkel, or my name isn't Lysistrata Cassandra Rendel."

Then Lyssa struggled to her feet, toppling her lap load as she ran to the bushes to throw up once again. "Lyssa-Whatever Cassandra Rendel *Kincaid*, you mean," Joie said meaningfully.

Then Joie herded the little ones back toward the cabin. "Time to feed the troops now," she said.

Suddenly Samson growled and his hackles rose. Delilah crept slowly toward the house where the baby still cried. Lyssa stood still and listened, motioning the others to do the same. She heard horses' hooves pounding in the distance. They did not sound like the shod feet of the militia. They must be Indians. Lyssa motioned for Delilah to return to the house. She disappeared inside, and the baby hushed. Lyssa and Joie kept the rest motionless. The horses slowed and stopped. It seemed like an eternity. Would they see their tracks? They'd been careful, brushing away their footprints whenever they ventured out of the immediate clearing. But they might have missed something.

At last, they heard the sound of the horses start up again and stayed quiet until they were sure they had passed in the distance. Lyssa and Joie ran immediately into the house to see about the baby. Delilah had quieted J.J. by licking him and making him smile and coo. Lyssa knelt and hugged Delilah. An emotional burst of tears surprised both her and Joie.

"I don't know why I'm crying," Lyssa said.

Godfrey watched pensively.

"Well, I do," Joie responded. "That Leona woman was fussin' and cryin' the whole time she carried J.J. I can tell you, this ain't gone be no picnic!" Joie flounced through the cabin and thrust an empty pot at her nemesis. Fortunately, Lyssa had gathered several when she'd braved going back to Fort Mims.

"Here's your damned pot, Godfrey Lewis Winkel. Now do your damned business and quit looking down your damned nose at me." Joie shoved the pot at Godfrey and then spun and ran from the room. Lyssa turned her back, tending to the little ones. When she was done, he was done, and she took the pot, kicked a hole in the ground, and emptied the contents.

Godfrey Lewis Winkel was better. The poultices and their constant application, nearly wearing both Lyssa and Joie out, had done their work, and the wound was well on its way to healing. As far as she could tell, the bone was healing straight. He was still weak, though two moons had passed since they had found their sanctuary.

Lately, there had been longer moments of lucidity when she could tell he was watching and weighing what was going on around him, but they were short and sporadic.

The day before, he suddenly seemed to wake up. Lyssa could tell the situation was going to be difficult. Godfrey turned red in the face every time she or Joie came near because he realized they had taken turns tending to his body functions, and if there was anything Godfrey Lewis Winkel was, he was modest to the point of prudishness.

Godfrey Lewis Winkel looks different today, Lyssa thought. The weeks of tending to sick people had made her analyze each of them, measuring their temperature with the palms of her hands, by the look in their eyes and the color of their skin. Godfrey just looked more...there. He had been deathly ill, in and out of consciousness, and in an extreme amount of pain from the time they had tossed him up on that horse with his badly broken and protruding leg bone until recently. Just as he would appear to be on the mend, another infection would occur and he would spiral down again. But within the past couple of days, he had been aware of his surroundings and particularly of the care for his basic needs that Lyssa and Joie had been performing for him. Lyssa guessed he was probably about fifteen, still growing, now gone from chubby and robust to pale and thin. Being of a pallid complexion common to redheads, his consternation was obvious. He turned bright red every time he looked at Joie particularly, knowing that she had seen all of his private parts. Lyssa understood. She'd been fifteen herself not so long ago.

That look on his face was always good for making Joie add a few more! Ever since he'd become more alert, Joie had delighted in making him blush. He responded with increased irritation that Lyssa suspected was to mask his embarrassment, and he became an extremely difficult patient. Since his interactions with Joie were about the only entertainment they had, Lyssa sat back and watched them unfold. She had become passive lately and was fighting a growing lethargy.

Joie had milked the nanny goat that they kept in an enclosure they had managed to create out of sticks and woven grape vines, and she took the milk in to feed J.J. Lyssa mixed the remaining milk with the sofkee for their morning meal. She wondered how the passing Indians had not noticed their smoke and then realized that the wind was blowing in just the right direction that morning to send the smoke away from the land toward the river. Lyssa said a silent prayer of thanks.

Later that day, she intended to bring clean rushes in to place in the corners. The others had flattened out and gotten soiled. Lyssa had read about rushes in the great halls of medieval homes and decided that if they had to have dirt floors, rushes could at least help make help make a more comfortable bed. And they had. She kept the floor brushed smooth and neat with a pine branch and the rushes clean and smelling fresh. A bucket hollowed out from a pine stump held fresh water, and they used a gourd dipper to take drinks. Lyssa had taught Joie the art of basket weaving. They gathered vines and grasses and the strips of white oak that grew near the swamps and then wove them into baskets for gathering the herbs and berries they found near their encampment. All in all, their hideaway had gotten cozy.

But now it was time to hunt for something to put in the pot besides sofkee. Lyssa procrastinated by taking a turn feeding J.J. She leaned back against the wall and closed her eyes for a few more minutes before duty took her away from the security of their haven.

Godfrey Lewis Winkel pushed himself up on his elbows, wincing. Mo and Meme had never paid attention to the boy before, but they responded to his observation by sitting down beside him. Godfrey obviously did not know what to think of small children. They simply sat and stared at each other for a long time. Lyssa watched as she fed J.J. and Joie stirred the sofkee. It only took a single sniff of it cooking early in the morning to send Lyssa to the bushes.

Meme stood up then and moved toward Godfrey, cupping his face in her hands as she looked directly into his eyes. She pointed to his leg and said, "Boo boo," and she pointed to a scrape on her arm. "Boo boo." Then she laid her soft, sweet cheek next to his to comfort him. Tears brimmed in the boy's eyes. He pulled himself away and back against the wall—away from the child, Lyssa thought, and almost called Meme to her. And then he opened his arms. Meme toddled forward, still careful of his "boo boo." She knew about "hurts" and avoided anything with a bandage on it. Godfrey pulled the little girl against his chest and patted her back awkwardly. Meme lay comfortably on his bony chest and cuddled closer. Her curly, silver-white hair covered the boy's smooth chest.

That was more than Mo could stand. Meme was getting attention and he wasn't. So he pulled himself up and crab-crawled over to his semi-twin and Godfrey Lewis Winkel. Mo was black and Meme was white...like Godfrey. Lyssa tensed. How would Godfrey react to the black child?

The older boy hesitated. Joie had told Lyssa how "high falutin'" Godfrey Lewis Winkel was. He might think he was too good to have anything to do with a black child. Mo pulled himself up on Godfrey's arm and stood looking straight into Godfrey's green eyes. Godfrey pushed himself further back on the rushes into a corner. Lyssa prepared to get up to rescue a rejected Mo and consign Godfrey Lewis Winkel to the farthest regions of Hades, but then Godfrey awkwardly pulled the boy into the curve of his arm. Mo cuddled into the boy's embrace, one hand on Meme's back patting her silky curls just like Godfrey did.

Lyssa sat back. Would wonders never cease.

Godfrey's eyes misted and he looked at Lyssa. Then he sat back and sighed. Lyssa watched as three pairs of eyelids lowered, and all fell asleep.

Joie and Lyssa looked at each other, barely believing what they had seen. "Well, hell," Joie said.

Lyssa nodded. She'd put it off as long as she could.

"Joie, take J.J. I need to do some foraging," she said.

Joie accepted the child reluctantly. "I wish you didn't have to do this, Lyssa."

"Well, I learned the Indian ways from the very best. Grandfather trained me as he did Lance, though I started learning much later than my brother did. Grandmother said he did not want me to be a 'victim' like she had been."

Just mentioning Chamay made Lyssa long for her. But her grandparents had prepared her for these trying times. Lyssa removed most of her clothing and wore only a skin shift. She had fashioned the shift from the carcass of a deer she had found recently shot on one of her forays for food. The clothing she had brought from Fort Mims was too brightly colored and would stand out in the woods when she needed to blend in. During the nights when she could not sleep, she had scraped the deer skin until it was soft and supple. Then she used the bones of the deer to make a needle and the sinew as thread, as she had been taught, to sew the shift and moccasins she now wore. She had also made a headband that effectively kept her hair out of her eyes.

She winked at Joie and ruffled Ben's hair as she passed him sitting on the front porch of the ramshackle cabin.

Keeping to the woods, using all the skills Pushmataha had taught her, staying in the shadows and leaving no tracks, Lyssa ventured out of the secure haven, carrying a basket and her bow and arrow.

15

Cade and Gabe found Judge Harry Toulmin and Jake Rendel in front of the dry goods store on the dusty street of St. Stephens, talking with someone Cade found vaguely familiar. He was dressed in the style of the territorial militia. Cade thought he remembered seeing the man at Fort Mims. Maybe he knew something about Joie. They hurried toward them, hoping to ask the man some questions.

Judge Toulmin was nearly fifty, but all the responsibilities and cares of his job had him looking much older. His white hair curled over his starched white collar, escaping the leather strip with which it was tied. Toulmin prided himself on the precision of language, and his speech was accentuated by a clipped British accent that some took as British arrogance. Yet his blue eyes shone kindly above a sharply pointed nose, and his demeanor bespoke humility. Judge Toulmin was highly regarded both for his wisdom and his humanity. He was a Unitarian minister who had left England to escape persecution for his beliefs and was recommended by his father's colleague, fellow Unitarian Joseph Priestly, to Thomas Jefferson and James Madison. They assisted him in acquiring a position at Transylvania College in Lexington, Kentucky. He became Secretary of State for the state of Kentucky and compiled the laws for that state. Thomas Jefferson then appointed him judge of the Federal Court for the Mississippi Territory. Toulmin and Benjamin Hawkins were good friends. Both had worked hard to avoid this day of war.

Rendel saw the twin brothers coming. "I haven't forgotten, Kincaid," he said. "An official marriage *will* take place."

Cade sputtered and balled his fists.

Toulmin coughed and caught Rendel's attention. Rendel remembered his manners and said, "Let me introduce Judge Harry Toulmin. Harry, this is apparently going to be my son-in-law, Cade Kincaid."

Cade tensed. Gabriel touched him gently, quieting him. Now was not the time. Cade regained control and inclined his head, acknowledging the introduction. He then gestured toward his brother.

"My brother, Gabriel...and that's Ned." Ned stood a deferential distance away.

"A pleasure," Rendel said, although he looked at Cade like he smelled something bad.

Cade wanted to punch him in the nose for the tone of his introduction. As if Cade were not good enough for his daughter! Even if it were true, Cade felt that he was the one who should be angry. Not Jake Rendel!

"How do you do, son," said Toulmin.

They all shook hands. Then they turned to the man with whom Toulmin and Rendel had been talking.

Toulmin said, "Private Sam Matthews, meet Cade and Gabe Kincaid." Cade eyed the man strangely. Matthews's eyes shifted and his hands trembled. He excused himself quickly and headed into Sexton's Tavern.

Jake Rendel's countenance, once merely shocked and concerned as he listened to Matthews, had now shifted to the stern outrage of a father who had just caught his daughter in a compromising act. Rendel was obviously not one of Cade's admirers.

"Did you bring my daughter for a real wedding?" Rendel demanded.

"When I left, she was with you!" Cade responded in surprise, preparing to break into a tirade on the injustice of it all. But the look on Rendel's face silenced him.

"Then she is still with Pushmataha and her grandmother," Rendel responded.

Toulmin got them back onto the subject at hand. "First, you must tell us about Fort Mims," he said. "Sam Matthews came in last night with Lieutenant Montgomery, who was bringing all the inhabitants of Fort Pierce down to Mobile after the Red Sticks attacked there. Matthews told us he made it to Fort Pierce, escaping after killing twenty Red Sticks even though he'd been bedridden with high fever. Several of those who escaped the fort have made it here, some seriously injured. We've not been able to question them."

"Were you involved in the battle, Cade?" Rendel asked.

"No. I went there to get my sister, Joie Kincaid, and Herman and Nicey Potts out. Gabe had said he'd heard there was gonna be a Red

Stick attack at the fort. I got in a pissin' contest with the man who sired me and Major Daniel Beasley. Beasley sent me to Claiborne with his report, or I'd a been there when the Red Sticks attacked. Gabe got captured and had to pretend to be one of them until he could escape. He never went into the fort, though. Old Interpreter didn't really trust him and kept him with him, guarding the camp. He escaped when he saw Ned and me on Boatyard Lake. We came right here to find out if those who survived know where our sister is."

"Apparently, we need to find a new little brother, too," Gabe added. Toulmin looked confused.

"After our mother died and our father took himself another wife, he refused to claim us as his sons and uses...used...our sister as his wife's slave," Cade explained. "Recently he had a baby by his new wife. I only just discovered that when I saw them briefly at the fort before I was sent to Fort Easley."

Here he took a breath. He was feeling the anger all over again. "Major Beasley commanded me to take his report to General Claiborne at Fort Pierce. Dixon Bailey backed him up. He is—was, actually—my commander with the Tensaw militia." Cade gulped. Those words had drawn up the images of the men in the militia—his friends.

"Joie just wouldn't leave," he continued. "My Pa got him another son, and Joie wouldn't leave the baby. But I was gonna come back and *make* them go with me!"

Toulmin and Rendel were visibly moved by the emotion in the young man's voice.

"I couldn't have been gone long before the attack started," he said. "Gabe said it started at noon, the same time that Caller attacked High Head Jim and Peter McQueen on their way back from Pensacola at Burnt Corn Creek."

Cade swallowed hard before continuing, avoiding the eyes of the men before him, afraid he might actually cry. Gabe tensed. Cade seemed so strong, but his brother knew how deep his feelings ran, and he had certainly been affected by what he had seen.

"There ain't nothin' living in that fort," Cade managed to say. "Dogs are runnin' around crazy, not even barking. Not a single living human being. All that were there are dead. They put up a damned good fight from the looks of it and fought till they were burnt out. Didn't see nothin' living at the fort except the vultures pickin' and pickin'...."

He paused, remembering. His eyes took on a faraway gaze, and he only brought himself back with effort.

"And I saw Zachariah McGirth buryin' his son. He and his man Ned had just left to go back to the plantation when they heard the shootin' commence right at noon. Said he heard a bagpipe."

"McQueen," Toulmin commented, nodding to Rendel. "Sounds like the same group that Caller fought at Burnt Corn Creek."

Cade nodded.

"It was payback," Gabe said.

"Payback?" Rendel asked.

"Yep," continued Cade. "The Red Sticks were going to take the guns and ammunition to Tukabatchee to fight Big Warrior and all those who mocked Francis and the cause. But after Burnt Corn Creek, they decided to go after Fort Mims. Dixon Bailey was with Caller at Burnt Corn. I know. I was there too." Unconsciously, he rubbed his wound.

"'Course, there weren't ever no love lost 'tween him and Weatherford."

Gabe picked up there. "After I dropped Cade off in the bayou to go to the fort and get Joie, I got captured by some of the Red Sticks and convinced 'em I was there to find Weatherford and join up with them. I did see they had captured some of the women, children, and slaves. Old Interpreter kept me close because he wasn't convinced I was really one of them. I couldn't say who was there, but there are survivors being held captive."

"One of them could be my sister," Cade said fiercely. "I've got to go find those captives and just hope...." Emotion filled his eyes at the thought of what could have happened to his sister. She was a beautiful child and would be a valuable captive with her Kincaid eyes, sky blue, and long, straight black hair. She would look like their mother, whom everyone had said was the most beautiful woman they had ever seen.

"Nicey and Herman were among the first killed," Cade said, swallowing hard. "Their bodies were just inside the gate. Herman still had his gun in his hand, and Nicey was sprawled over him, like she was trying to protect them." He looked into the distance. "Nobody else would have knowed it was them, but I saw Herman's gold tooth. They were both scalped, but Nicey being old as she was...." Moments passed as he saw something beyond the vision of the rest of them. "At least it didn't look like she was raped or brutalized like most of the others."

Cade shut up then, seeing the shocked expressions on the other men's faces. His words hadn't told the half of what he had seen.

Rendel stepped forward and grabbed Cade by the arm. "Those Red Sticks could be headed here! We heard they were supposed to attack Easley's when they attacked Fort Mims," he said. "Let's go get Lyssa and Lance from the village. We'll get you two married as quick as possible just in case there's already a baby planted there." He frowned at Cade. "Then we should go down to Mobile for safety."

Cade froze. A baby. He hadn't thought. Surely just the one time...well, maybe two. The first one didn't count because he was near asleep...or was it three? Gabe took him by the arm.

"Brother, your face has turned white and you look like you're about to pass out. Are you all right?"

Rendel eyed his future son-in-law. And then he turned and stalked toward his stables, shaking his head. "Come on, man. Let's get my daughter."

Jake Rendel looked back over his shoulder at Harry Toulmin and said, "I heard you say you were going back to your plantation at Fort Stoddard, right?"

Toulmin nodded.

"I'll stop by there before we go down to Mobile, if that is all right."

"I'll look for you," Toulmin said. "We may go with you to Mobile."

"Safety in numbers. Will you take Malee to the plantation with you? She'll be safe with you. I will get Lyssa and then we'll all go from there to Mobile. If you don't hear back from me in a few days, go ahead and we'll just meet you there."

"Fine. My wife will be glad for the company."

"If he's determined to go join the war, Lyssa may be difficult," Rendel said, indicating Cade.

Toulmin nodded. "You know your daughter."

Jake Rendel was already bracing himself for the problems he expected with Lyssa.

Cade and Gabriel mounted a pair of Rendel's prize Appaloosa horses. He used them for breeding stock for the Arabians he'd brought from England. As ordered by Zachariah McGirth, Ned stayed in St. Stephens. Rendel stroked Beast's neck as they headed out of town. There was obvious affection between the man and his horse. If horses could purr, this one would have done so. Gabe knew he'd like Jake Rendel. Cade would too, once they got over the jealousy they both felt regarding Lyssa.

They rode silently until they reached the Choctaw village where they had left Lyssa. Although they had not seen scouts along the way, they all knew they had been watched, and word had no doubt reached the village that they were coming. Cade expected to see Lyssa running out to meet him any minute.

He decided to act unmoved. He readied his expression and knew his countenance did not betray the tension and anticipation he felt. He would tell her that he was not ready to be a husband. He willed his Truth Teller to be still. They would refuse to go through with a marriage before Judge Toulmin; instead, they would, as was the custom of their people, renounce the marriage at the Busk celebration and go their separate ways.

It would be so. He was a man. That was as he willed it.

They approached the center of the village toward Pushmataha's cabin, passing many open doors filled with curious people. Chamay had been alerted of their approach and stood at the door of her cabin, awaiting their arrival.

Cade and Rendel expected to see Lyssa peeking out the door.

"I have come for Lyssa," Jake said.

"But she went with you," Chamay said, confusion written on her face.

Cade's heart clenched at her words.

"I left her here with you!" Jake said.

"Pushmataha said she was going back with you, Jake," Chamay said. "He said Cade had gone to Fort Mims...."

They both looked at him accusingly. Their expressions said this was *his* fault.

"No," he protested. "I got in that canoe with Gabe and left her with *you*, Rendel."

Silence. Appalled at what this meant, they all pondered the implications before Chamay spoke.

"At least she has Beauty, and Samson and Delilah must both be with her as well," she said, nearly in tears. She looked up at Pushmataha, imploring him to fix the situation. Cade now knew where Lyssa got her beautiful eyes. Lyssa was supposed to be here! She was supposed to be safe. He was not supposed to care.

Why did he suddenly feel like crying? He told himself to take a deep breath.

Once they stopped trying to blame each other, they realized what had happened. Lyssa—their impulsive, incautious, beautiful, loving, devoted daughter, granddaughter, friend, wife?—had simply, without thinking of the possible consequences, followed the man she loved.

Into hell, Cade thought.

"Oh, God," he groaned, with an agony coming from his soul. The woman he had tried to convince himself he could do without, would cast aside, had made love to, and might now be carrying his child had loved him enough to follow him into what he knew was hell.

He was ashamed.

He was confused.

He was afraid for her. He remembered Savannah Jack and knew the evil that waited on the other side of the river.

Oh, God. Had she made it into the fort before the attack? Had she been killed? Had she been captured? He covered his eyes as if to blot out the images. Was one of those burned and unidentifiable bodies that of the girl so full of life, so full of love, his Lyssa? He swayed in the saddle.

Gabe had his horse sidestep so that he could reach out and support his brother. Even in his own grief, Jake Rendel did not miss Cade's reaction. At Gabriel's touch, Cade quickly regained his outward composure, though the thoughts swirled in his mind. Surely Lyssa would be one of the survivors. She could not have gotten there so soon! Could she have arrived while the attack was going on? Had he walked past her dead body?

Good God Almighty.

She could be one of the captives. Just like Joie. And maybe even that new baby brother he just found out about. They could all be dead, and he hadn't recognized them!

How could he not have realized? Why had he denied it for so long?

He had *always* intended to return for her.

He had fought it with every thought of her. She had lingered in his mind long after he parted from her. And while Gabriel would frequently mention having seen her, Cade refused to speak of her. But Gabriel could tell, Cade knew, that he never interrupted when Gabe told him of her. And he spoke about Lyssa frequently. Only Cade had not believed him when he spoke of how she had grown into a beautiful woman, how skilled she was with her father's horses. But also of how misunderstood she was by her mother's people...and how she had been rejected by her father's world.

She was brilliant. That was a word he learned from the dictionary he now carried. A word he could read because she had taught him. They'd only had a short time together, but her willingness to see the best in him and encourage him had shifted his view of the world at a time when he could easily have lashed out and broken everyone.

She was brave. Braver than many men he had known. She loved him with a love courageous enough to walk into hell...for him. Oh, God, and how he had treated her! She deserved tenderness and soft words. But he had handled her so roughly...his virgin bride. He could not remember the words he spoke, only every touch, every flicker of her hand upon him and his upon her. He remembered the soft, tender love he saw in her amethyst eyes.

He'd looked up words in the dictionary he'd taken to carrying around to describe those eyes he'd remembered so well—amethyst, heliotrope, lavender, violet, wine—but no words could describe those thickly lashed eyes when they looked at him, lingered on him, enveloped him, soothed and thrilled him. So filled with life, with laughter, with indescribable love.

And then he thought of that buzzard plucking at the eyes of his stepmother. Her entrails spread about.

He shut his eyes and covered them, afraid the anguish would turn to tears. Always, he'd known she'd be waiting. But now. What if the world was empty of the one true soul he'd counted on for his tomorrows? He'd fought it. He did not want the responsibility that came with loving someone. But without it life was so empty, a gaping hole that threatened to suck him down.

There was no doubt that her love was wider than any river—she'd crossed it. Bigger than any war—she'd braved it.

The river was flooded with refugees from the Tensaw area. He would question them all. If she and—please, God—Joie were alive, *he would find them.*

Gabe, Cade, and Jake Rendel figured one of those refugees from the 'Bigbee country might know something that would help them find Joie and Lyssa. They were determined to question everyone who might have a clue. Were they dead or alive? Were they captives? Had someone seen them killed? They needed to know where to start looking. Jake Rendel had sent Malee to his friend Harry Toulmin. With refugees arriving all the time, Lyssa could be there! They felt it was logical to go there first.

16

Judge Harry Toulmin's plantation at Fort Stoddard seemed like a good place to begin their search. Since arriving in the Mississippi Territory, Judge Toulmin had become one of Jake Rendel's best friends. Toulmin acted as judge, diplomat, postmaster, and road surveyor. He performed weddings and funerals and practiced medicine. If anyone had acquired the information they needed, it would be Harry Toulmin. They discovered that Toulmin had already removed his family and others, including Malee Rendel, to Mobile. He left a message for Jake to follow them there. Only a few of his slaves remained to operate the plantation with orders to leave at the first whispers of Red Sticks. While they were there, Cade and Gabe found their first survivor of the Red Stick massacre.

Hester was Benjamin Steadham's slave. She had showed up at Fort Stoddard with a severe wound in her breast, battered, bruised, alone, and scared after clinging to a log to cross the river even though she could not swim. When Hester stumbled wet and bedraggled into Fort Stoddard, the slaves at Toulmin's plantation took her in. Hester told them she had prayed her way past water moccasins and alligators that were making their own progress before she at last kicked her log ashore on the west bank of the river.

Bandaged and in pain, the skinny, birdlike woman spoke with graceful hands, waving her pink palms up and down like a butterfly's wings, the brown tops of her strong hands roped with veins that told of her age. Her black eyes were big in her narrow face and rimmed red with crying. She was obviously distraught. She had seen Moses Steadham, her master's father, being cut to pieces while trying to defend his wife Elizabeth and their six daughters, one clinging tightly to Hester. The bullets missed Hester and killed the child. She had seen them all shot dead, and then she had run to the Mims house about the time the building was torched.

"Shot the baby in my arms! Po lil chile," she cried. "She was screamin', cryin' fo her ma and her pa tryin' to pull away and run to dem and der dey lay bleedin' on de groun' with lifeless eyes just starin'! Den all of a sudden she's quiet and I looked at those eyes and dey ain't nothin' der. I laid her on her ma and commenced ta runnin' till I made it to da Mims house. Why didn't dey shoot me?"

It took a long time to calm Hester enough to understand her. Finally, she was able to respond to their questions about Joie. "'Course I know dat girl," she said, her hands still fluttering. "She be Sarilee's bosom chile. Mostly we washed our close in the mo'nin' down by the creek bank. Sarilee stay near the camp to tend to dat woman. Dinah feeds de babe and Joie do mos' ever'thin' else."

"Did you see her leave the fort?" Gabriel asked.

"Naw. Fo I run out o' dat fort, I'se in de Mim's house with Dixon Bailey and his sister Lizzie Fletcher. Den de fightin' started. Miss Lizzie's man, Marse Josiah Fletcher, had been near the gate when they come a runnin' in shoutin' and shootin'. Moses Steadham, he'd just got back to where we's all gettin' ready to ladle out the stew when all hell broke loose. Heard a shoutin' at the gate and red and black devils ran into the fort. Somebody shot three of 'em, but others poured through befo' most could grab they's guns. Then the Red Sticks started shootin' into the fort from the holes in the logs. Folks uz fallin' ever'where. Black folks. White folks. Big folks. Li'l folks." She shook her head.

"Ever' man run to fetch his gun, knockin' over chillen who's playin' and then runnin', fallin', bleedin', all of the time the injuns was shooting. A tomahawk split Miz Lizzie's little girl head in two...lawd, lawd."

She put her head in her hands and pressed her eyes hard, trying to push the memory away. "Miss Lizzie's brother James had grabbed up all the chillens he could and run toward Mim's house. He made it, but was shot in the leg. Then he turned to fight. He din't have time to git his gun and the chillen too. Just had a knife and fought till he's shot full of bullets and fell down dead."

Tears streaked her cheeks, and she dashed them away with the back of her hand.

She looked off into the distance, remembering. "One injun ast Miss Lizzie ifn she uz related to anyone in the fort." Then Hester turned her gaze straight at Gabe and Cade. "He'd a let her go. I knowd it and I knowd she knowd it. At first they only killed the half-breeds and was lettin' others live. But that woman, I'll never forget it...she lifted her chin and pointed to the bloody body of her brother, James, who'd died tryin' to save her baby, and sez 'I am the sister of that great man you have murdered there.'"

They sat for a moment, thinking of the courage of that woman and the horror of her death. Cade paled. Gabe took over the questioning.

Gabe asked, "How did you get out?" But Hester was still reliving the moment.

"Hit was William Steadham, my marse's brother, whut killed Miss Lizzie. I sez 'William!' and he jes looked at me. Soon's he did, Dixon Bailey shot him through the head. Bailey shouted at me to 'get out through the hole while you can!'

"He told Caesar to grab his boy Ralph, who was limp as a dishrag with the sweatin' fever. Caesar grabbed Ralph and carried him through the hole Dixon Bailey'd cut earlier and then Marse Bailey ran out shootin', clearing a path for us. He got shot. Real bad, but Caesar made it out with Ralph. Marse Bailey passed out and Caesar, he don' know what to do, so he turned back around to the fort to turn hisself over to the Red Sticks. They killed po' lil' Ralph. Shot him. Scalped him. I'se too skeert t'stay so I runs fas' as I kin and then I seed this log a floatin' down the river. I figgahs I could drown or git kilt in a way I cain't even put to talk, like I seed 'em do fo' others, and so I waded out and pushed that log into the current and helt onto a leafy branch away from the Tensaw side."

Hester threw her apron over her head and cried.

Gabe patted her awkwardly on the shoulder, thanked her, and prodded Cade to stand up and leave. Words were inadequate. Cade had seen the inside of that fort. Good God. Once again, the thought that these were men he knew overcame him. Who could imagine them as savages? Killing children? Mutilating women?

They found Rendel with horses loaded, ready to leave Fort Stoddard. His green eyes were cold when he looked at Cade, who was still pale. Cade clenched his jaw and he gritted his teeth. He didn't say a word—just seethed—but at last he felt the blood return to his head. Toulmin had already taken Malee Rendel with him to Mobile, so Cade had to put up with traveling with the silently condemning father of his "bride."

"Listen, old man," Cade finally said. Rendel bristled, and his green eyes shot with anger. "I didn't go lookin' for a bride. And I didn't mean for her to follow me. So just quit blamin' me for Lyssa gettin' caught up in all of this. The important thing is findin' her and my sister."

Rendel rode on for miles, chewing on what Kincaid said. Cade Kincaid had turned into a much different kind of man than Jake had imagined he would. That mangy kid he'd seen on the pack train surely did not have much promise. But the boy had filled out. Cade Kincaid, had he been aware of how good-looking he was, could have been dangerous. But from all Jake had seen and heard, the young man had not played the games most young men play. It was almost like those swans he read of that recognized their mates and bonded for life. Lyssa seemed to have known it, and Cade was apparently just coming to the conscious realization of what she meant to him.

Lyssa had always insisted, even as a little girl, that Cade Kincaid was "her" boy.

Rendel watched Cade from the corner of his eye as they rode. With nothing else to occupy him on the miles they traveled, he studied the young man who was now, to all intents and purposes, his son-in-law. Cade was taller than average, perhaps a tad taller than Weatherford, the thoughts of whom made Rendel's heart beat fast and his hand itch for a gun and an opportunity. Cade's long dark hair had escaped the leather binding and lifted in the occasional breeze that drifted up from the river. Muscular, self-possessed, with pale blue eyes that were startling in his sun-browned face, Rendel had to admit he was a handsome man. He would give him that. And he had learned to use those eyes as his own sort of weapon to level on a person and peel away their armor as if he were able to see into a man's mind. Jake had seen him in action with some of the men they'd questioned.

They spent days together tracking down survivors to interrogate. Rendel learned to watch Cade's mouth, the only expressive part of him that could give away emotion. Cade sensed those who had run without fighting, like that man, Sam Matthews, at St. Stephens, the one he and Toulmin were interrogating when Cade and Gabe arrived. Cade had looked at him with eyebrows lifted as if sizing him up, and that sent the little man running. Hester had told them Matthews refused to fight even when Lizzie Bailey had poked him with a bayonet and threatened to shoot him. He'd just pushed his cowardly self through the hole Bailey had cut, nudging others out of the way. When Cade had first seen

Matthews, Rendel had noticed that the right corner of Cade's lip had turned down slightly, betraying his contempt...as if he knew the man was a coward. Jake had asked him later how he had known about Matthews just by looking at him. "It was the *way* he said it," Cade had explained. "Anyone who'd been there would not be *smiling*."

While it was fine for him to do that with others, Rendel did not like being sized up in such an unsettling manner. He guessed he had passed Kincaid's assessment because the younger men had not abandoned him and did defer to him with respect, something that Jake was surprised to realize actually pleased him.

And Cade rode the horse Jake had lent him with more grace than most of the jockeys he'd put on his racehorses. He controlled the horse Indian style, more with his legs, not needing a saddle. Indian boys were taught to guide their horses with their legs so they could handle their weapons and their horses at the same time. The hands that held the reins firmly and with unconscious skill were calloused with hard work—work he'd done for the Pottses if Jake had heard correctly. People who were of the same clan, but not even close blood kin. Just people who had shown him kindness and for whom he bore great affection...enough to risk his life for them.

But Rendel knew Cade had already spent his formative years with his remarkable mother, and perhaps she was the one who had taught him the values that made him, he thought grudgingly, a worthy mate for his daughter. Kincaid had shown his loyalty to his sister and foster parents by risking his life to rescue them. His twin brother, whom Rendel knew had Lyssa's gift of sensing the essence of an individual, be it beast or man, obviously respected Cade and loved him dearly. Their affection was nearly tangible.

Jake had actually thought Gabriel and his Lyssa would have been more suited for each other. He thought Gabe might have liked that himself, but Gabe must have realized early on that Lyssa saw only Cade when he was around. He could be her friend but nothing more. Jake had to accept the fact that he was angry because he had underestimated Lyssa's determination to be with the one she had selected and manipulated to her own advantage. If anyone was to blame for this situation, it was Lyssa herself. And she did it just by being Lyssa—brave, impetuous, impulsive, loving, and faithful. Oh, how he missed her! Since she wasn't there to berate, he berated himself.

"Well," he finally said, out of the blue, "if I don't blame you, I've got to blame me. I have never been so careless with my daughter. That's why she has Samson and Delilah."

Those words hung in the air for a few minutes.

Then Gabe said, "Maybe that ought to make us all a little more hopeful. No one we have talked to has mentioned seeing a bull mastiff. Wouldn't somebody take notice of a dog that big?"

This was the first positive thing anyone had said or thought. They all perked up.

Actually, Cade had preferred seeing Jake Rendel suffer. After all, he had left Lyssa in her father's capable hands! She was safe when he left her. Surely she understood he had to try to do something for his sister, who was just a child. Now he'd never forgive himself for not grabbing Joie up and taking her with him. Only he knew she'd have jumped off to go back for the baby. And then they couldn't have fed the baby without the nurse. And Beasley would probably have strung him up to the pole right along with poor old Jo and lashed him for disobedience. He'd have been tied there and torn limb from limb by the Red Sticks, too. So Beasley had saved his life by sending him to deliver that message. And that still wouldn't have kept Lyssa from following him and arriving right about the time those Red Sticks attacked the fort.

He was back to the beginning.

The closer they came to Mobile, the more the river was flooded with refugees. They came on boats, rafts, and logs. By the time they reached the city, the usual population of 500 had swelled to at least 3,000 as word of the massacre spread throughout the Tensaw area.

The first person they found to talk to was Lieutenant Andrew Montgomery, a member of the Tensaw militia who had commanded Fort Pierce, which was located about three miles south of Fort Mims. At Fort Pierce, the forty soldiers and about 150 settlers had heard the bagpipes and then listened to the sounds of the attack throughout the day.

"We heard the firing and yells of the Indians until after four o'clock in the afternoon when the firing ceased," Lieutenant Montgomery told them. A look of anguish marked his expression. "I wanted to saddle my horse and lead my men to their aid, but I was the commander of Fort

Pierce. We expected them to attack there at any moment. It was impossible to render them any assistance with my small force.

"We were on the alert through the night of August 30. I sent out a patrol on August 31 that returned, reporting that Fort Mims had fallen and the river swamp was full of Indians. There was absolutely no way I could defend Fort Pierce with the number of men I had. So I had to abandon the fort. We could not find any boats. My men said all the canoes along the banks had holes in the bottom. So we waited until dark and then we set out on foot, keeping to the woods. Longest, hardest thirty-five miles I've ever gone, with women with babies scared and not used to walking or going without food for so long."

"You did well, Lieutenant," Rendel said. "I hear you didn't lose anyone in that march."

"It was a miracle," the lieutenant replied. "There were many close calls."

Cade asked, "Did you see any evidence that others might be alive?"

"You're asking about your sister and Rendel's daughter. I've heard about your loss," he said, then took time to pack his corncob pipe with tobacco and take a draw. Slowly he allowed the smoke to escape from around the pipe. He leaned back in the chair and said, "Zachariah McGirth is here looking for his family and told us you'd be here soon. I wish I could say I had some good news for you. I can't say as I do."

Peggy Bailey, Richard and Mary McGillivray Bailey's daughter, gave them the first glimmer of hope. They found her at a rooming house near the river. She had swum across and gotten a boat that she brought back for the women and children who had been on the banks down by the water. She'd guided the boat down to Fort Pierce and then came with Lieutenant Montgomery to Mobile.

"Joie was hiding under a canoe last I saw her," Peggy said. "She wouldn't leave with us. She couldn't leave that baby. So she turned a canoe over and tossed a rock through it and hid herself under the other half of the canoe. She was smart enough to make it unusable and hopefully safer. But so much was happening that I really only took that in while I was pulling those who could fit into the boat back into the current. Many who tried to climb aboard fell bleeding into the water. Most of the militia that escaped is down at the tavern. You'll recognize

Dr. Ephraim Brevard Osborne…he's a tall, skinny, bookish man. Dr. Osborne strapped a little girl to his back and swam down the river."

Ephraim Osborne was indeed easy to spot when they entered the smoke-filled tavern. He was leaning against the bar, staring into his glass of white lightning, when they introduced themselves. As a way of opening the conversation, Gabe said, "Heard you rescued a little girl."

Osborne tossed down the liquid he'd been studying so seriously. "She was wandering around crying in the middle of a bunch of dead women and children when I got to the water," Osborne said. "Couldn't leave her there with the Red Sticks killing everything in sight. Leaving her would have been her death warrant."

Cade said, "Did you see our sister, Joie?"

"No, I had gone down by the river to get some fresh air after helping my brother with the sick in the militia all morning. So many were sick with bloody runs they couldn't get to the outhouse in time. They were lying there, weak and filthy. It took everything we could do just to try and keep them clean. We were exhausted."

"I left my brother Spruce tending to the patients. Lots of people were also sick of the sweatings sickness. Those who had family were being tended by them, but those in the militia were our responsibility. He probably didn't even have a gun close by. I stayed until staying didn't make sense. Couldn't do anything to save him or those in the fort, I told myself. So I grabbed the little girl and headed down river." He covered his eyes.

"I left my brother to die," he said, and turned away to sit alone at a table.

Cade recognized the ostler for the militia, Nehemiah Page, sitting at the wooden table in the far corner of the tavern great room, crouched over a glass of whisky. A big dog lay with his head on the man's foot, lifting his head every now and then for Page to slip him a piece of meat from the bowl of stew that sat to the left of his glass. His body language would discourage all but the most determined. Cade remembered the last time he had seen Page. He was going out of the fort about the time Cade was going in, a man in his early twenties, a happy-go-lucky guy with a broad, open face, pale skin with freckles, and sandy hair that now hung unkempt and stringy down his dirty homespun shirt. Cade pulled out a chair beside him and heard a growl.

"Page," he said. Nehemiah glanced his way through bleary eyes and, recognizing Cade, sat back in the chair.

"Kincaid," he said, unwillingly acknowledging him.

"My brother, Gabe," Cade said, introducing his brother. "We're looking for our sister, Joie, and need to hear your version of what happened at Fort Mims."

Gabe sat opposite Nehemiah Page. They were all quiet for a while. Gabe and Cade both ordered a whisky for themselves.

"Your dog?" Gabe asked.

Page shrugged.

"What do you call him?" Cade pressed.

"Damned Dog," Page said, and the dog lifted his head. "Damned Dog nearly got me killed!"

Then Page started talking. "I drank too much the night before the attack, and I thought my head was gonna bust wide open. Soon's formation was over, I headed out of the fort to tend and feed the horses. Didn't I see you comin' in about that time, Kincaid?"

Cade nodded. "Beasley sent me off with his report not long after."

Page grimaced and continued, "Soon's I did what I had to do with the horses, I lay down on the feed and went to sleep. 'Bout noon I heard a poundin'. The earth was vibratin'! I peeked through the boards of the barn. Hundreds of Red Skins ran past, wavin' their war clubs and shootin' at anything that moved. I crawled under the straw and stayed where I was. Damned Dog was runnin' after them like they was all playin' some kind of game or somethin', but soon's he saw me peekin' through the boards of the barn he started barkin' and waggin' his tail like I was somebody he'd been lookin' for. I was damned lucky they were focused on what was goin' inside that fort. They warnt no guns in the barn, and I sure as hell wasn't gonna try to make it back to the fort. I saw that crazy prophet runnin' around the fort shoutin' and shakin'.

"'Bout the middle of the afternoon, the Red Sticks retreated for a while, and I ran hell for leather for the swamps. Damned Dog followed me ever' step of the way." The dog looked up again, and Page slipped him another piece of stew.

"I hid in the woods for a while and then finally decided to take my chances in the river. Damned Dog jumped in with me. He'd get tired and climb onto my back. Near drowned me a couple of times. I finally made it to the other side and damned if the Damned Dog didn't follow me every step of the way here! He goes ever'where I go. Damndest thing!"

He retreated into silence, mulling over the memories. The dog sat up and laid his head on Page's lap, looking soulfully into his eyes. Page, showing unconscious affection, reached down and scratched behind his long, floppy ear.

"Did see somethin' funny, though," he finally said. "Damned Dog started barkin' a little ways out. Scared the shit out of me thinkin' he was gonna attract the attention of some of those crazy Injuns. Saw the biggest dog I ever seed. Just glimpsed it. Didn't look back. The log I was holdin' floated on, and I was lookin' for Red Sticks with guns. Didn't think about that till just then."

At the mention of the big dog, Cade and Gabe sat straight up in their chairs. Lyssa had been there that afternoon. "Oh, God," Cade whispered. His hand shook as he tried to raise the glass to his lips, but he wound up spilling most of the precious liquid on the table. He couldn't believe she had gotten to the fort in time to face the worst of the Red Stick attack.

Page lifted his glass to Cade. "Maybe with enough of this, I'll forget what I saw."

Gabe reached out and grabbed the man's hand. "Did you see our sister Joie or a real pretty girl with black hair and blue eyes with that big dog?"

"Hell, man. I told you what I seen!" His eyes got bleary trying to focus. He curled his lips and said, "Your pa, he's one mean son of a bitch."

"Tell us something we don't know," Cade said.

"But that wife of his…." He let his words hang there as the meaning sank in.

"Yeah," Cade pressed, "but we're askin' about Joie."

"Don't know. Didn't see her. I was too busy savin' my own worthless hide." With that, he tossed the remaining liquid down his throat and tears came to his eyes…with the liquor or the guilt, they couldn't tell.

Both Cade and Gabriel understood. They had all survived. Now they felt the guilt of that accomplishment. In their eyes, so many better men had died.

"It don't seem fair," said Nehemiah Page. He didn't have to articulate his thought any better; they all shared the feeling.

Cade turned to find another man at the adjoining table listening to their conversation. "And you are?" he asked.

"I'm Sam Smith," said the haggard, middle-aged man, who was already deep in his cups. "One of the few to escape. The Injuns retreated for about two hours, and Dixon Bailey gathered the women and children in the Mims root cellar. About eleven of us cut through the pickets and broke through the enclosure just as the injuns returned. Those damned Spanish had begged for their lives, telling them there was treasure buried in the fort, I heard one of the Injuns say. Damned lie far as I know, but it brought them back to find out if the damned Spaniards was telling the truth. Made them madder than hell when they didn't find anything."

Like so many of the others had done, he covered his eyes as if that would hide his memories. "They set fire to everything that hadn't already burned. The women and children in the root cellar musta got burned alive. I can still hear their cries!" Tears filled his eyes and spilled down his bearded face. "I made it through the hole in the pickets and into the swamps. We swam across".

The man sitting with him draped his arm across Smith's shoulders and said, "Smith here saved my life. He shot a Red Stick who was all set to hit me over the head with his tomahawk. Shot him and dragged me with him to the swamp." He gulped as he swallowed a drink of his own amber liquid. "Name's Stubblefield. I saw Joie leave the fort that morning following a bunch of women. Can't say I saw her after that. Sorry."

"Did you see the dog? Or a woman on a horse?"

"Saw one woman on a horse. That real pretty blonde girl, Betsy Hoven, came through the fence close behind us and spotted a horse runnin' loose. She grabbed the horse's mane and jumped up. She rode it past her brother, John, reached down and grabbed his hand as she rode past, and they both made it to the swamps," Stubblefield said. He spoke about her as if all the men knew Betsy. "Shore glad that pretty hair ain't on some Red Stick war club."

There were survivors! They were talking to them. Cade and Gabriel felt that they were accomplishing something as they developed a time line of events. Lyssa was at the fort sometime after the Red Sticks set fire to everything. But was she alive now?

Martin Rigdon, the militia drummer who had sounded the call at noon in the fort, pushed through the tavern door, ordered a whisky from the bar, and sat next to Nehemiah Page. He was in about the same shape as Page but had a bandage over his chest, a black eye, and an oozing scrape where a bullet had grazed his scalp.

"Rigdon," Cade said, acknowledging the drummer, a young man of medium height and slim build, his face still downy with whiskers that barely needed scraping. Everyone knew what a talented family the Rigdons were, and Beasley had actually written a request to General Claiborne to get a drum for Rigdon to play.

"They were waiting for the noon call to mess, I guess," Ridgon said. "I started playing the drum for the meal. That was when I felt the ground begin to shake. I looked out that east gate and there they were. As they made the gate, a loud whooping and hollering began. Beasley'd been doing some drinking, but soon's he realized what was happening, he ran to the gate to try to shut it. Too late. Four Red Sticks came through first, and three got shot. Others followed close behind. They sure had the advantage of surprise. Few men had their guns handy. Soon as they got their guns, the Red Sticks had taken command of the portholes and had proceeded through the fort, killing everything and everybody they could shoot. They got me first off. I was unconscious through most of the shooting, I guess. When I woke up, they were just leaving the fort. I pretended to be unconscious until they left, and then I crawled out of the fort and into the woods. I was passing in and out of consciousness."

He tossed back the whisky and indicated to the bartender to bring him another. "I should have stayed and fought. Should have tried to help others to get out."

He paused.

"When I finally woke up, it was dark as Hades, and the fort was shooting flames...and there was dead silence."

The barkeep brought another whisky. Cade and Gabe ordered more, too. Rigdon tossed his down. And then, with agony in his eyes, he whispered as much to himself as to them, "My mother and father and brother and sisters all died there that day. They'd come out to be with us, my brother and me. Maybe I could have saved them if I hadn't been such a damned coward."

After finishing their second drinks, Cade and Gabe stood to leave. They started for the door, but Gabe turned back.

"You were hit, Rigdon. Don't you think they'd want *somebody* from their family to survive?" Gabe said, attempting to comfort the man in his terrible agony.

By the time they left the tavern, both Cade and Gabe were staggering. They had shared their guilt with others who had lost family at Fort Mims and spent a maudlin afternoon. When they finally headed down the street toward the river, they literally bumped into Jake Rendel.

"Find out anything?" Jake asked, stepping back when Cade breathed on him.

Cade put his hand over his eyes and whispered, "I've let them both down. I couldn't find Joie, and now I've lost Pipsqueak."

There was no reason for him to linger here. He had Red Sticks to fight. He would find Zachariah McGirth, and together they would search to find those they could not admit to being dead. And if in the process they might also be killed, so be it. If Lyssa was dead, what would be the point of living, anyway?

"Soon as I find Zach McGriff, I'm headin' out to shoot some Red Sticks," he said, looking at Gabe. "And I hope I get Billy Weatherford in my sights. If I do, he's a dead man."

"Let's just hope Savannah Jack don't get us first," Gabe said, his amber eyes glinting with determination. "You ain't leavin' me behind."

As they stood there, others began to gather around.

Peter Randon, lieutenant of Citizens' Company of the Tensaw militia who'd been an officer at Fort Mims, asked them to give him time to let Dr. Thomas Holmes, assistant surgeon of the garrison who had escaped with them unwounded, tend to his wounds. He wanted to ride with them. His sister, Mary Louisa Randon Tait, and her little girls, along with his father John, John's wife Tura, his other sisters and brothers, and his uncle James had been killed in that damned massacre. Peter Randon's niece, Viney, survived only because she'd been picking muscadine on Nanahubba Island with Peter Durant when the attack occurred. Peter's family in the fort was wiped out as well. Cade and

Gabe followed him into the hotel where one of the bottom floor rooms had become a makeshift hospital.

Many other survivors had gathered there. Socca, a friendly Indian; Mourrice and Joseph Perry of the Mississippi volunteers; a man named Jones; Lieutenant W. R. Chambliss, also of the Mississippi volunteers; and Josiah Fletcher. Fletcher was by the east gate when the attack started. "Beasley had just ordered me to take my family from the fort by ten o'clock the next morning," he told them. "Oh, God, do I wish he'd ordered me out of the fort the day before. We'd have all been safe away from that hellhole. Why did *I* survive? Why did my brave Elizabeth and our children have to die?"

They didn't have the courage to ask him how he escaped or to tell him what Hester had said about his wife's bravery. The man was too distraught. He was wounded and bleeding and waiting his turn for Dr. Holmes's attention. He couldn't drink enough whisky to dull the pain of his own worthless scalp being intact while his Lizzie lay scalped and mutilated within the fort.

William Randon Hollinger, who had been raised by Davy Tait, told them that he saw Davy's brother William Weatherford lead the attack into the fort. Hollinger had actually witnessed his own wife and daughters murdered and mutilated. He was fighting hand to hand, trying to protect them, when he had seen them killed. Only then did he dive through the hole that he and Bailey had cut for their last-chance escape just as a tomahawk plunged into the wall behind him. He said Fletcher had followed him through after seeing Lizzie killed when she made her valiant declaration of loyalty about her brother.

Hollinger had bought himself a new gun and plenty of ammunition. "I'm joining Andrew Jackson," he said. "I hear he's bringing an army from Tennessee."

Jesse and Edward Steadham, who had lost thirteen family members at Fort Mims, would not be left behind, despite exhaustion and injuries.

"Our cousin William was with the Red Sticks," Jesse said, sick at heart. "I don't know his fate, but if I see him I will shoot him down myself!"

"Hester told us Dixon Bailey beat you to it," Gabe said.

"Does anyone know what happened to Betsy Hoven?" Edward Steadham asked.

"A man named Stubblefield said he saw her escape on a horse with her brother, John," Cade said.

"Thank God." At least some others had survived.

When they finally found the area where the assistant surgeon for Fort Mims, Dr. Thomas G. Holmes, had set up shop, he told them he had escaped from the burning fort and survived by hiding in a clay hole by the roots of a fallen tree. He saw Dixon Bailey get mortally wounded after he had helped him through the hole they had cut in the pickets.

"Dixon's man was carrying Ralph but turned back. Dixon cried out for him to come back, but the slave was determined to turn himself in to the Red Sticks and save his own hide. Dixon jerked from my arms and tried to follow, but he dropped dead along the way. There were Red Sticks stationed all around the perimeter to shoot those who tried to escape. I made it into a clay hole and hid out. I thought they'd hear my heart beating I was so damned scared!"

Apparently, Gabriel had distracted Old Interpreter away from Dr. Holmes and probably saved his life. Holmes had then wandered through the wilderness for nine days before being found by a friendly settler and brought to Mobile.

Cade knew details about Holmes that were not common knowledge from Nicey's gossip, though he had also seen him at several gatherings at Sam Mims's house in its glory days. Holmes was descended from George Galphin, an Indian trader who had made his outpost on the Silver Bluffs of South Carolina. He had once boasted to Nicey and Herman that his grandfather, the wealthy Galphin, had loaned Congress twenty thousand dollars towards equipping the fleet of John Paul Jones. Nicey had told Cade that Galphin's quadroon second wife was the illegitimate daughter of Moses Nunes, a wealthy Jewish merchant, and an Indian woman. Their daughter had married John Holmes, an Irishman who had worked with Galphin in the fur trade. This woman and John were Thomas's parents.

"We're glad you're here, Dr. Holmes," Cade said.

"I decided against joining Jackson, figuring I was needed in Mobile. There are so many wounded and ill!"

And then he recognized Gabe.

"You were with the Red Sticks," Dr. Holmes said accusingly, glancing up from wrapping Ned Steadham's head wound. Disbelief and anger flared in his eyes. If his hands hadn't been occupied, he'd have taken a swing at Gabe.

Cade stepped between Holmes and Gabriel. "Did you see him shoot anyone?"

"No," Holmes said. "But I was in the woods hiding in the roots of a tree."

"Oh, you're the one," Gabe said. "Then you saw me draw Old Interpreter away from where you were hiding, didn't you?"

Holmes looked confused but unconvinced.

Cade drew closer to the doctor. "We're looking for our sister Joie and a woman named Lyssa Rendel. Did you see them?"

"I saw only one other woman escape besides Betsy Hoven. Susan Hatterway, Henry's wife. She took Peter Randon's sister Elizabeth and a little slave girl by the hand and simply walked with them out the gate with the Red Stick I knew as Dog Warrior. One of the Cornells, I think."

It was something, anyway. Another of Peter Randon's relatives survived, though she was now being held by the Red Sticks.

Cade saw the doubt gather in the others' eyes as they studied Gabe. Cade could tell they were wondering if they could trust him. When Edward Steadham's eyes glittered wildly and he reached for his gun, Cade grabbed Gabe by the arm and pulled him out of the doctor's room. These people were beyond rational.

And Cade understood. He also wanted to shoot somebody!

"You can't go with us, Gabe," Cade said, leading his brother down the street to the hotel where Rendel and Toulmin had found accommodations for their wives. "They saw me leave the fort, so they're sure which side I was on. Holmes saw you painted for war. You wouldn't be safe. It's better if you go with Rendel. He's going to be searching through the countryside while I go with the army to see if they were captured. They may not be together, and we've got to divide up and cover more ground."

Cade explained the change in plans to Jake Rendel, who nodded and said, "I welcome Gabe and need his help in following whatever lead we can gather. What do you suggest?"

"Stubblefield said he saw a big dog. If we can find prints, perhaps they will lead us to Lyssa."

Gabe shrugged helplessly. "I want to go with you, Cade. Yet once again we must part, brother. Even though we shared the same womb, our blood shows differently in our appearance. The color of our skin has marked our destiny. I will do as you say, though I also wish to take up the gun and take vengeance."

Cade said, "Watch your back, brother. Savannah Jack is still out there, and his war is as much with us as with anyone else."

Gabe nodded and lifted his hand as Cade set off to rejoin the militia and find Jackson's troops to fight the Red Sticks.

17

Lyssa knew the time had come to leave the hollow that had been so secure. It had been their haven in the middle of a mad, mad world.

But today, dressed in her deerskin and moccasins, she had to find food. The Red Sticks had shot all of the livestock within their vicinity, and the meat rotted where it fell. The vegetables from the already-planted gardens had served them well. They and the animals had subsisted on corn, squash, beans, peppers, sweet potatoes, yams, and peanuts that appeared in those gardens, but now the season neared its end. Food was scarce—even acorns had been picked over—and there were days when she returned home nearly empty handed. Her children were hungry.

Keeping to the tree line and walking carefully to leave no tracks, Lyssa set out early. She must go further today to find a garden she had not already scavenged. She crawled to the top of a ridge and peeked down carefully. The air had cooled and the leaves were dropping, so their haven would soon be revealed to anyone riding the ridge above their hollow. She knew the danger remained. Today on her foraging foray, she had left Samson *and* Delilah behind with the children and Joie.

Godfrey had nearly regained his strength and was determined to assert his manly responsibilities, which Lyssa feared would put them all in greater danger. Godfrey had no concept of how his good intentions and obvious affection for her could actually endanger them all. The spoiled, pampered, scholarly boy who was so determined to experience an adventure was totally unprepared to be on his own alone in the wilderness. He had no idea of how to survive in the forest. One day of his tromping about through the soft red clay and there would be a trail directly to the place where they now were safe and secure.

But now the object at hand was gathering food to fill the empty, growling bellies of those who depended on her, to her constant amazement. With her bow on her back and a quiver of arrows attached to a belt at her waist, Lyssa inched forward.

Suddenly she noticed the stillness about her. While she had been lost in thought, something had silenced nature's sounds—a gopher had scurried into his hole, the birds had scattered, and the bushy-tailed fox squirrel had gone to nest in the longleaf pine. Even the crickets had suddenly quieted.

She hunkered down on a straw-covered hillock and listened. A twig crackled close by, and the hairs on the back of her neck stood on end. Slowly she turned her head and looked behind her.

A man's moccasins.

Oh, God.

Her eyes traveled to the breechclout and then further up to a raised tomahawk and recognition. She fainted.

Lyssa awoke to find herself in Savannah Jack's arms, riding through the clearing in front of the charred remains of Fort Mims. Another man, nearly as frightening, rode beside them. Her heart pounded, and she forced herself not to panic and scream. She had a baby to protect. Think, Lyssa. Had he brought her here to kill her? Why had he not gotten it over with when he found her?

Her sudden gasp got his attention, and he said, "Why are you alone, little mother?"

Lyssa blushed. His words brought about the realization that he had inspected her body in order to come to that conclusion, and her pregnancy had possibly saved her from being raped. Fortunately, her clothing and weapons were traditional Indian fashion.

She said the first thing she could think of in the dialect he used. "I followed my man and found him dead where his Red Stick friends left him in the cornfield." Such a statement made the tears of fright in her eyes seem justified.

"Your man was from which village?" he asked in a voice that rumbled ominously.

Lyssa remembered what she had heard about the villages that had taken the talk and said, "Tallusahatchee."

"We are going there ourselves. That is near the place our prophets have prepared as a safe haven. We will take you home."

The nanny goat bleated in the distance. Lyssa held her breath. She'd been careful to obscure her tracks. Let them take her, but she would do what was necessary to keep the men from finding the children. The two men halted abruptly, listening, and said, "Goat meat next time we come this way."

Now that she was awake, Savannah Jack put Lyssa behind him to ride the Appaloosa that looked amazingly like one that had been stolen from her father's stables. Savannah Jack's fiercely scarred face, shaved head, and cropped ears were just as frightening as she had been told, but apparently he believed her story. If he had any idea she was connected to Cade Kincaid, she had no doubt he would have killed her. Her Indian clothing had saved her life.

But what about the children? If she escaped, she knew Savannah Jack and his companion would follow her, believing from her actions that she had lied about being from Tallusahatchee. Otherwise, they would figure, she would have been glad to go with them to that town. She had to play it smart to stay alive. Her bare legs suddenly touched his, the man she knew hated whites in general and Cade specifically. That happened only once. She must not tempt him. She schooled herself not to move or let her face show her disgust.

"You ride much," Jack said after about an hour. "Your grip is strong."

His companion guffawed and gave a lewd gesture.

"Your man is dead," Jack said.

Lyssa knew immediately what he was thinking and slumped, pretending grief. "I carry my man's child," she said with pride. "He was a warrior. He must live on." Then she told Savannah Jack her name was Little Flower, her grandfather's pet name for her, and tried to remember to answer to it.

When they stopped for the night, Lyssa carried out the woman's jobs she had learned from her grandmother. Her grandmother had taken her with them when she followed Pushmataha on their hunting expeditions so that she would know how to perform the expected duties. Lyssa kept her head down and modestly prepared the meal, frying up cakes of ground corn and honey from the supplies Savannah Jack carried. She shook so badly that she could barely hold her pans.

The men licked their fingers with appreciation of her skills. Lyssa straightened the camp and then lay quietly beside the fire with her eyes closed, all the while aware of their watchful eyes. She sensed that Savannah Jack was not completely sure of her story and waited to catch her in the lie. His companion merely followed Savannah Jack's lead. That man had a strange look about him, and Lyssa wondered if he was right in the head. Jack's eyes shone bright with cunning intelligence, but the man he called Blue had no thoughts but food and sex, and it did not take a woman to satisfy his needs, as his actions on the other side of the fire made evident. He watched her, licking his lips as he performed his act. She'd gathered from his and Savannah Jack's few conversations—now arguments—that his name, Blue, came from what happened to him from performing those actions in the middle of the night. She was too afraid of them to turn her back to the fire.

Savannah Jack, his eyes glittering menacingly in the firelight, merely watched her discomfort, ignoring Blue's moans, and honed the knife with which he would slit her throat. She imagined her scalp could easily join the collection he wore tied to his breechclout. She did not allow herself to speculate on whose scalps hung from his belt. All it would take was one false word as she slept. As long as they thought she was one of them, she figured she was safe. If they knew the child she bore was Cade Kincaid's, she was certain that she and her child would not survive. She had to rely on her wits. And she must get as far away from the children as possible. That was all she could do to protect them. Though her mind raced trying to figure out ways to return to them, she knew she could not do so without bringing the wolves straight to her little sheep. But that night she could not sleep, worried about where they would find food. Would they expose themselves searching for her and be killed? Had they learned anything from her example?

She lay stiffly, restraining herself from running into the night to those she knew were calling for her, though miles prevented her from hearing their voices. Mo and Meme would not understand. Godfrey would go searching for her. Sister and Ben would be bewildered but would try to be brave, and Joie—well, even as young as she was, Joie was Lyssa's hope that they would survive.

She tried not to think of what she would do when they arrived at Tallusahatchee and no one knew her.

When Lyssa did not return by nightfall, Joie and Godfrey knew something bad had happened. They had no idea of where to start looking for her. But first things first. They had hungry babies to feed. Joie had checked the traps closest to the hollow and found nothing. She ventured out as she had watched Lyssa do, attempting to cover her tracks as she walked. Unfortunately, Samson followed her every step, so even when she covered her tracks, Samson's remained. Lyssa had told the dog to stay with Joie. He was obedient to Lyssa's command in spite of Joie's pleas that he remain in the hollow.

"Go back, Samson!" she said.

Samson cocked his head. Joie stepped forward. Samson picked his big self up and took a step forward. It was hopeless. The dog would do as Lyssa had commanded until Lyssa commanded differently. So together they foraged close to the cabin and found little.

Fortunately, the goat still gave milk, and there was sofkee in the pot that Lyssa had made that morning. But what about tomorrow?

Joie knew she couldn't leave Godfrey alone with the babies for long. They loved him, and he would hold them, but if one of them threw up or wet on him, his reaction really was funny to watch. He'd gag and choke, toss the child to her, and run to throw up. He'd come back mortified and red faced, every freckle popping.

Joie returned to the cabin to find Godfrey standing on the ridge above the hollow, anxiously watching for her. Night was falling.

"The babies are asleep and Ben will whistle if he needs me," he said in answer to her angry look. "Don't you do that to me again," he added. "I was standing there trying to figure out which way to go look for you if you did not come back! How would I find you if you got hurt?"

Then, to cover his concern for Joie, he said, "Tomorrow I'll go out and you can take care of the children. I'd rather get scalped by the Red Sticks than go through what I went through today."

Joie smiled to herself at what he had given away. For a moment there, she had really thought he cared about her. She gathered the bark they used for plates and divided all the sofkee they had left. "Feed the baby," she said to Godfrey, handing him the gourd.

Godfrey's face paled. He threw his hands in the air and said, "Please don't make me do that. You know what happens. You feed him. Then he burps and poops. I can't take it!"

Jay looked up from Joie's arms into Godfrey's eyes and laughed. Godfrey froze and said, "He couldn't have known what I said, could he?"

"No, he just likes you," Joie said. "Listen, you either feed him or help the other children…it's your choice. By the way, thanks for milking the goat."

"It wasn't me," Godfrey assured her. "It was Ben."

Ben ducked his head.

"He's obviously done it before," Joie said. "I guess he had little sisters or brothers."

Godfrey nodded. Their thoughts did not need to be spoken. Both wondered what had happened to the families of the ones they cared for. They dared not ask. The trauma in each of the children was too great to relive. And now the one they had looked to for courage and care had not returned, and all were worried. Each imagined the worst they had seen, and that was about as bad as it gets.

Godfrey took the baby and managed with great concentration. He was even able to clean up J.J., but when the baby burped on Godfrey's bare chest, Godfrey ran for the bushes.

"You're a brave man, Godfrey Lewis Winkel," Joie said, her exhaustion and hopelessness evident in each syllable.

Godfrey sagged against the doorframe. He did not miss the sarcasm in her voice and did not want her to know how much her low opinion wounded him. He did not want her to know he cared.

After they fed the children, they sat staring into the darkness as the younger ones reacted to Lyssa's absence in their own ways—silence, tears, and clinging—until at last they fell asleep. Joie had given the children as much comfort as she could and now lay holding J.J., with Meme on one side and Mo holding tightly to her on the other.

They never even heard the horses enter their hollow the next morning following Godfrey's footprints.

Joie awoke, suddenly aware. Someone big stood above her, and her scream awoke the entire group. Mo and Meme started crying and screaming and climbing all over her to get away from the scary man. And then more men entered their little cabin. Sister and Ben moved closer. Godfrey jumped to a crouch in front of them to protect them all, something that registered and amazed Joie even while she fought to sit up with the babies clinging to her. As soon as she lifted her Kincaid blue eyes to the man in front of her, he recognized her.

"Joie?" he said. "It's Gabe, Joie. I'm your brother."

Joie extricated herself from the crawling babies and, still holding her infant brother, launched herself into Gabe's arms. The toddlers followed, and soon Gabe had trouble standing with all the arms that embraced him. Jake Rendel could hardly keep from laughing at Gabe's discomfort. Joie thrust a peeing, obviously male, infant into Gabe's arms and said, "Meet your brother, Gabe. This is J.J., and we couldn't be happier to see you!"

Gabe tucked the baby under one arm and embraced Joie with the other. Godfrey now stood looking very much confused, his red hair tousled and wild.

"Have you seen my daughter, Lyssa Rendel?" Jake asked. Then remembering, he added, "Kincaid."

Tears filled Joie's eyes and she said, "She went hunting yesterday and hasn't returned. She's the reason we're all still alive."

Jake Rendel's face blanched. "I want to hear it all," he said.

"Wait. I'll set a guard," Gabe said. After giving the command, he sat cross-legged on the dirt floor holding his newfound brother. But his eyes focused completely on Joie as she related how they had come to be there and how they had searched for Lyssa to no avail. Godfrey Lewis Winkel nodded throughout Joie's tale, interjecting a comment now and then.

"We saw footprints and followed them here," Jake said.

Godfrey blushed. He had thought he was being so careful!

"Lyssa wouldn't let us leave the hollow because she was afraid our footprints would lead the Red Sticks to us," Joie said. "She was right. We were very lucky it was you and not them that found us!"

"She saved us all," Godfrey said. "If she could have come back, she would have. I am afraid she has been killed or captured by some of those Red Sticks who have kept returning, killing the livestock and raiding the abandoned homesteads."

Godfrey's clipped accent and cultured tones seemed out of place in the primitive surroundings. Gabe could not help noticing how the skinny boy with the wild hair watched Joie and how protectively he had stood before her and the children. There was more to him than one would guess by looking at his pale, freckled face and scrawny body.

"Now," said Joie. "Tell us how you found us. We've been here for months."

"We heard a goat bleat just as we were riding over the ridge above the cabin," Jake told them. "Gabe said he thought he smelled a fire. It was twilight and dark was falling, so we built a camp on the ridge. When dawn came, we followed some footprints, looked down into the hollow, and saw that goat in the makeshift pen." Godfrey hung his head at Joie's lifted eyebrow.

"Lyssa said we'd have to move," Joie said. "The leaves on the trees kept us hidden, and now they've fallen...." Her voice trailed off, and her eyes brimmed with tears again.

"We'll find her, Little Sister."

"*I'm* Sister," said the little girl who sat as if glued to Joie's right side.

"Yes," said Joie. "Forgive me for not introducing you. This is Sister."

"Is he our brother?" the child asked, lifting her hopeful green eyes to Gabe. This was a big man. He looked strong. He looked safe.

Joie had had never heard the child say so much at one time. She waited for Gabe to answer.

"Looks like the family keeps growing," Gabe said with only a moment's hesitation.

The little girl walked closer and framed his face in her two hands. She looked intently into his eyes. Then she walked back and sat next to Joie. "We'll keep him," she said matter-of-factly.

Joie lifted her eyebrow at Gabe, who smiled back at her. "Sister thinks all of us are her family." She indicated the brood around her.

Gabe nodded. "I guess we are. As far as we know, all the rest of our families were killed at Fort Mims. But still we're missing Cade and Lyssa."

Joie leaned forward and told Gabe, "Find her. She is your sister now as well."

Jake Rendel, though thrilled to find Joie alive, was chilled with the thought that a raiding party might have captured his daughter. He had heard what happened to those they chose to kill, and the thought of Lyssa's scalp hanging from some brave's belt terrified him.

"I am Lyssa's father. I will find her. Your brother Cade has joined the army to track Red Sticks and see if you and she might be among the captives."

"She was here. With us. Until yesterday morning. She wasn't captured at Fort Mims. You must start here and find her!" Joie insisted.

Mo and Meme started crying again. "Issie. Want Issie!"

Sister sniffed. Soon she took up the cry. "Find Issie! Pease!"

Ben just stuck his finger in his mouth and let the tears trickle down his flushed cheeks.

Godfrey stood up. "I shall go with you to find Lyssa."

Jay spit up again. Godfrey turned pale and swallowed hard. He planted his feet and refused to run outside.

"First things first," Gabe said. "We've got to get these little ones to safety."

Jake looked around, reluctantly coming to a conclusion. "There are not enough of us to split up and still be a strong enough party to defend the children. This place is no longer safe."

"We've got to take them to Pushmataha's town," Gabe said. "They'll be safe there. There's too much confusion and disease in Mobile. And all the settlers have cleared out in between."

Jake nodded. It would take precious time away from his search for Lyssa, but it was the only way to get them all to safety. Lyssa had risked her life to save theirs. He would honor her by keeping them safe.

18

"Today is November 9, 1813," remarked Cade's new friend, David Crockett, a scout with Andrew Jackson.

"And?" Cade questioned.

"Just like to keep up with the date. Remind myself so's I don't get lost in time."

Cade nodded. He had last seen Lyssa last on August 29. The massacre at Fort Mims happened on August 30. Word had come recently that Tecumseh had been killed on October 5 by a soldier under the command of General William Henry Harrison at the Battle of the Thames. While it seemed that Tecumseh had ignited the flame that finally became this bloody war, the tinder had already been laid over many years, he supposed. Perhaps it would all end for him today, he thought with resignation.

He slapped at a fly. Still hot as hell in November. Still no sign of Lyssa or Joie.

Cade had joined Zachariah McGirth in scouting for the militia. But when Zach had gone to deliver a message from General Coffee to Benjamin Hawkins, Cade had joined up with Jackson's scout, Davy Crockett. Together they would track down where the Red Sticks had gathered.

They had found a hornet's nest at Tallussahatchee. There appeared to be about two hundred gunmen in the village. After they reported back, Jackson ordered an attack. It was now just a little over two months since the massacre at Fort Mims. Wounds were still raw with the memory of how brutally the inhabitants of that fort were killed. Jackson kept the memory alive in the minds of his troops. It was what he fed them in place of bread and meat, which they had little of. In response, Jackson's troops were near mutiny. He needed a battle to keep them from abandoning the fight and going home.

Cade and Davy climbed the rise with Lieutenant Colonel Leroy Hammond's Rangers in the gray dawn of the new day and approached the sleeping Creek village of Tallussahatchee. One thousand cavalrymen under John Coffee gathered on the hills around the village.

"At least two hundred Red Stick Warriors in that village," Davy told Cade.

Cade's blood boiled at the memory of what he had seen at Fort Mims. He thought of Lyssa and how beautiful and full of life she had been the last time he had seen her. He remembered how her eyes grew hot with the passion he knew she saw in his own face, no matter how hard he had tried to deny it.

Joie's sweet face also flashed through his mind. She had so much life yet to live! She had been so brave in her determination to protect that baby, their brother. Now, both probably lay among the charred remains of the massacre back at Fort Mims.

These Red Sticks would pay.

Hammond ordered the attack. Smoke rose as guns were fired. Bullets pierced through the earthen cabins in the village. Men spilled from their doors, shooting back with a few guns and many bows, their ammunition having been sorely depleted.

Hammond's men were tired and hungry from the long march on half rations, but their hunger was soon forgotten in the battle, and a massacre quickly ensued in retribution for Fort Mims. The cry "Remember Mims" rang out above the fray each time the shooting faltered. The cavalry soon had the Red Sticks closed in on all sides, and the warriors retreated into the village.

Smoke filled the air, and the report of guns firing thundered throughout the encampment.

Cade shot furiously, killing Red Sticks, shooting them in the back as they retreated, his mind crazy with the thought that each could have been the man who murdered his sister or raped his Lyssa.

Then, through the carnage in that crazy montage of ruthless images—the furious visage of the warriors on both sides, the agonizing death mask of the dead, and the cries and groans of the stricken and dying—he realized there were women and children running from the doors of their cabins to gather their dying husbands, sons, and brothers in their arms. And where they sat cradling their loved one, the madness of war claimed them victim as well! Weaponless as they were, the bullets of the militiamen picked them off one after another.

Cade watched as a small boy child ran after his mother, who cradled her beloved and shrieked her grief. The child looked directly at

Cade with fear in his eyes; yet he stood before his mother as if to shield her.

A memory...elusive...one of nightmares...

And then a bullet struck the boy between the eyes, and his head shattered like a melon in target practice.

Dear God.

Suddenly, as if the bullet had pierced his own brain, he felt a pain so sharp that he grabbed his head and spun around in the middle of the battle. He stumbled over a dog whose tail lifted in a weak greeting, and Cade watched as the dog's eyes grew dim and the life force left him. The shooting had now become a flagrant massacre of all living things.

"Cade!" Crockett called. "Are you hit?" The battle raged as Crockett looked back.

Cade could not respond.

Not the women! Not the children! Regardless of his earlier need for vengeance, Cade was sickened by the callous disregard that had so disgusted him at Fort Mims.

"They're shooting them down like dogs!" Crockett shouted.

Cade stood in shock as he watched a large number of warriors gather in a single hut. One woman, middle-aged with graying hair, gesturing to one he took to be her son, sat boldly outside guarding the hut, a bow and arrow her only weapon. Surely they would surrender now. But the woman looked at them with contempt, and bracing the bow against her leg, she let loose a single arrow that struck a man named Moore who stood near Cade and Davy, killing him instantly. The enraged army set fire to the hut, and the woman ran into it as soon as her son ran past. The flames blazed higher. The fire burned hotter than any Cade had ever seen. Strangely, a smell oddly like potatoes baking filled the air.

When the shooting ceased because there was nothing living left to shoot, with even the dogs lying dead among the men, women, and children, Andrew Jackson cantered into the village. One man searching for treasure among the smoldering embers for treasure brought out a potato fried in the oils of the Red Sticks who had sought refuge in that last earthen cabin.

"Potatoes seasoned with Red Skins," the man shouted with a gap-toothed grin.

The hungry men surged forward, shifting the charred dead and dying into a single heap so they could gain greater access to the potatoes, which were hidden in a pit under the floor of the cabin, now cooked by the heat and seasoned with the oils of the Red Sticks. Remembering the tales of how the Red Sticks had used the scrotums of Americans slain at Burnt Corn Creek for tobacco pouches, Jackson's men mutilated the bodies of the warriors who lay strewn about on the ground in order to mete out their own primitive justice. When Cade saw what some of Coffee's men were doing to the women, all he could picture in his mind was Lyssa.

He staggered into the canes down by the river and vomited until he scarcely had the strength to stand.

Good God Almighty, any of those women could just as easily have been his Lyssa or Joie. His own loved ones had probably been murdered and mutilated in the same way. And here he was, no better than those he hated with such a vengeance. If fate operated in the universe, could the Almighty have punished them beforehand for the acts he now performed? What kind of world was this he lived in? How could he have participated in such a duck shoot and called it battle? Few of the Creeks even had guns and bullets. The boy's beseeching eyes appeared in his memory, and he lost all reason. An elusive memory from his long-buried past drew him down into the darkness.

Everyone he loved got killed. It just wasn't worth it anymore.

He threw himself into the river and made himself stay under the water until he was about to pass out, but his own sense of survival took over. He shot to the surface and gasped for breath.

He was a coward. Afraid to die, he thought, condemning himself. He realized he wasn't going to die in the river. He was too good a swimmer. So he allowed himself to float to the other side, where he knelt crying like a baby.

That boy's eyes became the eyes of another that was hidden in the recesses of his brain. But now he would have so many more. It wasn't those women or children that committed the atrocity at Fort Mims. How did it punish those who had committed the crimes to kill other innocents?

His powerful shoulders shook as he was racked with sobs.

Lyssa was thinking of Cade when she first sniffed the acrid smell of the smoke and the too-familiar smell of burning flesh. He had not been far from her thoughts during the past hour. With that strange second sense that she'd known since she first met him, Lyssa was aware of a crisis. Her own danger was real and present, but she had an odd uneasiness that told her Cade was near. Alert now to the sights and smells about her, she stiffened behind Jack, who looked up from following the trail on the ridge to see the smoke rising around the curve in the Alabama River. While Jack's attention was focused up the river toward the source of the smoke and the gunfire, Lyssa spotted a body floating in the water. And then the body pulled itself from the river and became a small, kneeling figure in the distance. Only Lyssa would recognize that figure as Cade in heart-rending distress.

Her immediate impulse was to cry out to him, but Jack reached for his gun and Lyssa thought he had seen Cade. She looked to where his attention focused and caught the movement of something running toward them down the path from the village.

"Just a child," he muttered. "One of ours."

He lowered the gun across his lap and kicked his horse into a gallop. Lyssa felt his body tense when he spotted a soldier with gun raised and aimed at the child. In one movement, Jack pulled his knife from his belt and tossed it straight into the man's chest. The soldier dropped the gun and reached to pull the knife from his chest. He looked into Lyssa's eyes and fell over with blood-laced bubbles coming from his mouth. Horses could be heard pounding on the path behind the soldier. Jack reached down to clasp the child's hand and lifted the boy across his lap. He kicked the horse into a gallop and kept going into the woods.

Lyssa did not dare look back for fear Jack's companion would notice her distress and look back also. Every fiber within her wanted to jump from the horse and run to her beloved. But if she did, there was no question they would both be killed. Now this young boy might reveal her lie by not recognizing her as one of the village. Still, it was possible the child was in such shock that she had a bit of time.

She wanted to cry out, "Live, my love. Live! I will find you." If there was to be a chance for them, she had to wait until an opportunity came for her to escape.

Cade felt a prickle on the back of his neck and quickly glanced over his shoulder at the ridge on the other side of the river. He saw a movement and could have sworn he glimpsed Lyssa. No! It couldn't have been her! But in his soul he felt a shift and thought he heard her say, "Live, my love. Live."

He would find her. If she lived, he would find her!

He staggered to his feet and headed back up the river. His head pounded and his eyes ached, but he had to get to his horse and see this through. He needed to search the ridge. Why would she be here? Was it just their strange connection that had him so sure she lived and willed him to live? Had Rendel and Gabriel found Lyssa and Joie?

Savannah Jack did not need to ask the boy what had happened. The child, Running Elk, was probably around seven or eight years old. He had scratches and a severe wound to the head where a bullet had grazed his scalp. It was a wonder he was still conscious with all the blood that poured from his head, but Lyssa knew even shallow scalp wounds bled profusely and were not life threatening. Her heart beat so quickly that she thought she might pass out, and so she broke her rule and clung to her enemy to keep from falling off. If she fell, he might stop, and if he stopped, he would go to the river to wash the boy's wounds. And if he went to the river, he would see Cade, who had seemed oblivious to anything around him. She could not tell anything about his possible wounds from that distance.

Lyssa took a deep breath and clamped her legs tighter around the horse. She eased her hold on Savannah Jack and struggled to support herself. Savannah Jack said, "You are brave, little mother. The child within you will have a warrior's heart. When the little one comes, you will need a warrior as his father."

He said no more. He needed to say no more. Her blood ran cold. She must escape before the baby was born.

"Where are we going?" Blue asked.

"Econochaca," Jack responded.

Blue nodded. "Holy Ground."

As they entered the woods, Jack tossed the boy to Blue, who swung him around behind him on the horse to hold on for dear life while they pounded the ground between the death and destruction of the village she had claimed as her own and their new destination of Econochaca.

Earlier in the summer of 1813, Josiah Francis had chosen Holy Ground as a sacred spot and secured its defense. Located on a high bluff along the south bank of the Alabama River between the Pintlala and the Big Swamp Creeks, Holy Ground had become the headquarters of Weatherford, Hossa Yahola, and the other chiefs and consisted of about two hundred Indian cabins arranged around a square.

The prophet Francis had ensured the security of the village, having the warriors erect stakes and obstacles and perform ceremonies to establish a spiritual barrier that he claimed would kill any white man who sought to breach it. Savannah Jack, who was at best a cynical believer of the prophet's power, still felt that the village was impregnable because of its position on the bluff, its vast stores of corn, and the large number of Red Stick warriors. Many of the Fort Mims captives had been taken there.

During the journey, Lyssa was so tired she could barely keep her eyes open to hold on to the horse behind Jack. Several times she awoke to find herself leaning against Savannah Jack, actually snoring! Once she woke herself and jerked upright. Savannah Jack chuckled, not a sound one expected from one so fearsome, therefore making it even more terrifying.

Sleep was something that came easily these days. She knew lethargy was a natural part of this time in a pregnancy. But she did not have that luxury. With sleep came nightmares. What if she spoke Cade's name? She could easily betray herself in her dreams. She had felt Cade's despair, experienced his pain, and yet could not go to him to ease it. She needed to eat to keep her strength up. If she was weak, she could not return to her children. And the baby growing within her needed nourishment too. For so many reasons, she needed to keep her wits about her.

Savannah Jack was just a man. That was something she now knew. And a man, though a fierce, blood-thirsty, hate-filled man, could be outwitted. When he allowed her to start a fire, Lyssa tried to prepare good meals because she knew that what she put into her body fed her growing child as well as the Creek child had won her heart and the two men who guarded her every move. She kept her mind active, mentally reciting Shakespeare's *Tempest*. Lyssa's father had said one of her ancestors had written the journal that Shakespeare used to inspire his play. "We are such stuff as dreams are made on; and our little life is rounded with a sleep." She would go on as she could and then....

If her ancestor could survive shipwreck, rebuild the boat, and make it to be a founder at Jamestown, she could outwit one crazy Creek. One day at a time.

By the time they made it to Holy Ground, exhausted as she was, Lyssa had won the adoration of the boy they had rescued. She had tended the bullet graze on his scalp and covered his other wounds with a salve that immediately eased the pain. Savannah Jack's frightening appearance scared the boy so badly that he cowered next to her throughout the nights.

"Never show your fear," Lyssa whispered to him as they picked up sticks for the fire. "Savannah Jack only keeps us alive because he thinks you will be a warrior for the Red Stick cause and I may carry one."

The boy's brown eyes grew large, but he nodded his understanding.

Since the nights were growing chillier, having the child's warm little body tucked up next to hers kept them both warm. Again, Shakespeare's words came to her: "Misery acquaints a man with strange bedfellows." A woman too, she thought to herself. The aptness of the phrase made her smile as she brushed her chin against the child's soft black hair. She could not trust the hot-eyed Blue with something so precious as this child. Both men had no value system except that which would prove most beneficial to them in whatever area they operated. Right now Blue's sexual urges took second place to the Red Stick cause. The Creeks needed warriors, and since Savannah Jack wanted to win the war, the baby she carried and the boy they had saved were potential warriors.

The baby was going to be a big one. Lyssa rolled over and situated herself so that Running Elk's little bottom warmed the small of her back, easing the pain she'd been having for a while. She knew she should slow down, but if she did Savannah Jack might find she could be dispensed with, and his way of dispensing with folks was permanent and not something she was ready to face. She must remain strong and continue her charade. For herself and the baby and Running Elk.

She allowed her mind to drift to Cade, and with his face in her thoughts she drifted to sleep.

19

Driven by the belief that Lyssa still lived, Cade made record time returning to St. Stephens to see if she had been found. Although his feelings about Joie were not so acute, his instinct was that if Lyssa lived, then surely Joie, his beloved sister, lived as well.

Shivering and shaking with that damned recurrent fever, he refused to slow down. He had seen so much death and felt such despair that he simply must return to a civilized setting to regain his bearings. He had literally *felt* Lyssa's presence as he knelt there on that bank, but there was nothing but death at Tallusahatchee and no sign that she had been there. He'd searched and searched but could find no clue. Nothing but horses' hoofprints were on the ridge above the river, and they merged with many that led toward Holy Ground, where he supposed some Indians had fled for safety.

Savannah Jack had been there. Cade had pulled one of his knives from the chest of a soldier on a path leading to the village. He would have recognized it anywhere. As a boy, he had sat and watched Jack carve the handle of just such a knife so that, wherever it was found, others would remember Savannah Jack had been there. Cade got the message and prayed to God that Lyssa and Joie never met up with that devil. For him to go alone to Holy Ground would be suicide, but it was truly something he considered before deciding it would be more rational to find out if she had been found first.

Davy Crockett had been concerned when Cade returned from the river. "Are you all right, Kincaid? Your face is red and your hands are shaking."

"I'm okay," he assured his friend, though he felt as if he were freezing while his skin burned to the touch. "But tell the general I'm takin' some time off. I'll be back."

"I'll tell him you're sick. You sure as hell look it. I wish we could have found whatever you were looking for," Crockett said. He touched his coonskin cap in salute as Cade rode away.

For miles the only company Cade had were his own thoughts. He now realized he'd *always* loved that quirky, curious, unusual girl. But the childhood affection between him and Lyssa had surely turned into the bonfire of true lovers. Then they were separated, and he realized that the strange emotion he was finally brave enough to admit he had was *love*, that the emotion he had tried so hard to stifle had grown despite his best efforts.

He had known her love for such a brief time, and yet it was long enough to shift his world.

How could a man *not* love a woman who loved him so much that she would go to the ends of the earth to show him? Even as far as following him into the hell that was Fort Mims. He would spend whatever time was left of his life searching for her as long as there was a chance she still lived. But a world without Lyssa suddenly seemed like the gaping abyss that had led him to throw himself into the river before he thought he heard her voice in his mind and her sighs in the wind.

Love, he finally realized, was a rare, beautiful, and often elusive thing. Sure it had made him vulnerable. It was something he'd always feared after the agony of his mother's death and the desperation he'd felt when he thought he wouldn't be able to save Gabe when they were captives of Bowles and Jack. But would he have traded the little time he'd had with Lyssa, those memories, for anything?

What if she had been found and his intuition that she lived meant he should return to where they began their search for her?

Cade rode his horse hard, though shaking with tremors that ran through his body and a fever that nearly drained him. He could barely stay on his horse. He finally made it to the ferry across the Alabama and Tombigbee rivers just above St. Stephens and went immediately to the Pebble Creek Jockey Club where her family would most likely be. The first thing he saw as he neared the track was his sister, Joie, surrounded by a group of children, some holding tiny swords made of sticks. Joie glanced up and recognized him. She ran to him, crying, "Have you found Lyssa?"

He stopped in mid-dismount, joyful in seeing the precious sister he had set out to save...alive. But when her words finally registered, he said in a weak, almost tremulous voice, "How do you know Lyssa, Joie?"

"She saved me and J.J. and the rest of these children at Fort Mims," Joie said, unable to hold back her tears. "Just before Papa Rendel and Gabriel found us in the hollow, she disappeared."

Cade looked up and saw Gabriel coming toward him just before his eyes rolled back in his head and he keeled over.

When they arrived at Econochaca, also known as Holy Ground, Savannah Jack delivered Lyssa to the women. When Jack told them of the death of Lyssa's husband at Fort Mims they clucked over her like mother hens.

Econochaca was located on a bluff at the fork of the Alabama and Tallapoosa rivers. After not bathing for weeks, Lyssa welcomed the trip to the river with the women who, being Creek, bathed daily despite the weather or water temperature. The chilly water was reviving. But before she took the plunge, she mixed up an herbal concoction with which she sudsed her hair, giving it such shine and luster that the other women quickly requested some for themselves. A concoction of boiled yellow spine thistle root mixed with tallow softened her roughened skin. They were gifts she was glad to share in return for the women's kindness.

Lyssa tried her best to remain anonymous but found the effort nearly impossible. Her unusual violet eyes set her apart, and her advancing and obvious pregnancy actually made her skin glow. She could tell by the look in Savannah Jack's eyes that he liked what he saw. And that frightened her. She had hoped her increasing girth would protect her. He came frequently to sit outside the hut merely to let the men who dared to look at her know he had staked his claim. Of course, his attention unsettled the women among whom she had hoped to find a friend.

Lyssa had not socialized much outside of the Tensaw area and had certainly been sheltered in her father's and grandfather's homes. The only one who might recognize her was William Weatherford, who had often come to the racetrack, just as her father had frequented Weatherford's, and had taken meals with her father. Lyssa knew he had led the battle at Fort Mims. She did not know what to expect from him, and so she decided to avoid him and remain anonymous among the women. They were in awe of her because Savannah Jack stood as her protector. She encouraged no confidences and friendships among the women because she had no idea if any were trustworthy. Her position with Savannah Jack was precarious. If even one misspeak were to return to him, she had no doubt that she would be killed. Always, she looked for an opportunity to escape and search for the children she worried about constantly. And Cade. She must find him. She could not forget her last glimpse of him and the feeling she got of his despair.

Now there was also Running Elk, her comfort and her grave concern. With no explanation, the women assumed the child was her relative, and the two preferred that so they could stay together. Their bond had been immediate. He had seen too much for a child and joined the ranks of the walking wounded that comprised the children of her heart if not of her flesh. He had no relatives left, having seen his entire family shot down before his eyes, and Lyssa's heart had opened to him from the first.

"The children ask me if you are my sister," he whispered to her one night. "What should I tell them?"

Lyssa was amazed at how perceptive Running Elk was. When Savannah Jack had told the women that she was from Tallusahatchee and her man had been killed at Fort Mims, she had noticed the child looking at her strangely. She had given a slight shake of her head, and he immediately knew to hold his tongue. But now he needed to know how to explain their relationship.

"Perhaps your cousin," she suggested. "That would account to Jack for us not being more demonstrative when we found one another."

He nodded and they quieted, concerned that others might overhear.

The women did inquire as to when the baby was due, and when she told them they could not believe her date was right.

"You are much too large for that date," muttered the woman who served as midwife. But Lyssa knew the date with no question. Before she could confer with the midwife about her challenge to the date, the old woman's gaze was drawn to something behind her. Lyssa turned around and started, catching the scream before it escaped and thankfully succeeding in presenting a calm front. That sort of effort did not come naturally to Lyssa. As a child she was teased by her parents that her every thought could be read on her face. But too much depended on her not betraying a single thought or emotion.

Savannah Jack watched her for long, tense moments. Then he dropped skins and deer meat at her feet.

"You make clothes. Eat meat. Young warrior grows."

242

He had apparently used up all of his words and walked away. The old woman grabbed up the meat greedily and scurried about to prepare a fire with which to cook it. It had been a long time since these women without a man had meat. It was a luxury to women in the cabin where she dwelt, widow women from other villages whose men had been killed in battle. While the midsife cooked, Lyssa scraped the pelts to make them supple and then sewed them together to fashion a mantle and skirt. The women commented that her methods were not those of the Creek. Lyssa merely smiled and evaded their curiosity.

The smell of meat set her stomach to growling. She knew the others were as hungry as she was. Reluctantly, they served her first. The women, young and old, envied the attention Savannah Jack paid her in spite of his horrific appearance. To them, the scars represented badges of his courage. Hideous though he was to her, to these women without men, Savannah Jack was a man of strength who could provide meat. Their jealousy grew more apparent every day. As their jealousy grew, they set her to the more distasteful tasks, which she completed with no complaint until Savannah Jack noticed how thin her wrists had become.

"I will bring no more meat to this hut if you do not show more concern for this one who will be my woman," he said to the widows. "The meat comes to this dwelling because it is the fire at which this woman eats." He grabbed Lyssa's wrist and held it up for all to see. "Yet as her baby grows, she grows thinner. You take the food that she must have. This will not continue." He spoke in a voice so soft as to be chilling. The women shivered. They bowed their heads and nodded. Lyssa kept her eyes cast down.

The store of corn the Red Stick leaders had deposited there kept them from starving, but hardships caused by having to stay close to the village due to threats made for a tense situation.

Lyssa kept quiet and close to the hearth of the women with whom she lived, mainly preparing the meat Savannah Jack provided. Her herbs seasoned the meats in such a manner that many single men began adding their game to her fire and gathering at mealtime. That was the only good thing the other women could find about her. And, since Savannah Jack was so fiercely possessive, the men made it a point to ignore her and focus on the other women, but it was obvious to all that she was their object of their attention, though they watched her surreptitiously beneath hooded eyes. She shared whatever Savannah Jack brought her, made her salves and herbal concoctions and gave them freely, hoping to make a contribution to those who sheltered her. But these women, like most were a sociable species, and they expected to get confidences in return for those they shared. Lyssa dared not speak. The words she chose and their inflection would give her away. She pretended a shyness that was not her natural inclination. And still they were mistrustful. They saw her actions as setting herself above the others.

Early on the morning of December 23, a hunter cantered into camp and reported having seen General Claiborne's army approaching, led by Sam Moniac, William Weatherford's kinsman and dearest friend. The warriors took to the trees to hold off the attack until the women and children could cross the river to its western bank. The horrible massacres of Fort Mims and Tallusahatchee would not be repeated if he could help it. Sapothlane, Weatherford's pregnant wife, and his children Polly and Charles were to go on to Dutch Bend through treacherous ravines and marshes, though it was only about five miles as the crow flies across the Alabama River. Weatherford feared for Sapothlane's safety. She was very weak and in much pain. The babe threatened to arrive too early. He wished it were safe for her to return to the comfort of his plantation, which was less than twenty miles away on the Holy Ground side of the River.

Lyssa grabbed Running Elk by the hand and ran with the women. Savannah Jack yanked her by the hair as she ran past.

"I will come for you," he said, twisting her hair and bringing her so close she could feel the heat of his breath. The warning was evident in his voice. If she tried to escape, it would be the end of his protection and the beginning of his search for her. He would then kill her. She had no doubt.

Lyssa shivered and lowered her eyes. She nodded, but inside her mind raced. Perhaps now was her opportunity to escape.

Weatherford rode past on his horse, Arrow. "To the barricade, Jack," he commanded. His eyes lingered on Lyssa when she glanced up at him, forgetting herself in her eagerness to get away from Savannah Jack. Unfortunately, her thickly lashed violet eyes were so unique as to be unforgettable. She saw the recognition in his eyes and then his glance at Jack's tight hold on her hair.

Jack looked at Weatherford with arrogant disdain. "She will be my woman when the Tallusahatchee warrior's son is born," he said.

"First Claiborne and the army, Jack," Weatherford commanded as he wheeled Arrow back to prepare for the attack.

Lyssa lowered her head and grabbed Running Elk's hand, guiding him toward the waiting canoe to go across the river. As the other women, carrying as many supplies as they could grab, proceeded to the caves and bayous where they would hide from the Americans, Lyssa hung back with Running Elk, claiming fatigue due to her pregnancy. The truth was that she had noticed spotting earlier and feared for her unborn child. No one offered to linger with her. They had heard what happened to the Hillabees, who thought they had a truce with Jackson. They were sure they would be slaughtered by the Americans just as the Hillabees had been only a month before.

The women had noticed the attention William Weatherford had paid to Savannah Jack's woman. They were jealous of the violet-eyed widow who spoke strangely, made potions, and captured the attention of the men all the others had hoped to attract. The war had claimed many of their men.

They turned their backs, leaving her in the danger of her choosing while they hurried to their hiding place.

"Running Elk, I am in pain, and I am afraid I will lose this baby if I do not find a place to rest immediately. You will be safer with the others. Please go with them," she said.

"I stay with you," the boy replied, guiding her to a tree that slanted so that one who lay against it could be comfortable looking through a canopy to an open meadow. It was a balmy December day, neither too hot nor too cold, and a slight breeze rippled the remaining leaves and sighed through the pine trees. Lyssa dozed off. Running Elk found a spot where he could watch the action across the river.

Several hours later, about an hour before the sun reached its midpoint in the sky, gunshots were heard across the river at Holy Ground. Three columns of Claiborne's nearly one thousand men and a band of Choctaw warriors led by Lyssa's grandfather, Chief Pushmataha, surrounded the town. In spite of Josiah Francis's incantations to make the town impregnable, the battle lasted only about an hour before Weatherford recognized its futility and ordered his vastly outnumbered band of 120 to fall back to the river.

Pushmataha and his Choctaw warriors had followed behind Claiborne's men and were securing the 1,200 barrels of corn the Red Sticks had stockpiled to feed their people during the winter months, provisions Jackson's army desperately needed. They then began setting fire to the village.

Weatherford watched the conflagration from the bluff, waiting to follow at the rear of his retreating warriors as they paddled their canoes to cross the river. With bullets pelting around him, Weatherford kicked Arrow's sides and leaned low over his neck. The horse pounded along edge of the ridge. Lyssa's heart clenched when, at the last second, Arrow leapt from the fifteen-foot bluff and floated for seconds in midair before descending into the depths of the river. After several anxious seconds, Arrow popped up with Weatherford, also known as Red Eagle, holding tightly to his flowing white mane.

Lyssa gasped as Weatherford clamored from the water, having survived a jump that would have killed a lesser man. The soldiers now standing on the bluff watched in amazement, a few attempting to shoot him as he made his way ashore. Bullets spattered the water about them. Finally Arrow found his footing on the opposite bank and bounded away from the range of the bullets. Weatherford dismounted to inspect his horse for wounds. Only a lock of his mane had been shot off by the soldier's bullets. Weatherford remounted and turned to the watching soldiers. The valiant Weatherford sat proudly astride Arrow, straight and untouched, looking boldly into Claiborne's eyes. He lifted his hand, giving an easily interpreted salute of defiance.

He then turned into the woods where he had spotted Running Elk and knew Lyssa was nearby. There he found her reclining against a tree where she could see but not be seen. Running Elk sat close at hand.

Savannah Jack had crossed the river earlier on horseback, where he had watched Weatherford's spectacular escape. He followed him into the woods. Weatherford indicated Lyssa and said to him, "I have heard of this woman. I need her herbal skills with Sapothlane. She will go with me."

Savannah Jack glowered. He was big and muscular. His grotesque face was even more startling painted as it was for war and splattered with the blood of enemies he had killed. Lyssa looked up from where she sat and refused to shiver. She summoned her courage and stood awkwardly, clutching her abdomen as she rose.

Lyssa sensed the boy's fear and said, "Running Elk stays with me."

She stood proudly and refused to be intimidated by the look Weatherford aimed at her. He was a stranger to her now. The man she had known who visited with her father was civilized, wore the clothes of an American, and spoke that language well. He was charming and kind and associated on equal footing with other Americans who came to the racetrack. But in this man, painted red and black and wearing only a breechclout, she saw Red Eagle, Lamochattee Hopnicafutsahia, the war chief who had led the attack at Fort Mims that had brought about the deaths and mutilations of over four hundred inhabitants—his relatives and friends.

To her, he was no better than Savannah Jack.

Those horrible betraying tears once again filled her eyes.

Weatherford felt her fear. Of him as much as of Savannah Jack. Had he come to this?

She slapped at the tears with the back of her hand, angry with herself for her weakness. But she missed Cade so much, and here was the man he resembled threatening her. Was Cade here? She did not sense him. Did that mean he had died and she would never see him again? Cade had been alive on November 3 at Tallusahatchee, but she knew he was in distress then. And how could she find him? He could be across the river with her grandfather Pushmataha and Claiborne's army now looting and burning Holy Ground.

Even if Savannah Jack left her with William Weatherford, had she improved her situation? Could she keep Running Elk alive? Were her children in the hollow near Fort Mims alive? Running Elk hugged close to her, slipping his hand in hers when he saw her tremble.

Weatherford had to navigate this dilemma carefully. The first Choctaw to enter Holy Ground had been Lyssa's grandfather Pushmataha. Weatherford had only known the woman who dwelt among the other widows as Savannah Jack's captive. Jack had found her at Fort Mims, and she claimed to be the pregnant widow of a slain warrior from Tallusahatchee. The boy that Savannah Jack had captured fleeing a soldier at Tallusahatchee seemed to confirm that. But it only took one look at that beautiful face and those distinctive violet eyes for Weatherford to recall the girl and remember that she was the granddaughter of Pushmataha, chief of the Choctaw, who now pillaged Holy Ground and would soon be pursuing him. If other Red Sticks knew who she was, he would never be able to protect her. Without another word, he pulled her onto the horse with him, cradling her in front of him.

"Take the others to the caves," Weatherford commanded Savannah Jack. "I will question this medicine woman of her remedies before allowing her to help Sapothlane. I need you now to protect our people."

Savannah Jack muttered but nodded and then pulled Running Elk onto the horse despite Lyssa's protests.

Sapothlane *was* having difficulty with her pregnancy. As soon as the armies had been reported approaching Holy Ground, Weatherford had sent Sapothlane and his family along with the other women and children into hiding. They could not go home to his plantation because Hickory Ground would surely be a target for the Americans. Running Elk looked back at Lyssa helplessly.

They were the last to leave. Weatherford checked around to make sure no stragglers needed his help. He then pulled Lyssa onto the horse and held her to his chest. He did not miss the clenching of her teeth as the horse cantered forward. When they had gone a distance, he shifted her in his arms to accommodate her ample stomach.

"When is the baby due, Lyssa Rendel?" he asked.

So he did recognize her.

She lowered her eyes, shrugged, and said reluctantly, "The baby is due in May, William Weatherford."

"Why are you not safe in your grandfather's village?" he asked.

Lyssa looked back at him and studied his expression. His black eyes regarded her with kindness. Worry lines now etched his eyes. This war had aged him. Gray glistened in his hair with just enough red that it glowed like fire when the sun hit. Her father had always thought Weatherford was a good man and enjoyed his company. How could such a man have participated in the horrible massacre at Fort Mims?

Lyssa had always trusted her instincts. But look where that had gotten her. She was inclined to trust him, but war had made enemies of friends and now she was unsure. She looked down at his hands holding the reins loosely and at his legs, guiding the horse while he supported her. He had long, tapered fingers, calloused from practice with the bow. His arms were roped with muscles. He was a strong man but held her gently. He was a warrior but now showed her kindness. He was a paradox.

Just then she felt a pain and grimaced, grabbing her abdomen. "I need to rest, William Weatherford, and make a tea from some herbs in my pouch," she said. "If I do not, I may lose this child."

She could not keep the apprehension from her voice. She could not, would not, lose all she had left of Cade. They were quite a distance from the river but near a stream that fed into it. Weatherford guided the horse beside the stream and dismounted. He then lifted Lyssa from the horse and settled her in the straw while he built a small fire for her to brew her tea.

Would such a gentle man betray her?

"We are not far from Dutch Bend where my family hides," Weatherford said. "I did not lie when I said Sapothlane was in need of your herbs. She also is pregnant and bleeds. If your herbs are effective, they may also help her. You must rest. When you are ready, I will travel slowly and jostle you as little as possible."

Lyssa drank the tea and then lay back on her side, curled away from the man who now held her captive. She stilled her mind and forced herself to be calm. Cade's face kept popping up, and she focused at last on the time she had with him before the world intruded and once again separated them. Tears spilled from her eyes as she thought of the anguish she had felt when she saw him beneath the ridge. At last the herbs eased the slight contractions, and she went to sleep.

Weatherford watched as her breathing became the even breaths of a deep sleep. Her hand held her abdomen protectively. He lifted a straw and stuck it between his lips, and when he did so, he glanced down his body and for the first time noticed the blood from the men he had killed. Yet he was too emotionally exhausted to go to the stream to wash it off.

Fortunately, the girl had given him an excuse to take some time to himself. He was a man and a warrior, and he had chosen his path. He was a leader, and that meant he must keep his focus on the goal of the war. Yet, the irony was that he knew in his heart of hearts that the goal of his people to return to the old ways could really never be. They had been reduced to using their bows and arrows and now suffered defeat after defeat because they did not have the ammunition they depended on the white man to provide.

He grimaced. This time last year he had probably been at the racetrack watching his horses perform. He had likely worn his white man's clothes. At that point, he had not totally decided which path he would take in the war. He lived in a white man's plantation house, and it was so close to here. When he had hunted this land and fished in the creeks and bayous they passed, he had never thought he would be hiding from soldiers in this place, this land that was his home. But was that not *why* they fought?

They had been pushed this far and no further, as Far Off Warrior had said.

When Weatherford went to Mobile or Pensacola dressed in his white man's clothes, no one treated him differently than any other white man. His father was a Scot. His mother's mother was half French.

There were few in this war who did not have white blood. Even his woman, Sapothlane Moniac, had a white father. Yet she had taken the talk along with many of his other relatives, while some remained faithful to the Americans. His best friend, Sam Moniac, wore the medal George Washington gave him like a talisman, never removing it.

Weatherford had heard it was Sam Moniac who led the Americans to Holy Ground. Was he any different than Weatherford? Sam was leading the Americans to fight and kill members of his own family at Holy Ground just as Weatherford had done at Fort Mims. He had tried to warn the inhabitants of Fort Mims by letting Jo go, and then he found him strung up and beaten inside the fort. Old man Beasley, he thought. Arrogant son of a bitch. He shook his head, remembering.

On the road the day of the massacre, David Tait, Weatherford's gentle, scholarly brother, had said he'd gone out to check on the cattle. When he returned, his wife Mary Louisa had taken two of their girls to visit her parents at the fort. Davy had told her about William's warning. Unfortunately, she felt compelled to go and deliver the warning in person to her family. He was sure her father had convinced her that they were safer staying at Fort Mims. The word was out that the Red Sticks were headed toward another fort, so he would have reasoned that their plantation was in more danger than Fort Mims.

If it had not been for the fact that Dixon Bailey and his brothers— along with the others in the militia that had attacked the Red Sticks at Burnt Corn—were at Fort Mims, that would probably have been the case.

Davy had been afoot on his way to retrieve his family. His horses had already been stolen by the Red Sticks. Weatherford had met him on the road, the blood of the battle evident on his body. He had already delivered Far Off Warrior to the women who now tended him.

Upon seeing him, Davy Tait had stood stock still. His face paled, and he swayed. One look at his brother sitting on his horse told him that Weatherford's news was not good.

"Why are you here now, while your *braves* are in the battle?" Davy had asked him apprehensively.

Weatherford slid down from his horse and approached his brother. "I had given orders that our fight was not with women and children, but my command was ignored. I could not stop the killing. Savannah Jack and…I could no longer stand to see it."

He stopped, unable to say or do anything more. He watched the understanding come into his brother's eyes. And then they turned bleak and deadly cold. His brother had clenched his fists to strike him. But, gentle man that he was, he had turned and stumbled away, his grief and anger evident in every step.

"I sent the slave back to warn you," Weatherford had whispered. Why had no one heeded the slaves he had allowed to escape?

"Please," he called after his brother. "Take the others and go to Mobile!"

Sitting beside Lyssa Rendel now, Weatherford groaned as he thought of what he had seen during the past months. But a warrior does not show emotion. He must pull the shell again over his aching heart.

Lyssa stirred and muttered a name that he could not quite make out.

Savannah Jack had said he'd found the girl at Fort Mims. What was she doing there? The story she'd concocted about being married to a warrior from Tallusahatchee was an obvious lie. Weatherford would bet she'd never been to Tallusahatchee. Why was Pushmataha's granddaughter at Fort Mims? And, more important, who was the father of her child?

Dark was falling. He should be following his people to Dutch Bend. His wife Sapothlane had been in pain when she left that morning. But there were others taking care of her, and there was too much plunder at Holy Ground for a hungry army and their Choctaw friends to ignore in order to follow their ragged band. He would stay here for the moment and let Pushmataha's granddaughter rest. And then he would have her story.

Sapothlane would worry, but he did not want to think about her now. If his first wife Mary had still been alive, he wondered if he would have joined with the Red Sticks. Mary and Sam Moniac were brother and sister. They were both realistic about the might of the Americans and the eventual fate of the Creek. Mary had been dead for nine years, and he had missed her so. When Sapothlane Moniac had shown up, looking much like his Mary, showering their children with the woman's love they'd been without, singing to them with that voice so beautiful the birds stilled, he'd listened to her romantic notions about the return to the life the Great Spirit had intended for his people. His sister, Hannah, and her husband Josiah Francis had encouraged him to join them, emphasizing his duty as a leader of the Clan of the Wind to support their spiritual quest and honor their ancestors. They wanted him to resist the encroachment of those who would steal their land and their traditional ways. Those who followed the white man's ways must be scourged, they believed, or all would be lost for their children.

It had made sense by the fireside as they reminisced about the old ways and their family members who had made them proud.

It seemed folly now by the creek with his enemy's pregnant daughter by his side.

She could be a valuable tool in negotiations. Or, if others found out who she was, she would be another victim in this awful war. He thought long and hard about what would be the honorable thing to do.

He could not leave the people he promised to lead. He could not abandon his duties. But he would not reveal this girl's identity. Her face became the symbol of all the faces he would not see again. He remembered Lyssa as the shy little girl who stayed close to her father, who shared Rendel's love of books and always carried one in her hand.

When dawn finally came and the first rays of sun streaked through the branches of the trees, Lyssa stirred. She lay back and brushed her hand across her eyes, finally focusing on William Weatherford, who sat cross-legged watching her.

"Now you will tell me who is the father of this child," he said, authority ringing in his voice. He sensed that the rest of the story would revolve around the answer to his question.

Lyssa blinked. "I don't suppose you believe it was a warrior from Tallusahatchee."

Weatherford did not dignify her words with a single utterance. His black eyes bored into her, and she knew prevaricating was useless.

Lyssa struggled awkwardly to sit up. She was surely at a disadvantage lying down.

"Cade Kincaid," she said reluctantly.

Weatherford stood and looked down at her, shaking his head. "The news gets worse. If there is anyone in this world that Savannah Jack hates, it is Cade Kincaid—or any Kincaid, in general."

Lyssa nodded. "I know. That is why I had to concoct that story when Savannah Jack appeared."

"Now you must tell me how you came to be at Fort Mims. Surely Kincaid did not bring you there."

She hung her head and admitted, "Gabe came to the village to tell Cade that their sister and their foster parents, the Pottses, were there. He thought the attack would be imminent, and since Gabe could not go in because of his relationship with you, he came to get Cade to get them out. I followed him."

"Lyssa Rendel, I know how your father and grandfather have protected you. How did you get them to let you go?"

"Each of them thought I was with the other. And so, when Cade left on the morning after our marriage, I followed."

"And now they are all probably aware that you are missing. Is that why Pushmataha was so furiously searching Holy Ground?"

Lyssa shrugged. "I don't know. I have not seen any of them since the day before Fort Mims." Tears filled her eyes. "Cade's sister Joie is alive. Other children joined us, and they were alive before Savannah Jack took me. I was hunting and he captured me without discovering the others. And I saw Cade briefly, though he did not see me, at Tallusahatchee."

She looked at William Weatherford, her beautiful violet eyes filled with tears and emotion, and pleaded, "Please let me go and find them all. I must take care of them."

The dark circles under Lyssa's eyes told him her physical condition. She was just a little thing, and yet her pregnancy seemed advanced. She thought she could care for those she loved, but she needed someone to take care of her. She would not survive on her own for long, especially with Savannah Jack in pursuit.

"Lyssa, think of Running Elk," he said, knowing her own welfare would mean nothing to her. "He thinks you are coming to where he is. Would you abandon him?"

He watched as she debated with herself. She was such a brave one.

During her rest, he had trapped a fish and baked it in a smothered fire. He laid it out while she went to tend to her private business in the bushes.

When she returned, he looked at her with a question that did not need to be said. She nodded and replied, "I am well."

"Good," he said. "Let us eat and continue on to the cave."

When she had eaten what he gave her, he mounted the horse and pulled her onto his lap where he cradled her, taking the horse at as slow and gentle a pace as he possibly could.

At last they reached the caves where the women and children had hidden. Savannah Jack met them.

"Claiborne has pitched his tent at your plantation," he informed Weatherford.

Weatherford acknowledged Savannah Jack's words with a nod. "Set the sentries and tell the warriors to remain alert."

Lyssa slid from the horse before Savannah Jack could get close enough to reach for her. At a look from Weatherford, Jack reluctantly went to do his bidding.

Polly and Charles came running out to meet him. Weatherford spun his children around one at a time.

"This is Charles," he said, introducing the oldest, who appeared to be about ten. Joie's age, Lyssa thought. Then came his sister, squealing

Polly who was about eight, perhaps Running Elk and Ben's age. Behind them, smiling enigmatically, stood the most beautiful woman Lyssa had ever seen. Sapothlane Moniac Weatherford was graceful and tall, with a swanlike neck, golden, almond-shaped eyes, and long, lustrous black hair. She was also obviously pregnant. Lyssa caught the question in her eyes. Who was this woman her husband had brought cradled in his arms?

"I am glad you are here and safe," she said in a sultry, husky voice. William reached for her, and she entered his embrace as if he were the center of her world.

Oh, she wanted that for her and Cade.

At last Sapothlane released him, and Weatherford stepped back as if released from a spell, forcing himself to focus. "Sapothlane, I want you to meet Little Flower, whose husband was killed at Tallusahatchee. She is a medicine woman of some skill who is also pregnant and is experiencing the same problems that you are. I have brought her to share our cave and her herbs with you."

Sapothlane looked at Weatherford and weighed his words. Lyssa saw the doubt and reluctance in her eyes. But she played her part well. She turned and extended her hand to Lyssa and led her into the cave. "I think we have much to talk about," she said. "But first, I think we both need to lie down for a while."

"I have an herbal tea that I would like to prepare for us before we rest," Lyssa countered.

"That is good," Sapothlane agreed.

She guided Lyssa into the cave. Lyssa saw her glance back and give William a private smile to which he responded with heat in his eyes but no change in expression. Charles and Polly danced around his legs. But when Savannah Jack, returned the children ran for the cave.

"You stayed the night with her," he said to Weatherford accusingly.

"The girl did not tell you of her woman's problems. Had we not delayed for her medicinal tea to halt the pains, she would have lost her child," he said.

Savannah Jack looked confused. Woman's problems were nothing he understood.

"I decided her gift with herbs will also benefit my woman, who shares those problems."

"Is that so," said Jack. He tried to glimpse the woman he knew as Little Flower in the cave but could not. Just the talk of "woman's problems" was disturbing. He did not like to think of a woman being anything but a mate in bed and a bearer of children. The whole process between was appalling, not something for a warrior to deal with.

"I go to sharpen my knife and make tips for my arrows," said Savannah Jack.

"That is good," said Weatherford.

Lyssa was safe for the moment, but Weatherford was in a dilemma. If he revealed to anyone her true identity, she would be killed because of their resentment that Pushmataha had chosen to support the Americans. Savannah Jack would oblige them as soon as he heard the baby she carried was also a Kincaid. So he could not send her with anyone to her family. No one could be trusted except himself, so he must keep her close enough but not too close, or Sapothlane would be jealous. He had not missed the look in her eyes.

Now to the business of war, he thought. Where should they go from here?

20

The entrance to the cave was well hidden by vines. Sapothlane lifted the curtain of vines on the wall of the hill and looked out at the sun-dappled morning. Two days had passed since their flight from Holy Ground. The contractions had intensified, though the strange medicine woman's teas had slowed them yesterday and enabled her to rest during the night. She drew a blanket about her, shivering with the chill of the December day. Behind her, the shallow cave in the ravine, though cold, dark, and dank, had been made comfortable with the women's blankets. Baskets were set about containing what they could grab upon running from Holy Ground. They were warmed only by small fires laid on the sandy bottom away from the entrance.

A wounded warrior did not cry out, but the moans of those injured and in pain could be heard all around them. Sapothlane knew that Savannah Jack's woman feared losing her babe and took the same teas she had given Sapothlane. The woman had also busied herself making potions and teas to ease the pain of the injured men, as well as poultices from her herb bag to combat their weeping sores. She had the boy Running Elk take these medicines and instructions to the women tending the men, and did not seek recognition. She then directed Running Elk to go with Charles and Polly to find branches that might be used as crutches, which they took to the proud warriors who would never ask for help. She told them to offer them as if the children themselves had thought of the idea.

Sapothlane watched Lyssa carefully and wondered at her actions. Even though William appeared to pay her no more attention than he did Running Elk, who came to live with them also, she was curious. Why would a tustenuggee, a war chief of the Red Sticks, concern himself with a woman if she were merely the widow of a Tallusahatchee warrior? How had this mystery widow of a Tallusahatchee warrior come by her knowledge of herbs and medicine?

Sapothlane returned to her bed to fret. She had been made as comfortable as possible on a pile of moss. She thought longingly of the comforts she had renounced to follow the prophets. Only a few miles away at Weatherford's home at Hickory Ground, she had a comfortable feather bed. She felt guilty for thinking such. Reluctantly, Sapothlane accepted the herbal concoction Lyssa provided.

When the curtain of darkness had fallen beyond the opening of their refuge and the fire flickered with shadows on the walls, Lyssa told stories of mighty quests of men with strange names like Odysseus and Agamemnon. Charles, Polly, Running Elk, and other children, as well as adults who pretended not to listen, hung on her every word. Sapothlane was unaccustomed to the lack of attention. She was ill and grew more and more irritated as she listened.

"You teach the children white man's stories and undermine our traditional ways," she told Lyssa accusingly.

So then Lyssa told only made-up stories playacting the thoughts of animals, which fascinated the children and taught lessons of gentleness and understanding.

"Witches talk with animals," Sapothlane said.

Lyssa found this ironic, as she knew many other Creek tales that included animals and their thoughts. But she tried to be understanding. Sapothlane was uncomfortable and in pain.

Sapothlane knew only one story with which to compete for the children's attention. She struggled to sit up and made a great ceremony as she told it, gathering all the children about her.

"Three Indians went out hunting. One found a nice hole of water but was afraid to drink. Another went down to it, dipped his fingers in, and said, 'It is good. Let us go into it.' So he dived in and came out white. From him came the white people. The second dived in oily water and came out darker. From him came the Indians. The third dived very dark water and from him came the Negroes.

"Just before the white man had dived into the water, he felt the rocks rattle. As they traveled, the Indians found a book. The white man picked it up and asked the Indians to read. They could not. The white man *could* read it, and it told him those rocks were gold. The book gave him this advantage. The whites were terrible people to take that advantage."

She nodded at Lyssa and said, "And that is the story of our people."

Her voice was melodious, but her story was lifeless. The children did not ask Sapothlane for another. Perhaps that was for the best. Sapothlane looked exhausted.

The children turned their back on her and begged Lyssa for a story. Lyssa's stories were told animatedly with varying voices so that the characters came alive. Lyssa cringed, knowing how that would play with Sapothlane.

Sapothlane filed it away as another reason to hate the beautiful violet-eyed girl who, despite her advanced pregnancy, garnered looks of appreciation from the warriors who once only had eyes for Sapothlane.

She lay back on her bed of moss and deerskin and covered her eyes with her hand. The potion had finally kicked in.

Running Elk had quickly become best friends with Charles, Weatherford's son by Mary Moniac, Sapothlane's cousin. Lyssa thought Sapothlane's eyes made a lie of the love her lips proclaimed for Weatherford's children.

Sapothlane reluctantly submitted to Lyssa's personal attention at Weatherford's command. Hoping to calm her, Lyssa massaged her skin with creams. Fortunately, Lyssa's herbal teas eased the contractions that had Sapothlane fearing she would lose the active child she carried.

Other than giving her treatments, Lyssa decided it would be prudent to stay away from Sapothlane as much as possible, so she took the children with her to find food and herbs. The men were busy preparing more arrows, hunting larger game, and scouting the area to make sure Jackson and Claiborne's men had not followed them. Therefore, Savannah Jack was otherwise occupied. Had she felt she had any chance of escape, she would have taken it. But the spotting had scared her, and she was determined to do what she must to protect her child. The primary focus now must be food. That was something she could guide the children in doing while she rested.

She made Charles and Running Elk a cohamoteker, a blow gun, that was familiar to the boys and frequently used for hunting. Then she set up a competition of skill to see who could bring back the most game. Scarce as food was after fleeing Holy Ground, they would all be glad of the rabbits, small rodents, lizards, and snakes the boys would be able to provide. Although Lyssa's delicate appetite rebelled at the idea of what she ate, her determination to remain strong for her child overcame the revulsion.

She and Polly found a stream near a beaver dam where the children could dig for the bog potato, a large tuberous root that, when pounded and washed repeatedly, could be mixed with honey to make little cakes. She directed them to gather the seeds of cockspurgrass and the water lily to grind into meal since their supply or corn was low. While sitting on the bank watching them, Lyssa wove a basket of reeds, and they managed to trap some fish in it.

The day glittered with sunlight, though the air was brisk. Squirrels frolicked from limb to limb among the boughs of the prickly pines, chattering all the while as if challenging the boys. The boys accepted their challenge quite effectively with their blow guns. After all the death she had seen, Lyssa marveled that birds still swooped and soared in the clear blue skies above them. A song of life played about them in the music of the wind and the song of the bird. There below, the emaciated children scavenged for food amid the bounty of the provisions of the Master of Breath—a dissonance in the majesty of life's chorus that played about them.

Lyssa lay back and let the sun warm her. Then, suddenly, her soul was chilled at the sight of the children cowering at the boom of thunder in the distance, a harbinger of a coming storm, afraid lest some mighty hunter of men choose to make them a target for their war.

Lyssa called the children to collect what they had gathered. The wind had freshened and she smelled rain. They should return before they were all soaked. Lyssa moved slowly these days, and she did not want to start bleeding again.

Though the other women ignored Lyssa upon their return, they praised the children. They eagerly took the food and prepared what to all of them, as hungry as they were, was a feast. Lyssa prepared the biggest fish to reward the children and to tempt the irritable Sapothlane. She had Charles deliver her portion of it in the name of another woman.

That night, Running Elk kept his blow gun handy and promised Lyssa that he would keep her safe, though his eyes closed the moment he fell on the blanket they shared on the hard, cold ground. Both of them were exhausted. Lyssa listened to his regular breathing and cuddled him close for warmth. The wind blew eerily, scattering leaves while the rain pounded beyond their shelter, making the fire blaze higher when it whipped into the entrance of the cave. Bare tree limbs made scratching noises. Her heart ached for the wounded who were wrapped in their thin blankets in the rain and the cold March wind. In spite of the strange noises, they felt secure inside the cave, knowing the warriors were at their posts. Running Elk was a comfort...her only comfort.

That evening by the fire after Lyssa had begged off telling more stories, she had listened respectfully to Sapothlane's ramblings over the return to the old ways. Lyssa wondered whom she was trying to convince. Herself?

Lyssa's girth had grown far beyond Sapothlane's, though her due date was much further in the future. Weatherford watched Lyssa closely, knowing the danger she would face if anyone knew her true identity. Many Red Sticks had been killed by the Choctaw. Who knew where they might decide to take vengeance?

Morale was low. Being defeated in Holy Ground had a devastating effect on the Red Sticks, even though only twenty-one Indians were killed and twenty wounded. Those numbers reflected lack of ammunition, not lack of courage. The much-needed, scarce supplies left at Holy Ground had been pillaged by Pushmataha's warriors. Weatherford had heard that when the soldiers discovered the pole in the center of the public square containing several hundred scalps they believed to have been taken at Fort Mims, Jackson's men became enraged and wreaked their vengeance on the village.

If the Red Sticks discovered who she was, Lyssa knew she might be the scapegoat for the prophets for the defeat at Holy Ground.

Weatherford, too, knew her safety was tenuous.

Despite Lyssa's herbs, the flight and scare had an effect on Sapothlane, and on December 25, 1813, two days after they had left Holy Ground, Sapothlane's water broke. Her women settled her on her deerskin bed, and within hours her son was born, but the babe was small. Much too small. And the cord around his neck had nearly suffocated the life from him.

He was perfect in form but lay tiny and lifeless in Sapothlane's arms where the midwife had placed him. Sapothlane held him from her and began to cry.

"An omen," one woman whispered, taking the child from Sapothlane, assuming he was dead.

They were doing nothing! Lyssa restrained herself and kept to the dark shadows as long as she could, but finally she rushed forward and grabbed for the babe.

Sapothlane shouted, "Do not let her touch the child! It was her *cures* that killed my baby! She is a *witch*! She has put a curse on me because she wants my husband. My baby's death is an omen that this one has brought destruction upon our people and our cause."

"I will give him *my* breath," Lyssa told them. And before they could take the child from her, she breathed into the child's mouth. Once. Then twice.

And then the child took a breath. The women who had been surprised into inaction had just reached her to grab the child from her arms. Now they stood back, watching. Color came into his face and he began to cry. The cry grew stronger, and the women looked at Lyssa in awe. Lyssa handed the baby to the midwife, who handed him to his mother.

"Heat some rocks and wrap them well. Use them to keep the babe as warm as possible," she whispered. "Feed him frequently."

No one acknowledged her, and Lyssa went back to her dark corner. Yet they followed her instructions and the babe lived.

Savannah Jack had just arrived with a message from the scouts when he heard Sapothlane's words accusing Lyssa of being a witch. He turned his reptilian eye on her. Could Sapothlane be telling the truth? There was indeed something different about Little Flower. What drew him to her? Had she cast a spell on him? From the shadows where she had retreated, Lyssa did not see Savannah Jack.

But Sapothlane read the doubt in his eyes and smiled to herself. She would soon be rid of the only woman beautiful enough to compete with her now that she would have her figure back.

"I heard of such a one among the Choctaw," said a young widow who had most resented Savannah Jack's attention to Lyssa when she had first come. She'd started a whisper campaign against Lyssa as soon as Weatherford had befriended her. Sapothlane had listened eagerly. But now Weatherford owed Lyssa for his own child's life.

"The babe's near death is an omen," the women said in their jealousy, picking up on Sapothlane's words.

Sapothlane looked at Lyssa accusingly. She had seen the doubt in Savannah Jack's eyes. She would get rid of that woman. "Witch!" she shrieked. "Depart from me. I do not want to see you."

Weatherford held Sapothlane while she tried to nurse their tiny baby. Sapothlane cried. Her milk would not descend, and the little one cried also. Now that the babe was born, the frailty that had been disguised by baby weight was now apparent to Weatherford. Though he had made sure Sapothlane had been given more than her share of food—indeed, he had given his own portion for her to eat—she felt like a leaf in his arms.

She needed reassurance. Weatherford did not bother to reason with Sapothlane because hers were the words of a weak woman. Women bearing a child were filled with tears...or such was his experience. And this one had endured much.

A young mother whose child had fallen from her arms into the deep waters of the Alabama during their frantic escape from Holy Ground gladly nursed Weatherford's son.

Weatherford was caught up in his own worries for his wife, his people, and his cause, but not so much that he did not consider the consequences of Sapothlane's words on Lyssa's future. He had seen much death and wondered whether life should be brought into this crazy world. He thought of the babes at Fort Mims and their fate in this war. He had just learned of the death of his cousin Will Milfort, who had been killed by their friend Sam Dale in a cane break near Randon's plantation. Dale, now a captain in the militia, had shot Milfort, the leader of a small group of warriors in a canoe. Those who escaped said Milfort and Dale had recognized one another just as Dale pulled the trigger of the gun. Their leader fell dead with his friend's name on his lips. They heard Sam Dale cry out in disbelief.

Then Dale got into a canoe along with a slave named Cesar, James Smith, and Jeremiah Austill to pursue the rest of the fleeing warriors. They pulled even to the warriors and wound up killing eight of the eleven in the canoe in hand-to-hand combat there on the Alabama River. The news spread quickly, carried by the three Indians who had survived.

So many with whom he had shared a happy childhood were now gone from this blood-soaked land.

Will Milfort. Killed by their friend Sam Dale.

Somehow he must send word to Will's father. In his mind's eye, he pictured the day in the forest when they had shared the joy of Will's first deer. He remembered Will's eager eyes as he had absorbed the tales that Weatherford told him of mighty warriors in times past and lands far away...and the stories of LeClerc Milfort's own exploits as war chief of the Creek. Weatherford's heart ached.

But he was a man and he remained stoic.

He looked at Lyssa and those at his fire who depended on him. He gently laid Sapothlane back against the skins and whispered, "Must go." Then he strode out of the dark cave, passing Savannah Jack without even seeing him. Lyssa thought she saw tears in Weatherford's eyes.

Lyssa had kept to the shadows, letting his clan's midwife and medicine woman tend Sapothlane. At last, with great compassion Lyssa brought Sapothlane a tea she brewed to calm her and help her womb heal, but Sapothlane slapped the cup from her hand.

"You are the reason I nearly lost the child," she hissed with venom in her whispered words. "You are a witch...with *your potions*! Leave me!"

The woman was distraught. Surely she did not mean it. But the other women looked at her with fear and shrank away. Lyssa knew what they did to witches. It was then that she spotted Savannah Jack, his head cocked, eyeing her speculatively.

Lyssa returned to the shadows.

She thought about her own impending childbirth. Counting the months, she figured herself to be about five months along. Four more months to go, and yet she waddled like a duck when she walked. She felt like she was all belly. Just recently her child had started moving and kicking. How strange it was to see a bulge in the middle of her belly and think of someone's foot pressing from the inside! She patted her belly and tried to soothe the little one within. What would happen if her babe had blue eyes? Who would believe her husband had been a Tallusahatchee warrior then? Please, Yahola, Great Spirit, God, whatever your name, please keep my baby safe...and let me find Cade.

Lyssa remained at Weatherford's fire, continuing to take the children out to forage for food, but she was shunned now by all the women. She took pleasure in watching Running Elk play with Charles and Polly but stayed as far from Sapothlane as possible. She tried to call little attention to herself. If they knew who she was, her life would be worthless. Only Weatherford's protection and the other women's fear of Savannah Jack kept her safe.

But Weatherford was frequently away. Led by Peter McQueen and Josiah Francis, the Red Sticks fought Jackson at Emuckfaw on January 22, 1814, and Enotachopo Creek on January 24, approximately twenty to fifty miles northeast of Tahopeka. Weatherford oversaw the building of a barricade at Tahopeka, sometimes called Horseshoe Bend, where the war chief of the Okfuskee, Menawa, was preparing what they called an impregnable defense in the horseshoe bend of the Tallapoosa River. It was there that Weatherford saw Far Off Warrior, who had survived but still suffered from his wounds at Fort Mims.

Far Off Warrior told him, "Little Warrior was with Tecumseh when he was slain at the Battle of the Thames in October. The bodies of the warriors were so mutilated after the battle that no one could not positively identify Tecumseh. However, Little Warrior claims that he and others managed to carry him through the dense smoke from the battlefield and bury him in a place where no one will find his body."

Tecumseh had fought for his people for most of his forty-two years and had foreseen his death in the coming battle. News of Tecumseh's death spread from village to village. How would this news affect their cause? Weatherford led his warriors from town to town to bolster support for the Red Sticks.

Scouts reported that the Americans approached and were setting up camp near Calabee Creek. The Red Sticks burnt-earth policy, leaving no viable crops, made it difficult for the Americans to live off the land. But that policy also affected the Red Sticks, whose stores had mostly been burned at Holy Ground. Yet the Americans continued pursuing. A Creek scout reported their approach.

Paddy Walsh sent out a call to join in battle, and 1,274 fighting men soon appeared at their camp. While General Floyd gathered his army at Calabee Creek, a war council ensued between William Weatherford, his cousin Malcolm McPherson, Paddy Walsh, and High Head Jim as to the best plan for attack. The meeting between the Red Stick leaders for discussing strategy was held at Weatherford's fire. Lyssa overheard the debate over the impending attack on the American forces gathering at Calabee Creek. All agreed the force must be dislodged before it became too strong in that position. But fierce disagreement occurred as to strategy.

Lyssa studied the gathering of warriors from the dark shadows of their camp where the women waited to be called on to serve the men. She had the opportunity to observe the men as they spoke, as their faces were reflected in the flames of Weatherford's fire.

Paddy Walsh was a contradiction. He was only about her height—five foot two or three—with a wide mouth that made him look like the image of a demon. In truth, he was nearly as ugly as Savannah Jack, who was in her opinion the ugliest human being she had ever seen. At first his appearance frightened and repulsed her. But she learned that Walsh was a gifted linguist who spoke Creek, Alabama, Chickasaw, and Choctaw languages fluently, and he rivaled Weatherford as an orator. She could tell as she watched the men listen to his words that the warriors respected him and responded to him.

It was Paddy Walsh who, along with Far Off Warrior, Red Eagle, and the chief of Wewauka, had led the attack on Fort Mims. While his stature as a prophet was greatly diminished, he had regained their respect because of his courage on entering the fort ahead of anyone else. He survived the barrage of bullets and his near-mortal injuries.

"Americans place their leaders in the middle of their camp for their protection," Weatherford said, explaining his plan for the attack on Calabee Creek. "If we send a small force of 300 warriors under Paddy Walsh directly into the center of the camp and kill the leaders, the rest will run. When the head is cut off of the serpent, the rest has no direction."

Walsh allowed contempt to show on his face, and the others looked dubious.

"We have little ammunition with which to fight," Weatherford continued, undaunted. "We must design our attack to make the most of our weapons...our tomahawks and war clubs. They might be effective if we can get to the leaders before they have time to organize to fight us with their guns and bayonettes."

"Foolishness!" Walsh shouted. "You would cause the needless deaths of 300 warriors in an attack in which you will not personally participate. We should attack two sides of the camp, with a feinting attack elsewhere and fight until dawn, at which point we will withdraw."

"Men will not give their all in battle if they know there is a deadline at which they may leave it," Weatherford insisted, his black eyes flashing. "*I* will lead them into the center of the camp, though I thought the prophet Paddy Walsh would want to do so." He spoke even more softly so that all had to quiet to hear him speak. "*This plan will work!*"

To the other warriors assembled, he said, "Who will go with me?"

After an uncomfortable few moments when only a few stood, Weatherford was stunned, shocked, and insulted at the lack of support. He stood tall before them. "You may continue your cautious half-fights," he said, turning his back on Walsh. "I am leaving it to you." He walked away from the fire and mounted Arrow to ride into the cold forest and think.

The warriors left with plans to attack Floyd's army at around five o'clock on the morning of January 27, 1814.

Though he did not take part in the battle, the fight was never far from Weatherford's thoughts. He knew his brothers would die because of the foolish decisions of their leaders. He sat alone that night waiting for the dawn, when he knew they would attack, and prayed for their success.

Weatherford's personal life was no less wrought with danger. He had considered his options from this point forward, and he reluctantly came to the conclusion that for Lyssa's safety, she and Sapothlane must be separated. Sapothlane's jealousy was insane. But their separation would make Sapothlane happy.

Not long after sunrise, Savannah Jack appeared in the dark before him, bloody from the battle he had just left.

"High Head Jim is near death. We fought well until daylight came, and then they drove us back with their bayonets, just as you said."

"We have lost a mighty warrior, and I have lost another friend," Weatherford said, trying to maintain his stoic demeanor. High Head Jim, a tustenuggee from Autauga, though fifteen years older than he, had been a like a brother. His cousin, Polly Durant, would be heartbroken.

So many of their honored leaders and brave young warriors had fallen to the cause. Ten warriors killed at Burnt Corn, fifty at Fort Mims, 186 at Tallusahatchee, 300 at Talladega, twenty-five at Holy Ground, fifty-four at Emuckfaw and Enotachopo Creek, and now forty-nine had fallen at Calabee Creek. His heart, if not already broken, would surely fail him.

He had a new son...another William. Yet his brother's wife and children had been brutally murdered. He had held those children when they were no older than his new son. That image—that nightmare of their deaths—would never go away. And now his own children, his people, were in danger of starving.

"Many go to Tahopeka in the bend of the Tallapoosa to make camp with Menawa and prepare a defense at which the Red Sticks might gather and make one mighty battle against the weakened Americans," Savannah Jack said. "However, Paddy Walsh has decided that we cannot defeat the Americans. He sends you this message: the best plan would be to go to Pensacola with the Spanish and get out of the way of harm until the nation can affect peace."

Weatherford recalled the Hillabees' belief that *they* had a truce with Andrew Jackson, only to be betrayed and have their village destroyed, their people shot and bayonetted. Sixty men, women, and children of that village were slaughtered in fifteen minutes. The memory of what happened to the Hillabees led to Walsh's decision not to pursue a truce and instead to leave Creek country altogether.

Weatherford was inclined to fight rather than surrender. He went to tell Sapothlane what had happened at Calabee Creek and inform her that other leaders wanted him to join them at Tahopeka.

"I will not go to Tahopeka," Sapothlane declared. ""I am going to Moniac's Island. There we will be safe with my family. You kept that woman here with the excuse that I needed her remedies. I am no longer pregnant. Our son is here and strong, and I want her gone. What is there about this woman that makes her different than any of the other many widows?" she demanded.

"Tell the women to pack up and break camp. We are leaving," he said.

Sapothlane gladly commanded Weatherford's slaves to gather their supplies together. "Little Flower remains," she said. Weatherford gave a brusque assent and rode away to prepare for their departure.

Lyssa watched as Running Elk scampered after Charles and Polly, mounting the horse behind Charles. Running Elk thought Lyssa would follow. Lyssa was gathering her possessions when Sapothlane approached.

"Running Elk will go with us, but you stay with Savannah Jack." Coldly, she turned her back and followed the woman who carried her child.

Lyssa watched as Weatherford smiled and reached down for her to ride with him. Sapothlane cuddled close, and, touching his cheek, gave him her siren's smile. Dark shadows circled her eyes.

Lyssa shivered, but not with cold. Sapothlane had refused her help and bled heavily. She was not strong enough to travel. Yet Lyssa was helpless with her premonition. Sapothlane would misinterpret her warning.

Weatherford held Sapothlane and tried to cushion her from jolts as they rode to Moniac's Island, a small cay near the mouth of Catoma Creek, a tributary of the Alabama. It was all he could do. He must let Savannah Jack take Lyssa with him to Horseshoe Bend. He forced his mind to the dangers at hand.

He was a man, the son of Sehoy of the Clan of the Wind, who had died only last year at fifty-three. He knew her spirit lingered to give him strength.

He had fought with his people for their traditions as she would have wished.

He had done all he could to protect Lyssa Rendel, granddaughter of Pushmataha and woman of Cade Kincaid. Now his own family was a threat to her. He would get a message to Pushmataha if he could.

Lyssa lay listlessly on her pallet amid women whose husbands did not follow Weatherford. Some were widows whose men had been killed in battle.

Cade was never far from her thoughts.

She had tried over and over in her mind to figure *some way* to escape. Unfortunately, she realized she had never been gifted with a good sense of direction and was just as likely to wander into the field of battle as away from it. She knew that physically she was in no condition to venture forth alone and elude Savannah Jack's tracking skills. She was frightened. She was exhausted. And she feared she might actually be the widow she claimed to be. She had not *felt* her boy's presence for a long, long time. Though she had not given over to tears before, they now flowed uncontrollably. She felt hopeless.

Weatherford had left her to Savannah Jack. The time she had dreaded had arrived. Now what?

Sapothlane had tricked Running Elk and Lyssa into thinking they would both accompany Weatherford. It was another of her cruelties. As the days passed, Lyssa missed Running Elk terribly. She cried so hard that even Savannah Jack feared for her health. He ordered the preparation of one of her own potions to calm her. When she awoke, she was cradled in his arms, heading toward Horseshoe Bend.

The spring rains had the streams and rivers rising above their normal boundaries, and horse paths had become tiny rivulets, making their journey even more precarious. Lyssa was exhausted and despondent.

Once they made it to Horseshoe Bend, Lyssa found that day followed day with little distinction. Word came through scouts that the American leader Russell had led his 3rd US Infantry and a contingent of Choctaw and Chickasaw against the refugee camps of Red Sticks and burned abandoned Red Stick towns. With the Americans' woefully inadequate supply lines, they were reduced to eating their horses just to reach their base at Fort Claiborne. Meanwhile, Josiah Francis harassed settlers who might attempt to resettle on their farms and plantations in the Tensaw country from his base at Moniac's Island, where Weatherford had resettled his family.

As war chief, Menawa of Okfuskee had gathered about 1,000 warriors and more than 300 women and children inside the loop of the Tallapoosa River. Under the direction of William Weatherford, he had built about 400 feet of breastworks to close the loop on the land side. The breastworks provided portholes at a height to be defensive and yet with a clear shot on advancing adversaries. The Red Sticks had learned their lesson from the errors at Fort Mims. The Tallapoosa would be their defense on the other three sides. The head chief of the Okfuskee, their medicine man, said the Americans would attack at the back of the horseshoe at the river, so it was there that Menawa, relying on the predictions of the prophet, planned his strategy.

Menawa, forty-seven, was one of the wealthiest of all the Creeks. He was famous for his herds of cattle and horses and his large quantity of hogs. As a youth, he had conducted annual horse-stealing forays into Tennessee that earned him his name, Hothelepoya or Crazy Trouble Hunter. When he became war chief, he gained the name Menawa. Before the war broke out, he was operating a store and enjoying his prosperity at Okfuskee. But now he prepared to fight.

It was the end of March. Jackson's army approached Horseshoe Bend. His scouts reported that Menawa had listened to the head chief, the medicine man, who said the Americans would attack from the across the river at the back of the loop. Jackson adjusted his tactics and situated his cannons at the breastworks in preparation of attack. An infuriated Menawa struck the hapless prophet with his war club and killed him. Ferociously, he redirected his warriors toward the breastworks where Jackson had now established his line of attack.

Though scouts had reported the approach of Jackson's army and there was confusion as to where to establish their major line, the Red Sticks were still confident that they had produced an impenetrable and unconquerable position there in the loop of the river, accessible only through the narrow mouth of the loop. A raging river surrounded them, fueled by the spring rains on the three remaining sides.

Savannah Jack strutted about, wearing only his breechclout, the wounds and scars of many battles evident on his muscled body, exhorting the others and exuding bloodlust and confidence. As a precaution, Peter McQueen had sent his sister Nancy, her daughter Polly Coppinger, Polly's ten-year-old son Billy, her daughters Hepsy and Missouri, and others into the safety of the swamp. His sons fought with him.

Though the warriors fasted and purged with the Black Drink, women and children still had to eat. Lyssa made it through each day by surviving on routine. Chaos swirled around her, with prophets chanting their incantations, women trying to gather up their little ones and hurry them along to safety, children crying, mothers crying along with the children as they remembered Tallusahatchee and what happened to the Hillabees, dogs barking and chasing, wondering what game was afoot, and warriors shouting to one another about changes in strategy and planning. In the midst of the reign of terror, a despondent Lyssa listlessly, hopelessly, hummed the tune with which she had successfully convinced all but Savannah Jack, who was oblivious, that madness had possessed her...and stirred the sofkee that bubbled in her pot.

Wearing only a thin ragged blanket about her shoulders to cover her deerskin mantle and skirt, with moccasins flapping at her feet, she spread her hands over the fire to warm them against the chill. Seven months into her pregnancy, Lyssa was so large that when she lay on her back she could barely breathe. The sight of her toes was a mere memory. Weeks before, Running Elk, Charles, and Polly had giggled at her pitiful efforts at pulling on her moccasins and had taken mercy on her by helping her tie them on. Now there was no one to take mercy on her. Here she was at the beck and call of Savannah Jack, for whom she prepared meals and tended the fire.

Oblivious to the running back and forth, Lyssa, now an island unto herself, stirred absently with her mind on the man she loved, wondering where he was and if she would ever see him again.

A sound. She stiffened and listened. There. She heard it again. Her eyes darted here and there, looking for the source of that sound floating on the wind. She rubbed her aching back and blew back the hair from her eyes, but the lethargy of moments before had disappeared.

The notes of a flute? Gabe's flute? Somehow she knew that the prickle of apprehension she had fought to hold at bay was somehow connected with Cade. He must be near! Was that despair she felt from him? "Hold on. Do not give up," she whispered to him in her mind.

She felt his desperation, but what could she do? She could barely tend to her own basic needs. The baby moved and kicked and tumbled about inside of her, reassuring her that he was healthy. Unconsciously, she stroked her belly, soothing the life within.

Jackson's army approached. The chaos became a whirlwind of purposeful activity. The men directed the women to take the children and move to the woods further inside curve of the horseshoe. A jubilant Savannah Jack ran past her, painted red and black for war. "Scouts have spotted Jackson's approach at the breastworks!" he shouted. "Go to the woods!" Jack held his gun in one hand and brandished his war club with the other as if itching for battle. His distinctive knife was tucked into the band of his breechclout. Excitement glittered in his eyes at the thought of war and blood.

The red-and-black-painted prophets, feathers bobbing about on their shoulders and heads, danced frantically, shouting their incantations and declaring that the land on which they fought was holy ground and impenetrable to the enemy. The look in their eyes was more desperate than convinced after seeing one of their own struck dead by Menawa.

Perhaps this is my chance, Lyssa thought. There are canoes on the river. Perhaps I can steal one.

21

Lyssa hurried through the trees to the river, carrying a pail as if going for water. The river was a torrent with all the streams and rivulets full and flowing forth with spring rains. As she was about to step out from the woods onto the bank of the river, she spotted black-faced Indians friendly to the Americans swimming and pushing the Red Stick canoes positioned for escape to the other side of the river. They dodged the debris the heavy storms had dumped into the water.

So the prophet's prediction was partially true. The Americans would use the Red Sticks' own canoes to transport a wing of their army across the swiftly flowing Tallapoosa onto the peninsula for a rear attack!

Lyssa hid her bulk behind the veil of moss and the massive trunk of an ancient oak. Perhaps she blended. Her mantle and skirt were of deerskin. Would these Americans and their allies kill women? They had before. She was unexceptional and would be treated like the women at Tallusahatchee. Lyssa slid down the tree trunk and put her head in her hands.

There would be no escape.

She glanced back to the river. A lone egret, snowy white and stark against the raging, silt-filled waters of the Tallapoosa and the still barren landscape, stood on one foot and cocked its head, eying her speculatively. It then took flight, soaring into the brilliant blue sky and over the treetops back toward the barricade where the battle would soon begin.

Despondently, Lyssa gathered herself together and stumbled back to where the other women were huddled with their children. Would this be the end for her and her child? She looked toward the barricade that had been built under the direction of William Weatherford, who had studied the defensive works at Mobile and Pensacola. It was massive, five to eight feet high, made of stacked logs with portholes of staggered height and sharpened poles pointing outward toward the expected attackers.

She looked to see the egret once again, and that was when something glistened in the sun's rays and caught her eye through one of the portholes at the lowest point of the barricade. It was a horse whose coat shone brilliant white. It was Beauty. And on her back was the man Lyssa loved. She unconsciously stepped forward, no longer hidden by the copse of trees.

At Beauty's feet loped the two dogs who would know her scent. Their heads rose as the wind shifted to come from the river through the trees and over the barricade. They set up a howl as the first barrage of shooting commenced. Beauty's head lifted, and Cade, who had almost given up on ever seeing Lyssa again, looked over the barricade. In his anguish, he had actually viewed this battle as his last. But now, as the smoke rose about them, he locked eyes with Lyssa. His heart leapt within him.

She lived!

Oblivious to the war raging about him or the danger to which he exposed himself, Cade kicked Beauty into action, never taking his gaze from Lyssa's. If he were to look away, she might disappear!

Cade and Beauty galloped toward the barricade. Arrows flew around him from the Red Sticks, whose ammunition had nearly given out. Bullets flew behind him from Jackson's army. Beauty responded to his command and lifted off, sailing over the heads of the Red Sticks manning the portholes. To his right, he glimpsed Major Montgomery fall from atop the barricade with a bullet in the middle of his forehead. Samson and Delilah both climbed the barricade in pursuit. Cade barely noticed when an arrow grazed his arm and a bullet lodged in his leg. Samson attacked a warrior whose hatchet was set to sail straight into Cade's chest, and Delilah jumped a warrior who was about to grab him and pull him from the horse. Through the melee he rode, with bullets wounding him, but not seriously enough to deter him from his goal.

Savannah Jack was in the first line of battle, a savage painted for war. The newest scars from the battle at Calabee Creek puckered and made his face even more frightening. He spotted the white horse as it gracefully bounded over the barricade. Then he caught the focus in Cade Kincaid's eyes and turned to see where he looked.

The woman?

With a roar of rage, the black-and-red-painted warrior, the most feared of all the Creeks, turned from the barricade and ran to the woman he knew as Little Flower, the widow of a Tallusahatchee warrior. His eyes glittered maniacally as Cade pounded toward him through the smoke of battle.

Savannah Jack beat Cade to her and held his knife to her throat. Lyssa nearly fainted, but she would not break her gaze from the man she had loved since she had first seen him those years ago when they were children on Twiggs's pack train. An ungodly howl erupted from Savannah Jack as he put the pieces together.

He had sheltered Cade Kincaid's woman!

He had protected the whelp of his greatest enemy! Bowles had mocked him ceaselessly about letting Cade and Gabe Kincaid escape. Those twin brothers and their father had been his greatest failure. He'd finally gotten his vengeance on their father. But those two....

And now....

He tightened his grip on the bitch he'd captured and backed with her toward the loop of the bend where canoes had been hidden. Today she would die. And Cade Kincaid would watch him kill her! He stopped on the ridge above the river and pricked Lyssa's skin with the tip of his knife. His eyes glittered as he licked the blood from her neck.

He saw Cade flinch but still he pursued.

Gabriel, who had been beside Cade in the battle line, glanced beside him, wondering why his brother's gun had grown silent. Following Cade's insane advance, he saw Savannah Jack pull Lyssa into the woods. Gabriel kicked his own horse and followed Cade over the barricade. He shot past Sam Houston, wounded by an arrow in his upper thigh. Gabe hacked and slashed his way forward, trying to protect his brother's back. They had become a war unto themselves, and Savannah Jack was the only enemy.

Savannah Jack had Lyssa! Finally the battle was behind Cade, and he was pursuing Savannah Jack and Lyssa through the woods. At the shore of the river, Jack saw that the canoes were now ferrying Americans across the river.

The pregnant Lyssa had become dead weight, and Cade was on Jack's heels.

"Bitch!" Savannah Jack cried and threw her from the embankment into the swirling, raging current of the river as he turned to fight Cade Kincaid.

Cade was bleeding from the many wounds he had taken in his race through the battlefield. He prepared to jump after Lyssa, but Savannah Jack readied to toss his knife at her! He must survive to save Lyssa. Cade drew the knife he had pulled from the soldier's chest at Tallusahatchee and flung himself from Beauty's back, taking Jack tumbling backwards into the current. Over and over they went, choking, gouging, and slashing at each other, each man gasping for breath when they chanced to surface. Lyssa saw Cade come to the surface, draw back the knife, and then the two went under once again. Blood came to the surface, but no Cade...and no Jack.

Lyssa, caught in the current, could not swim to reach Cade. She could not see him! She was sinking, the weight of her mantle and skirt taking her down. Savannah Jack could appear at any moment. Cade had not surfaced...and she was sinking!

Suddenly, she was being pulled up. Samson had grabbed her mantle and pulled her to the surface. Beauty came up beside her, and Lyssa grabbed her mane, gasping for breath. Still Cade was nowhere to be seen. And Savannah Jack had disappeared.

"Samson, find Cade!" she shouted.

The dog immediately dove under. Lyssa pulled the heavy clothing from her body and dove under to where she had seen Samson disappear. There! She saw Cade. His clothing was caught on a log and his eyes were open and unseeing. His hands lifted as if in prayer to the surface, swaying where the sunlight caught his movements through the amber water in a strange sort of glow. Lyssa grabbed his shirt and twisted until she could rip it from the limb that held him captive. She gripped him under the chin and shot toward the surface. Samson grabbed Cade's shirt and pulled also. Finally, she reached the surface and gasped for air. She grabbed Cade's chin and lifted his face above the rippling waters as they floated down the river away from the noise, the smoke, and the carnage.

Lyssa finally got enough air to whistle for Beauty. The horse swam against the current, dodging debris in the angry waters until Lyssa could grab her mane. Samson and Delilah swam on either side, helping her hold Cade while the current carried them down until they reached an island.

Lyssa pulled Cade from the river with the help of the animals. "Breathe, my love, breathe!" she cried, pressing his chest to push the water from his lungs and then giving him a breath of her own air. Naked as the day she was born, she straddled him and demanded that he live. The babe between them made her wild efforts awkward and less powerful than she needed.

"Please don't leave me now that I have found you!"

Lyssa willed herself to have the strength to roll Cade onto his stomach and push and pound on his back just as she had done when she had pulled him from the river years ago. Then she turned him again. She cupped his head and blew into his mouth as she had with Weatherford's babe. Finally, he vomited the waters of the river and began to breathe. Exhausted now, she lay beside him and fell asleep, but just for a moment. Delilah's harsh tongue licking her cheeks woke her. Cade lay beside her, breathing but unconscious. He was bleeding...and she slept!

Lyssa stripped him of his torn and bloodied shirt. She ripped the sleeves from the shirt and made a tourniquet around his leg above the most serious wound. She had to stop the bleeding and find the herbs she needed to make a poultice to prevent infection. She slipped the sleeveless shirt over her naked body.

He lived! In the fading light, Lyssa took time to look about her. They needed shelter. On a bank on the other side of the river she thought she could make out a cabin. It was March, and the water had been freezing cold. The weather was unpredictable. Weeks of rains had made the river swift and dangerous. But now hypothermia threatened their lives more than bullet wounds. In truth, the freezing water had probably saved Cade's life by making his blood flow slower from his wounds. Lyssa reached for Beauty, who had stayed close. At her command, Beauty knelt, and Lyssa managed to get Cade onto the horse's back. Then she climbed up too, and the horse bore the weight of both of them. Lyssa held tightly to Beauty's mane and guided her back into the water to swim across the river and up the bank.

There was indeed a cabin there, sheltered by woods in the back. Beauty struggled and slipped in the wet mud, but she made it up the hill. Samson and Delilah sniffed out the cabin, and by the time Lyssa was there, the scurrying noises from the interior had ceased. Beauty knelt at the porch, and Lyssa pulled Cade into the cabin, where to her surprise she found a fire laid and ready to light. She looked around her. Someone had fled in a hurry. She lit the fire and laid a blanket on the floor in front of it. She pulled Cade onto the blanket. Tafia rum in a jug would do to wash his wounds. But she noticed that several of them still contained bullets. She found a knife and seared it in the fire before she dug around, trying to remove the bullets and the debris that had entered the wounds. Hours passed. She sweated with her nerves and the effort of her concentration.

When she felt she had done all she could do, she washed the wounds once again with the rum, bound them with sheets she found in the cabin, and lay down beside Cade, cuddling him and covering them both with the beautiful log cabin quilt the woman of the house had lovingly pieced together. Lyssa was shivering with shock and cold. She turned the jug up and took a drink herself, welcoming the warmth.

Samson stationed himself at the door of the cabin. He would alert her to anyone who might venture near. Delilah lay close to Lyssa as if she knew she needed warming. Lyssa rested only a short while, warming Cade with her body heat. Between Cade's fevered heat and body warmth of Delilah, she had warmed quickly.

Cade moaned when she rose. "I will not leave you, my love," she whispered. Delilah moved closer to Cade to watch and warm.

Lyssa checked out their surroundings. Beauty had found a shed with a manger where someone had left parched corn. Beauty had been wounded herself, though not seriously. Lyssa used the same poultices and cleaning methods on the horse. And then she just held her for a while, stroking her mane and murmuring her gratitude. It was Beauty who had brought them all to safety.

A storm cellar revealed a bounty of produce and supplies. Lyssa wondered to whom the cabin belonged. She had not seen such a store in so long that she had almost forgotten what it was like to have smoked ham in the smokehouse. The Red Sticks had only ravaged the Tensaw area, she supposed, viewing it as the rebellious daughter of the mother villages. The area closer to the mother village had remained untouched.

She took onions, beans, and potatoes from the cellar and set them on the fire to boil with a ham bone and chopped ham. Only then did she think of washing herself and finding something warm to wear. The lady of the house had left all of her clothing, and Lyssa chose a white cotton nightgown that would be comfortable over her bulging belly.

Then she allowed herself the pleasure of lying close to Cade once more, her hand over his heart to be sure it was beating, her face close to his to breathe his breath. "Please, God," she whispered. "Let him live."

As the hours passed, she found life much easier here than it had been in the hollow with the children. She knew now how to deal with the infection that came with serious wounds. The lung fever that resulted from inhaling so much water was what she feared the most. Cade's breaths had come in such shallow gasps that she kept expecting each one to be his last. Yet somehow he survived, though there were times she had almost given up hope. Just as she thought the tide had turned and he was on his way to recovery, the shaking sickness beset him and he relapsed.

She prepared the same remedy she remembered Nicey Potts preparing, a tea from willow bark. She fed him the tea and soups, spooning the liquids into his mouth and stroking his throat to make him swallow. Oh, how she longed for him to open his eyes.

Day turned into night and night into another day with the same routine. Weeks passed. Samson was their hunter and brought meat— rabbit, squirrel, dove, and amazingly a turtle. Delilah stood as sentinel, watching the river and trails. Lyssa continued to tend Cade's wounds and keep him clean and dry, using wet cloths to cool him when the sweating sickness came upon him and cuddling with him when he began to shiver.

Lyssa conclued that Cade must have been sick recently, before coming to Horseshoe Bend. He probably should not have come to the battle. He had few reserves to draw upon. He was so thin that she despaired. He continued to lose weight despite her constantly forcing nourishing fluids into him. His hair was tangled and matted, so she finally found scissors and cut it herself. She took the man of the house's razor strap and shaved her boy's handsome face. If it hadn't been for the dark hollows around his eyes, he would have looked like her old Cade. In his delirium, he called her name.

"I am here, my love," she whispered, and held him close, caressing him with her tender touch and gentle kisses. "You are no longer alone."

He calmed to the sound of her voice.

"Tell me," she said to him. "Please tell me. Let me share your pain."

He was so alone with his nightmares. Finally, as weak as he was, her comfort drew the words from him. His brilliant blue eyes were wide and staring but unseeing. His voice was faint, but she nestled closer.

"Savannah Jack comes for us," he whispered, but she knew he did not mean the two of them. He had reverted to the time when he was a boy.

"Bowles and Jack take us down the Flint to the Apalachicola River. We cross the bay to St. Marks, and they keep us in a cage hangin' from a tree. The women of the village bring sharp, pointed sticks and torment us by day. The swarms of mosquitoes torment us at night." His voice was so weak it was almost a whisper.

Cade began to thrash about. Lyssa threw a leg over him to hold him still. She cuddled closer and stroked his cheek. He calmed, but the agitation continued in the expression of his face and the tension in his hands as he clenched his fists.

"No, I will go. Gabe's too sick to walk. I'll go with you. Just bring Gabe some food and water," he pleaded, reverting back to living the moment.

In his delirium he narrated what he saw.

"The path through the cane and rush looks too thick, but Savannah Jack has a machete. I've got to remember this place. I've got to remember the landmarks. If I can remember, maybe we can escape and I can save Gabe.

"Savannah Jack settles behind some rocks above a canyon to watch the trail. He spots a pack train with some settlers. Separated from the others at the end, a boy about eight years old walks beside his mother's horse, holdin' a squirrel he's shot with a gun that looks brand new. She's laughin'. The father looks back at them with his own gun restin' against his shoulder. He smiles.

"They don't know we wait for them. I *want* to shout. But then Gabriel would die.

"Savannah Jack lets out a whoop, and before the man can bring his gun from his shoulder a tomahawk splits his head. The boy stares with shock in his big green eyes, and Savannah Jack's knife is in his chest. Savannah Jack's men—Blue and the others—decide to have sport with the woman.

"'Come, boy,' Jack says. 'It is time for you to become a man after I take my turn.'

"'Not the woman. I can't!'"

Cade stiffened in remembrance.

"'Watch and learn,' Jack says.

"Jack forces me to watch. The woman's eyes hold mine. She knows I'm horrified. She wishes she could spare me like she would her son. I hold her gaze. It's all I can give her. I'm not strong enough to fight those men. I'm helpless and weak...and angry.

"Her insides are so damaged she's bleedin'," Cade continued with tears in his eyes. "Yet the more the blood, the more excited it gets Savannah Jack. He parades around in front of his men. And they cheer him on.

"Jack sits back on his feet between the woman's legs. But she has enough life left in her that she kicks Jack, sendin' him sprawlin' back. Jack is so furious he pounces on her and slits her throat with that knife he sharpens over and over. The blood spurts and covers him. But she's saved me. She knows it and looks at me as death comes into her big green eyes, her boy's eyes. She smiles, gives me her forgiveness.

"Please don't mutilate the woman. Good God, he's skinnin' that boy as if he were a deer!" Cade cried out, tossing and flailing. "Savannah Jack promises to do it to Gabe next. I must escape. I must save Gabriel. Jack throws me into the cage when we get back to camp. Tomorrow we will die.

"Must leave," Cade muttered. "Pretend to be sick. Isn't hard since I've also got the swamp fever. But the woman with the kind eyes left me a sharp stick in the cage. When the guard brings the gruel, I'm ready." Lyssa was quiet, listening. She doubted Cade even knew he was talking.

"The guard thinks we're both too weak for him to worry about. But with a jab through his eyes and into his brain, we have a chance to escape," he said. "I grab his arms and hold on to him until I can reach his knife. Then I cut through the ropes bindin' the sticks of the pen and pull Gabe out.

"Carryin' Gabe on my back, I go down to the river. Once again I use the stick and find the heart of Blue's brother. I kill him, thinkin' of the woman he violated. I pick Gabe up and carry him to a rowboat rigged with a sail and manage to get him aboard. I have watched that fisherman come in with his catch of fresh fish every day, and I think I can handle it. I find a strength I didn't know I had to put up the sail and round the point. The wind picks up, and I get us out into the still waters of the Apalachee Bay. I can see a point of land in the moonlight. Beyond its white sand beaches is the Apalachee River. If I can make it up that river, we'll come to the Chattahoochee and Flint Rivers. I look back. So far no one follows.

"Savannah Jack has taken the tafia rum he stole from the settlers and gone to his cabin with the strangers who've come to gamble. The dogs bark and howl with all the strangers in the camp, so no one notices when they bark at us. My heart beats so loud I think they must be able to hear it! But Jack doesn't think me strong enough to escape.

"I sail until I see the entrance to the Apalachicola River. The wind dies, so I lower the sail and row. Snakes and alligators are all around us. A panther roars in the dark. I dare not beach the boat.

"Finally, I have to rest. Pull the boat ashore. I gather driftwood for a small fire, leaving Gabe on the shore. A bull gator sounds, and I look back to see the eyes of a gator in the shallow water next to Gabe, creepin' up on his prey. I run back and snatch Gabe under the arms, pullin' him as fast as I can to the river oak leanin' over the water.

"The water beneath the tree thrashes with a number of gators so great you could walk across the river on their backs! Where are these gators comin' from? I push Gabe up into the tree and keep pushin' and pullin' until we reach the top. Then I hold him on the branches through the night. My eyes close and we wobble. I nearly lose hold of Gabe. I will not. I will not!

"Mornin' comes and the gators return to the water. One by one. Their eyes stay just above the water, but they back off. I run with Gabe on my back to the boat and paddle as hard as I can between the giant creatures.

"At last I think I can go no further. It's rainin'. The rain cools my skin and feels peaceful. I lie back. I look up at the dark sky and open my mouth to the rain. The rain is cool. A white egret dives and, with bright eyes that look directly into mine, lights upon the boat. I'll die here, I think, and I'm at peace. I close my eyes.

"When I open them I'm again in my mother's village. High Head Jim stands with my father and talks of how brave I am, how I'm a warrior, killin' two braves to make our escape. It's a miracle.

"Father only says he wasted his money on the ransom if we were going to escape. Wouldn't have agreed to give Bowles his trading territory."

Lyssa figured Bowles must have been making his deal with Cade's father the day Jack had taken Cade on his little foray to rape and murder an innocent family. Savannah Jack had apparently decided to "play" with the boys. If Bowles had been at St. Marks, Cade and Gabe would not have been able to escape. Savannah Jack wouldn't have been drunk with the tafia. And there was no assurance that Savannah Jack and William Augustus Bowles would have handed them over alive.

"Polly argues that we aren't strong enough to leave. But Father takes us to a hilltop above the river where he first saw Mother as he paddled toward her village. 'She was so beautiful standin' there on the hill,' he says. 'I knew she was to be my woman. And now she's buried here.' He hands the cryin' baby to me and lays down on the grave of my mother. Tears flow from his eyes.

"I hear him say, 'Goodbye, Snow Bird. Goodbye, my love.' And then he turns to me and says, 'You and your brother killed your mother.'

"He stalks away, leavin' me holdin' Joie and supportin' Gabe, who can barely stand. My own eyes ache with fever, and I'm afraid I'll crumble with each step. I take one step at a time."

Cade fell back then, exhausted with the telling. But at last he did not toss and turn. His body could relax, and Lyssa thought that perhaps now he could heal. Telling the story had excised his soul.

Cade's story explained his torment. Now she understood.

22

More weeks passed. Cade's fever was at last at bay. But still, he did not seem to see with his eyes.

And then early one morning, the first pain cut through Lyssa's body with a fierce, shooting suddenness. The beautiful white nightgown she wore was wet with a bloody moistness. When the pain passed and Lyssa could breathe again, she rolled from the pallet where she lay next to Cade and crawled to a chair, where she pulled herself up. She clenched for another pain, toppling the chair in the process. Slowly she moved toward the bedroom she had prepared for having to deliver her child alone. Along the way, she managed to remove the soiled nightgown, dropping it as another pain possessed her. Lyssa forced herself to walk. She concentrated on breathing between the pains, knowing that tensing in anticipation of the pains would only make them worse. And then the pains came so frequently and so fiercely that she had to lie down before finding another gown or a quilt with which to cover herself.

When the contractions possessed her, she pulled on the strips of cloth she had tied to the sides of the bed and pushed to help the baby come. Time passed and became nothing to her. Cries escaped her that she could not control.

Lyssa. He heard Lyssa. But something held him down. He was in a dark and lonely place, afraid to come out. Here he could hear her, see her in his memory. But leaving the safety of the darkness seemed like more than he could do.

Something beyond where he lingered pulled him forward. He heard her cries! Finally, he broke through and his eyes popped open. A chair lay overturned. A bloody white nightgown littered the floor.

Where was he? What was this strange place? He lay on the floor in front of a fire.

Another cry. A moan. Lyssa?

At last he remembered. Savannah Jack had thrown her into the rushing current.

Lyssa!

Cade rolled onto his side. There beyond the door. He heard it again. He turned over to his stomach and pushed himself into a crouch, finally pulling himself to his feet and oversetting the chair he used for support.

Weak. He was so weak. He stumbled toward the open door of the bedroom.

Samson and Delilah stood on either side of the bed watching, only able to give Lyssa their moral support. They could not help her with this.

She cried again and strained, pulling on the restraints on the bed. Her body was distorted, her belly a hard knot.

Hearing a sound at the door, she turned her head in alarm. Had Savannah Jack survived and found them? Her violet eyes opened wide with fear.

And then she saw Cade's beloved face, anguished at her distress. A cry escaped...joy...pain.

He watched as the violet eyes grew soft and dewy with such love that it pierced his heart with a fierce, responding ache. He'd sought her for so long. He'd longed to tell her how much he loved her before it was too late.

Could it be too late? She lay naked and writhing and tied to the bed. Why? Who had tied her?

She was pregnant! And the child was coming! The situation finally registered in his befuddled brain.

"Help me!" she pleaded, beyond knowing how to make words to explain. His brain cleared with her need.

Instinct kicked in, and Cade situated himself at the foot of the bed and pulled her legs apart. A bulge and what looked like a tiny head appeared with the contraction.

"The child is coming, Lyssa."

With a grimace and a shout, Lyssa pushed. A gush of blood and a head appeared.

Cade went so white she thought he would pass out. "I have killed you," he said. Lyssa knew he was going back to the stories he heard of his mother and the woman he had seen Savannah Jack kill.

"Cade. Look at me. Look into my eyes." At last she got his attention. "Focus on my eyes, my love. I am not your mother. I am not that poor woman Savannah Jack killed. Look at me. I am Lyssa. I am your love. I will not die. I will not leave you. This is how babies come."

She had to push. The pain seemed to rip through her, but she did not cry out. She kept her eyes focused on Cade.

"We will do this together," she said. "But you must help me."

"I don't know if I can," he whispered, wobbling before her.

"You are strong. You are my brave warrior. You fought Savannah Jack for me. I would be dead if you had not taken bullets and arrows to get to me."

Another pain. She held her breath and pushed but never faltered from her focus.

"Our babe, Cade Kincaid. You must help our child into this world."

With a wild scream, Lyssa tossed her head back and pushed. Instinctively, he held out his big, calloused hands and the tiny body slid into them...a little girl with rosebud lips pursed in discontent. Unsure what to do next, Cade looked at an anxious Lyssa. When the baby's discontent turned into a strong wail, Lyssa smiled.

"Tie the cord that binds us twice with the string, and then cut between your knots," she managed to say.

Shouldn't she be comfortable now? Should expelling the afterbirth be this painful? She could not let Cade sense her anxiety. He tied the cord with the string beside the bed. And just as he was cutting the cord as she commanded, Lyssa felt the urge to push again. Cade looked between her legs and then nearly tossed the little girl into Lyssa's arms. Another child, this one a boy came out and commenced an immediate wail.

Lyssa looked at Cade in shock. Two?

"Mine...?"

The joy in her eyes turned to fury. "Of course yours, you fool."

"But..."

"Don't you dare question me now!"

She was furious. Furious and exhausted. She directed him to do for his son as he had done for his daughter. She only wanted to hold her babies. He dared to question! As if there could ever be anyone else but him. How could he question that those babies were his! She just wanted him to hold her, but now she had to push again.

The look on his face with the gush of blood and the blatant fear that she would bleed to death changed her anger to compassion. She understood how all he had endured had made him shield his heart. Yet she knew she held a place in his heart, and he was scared to death he would lose her.

"Look into my eyes," she said. "I am not dying. This is the natural way of things. The Master of Breath is done with the nest he made for our babies."

Her voice soothed him, this man who was a man and knew little of womanly things. She had made two babies for him. She must guide him gently. Together they would conquer those horrible memories.

When the afterbirth spilled from her womb, Cade looked like he was about to pass out. He had awakened to her cries, been pulled from the dark tunnel in which he had been lurking behind the pain of his reality and the fever from the sickness. He had only barely managed to shuffle into the bedroom to find the woman he had been searching for in the throes of childbirth.

"Look at me, Cade Kincaid," she demanded.

"One night?" he said.

"It only took one night for you, but I have carried the fruit of that night for nearly nine months. They are early. I thought it was only one and now there are two. Like you and Gabriel, twins. A boy and a girl."

She looked at him, her eyes glowing with joy and love...and frustration.

"Give me my baby boy," she commanded, once again the Choctaw princess. "I will roll over and you can take that soiled top quilt away from beneath me."

He followed her instructions, and then he tenderly took the cloths hanging on the bucket to wash the blood from her body. Lyssa blushed at the intimacy but was immediately distracted when their little boy found a nipple and began to suckle.

"Oh!" she yelped.

Cade jumped. "Did I hurt you?"

"This one surprised me."

Together they marveled as his tiny fists kneaded her swollen breast. The little girl kicked her brother and tried to fasten onto the other breast.

Lyssa watched as color returned to Cade's face. She struggled to sit up in a position where she could better accommodate her babies. Cade adjusted the pillows behind her so that she could hold both at her large breasts, which he found himself leering at. A stirring told him he wasn't dead yet.

Lyssa looked up and blushed again at the heat in his eyes. "You are about to fall over. Lie down here with us."

The knotted cords of the cornshuck bed creaked as he lay beside her, afraid to touch her. Then the need to be close overcame his fear of hurting the three of them, the desire to be a part of that tableau drew him nearer and nearer. Lyssa was achingly aware of his every move, afraid to speak, afraid a word would drive him away. For weeks...no months...she had wondered if he would live. And yet she never lost hope.

And now, she wasn't sure he was ready for this. All of this. Her. The babies.

Almost losing her had nearly driven him over the edge, and having her so close now, he had to be closer. He had to touch her and make sure she was real. Touch her and never let go. Slowly he worked his hand behind her head and closed the distance between them. He pushed at the pillows and managed to maneuver himself so he supported Lyssa while she nursed the babies.

A sound beyond the cabin captured his attention. It was a flute. And the tune it played was the tune Gabe played his horses. Could it be?

Samson cocked his head on the other side of the bed. He heard it also. "Samson. Find Gabriel," Cade commanded. Samson set off at a run.

Could it be his brother? Please, God.

Lyssa sighed. Cade brushed his hand across the downy hair on the heads of his babies. Their babies. He listened to the sounds of contentment as they smacked and sighed and kneaded. Lyssa brushed his hand with her cheek, and he placed soft kisses in her hair. Exhausted, they all fell asleep cuddled together.

Samson followed the sound of the flute and found Gabe and Pushmataha camped not far away. The two men had searched and searched and despaired of ever finding Cade and Lyssa alive. They had almost reconciled themselves to perhaps, if they were lucky, finding their bodies. And then Samson appeared from nowhere. Agitated and pushing Gabe back in the direction he had come, Samson led them to the cabin beneath the hill on which they had camped. They joyfully bounded up the stairs and through the open front door. And there they stopped, surveying the overturned chairs and the bloody trail to the door of the bedroom. Gabe stopped to pick up the bloody gown while Pushmataha stepped forward into the room. They approached the door to the bedroom with knives in hand.

Gabe looked to the door and saw tears in the eyes of the Choctaw's greatest warrior.

"Are they...?" He rushed to look inside.

No, not dead. But Gabe felt the same emotion that Lyssa's grandfather did when he saw his brother embracing his little family. The baby girl opened her eyes and looked straight at Gabe. His heart quickened, and he felt the tears gather in his own eyes.

They lived. In the land so devastated by hatred, killing, and death, they lived.

Pushmataha lifted a quilt from a chest beside the bed and tucked it around his granddaughter and her husband. Pushmataha lifted the infant boy, who immediately cuffed him with his tiny fist, not happy to be taken from his mother.

Lyssa's eyes popped open in alarm the minute the child was taken from her arms, and Pushmataha saw joy in her eyes at the sight of him. "Grandfather," she said with love and relief.

"Rest, little one, I am here now. You are safe. We will care for your babes."

Lyssa nodded and closed her eyes. Then he took the little girl from her arms and handed her to Gabe, who wrapped her in the cloth laid neatly beside the bed for the one child Lyssa had expected. Pushmataha found another cloth and wrapped the boy child.

Gabriel had last seen Lyssa when Savannah Jack had thrown her into the river. When Cade had disappeared fighting Savannah Jack, it was Jack who had climbed back onto the bank. Gabe had fought him, determined to kill the man who had killed his brother. But Savannah Jack had managed to escape once again when other Red Sticks came to his rescue. Jack was bleeding profusely from Cade's knife, which protruded from his shoulder. It was a knife Jack himself had carved.

When at last the battle was over and Gabe was free to look for Savannah Jack, he had disappeared. They did not find his body among the 557 Red Sticks killed on the battlefield at Horseshoe Bend or the 300 in the river who tried to escape and were killed. Neither did Gabe know if Cade and Lyssa had survived the river. But Beauty, Samson, and Delilah disappeared at the same time. That gave them hope.

For weeks Gabe himself had to heal from the many wounds he suffered. Pushmataha had to fulfill his duties as a chief, and only afterward could he and Pushmataha search the east side of the river for Cade and Lyssa. They would have missed the cabin on the embankment on the east side of the Tallapoosa had Samson not led them there. The trees had leafed out and hid what once was barely visible. Nature had reclaimed its land quickly in the spring rains, which had also managed to wash away whatever tracks might have led the searchers to their hideaway. Fortunately, it also kept them safe from a predator like Jack.

The door to the cabin closed.

Unconsciously, Cade pulled Lyssa tighter into his arms. Lyssa sighed.

Safe at last.

Quietly, Gabe and Pushmataha carried the babies with them as they left the room and went to sit on the steps of the cabin. The sky was a glorious shade of blue.

Kincaid blue, with not a single cloud.

23

Gabriel left them at the cabin only briefly while he found canoes in which to ease Cade and Lyssa's travel home. Pushmataha stayed back at the cabin to guard his granddaughter and great-grandchildren. The threat that they might yet be discovered by Savannah Jack was real. If he still lived, Gabe had no doubt that Jack would never give up. Gabe would never underestimate Jack's ability to survive. They sent several of the braves who had come with them back to St. Stephens to prepare the others for their return. They had orders not to tell about the babies. Pushmataha, with his odd sense of humor, wanted to witness Jake Rendel's expression when he saw the grandchildren they shared...and of course experience the joy of his Chamay and Malee as they learned about the babies.

They decided it was safest to travel with Gabriel and Cade in one canoe and Pushmataha in the other with Lyssa and the babies. Samson and Delilah trotted along beside the river.

The travel was slow, but Cade and Lyssa were so exhausted that they slept most of the way. Pushmataha and Gabriel made camp for them every night. Cade was still so weak. Gabe dipped an oar in the water and guided the canoe day after day. Finally, Cade became alert enough to want news.

"I've been saving word of Zach McGirth until you were strong enough to take it," Gabe said.

Cade prepared himself for the worst about his friend, with whom he had scouted and fought side by side. Zach had been beside himself with grief...losing his son James and his wife Vicey and all their girls. Cade had been with him when he'd buried the son he'd pulled from that inferno. He'd had no hope of finding Zach's wife and girls.

"Zach and I both thought death would be better than the hell we were in," Cade said quietly. "Did death finally catch up to him?"

"Zach was in Mobile one day when someone came up to him and told him that there were people down at the docks asking for him," Gabe said. "Zach hurried to where the man said those people were, and there was Vicey and his girls."

"How did they survive?" Cade asked, remembering the devastation at Fort Mims.

"That boy they raised...Sanota...took them from the fort as his hostages. He was shocked to see them there. But he protected them while the battle raged and then just walked them out the gate. He kept them fed and safe until Horseshoe Bend. Then he told them he might not make it back."

Cade looked off into the distance. He remembered Sanota. He remembered Horseshoe Bend. "He didn't make it back," he said.

Gabe shook his head. "The family made their way to the Tombigbee and managed to find a guy with a flatboat to go the rest of the way. They'd just gotten to the dock and started asking around for McGirth when Zach got there."

Too weak to maintain his usual composure, Cade found himself crying with joy for his friend. Once he started, he could not stop, and he wept for all of his friends who had died in the senseless conflagration.

Gabe pulled ashore, telling Pushmataha it was time to make camp. When the canoe touched ground, Cade had regained control of himself, but the tears had been healing. That night he lay next to Lyssa on the deerskin and quilts that Gabe and Pushmataha brought from the cabin, holding her tighter and cuddling her and the babies with an even greater appreciation of his good fortune.

They had all been near death. His Lyssa had saved him.

He might not be a strong fighter at the moment, but he knew he could be quick enough to cover them with his own body if trouble came.

The stronger he got, the more Cade nearly drove Gabriel crazy, insisting that he maneuver the canoe close enough for Cade to see Lyssa and the babies. He could not abide the possibility that they might get out of his sight or his reach.

Gabe could only shake his head in wonder. This brother he had despaired of ever allowing himself to love anyone was close to overdoing his new roles of husband and father!

It was several weeks of slow travel before they finally arrived at the Hobuckintopa Bluff where Lyssa had waited for Cade that morning nine months ago. As they rounded the bend, she saw a group of people gathered there. At the sight of the canoes, an excited cheer rang out and the crowd ran to the ruins of the Old Spanish Fort where the canoes would land.

Cade jumped from the first canoe and went to lift Lyssa from the second. The weeks of travel had given both of them time to heal physically. The babes had grown and were developing personalities. The haggard, emaciated man they had found in the cabin had regained his strength under the careful watch of Gabe and Pushmataha.

The couple's physical separation as the result of riding in two different canoes during the day and caring for two nursing babes on the deerskins at night had become a torment to Cade, and from the blushes on Lyssa's face when they caught themselves staring longingly into one another's eyes, he knew it tormented her as well.

Gabe tried his best not to look at them. He hoped he never got himself into that fix!

Pushmataha kept his stoic expression, but it covered a joy that his Little Flower had found her boy and that her boy returned her love.

As children ran up to greet them, Cade reluctantly put Lyssa on her feet. Pushmataha and Gabriel followed with the babies.

Joie jumped up and down just looking at Lyssa before she threw herself into her arms. "You're here, finally!"

Godfrey Lewis Winkel abandoned his usual reserve and embraced the two of them awkwardly. "We were so worried."

Ben and Sister pushed into the circle.

Mo and Meme followed as fast as their chubby little legs would go, shouting "Issie, Issie!"

With tears in her eyes, she knelt and pulled all of the little ones into her arms. "Mo, how you're grown!" she exclaimed.

They all tried to talk at once. They had so much to tell her! She glanced up at a bewildered Cade. Lyssa felt a bit guilty about not warning him of the children.

But then Mo pulled her to him and said, "No Mo." He folded his arms across his chest. "Androkeez."

"Papa Rendel told him the story of Androcles and the Lion," Joie explained. "He thinks he should be Androcles and make friends with the lions."

Papa Rendel? Cade thought.

Jake Rendel smiled at him broadly, enjoying Cade's discomfort. Being accepted by the rest of Cade's family would make it harder for Cade to take his Lyssa away from him.

Lyssa smiled. "So do I," and she gave Mo a fierce hug.

"Are you still Meme?" she asked the beautiful blonde cherub.

The little girl balled up her fist and gave a ferocious roar. "Me Lion."

Everyone laughed.

Lyssa finally spotted her mother. Once again laughing and crying, Lyssa gave a shout and rushed to embrace Malee. Jake gathered them both into his arms with tears of gratitude and joy in his eyes.

"I was so worried," her mother said.

A newborn's cry was different from any other. When two separate wails came from behind and her parents' attention was drawn to the noise, Lyssa turned to make introductions. Cade took an unhappy little girl from Gabriel, and Lyssa took her son from Pushmataha.

"Meet your grandson and granddaughter, Marylyssa and Jacob Gabriel Kincaid."

"Oh, Lyssa," her mother cried as she touched each child's tiny head. The thought of what Lyssa must have gone through while carrying those babies was scary even now. Her little girl.

Jake thought of how fragile he had once considered his daughter to be. Now, standing before him was a woman, strong and competent. He held out his open hands and took the baby boy—his grandson—from Lyssa.

Beauty, healed from the many wounds she had taken at Horseshoe Bend, waited patiently. The children had woven ribbons into her mane.

It was Cade who embraced her first. "Thank you, dear friend," he said as he stroked Beauty's mane, remembering her jump over the battlement and charge straight toward Lyssa. Beauty nickered and nudged him modestly.

Lyssa laughed and also hugged the horse. Cade lifted Lyssa onto Beauty's back and took the reins to guide her down the path to town.

They followed her father, still holding his grandson, to the welcome they had expected. But instead of guiding them to the racetrack or to the Globe Hotel, where a bath and a meal might await, Lyssa's father stopped in front of Sexton's Tavern, now bedecked in spring flowers and ivy, with Judge Toulmin standing at the door in his fine, shiny suit.

"There's no church in St. Stephens, but Harry Toulmin's a minister as well as a judge," Jake said.

The scent of the sweet peas in the bouquet her mother thrust into her hands once again brought tears to Lyssa's eyes.

"Scouts told us they'd seen you," Malee explained, rolling her eyes at Jake.

"We were on our way to a wedding when a war happened," her father said.

Cade smiled and said, "Let me do this right." He gently handed his daughter to Malee, who cuddled the baby close, and then turned to Lyssa. There on the dusty street of St. Stephens in front of Sexton's Tavern, he knelt before his beloved. "There is no other woman for me, Lyssa Rendel. You are the most beautiful woman I have ever seen. I look at you and you take my breath away."

His eyes misted as he remembered all they had been through. And then he said, "You are the bravest woman I have ever known. I want to live with you as long as I have breath, and if the Great Spirit allows, I'll follow you through eternity. Will you be my wife?"

Lyssa laughed and cried at the same time. "Look around you, Cade Kincaid. Can you make room for all of us in your heart?"

The children looked at him, earnest and intent on the seriousness of the occasion. Ben's green eyes took Cade back to a ravine and a boy he had known years ago.

Perhaps he had a chance for redemption.

Was he good enough for their Lyssa? Even the animals cocked their heads as if wondering the same thing. Cade wondered that himself. But he would spend his life trying to be worthy of their trust and love.

He lived.

For some reason.

"I already have," he said honestly.

He was sure he could get used to the animals.

Lyssa knelt with him in the street and said, "My love, my life, my heart, yes, yes, yes."

The ceremony was a strange one with the young bride and groom surrounded by children, crying babies, joyous parents, and every citizen of St. Stephens that could fit into the tavern.

Jake then led them up High Street to the Globe Hotel, where a wedding meal had been prepared. After she had eaten and the gentlemen had progressed to toasting and cigars, Lyssa's mother led her upstairs, where a bath had been provided and beautiful clothes hung in the wardrobe. Across the tester bed on the golden velvet coverlet lay a pink silk negligee and robe. Lyssa raised an eyebrow at her mother.

"I would have had you prepare for your wedding first, but your father was afraid we wouldn't get you out of the room and across the street," Malee said matter-of-factly.

Lyssa blushed like an innocent bride, even after birthing two babies.

"Bathe," her mother said. "Nurse the babies. Then your father and I will keep the little ones for you and Cade to have your wedding night."

When at last her babies were replete and sleeping, Malee carried them out the door. She had barely left the room when Cade knocked and then entered.

He had apparently gotten a bath of his own because he'd had a shave and a haircut and smelled of bay rum. The sight of Lyssa in the filmy gown with her shining ebony hair loose and flowing stopped him at the door.

"You are the most beautiful woman in the world," he declared when he had caught his breath.

"Come, let me touch you," she whispered, suddenly breathless at the sight of him. "Let me know this is real and not a dream." By now tears spilled from her eyes with the emotion of seeing him standing there. His eyes filled with love and the passion she now recognized, knowing that it mirrored her own. A lifetime of loving him could never be enough.

He took her into his arms and held her. She fit in his embrace as if made for him. And she was. With her he was complete. How had he ever thought to walk this world without her?

"You are a wise woman, Lyssa Rendel Kincaid."

"Yes," she said, smiling and teasing. "But what exactly are you talking about?"

"You knew how much I needed you. And you are so brave. You saved me once again."

His lips were on her neck, behind her ear, drifting down.

"Once again?" she gasped. He pulled down the straps of the pink silk gown. His tongue teased her nipple, and he chuckled as milk suddenly spurted onto his lips.

"You told me my life was yours when you pulled me out from under that horse in the Flint River when you were eight years old," he explained.

"I did?" What was he babbling about?

He chuckled. "Your father warned me...."

She pulled his lips to hers and they sank into a soul-stirring kiss. "Less talk," she said. "More action." Her hands were busily touching, stroking, pulling him closer and closer.

He laughed as she arched into his embrace.

"Hurry," she said.

Needing no further encouragement, Cade removed his shirt and unbuttoned his pants. The Kraken broke from its constraints. No bent arrow here.

Cade stumbled as he stepped from his pants, and the two fell onto the feather bed. He wanted to go slow. She'd never had a wedding night. But the passion was too intense. She wrapped her legs around him and pulled him toward her.

He kissed her deeply and sweetly with all the love he'd fought and never dreamed he could feel. She pulled him into her embrace, refusing to let him break the connection even when they were finished.

"Never leave me," she said.

Once again, their passion consumed them. They had to make up for many months of time. Finally, as the sun was beginning to chase away the shadows, Cade was pleased that he had acquitted himself with such honor that even Will Milfort would have approved. After having given his bride the attention she deserved on their wedding night, he rolled over with her in his arms and they slept.

Together and safe at last.

Epilogue

The knock at the door became so insistent that it could not be ignored. It was morning, and consolation with sugar tits no longer worked for the infant twins. Lyssa's mother's soft voice rose to a level rare in Malee in order to be heard above the cries of two obviously hungry babies. Lyssa straightened her gown, fluffed the pillows, smoothed the covers, and lay back against them. She smiled a sweetly contented smile, looking regal in her pink silk gown contrasted against the downy white pillows and illuminated by the rays of the morning sun.

So beautiful.

Reluctantly, Cade pulled on his pants and went to the door.

"They need their mother," Malee said, handing him Marylyssa.

"The best thing about being a grandparent is being able to give them back to their parents," Jake Rendel said as he thrust his grandson into his son-in-law's other arm.

Cade laughed and turned with his screaming, red-faced babes in his arms. How could a man be happier than he felt when looking into the eyes of his passion-tousled wife, with his two beautiful infants in his arms?

Unless the two babies were sound asleep and he was looking at his passion-tousled wife with all the time in the world to show her how much he loved her.

He had no sooner deposited the two babies in their mother's arms than another knock sounded much lower and much softer. He opened the door and looked out...and then down...as two little people scurried through the open door. And then they were pulling on the brocade coverlet, crying, "Issie, Issie!" at the top of their lungs. They finally managed to pull themselves onto the bed, joining the babies who now hungrily nursed at their mother's breasts. Brown-eyed, kinky-haired Mo and his shadow, the fair-skinned, flaxen-haired, periwinkle-eyed Meme, leaned back against the pillows on either side of Lyssa, watching the infants knead and grunt as they enjoyed their meal. Gently, the toddlers reached out and stroked the dark, downy heads of the babies.

"When dey eat at de table?" asked Mo, with great disapproval and a frown on his face.

Cade followed them to the bed. He was about to comment when there was another knock. He opened the door again, and two more shy little people crept through into the room and lingered there, unsure of their welcome. Then Lyssa's warm amethyst eyes and bright smile drew them forward.

"Come, dear ones," she urged and patted the bed near her legs. Cade lifted Ben and Sister onto the foot of the bed, where they leaned against the posters, watching the little ones nurse.

Before he could get the door closed, Joie came in carrying J.J., and Lyssa indicated that he should go into the little nest made by her legs where she sat cross-legged on the bed. Godfrey followed Joie and peeked in, but then he stepped back outside, reluctant to intrude.

"You might as well come on in," Cade said, and the teenaged boy blushed beet red at Lyssa's bare chest and immodest nursing of the newborns. "Lyssa will not be happy if you are not a part of this gathering."

"They are so little; they must nurse," Lyssa explained to Godfrey. "And I am so glad to see all of you, I will not deny myself your company for the time they must eat."

Godfrey nodded but looked away. Joie helped by standing between him and Lyssa.

They all laughed as J.J. crawled forward, ready to push a yelling Marylyssa aside as he bellied up for a taste himself. She kicked and he yelled.

Joie frowned and made a futile attempt to adjust the covers, the babies, something to shield Lyssa's breast from public viewing. Finally giving up the effort, she shrugged and pulled J.J. back so he didn't squish Marylyssa. Lyssa smiled her understanding and rolled her eyes at the futility of the effort, making Joie show her dimples again with the smile that lit her face and made her beautiful.

Looking directly at Joie, but including them all, Lyssa said, "I missed you all so much." Her voice was filled with emotion, and her eyes brimmed with tears.

Samson and Delilah pushed open the cracked door, their tongues lolling and their jowls lifted as if they were smiling and happy themselves. There was such joy being there together, welcoming the little ones into the family.

With a shock, Cade realized that the word "family" was exactly what he felt about all the individuals in that room. This was his family.

The very thing he had fought so hard against, yet hee it was and it was right. If he'd planned it, it would never have happened. But someone smarter (he looked at Lyssa), but perhaps more powerful (his thoughts went to the God Nicey had always said was in control) knew better than he did what he really needed.

He wanted to wipe that damned smirk off Gabe's face! Someday he'd get him back. And that thought made him smile.

The room had gotten crowded. Everyone watched each tiny movement of the new infants.

But when Lyssa's eyes met Cade's, it was as if there was only the two of them in that room. She reached out her hand, beckoning him to her. The distance was further than she ever wanted them to be again. He pushed himself onto the bed, taking them all into his arms...welcoming them into his heart.

From the door, Jake, Malee, and Gabe watched with grateful, damp eyes. They'd been so afraid Lyssa had been one of the many victims of the Red Stick War.

And then the group parted as Pushmataha made his way through the crowd, leading a small boy about Sister and Ben's age.

"Running Elk!" Lyssa cried and pushed Cade off the bed. "Come here and let me hug you!"

She looked at Cade and said, "Running Elk is my 'cousin,' or so we have decided. We were both captured by Savannah Jack and managed to keep each other alive." Running Elk preened at her introduction and submitted to her kisses.

"Red Eagle sent me to Pushmataha," he told her eagerly. "Abraham Mordecai was at his cotton gin near Hickory Ground by the racetrack where Red Eagle went to forage food. There was too little food." Sorrow suddenly clouded the boy's face. "Sapothlane grew weaker and weaker and finally...." His voice trailed off, and he swallowed hard as he remembered.

Too much for such a little boy. Lyssa stroked his arm to soothe those sad memories.

"Josiah Francis took Red Eagle's sister Hannah and Millea to St. Marks. They're going to get on a big ship to go across the water to a place called England. Millea was real happy. She said she knew one of her father's uncles. He's a British agent like her great-grandfather. He brought them presents at Tukabatchee once," he said excitedly.

"Weatherford went to turn himself in to Jackson to save the rest. He took me to Abraham Mordecai first."

Weatherford had turned himself in to Jackson! Lyssa's heart clenched. He had always been good to her. She was saddened to hear of Sapothlane's death. Lyssa had never warmed to Sapothlane, but neither had she wished her ill. Lyssa looked at her babies and wondered about Sapothlane's baby to whom she had given the breath of life…and about the babe's half-siblings, Polly and Charles Weatherford.

Running Elk pulled himself up proudly to relate his important news. He said, "I was supposed to tell Chief Pushmataha you were alive."

Weatherford had managed to tell her before he left to for Moniac's Island that he would get word to her grandfather. Abraham Mordecai, the wiry little Jewish man who traded his wares for ginseng root, hickory nut oil, and pelts and operated a cotton gin at Hickory Ground near Weatherford's racetrack, was well known among the Creek and would have been the perfect envoy. He certainly had a distinctive appearance. He had been caught in the act of adultery with a Creek woman and had his ears cropped by her irate husband.

"Running Elk has been eating ever since he got here, Chamay says," said Pushmataha.

Running Elk's face was still gaunt, and Lyssa was glad he was eating.

"Meet your new family," Lyssa said, looking over Running Elk at Cade, who was watching thoughtfully. What was one more in that brood? It was kind of like the twins. It wasn't like you could just send one back.

"Mordecai found something else along the Natchez Trace," said Pushmataha.

"*More* children?" Cade said, starting to feel overwhelmed.

Everyone laughed.

Chamay entered, followed by a stately, elegant older lady wearing a gold silk day dress with lace fichu.

"I think you two are acquainted," Chamay said to Jake.

Chamay then moved directly to the bed and the babies, lifting Marylyssa against her shoulder. The baby girl was about to be pushed off the bed as J.J. moved to take her place at Lyssa's breast. Joie reached for him, but Lyssa held up her hand.

"Let him nurse. He is my baby also," she said.

Joie smiled. Cade demonstrated his approval by removing the pillows and putting himself behind Lyssa for her to lean against. The children filled in around them like a stack of puppies.

Dressed only in his breechclout, Little Arrow, or Lancelot Rendel, his new brother-in-law as Cade had now come to accept, stepped across the threshold to stand just inside the door beside Gabriel, who also was bare-chested and wearing only buckskin trousers. His eyes sparkled. Cade smiled watching Lance emulate Gabe's stance.

The lady surveyed the scene through a lorgnette while a younger lady with sparkling green eyes that Lyssa noted were identical to those of her father, Jake Rendel, held off two excited dogs.

Jake gaped at his mother, Theodora Palmer Rendel. "Well, Mother, I do believe you are the last person I would have expected to walk through that door. Push, where did you find her...and my sister Felecia? Malee, you remember Mother and Felecia? Mother and Felecia, you have already met Chief Pushmataha, chief of the Choctaw Indians, and Chamay, his wife, my wife Malee's mother and father."

His blueblood mother was speechless. She was not the snob his father was, but he couldn't help getting a kick out of her astonishment at his and Malee's band of children.

"Abraham Mordecai met them on the Natchez Trace and brought them to St. Stephens, where they understood you operated something like a place called Ascot," Chamay explained.

Jake laughed at that. The thought of comparing the Pebble Creek Jockey Club and *its* patrons with the august patrons of Ascot was like comparing the queen of England with...the wife of Pushmataha. Well, maybe that analogy was lopsided. He knew he'd prefer Chamay any day. And accompanying Abraham Mordecai? She must have really been desperate for a guide.

"Mother, I am glad to see you. We are celebrating the marriage of our daughter Lyssa and her husband Cade Kincaid. This is Cade's brother, Gabriel, his sister, Joie, and their little brother, J.J." He watched the shock on her face when she realized J.J. was one of the infants nursing at her granddaughter's breast.

"You are just in time to meet the newest members of the Rendel family, Marylyssa and Jacob Gabriel Kincaid. They are Lyssa and Cade's newest additions. And you must also make the acquaintance of their other children, Ben, Sister, Running Elk, Mo, and Meme."

Felecia looked at Godfrey Lewis Winkel.

"I'm just a friend," Godfrey assured her.

"Probably the only one in this room not related to you," Jake quipped.

"I'm Godfrey Lewis Winkel, ma'am. And I want to tell you, your granddaughter saved all of our lives. We would all have been casualties of that tragedy at Fort Mims without her."

Jake's mother blinked.

There were children of all ages, races, and colors, and this well-mannered young gentleman, the only gentleman in the room, she noted, said her granddaughter had saved them? And now her son indicated that they all belonged to her granddaughter and her granddaughter's husband?

The lorgnette fell from Theodora Rendel's eye. Her unfamiliarity with the eyepiece had been evident from the moment she first entered the room.

"Mother, when did you begin using that lorgnette?"

His mother frowned and sniffed. His sister answered, "When the news came from England."

Jake looked confused.

"It seemed appropriate for her new station in life, I think she said."

The dogs nudged his sister, distracting her. Felecia laughed and said, "I think Samson and Delilah remember me." She knelt to receive the kisses from the two "puppies" she had given Jake when he first brought Malee and Lyssa to meet the family.

She looked up from where she knelt and said, "Mother, tell Jake the news."

The crowded room stilled, and all eyes focused on the bewildered woman.

"Jake, your grandfather has passed away."

Jake frowned. His grandfather was an old man whom Jake had seen perhaps once. It was expected that a man of his age would pass away. "I am sorry, Mother. But surely that news would not have you leaving the comfort of the plantation…especially now."

"His other sons never produced any sons."

"Again, my regrets," Jake said.

By now the others were beginning to pick up on the point toward which she was leading.

"Your uncles have passed."

"Father must be saddened at their loss."

"Jake, your father passed away six months ago."

"And you have just found it necessary to tell me?" Jake said.

Felecia could not stand it any longer. "You, dear brother, are the only surviving male heir to the Duke of Penbrooke. You are the Duke of Penbrooke, and your wife, Malee, is a Duchess."

His mother looked sick.

"Lancelot Rendel, in the loincloth over there, is the heir apparent to one of the largest estates in all of England," Felecia continued gleefully. She surveyed the room and said, "May I go with you to claim your inheritance? This family will surely set British society on its heels!"

Well, this is one hell of an end to a wedding night, Cade thought. The shock on Jake Rendel's face was almost—*almost*—worth the intrusion into what the Krakon thought should be the business of the day. Lyssa wiggled a bit there between his legs and looked at him, her violet eyes glittering with mischief, knowing full well what she was doing.

Life was not going to be dull.

Through the window came a slight breeze. Like a mother's gentle touch, the wind lifted a tendril of Joie's blue-black hair and let it slip loose, drifted on and rippled Cade's hair lying unbound and long in his happy languor, and then moved on to touch Gabriel like a goodbye kiss. The sigh of the wind drew their attention to the open window, where a snowy white egret lifted from sill and soared into the brilliant blue sky.

Acknowledgments

This is first and foremost a work of fiction. In writing historical fiction one cannot, of course, recreate the situations and conversations exactly. One can only imagine them by knowing as much as possible about the people, places, and events about which one writes and then applying the timeless universals of human nature and personalities to historical figures.

I would like to thank David Mason, author of *Five Dollars a Scalp: The Last Whoop of the Creek Indians,* for sharing the story of his ancestors, James and Aletha Arundel Smith, who, along with James's twin brother Samuel, were the inspiration for this novel. Some of the experiences of these people have been fictionalized so that I might create characters who would have been in a similar situation to experience these pivotal events in the history of the United States. I hope readers of my novel will want to read Dr. Mason's story of his ancestors who actually survived the Creek War. His book made me want to know more about *all* of those involved.

I would also like to thank Dr. Gregory Waselkov, author of *A Conquering Spirit: Fort Mims and the Redstick War of 1813–1814,* for his scholarly work on the Fort Mims Massacre and the Creek War. Dr. Waselkov is a Professor of Anthropology and is the director for Archaeological Studies at the University of South Alabama who is excavating the site of the Fort Mims Massacre.

I owe a debt of gratitude to Don Greene, author of *Shawnee Heritage I and II,* for sharing his prodigious accumulation of research on the genealogy of our Native American ancestors. Don provided information about Mary Bailey, Dixon Bailey's mother, being one of Alexander McGillivray's sisters. The conflict between Weatherford and Bailey is mentioned frequently, and it is common knowledge that Dixon Bailey and his brother James, along with cousins John and Sandy Durant, were selected by Alexander McGillivray to be educated by the Quakers in Philadelphia. Personality conjecture is my own based on Benjamin Hawkins's writings and observation of human nature.

Discovering the friendship between Benjamin Jernigan and Andrew Jackson and the Native American ancestry of Vashti Vann Jernigan, Benjamin's wife, my fourth great-grandparents, certainly provoked my interest in this time, place, and people. There is nothing like discovering that history is actually *your* story to make you want to know more!

I also want to express my thanks to my tenth grade English teacher at Dothan High School, Julie Wauthena Nall Knowles, who told me I could write, and to my eleventh grade History teacher, Mary Turner Hamner, who played "There'll Be Bluebirds Over the White Cliffs of Dover" for our class on World War II and made history more than facts. At that moment, I felt just as millions during that time would have felt, and the moment became mine as well.

This book would never have made it to publication without the encouragement of my dear friends, Kathie Bennett, Karen Spears Zacharias, Janis Owens, and Cassandra King.

Though words must be my instrument, I hope that my readers will experience the moments recreated in this book.

Visit my website, Southern-style.com, for maps, family trees, and other details that did not make it into the book.

Sharman Ramsey
May 31, 2011
Dothan, Alabama